the
GOD *of* D
BATTLES

THE GYPSY DREAMWALKER. BOOK TWO

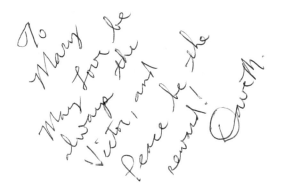

To Mary be
May love be
always the
Victor; and
Peace be the
reward!
Gareth.

the GOD *of* BATTLES

THE GYPSY DREAMWALKER. BOOK TWO

DAVID MENEFEE

Sophic Arts
2015

Cover design by Clarissa Yeo / Yocla Designs
Content editing by Jessica Anderegg / Red Adept Editing
Line Editing by Sarah Carleton / Red Adept Editing.
Proofread by Virge Buck / Red Adept Editing

Printed in the United States of America
First Printing: 2015

ISBN: 0692324828
ISBN-13: 978-0692324820

Sophic Arts
PO Box 1183
Hayfork, CA 96041
U.S. trade bookstores and wholesalers, please contact Sophic Arts Tel: (530) 628-6363 or email info@sophicarts.com

DEDICATION

This book is dedicated to Sekhmet,
Sacred Partner
Beloved Soul of Re

ACKNOWLEDGMENTS

First, this book would never have been written without the gracious and loving support of my partner Rachel. She patiently performed the first corrections as an alpha reader, night after night, for over a month. Thank you, beloved. My other alpha reader, David, provided much-needed encouragement and advice on this story, and it is the better for it. My study group friends, Judy, Tanya and Kate, cheered me on and helped me with important philosophical elements, including the idea of "meme angels." My faithful readers, having completed The Soul Thief, kept asking me when the second book would come out, and this spurred me on through the harder patches. Thank you all! Finally, I would never have considered publishing this book without the ever-patient work by my editors, Jessica Anderegg and Sarah Carleton, and my proofreader, Virge Buck, all from Red Adept Publishing. A deep bow of gratitude to you and to Lynn McNamee

CONTENTS

A CONVERSATION

War: Beloved, come rest with me and behold my greatest work. I have conquered the Heavens with my strong right arm and would lay them at your feet as a bridal gift.

Love: I would that you come to me instead and lay down your Sword and Spear. As for wedding me, my Lord, that must not be. For we hold the worlds within our hands, and to become one in spirit would be to return those realms to the Light from whence they came.

War: Would you challenge me, then? The winner may claim his heart's desire.

Love: Or hers.

CHAPTER ONE
A WARRIOR'S NIGHTMARE

The Rubaiyat of Iron Star

A Child of War despising strife,

A bitter foe of poisoned knife,

Is bound to bitter stink of death

That plunders him of joyous life.

CHECKPOINT 4, *Baghdad, Iraq,* 012134CJUN14

"Mom sent chocolate." Simon grinned at the other man, Sam —or was it Bill?—and shivered in the night breeze.

"Oh, man." His buddy chuckled.

"Yeah. It squirted when I opened it. But ya gotta love her for trying." Simon had received his birthday gift a month late, and Iraq's merciless summer heat had reduced the gourmet dark-chocolate bar to a softened blob.

Bill—Sam?—straightened and stared down the road. Simon peered in that direction and, seeing headlights, assumed a ready stance. As the lights neared, both men readied their M16A4s. The other soldiers stationed at the checkpoint followed suit as they prepared for the tenth vehicular stop that night.

The loudspeaker crackled. "Stop your vehicle!"

The amplified voice cut the night air. Simon glanced at his buddy and nodded, raising his weapon to ready position. The oncoming headlights, resembling those of a passenger car, were not slowing. Several other Marines began to wave high-powered flashlights at it, signaling it to stop.

"I repeat, stop your vehicle, or we'll open fire."

The car accelerated with a roar. Simon felt himself tense as he lifted the rifle to take aim. Suddenly, his mind swam with vertigo, and he blinked, shaking his head. Something was wrong with the situation. Was it the strange glowing red clouds in the sky? Or maybe the fact that Simon could not recognize anyone else at the checkpoint, not even his buddy? As his finger began to squeeze, the realization struck him and took his breath away.

This was the nightmare again. His mind clear within the dream, Simon pulled his finger away from the trigger guard and lowered the weapon. "No. Not this time. I'm not gonna kill them again." No one else noticed as they were all intent on the oncoming vehicle.

He set the rifle down. All movement slowed to a crawl, including the car, and he walked away from the checkpoint into what had become featureless darkness beyond. His shoulders relaxed, and he sighed. It was just a nightmare; he had succeeded in escaping it, and he would wake up in a moment.

"Halt, soldier!"

Simon froze automatically, his hands going up. Then, realizing his error, he crouched, ready to fight. A group of Marines was running to intercept him, spreading out to cut off his escape. Behind them was a much larger man dressed in a general's uniform. All that was visible of his shadowy face was a pair of glowing eyes.

Simon dove toward an opening. The soldiers intercepted him easily and hauled him toward General Iron Star. Iron Star? Why did Simon know the giant man's name and no one else's?

"Back to work." Iron Star spoke in a grating, repulsive voice. He gestured to Simon's station, and the soldiers dragged him to where his rifle lay on the ground. The car was about ten yards from the checkpoint, clouds of dust hanging suspended in the air behind it.

"No. Please. Not again," Simon sobbed.

One of the soldiers thrust the rifle into Simon's hands while another held him fast in an iron grip. Iron Star reached over with a massive hand and shoved the rifle into aiming position against Simon's cheek. His tear-blurred vision swam with images of the dead woman and her two children, killed when the soldiers had opened fire on the onrushing car five years ago. He clenched his eyes shut and screamed as the gun bucked in his hands.

WAR IN HEAVEN: BALD EAGLE

"So, you think you are able to resist," Iron Star muttered. "That is not permitted." His hands clasped behind his back, he stood at the lip of a pool of steaming yellow coolant and gazed into the gigantic crystal resting in its center. Faces of warriors of all ages and from all places, embroiled in nightmarish battle scenes, appeared and vanished in its facets. He exerted his will, causing the crystal to show just one of those faces. It was that of an agonized soldier, eyes closed, screaming as his rifle kicked in his arms. One of the power cables that festooned the great artifact crackled at the surge of power from the nightmare, and Iron Star smiled with grim satisfaction.

He turned to one of the guardian angels who was stationed there. "I must report to my master. For now, I will leave my projected image in place within the Root Hexagon. It should be able to respond to minor fluctuations. If you see any signs of major power loss again, let me know immediately."

The angel snapped a salute. "Yes, sir."

Iron Star left the side of the pool and crossed the rubble-strewn floor of the Great Crater. As he climbed the sloping wall, he glanced up. Great red clouds swept across the sky, forming a dramatic backdrop to the semiorganic structures of Bald Eagle's skyline beyond the rim of the crater. Iron Star would have rather been on the front lines, managing the war with Silver Scimitar, but his master, the great Egregore Bald Eagle, expected a report on this most recent power loss.

CHAPTER TWO
BROOKLYN BASIN MENTAL HEALTH, OAKLAND, CA

DR. ANGELA Cooper wrinkled her nose. The smell of paint lingered in her office, despite two months of opened windows. She leaned forward over her desk in the creaky swiveling chair and handed a folder to her partner, Dr. Eric Weiser.

"The clinic is finally approved to accept VA patients."

"Cool." Eric straightened from his slouch in the chair opposite her.

She continued. "Well, I'm approved, anyway. We need to send you to training next month to get you certified. Unfortunately, it's not going to be cheap, but we've got enough budgeted for it if everything goes according to schedule."

Eric flipped the folder open and riffled through the colorful brochures, his forehead creased with concern. He ran a hand across his shock of platinum-blond hair. "So what's up with the funding?"

"It's coming in really slowly. Money always does." Angela stifled a yawn. Sometimes it seemed that business offices were designed to drain their occupants of all energy and enthusiasm. "I need you to do me a favor and meet with the Department of Mental Health office to clear up some questions they have. Seems that last year's incident at the hospital got their attention."

Eric lifted an eyebrow. "Took them long enough. I assume we're ready for their questions."

Angela nodded. "Yup. I told them we would pull those files

and take them with us to the meeting." She sighed and tapped her tablet with a finger, ticking off an item on the to-do list. "The next step is to get community buy-in. We're meeting with City Council in a week. It's mental health awareness month, so I'm going to capitalize on that."

The office phone warbled, and Angela picked it up. "Brooklyn Basin Mental Health, Dr. Cooper."

"Hi, Angela."

She recognized the light, pleasant voice. "Oh. Hi, Hector. We were just discussing the meeting."

"Good. Can you bring those materials we talked about?"

"Eric will be there with the records. I've got a prior commitment and can't make it."

"That's fine. I don't think there'll be any problem securing your funds."

"That's good to hear." Angela gave Eric a thumbs-up, and he grinned.

"Have you had any luck finding staff?"

"It's been a little slow, but I think we'll be fully staffed by August. I've got some excellent resumes on my desk." She glanced at the stack of hard-won folders on her desk.

"That's fast work. Sounds like you'll be ready for business soon."

"True, but don't forget that we still need that funding."

"I won't forget. Listen, I've got to run. Tell Eric we're looking forward to seeing him at the meeting."

"Okay, I'll let him know. Thanks."

She hung up and grinned at Eric. "Hector Jameson at the Sacramento office thinks we'll have no trouble getting funding."

"That's great news!" He got up to leave. On his way out, Eric placed a hand on the doorjamb and grinned at Angela. "This calls for a celebration. How about Beer and Far? They've got a Czech pilsner on draft that's to die for."

Angela shook her head. "I wish I could. Cassie and I are heading over to Nadia's after work. But after that, we're hitting the Rings. We'll see you there."

CHAPTER THREE
CASHIER

THERE WAS no better place for people watching than NutriMart in Berkeley, Cassandra decided. You'd see hipsters trolling the produce aisle for hookups, neo-hippies browsing the supplements for quick fixes, and glassy-eyed students stumbling through the selection of international beers for that night's pants party.

"That'll be sixty-three dollars and forty-two cents." She waited for the customer to swipe her card and key in a PIN. Cassandra tore off the enormous receipt and handed it to her with a plastic smile. "Have a good day."

The woman nodded her thanks and disappeared into the river of outgoing shoppers. As Cassandra looked at the next person in checkout, a babble of voices arose. It sounded like an argument. She scanned the crowd for trouble, but then she realized that the voices were in her own head.

She winced as a twinge of pain shot across her forehead. She reached into her pocket and pinched her index finger and thumb together in a gesture that Angela had taught her. The voices immediately died away, along with the pain, and she relaxed and began checking the next customer.

"Hey Cassie, need a break?"

She jumped and turned her head. Jeremy must have come over while she was dealing with the voices. Cassandra rolled her eyes.

"Hell, yeah. Thanks." She realized she was swearing in front of customers and touched her fingers to her lips. "Sorry."

They switched places awkwardly, Jeremy squeezing his bulk past her, and then Cassandra eeled her way through the crush toward the stairs up to the employee break room. On the way, she waved to a fellow cashier. "Janet! Are you going to the Rings tonight?"

Janet glanced at Cassandra as she swept an item through the scanner. "Yeah. About eight thirty."

"Awesome. Angela's going too."

"Angela? Rad. See you guys there."

Cassandra grinned. Janet reminded her of some of the friends she had made when she was much younger, when she and her family had gone on extended vacations all over the country. A slim, dreadlocked blonde with a nose ring, she was a little bit of a rebel and someone you could count on when you were in a fix.

Cassandra pressed on through the crowd until she got to the stairwell. Whistling a tune from one of her favorite electronica bands, Cassandra ran up the stairs two at a time and went into the break room. Both computer stations were occupied, so she poured herself a cup of sludgy brew and leaned on the counter to wait.

One of the computer users, Rhonda, a thin young woman with small eyes and mousy brown hair, looked up at her. "Hey, Cassie. I'm almost done. I heard the boss wants to talk to you about something."

In Cassandra's limited experience, a word from the boss usually meant trouble. "Oh, fuck. What about?"

Rhonda clicked the mouse, logged off of Facebook, and got up. "The usual. Your team leader came in earlier. He said something, and I heard your name. Then Janelle said something about calling you up to the office."

Cassandra sipped her coffee and grimaced at the bitterness. "I hope this won't take long. I'm going out tonight." She sat down at the computer Rhonda had just vacated.

"I think you'll hear from her tomorrow. She doesn't usually go for afternoon meetings with employees. So, where're you going?"

"The Rings."

Rhonda walked over to pour herself some coffee. "The what?"

"Saturn's Rings. It's a goth dance club in the City."

Rhonda grinned. "You're a goth?"

Cassandra gave Rhonda a steady stare and said nothing, waiting for the other woman's composure to crack.

Rhonda's eyes flicked to the clock then back to Cassandra. "Well, anyway, have fun."

Cassandra nodded, hiding her satisfaction, and turned back to the computer to check her e-mail. She had a feeling she might be unemployed after tomorrow. She fought a momentary urge to lurk by the manager's door and telepathically snoop. Her boss's head was probably full of skank Cassandra didn't want to know anyway.

CHAPTER FOUR
AT DAY'S END

ANGELA PAUSED to run her fingers along the teak railing above the companionway, where the varnish was lightly chipped. Her grandfather George had often complained that the finish wore off faster there than anywhere else. She made a mental note to repair it sometime soon.

She removed the hatch boards, set them aside, and descended the steep ladder into the dining salon. Sometimes Cassandra would draw the emerald green curtains shut, leaving the interior in a gray gloom. But the curtains were open now, allowing warm daylight to stream in through the portholes to gleam on brass accents and make the upholstered red cushions glow.

The day's concerns receded from her mind as she turned left and walked along the short passageway to the master berth at the stern. Unlike the dining salon, the curtains were still drawn, and the aft cabin was dark and cool. She switched on the light and unbuttoned her work blouse.

She had finished pulling on a pair of comfortable sweat pants and a T-shirt when she heard the clump of boots above. Angela sighed. Cassandra was scuffing up the deck with her army boots. Again. "Hey, Cassie. Boots?"

"Sorry." There was a double thump as Cassandra pulled off her shoes. "I'm starving."

"There's leftovers in the fridge." Angela finished changing and came out of the master cabin. Seeing Cassandra, she paused for the tiniest moment.

Even tired, the younger woman was beautiful. Her dark eyes, as well as her classic Roma features, gave her an exotic look that turned heads. Cassandra brushed her short hair away from those eyes as she set her backpack down. Catching Angela's stare, she smiled and then began rummaging in the small propane refrigerator.

Angela made her way to the galley in time to see Cassandra pull a Tupperware tub out and hold it up to the light, frowning. "How old is this?"

She grabbed it out of Cassandra's hand and popped it open. "If you have to ask, it's too old." She dumped it into the compost bucket on the counter and dropped the container in the sink. "So, how was your day?"

Cassandra emptied a tub of leftover soup into a saucepan and lit the burner. "Okay. The floor manager wants to see me tomorrow."

"Is this the manager you called 'the bitch from hell'?"

"Yeah."

"Uh-oh." Cassandra had an issue with authority figures. Angela made a mental note to call around to find her another job in case she got fired.

Cassandra pulled out a couple of soup bowls. "Well, anyway, other than that it was good."

Angela found a tub of salad and unloaded it into a couple of bowls. "How about your telepathy?"

Cassandra shrugged. "No problem. The voices got kinda loud, but I pushed them away. No sweat. In fact, I think I'm ready to start tuning in on people there."

"Are you sure? I mean, that's a lot of random minds to keep

track of. You could undo months of work." Angela cleared her throat. "Nadia thinks you need more training."

Cassandra hesitated for a moment then resumed stirring. "I'm fine, and I think I'm ready. So, what's the plan this evening?"

Angela squirted dressing on the salad and watched her girlfriend stir the soup. "I want to drop off the vacuum cleaner at Nadia's on the way to the Rings. I picked it up today at the shop."

Cassandra stared at the wall, unspeaking, her face blank, the spoon resting in her hand.

"Is that okay?" Angela asked.

Cassandra nodded and resumed stirring. "Sure. No prob."

Soon the soup was ready, and they both sat at the dinette table to eat.

"Eric'll be at the Rings," Angela said. "He broke up with Jason, you know. So he'll be hunting." She grinned at the thought of her friend prowling amongst the unwitting goths. They'd never know what hit them.

"I invited a couple of friends at work, too." Cassandra paused. "I couldn't find a card for Nadia. Nothing that I thought she'd like, anyway."

"It's okay. I got one. We can both sign it." Angela poked at a half-submerged piece of carrot. "So, why do you want to read minds at work?"

"Because it's my talent, and I want to use it." Cassandra glanced up at Angela, a challenge in her eyes. "Besides, I've been opening up at the Rings. That's why I think I can handle the hippies at work."

"No shit." A grin spread on Angela's face. "If you can handle the Rings, a bunch of granola munchers shouldn't bug you."

Cassandra grinned back at her and slurped down the rest of her soup.

Great-aunt Nadia's home had become a welcome sight for Angela since the Romani clans had lifted the stigma of *marimé* from her the previous June. At that time, Angela's great-aunt had lived in a gaudily decorated trailer in Daly City. However, when the trailer park was sold to a developer who was building condos, Nadia's entire clan had turned out to help her move into a somewhat weather-beaten Victorian-era rental house in Oakland, not far from Angela's clinic. Being Nadia, she had immediately set to work redecorating. Or rather, she had set a team of grandsons and great-nephews to work, overseeing them with her critical eye as they hung charms, painted elaborate glyphs on the chipped frames of the doors and windows, and—as she put it—"made a home" out of her house.

Since June, when the Soul Thief had killed George, Angela had grown closer to her older relatives. She made an effort to visit Nadia and Nadia's brother Michael, who shared the house, every week.

Nadia greeted them at the door. "My dear Angela. And Cassandra. Please come in."

They entered the warm house, and Angela frowned at the smudged carpeting and world-class dust bunnies peeking out from underneath the furniture. While the vacuum cleaner had been out for repairs, Nadia had created a real mess to test it with.

Nadia turned to hobble back to her chair, leaning on her cane and puffing with exertion. Her hip problem had worsened in the last six months, but Nadia steadfastly refused to seek medical treatment.

"Nana, let me help," Angela said, offering her arm.

Nadia waved her off. "No, thank you, dear. Put on a kettle, will you?" She sat down with a grunt in her customary overstuffed chair.

Angela sighed in resignation and went into the kitchen. As she began filling the kettle, she noticed that Cassandra was still standing awkwardly near the door. Angela caught her eye and lifted an eyebrow. Cassandra shrugged and walked over to the couch.

"Cassandra?" Nadia said. "There are cookies in the cupboard. Would you mind getting those?"

"Sure." Cassandra came into the kitchen and began hunting through the cabinets.

Angela pointed to the one to the right of the sink. "In there, I think."

Cassandra opened it, retrieved a large glass jar with a flip-top lid, and returned to the living room to place it on the coffee table. She took out two cookies and brought them to Nadia.

"Thank you." Nadia sounded pleased. "That's just what I wanted."

"You're welcome," Cassandra mumbled. She went back to perch on the edge of the couch.

Angela returned to the living room couch to wait for the kettle to boil. "Nana, the vacuum's out in the car. Where do you want me to put it?"

"Don't bother yourself." Nadia looked toward the corridor and raised her voice. "Michael! Are you awake?"

A muffled response came from her brother's bedroom, and the door opened. Michael poked his head out, rubbing his eyes groggily. "I am now, Nadia."

He came into the living room dressed in shorts and an undershirt that was stretched over his hairy belly. The beard he had grown in memory of his brother George looked like a bird's nest. His face lit up when he saw Angela. "Angel! I didn't hear you come in."

She rose to give him a hug, which he returned with a fraction of his old strength. She wrinkled her nose at the odor of stale sweat, beer, and for some reason, green beans. He was a heavy drinker, and some people with liver problems developed odd body odors, so she added this to her catalog of worries about her great-uncle.

Michael patted her shoulder and shuffled to the other overstuffed chair, groaning as he settled into it. "Hello, Cassandra," he said with a broad grin. "How are you today? I don't see you often enough."

Cassandra returned his smile with warmth. "Great. I got that job at NutriMart."

"Good, good! I thought you would. Angel, can you get me one of those cookies? My back is out again."

Angela, who had just sat down, hopped back up and fetched one for him. The kettle started to scream, so she returned to the kitchen to busy herself making tea.

"Michael," Nadia said. "I need you to go get the vacuum cleaner out of Angela's trunk."

He looked pleadingly at Nadia for a moment. He started to rise from the chair.

Angela shook her head. "Uncle, no. Don't try to carry that with your back out." She glanced at Nadia. "I'll go get it."

"Very well, but you shouldn't have to. After tea—not right now."

Angela brought in a tray with teacups and the pot and set it on the table.

Nadia looked for a moment at Cassandra then back at Angela. "You are both coming to my birthday party tomorrow, aren't you?"

"Of course." Angela poured tea for Nadia and Michael. "Cassie's taking the evening off at work. Right?"

Cassandra nodded. "Sure am."

Silence fell for a moment as everyone picked up their cups and blew across the top of the hot tea. Nadia looked at Angela again with a slight frown. "Angela. Have you thought about my offer? To teach you?"

Angela paused before answering the dreaded question. Placing herself under Nadia's tutelage would create an unwanted obligation to the Roma path of the *chovihani*. She decided to dissemble. "Nana, I... I've been so busy lately with all the paperwork involved in setting up the new clinic."

Nadia's eyes glittered. "There's a lot you need to learn."

Angela shook her head. "I know, I know. It's just... I want to be in the right frame of mind."

Nadia set her cup down. "Your power won't wait. Angela, you may not want to admit it, but your decision affects us all." She glanced at Cassandra. "You know what happens when you choose to ignore your strength."

Cassandra flushed. "She's not kidding about being busy. Angela's working eighteen-hour days. I had to yell at her about it." She glanced at her girlfriend, who smiled with understanding. "I told her to take tonight and tomorrow night off so she could have some fun."

Nadia's frown deepened as she stared at Cassandra for a moment in silence. Then she turned her attention back to Angela. "Just don't wait too long, dear. Please give me an answer soon."

"Of course. When the dust settles at the clinic, I'm going to give serious thought to that commitment."

Nadia nodded. "Good. Michael, go get that vacuum cleaner, will you?"

Michael groaned.

Angela got to her feet. "I'll be right back."

The air had been heavy with the tension between Nadia and Cassandra, so Angela was relieved to get out of there for a moment. However, she was afraid that Cassandra would be uncomfortable spending time alone with Nadia, so she hurried to unlock the trunk of the car and retrieve the vacuum cleaner.

After lugging it back up the porch steps, Angela barged through the door. "Where can I put it?"

Nadia waved toward the corridor. "Take it into the back, will you?"

"Sure thing." Angela carried it into Nadia's bedroom and returned to the living room. "Nana, we've got to go. We're meeting some friends for dinner before heading over to the Rings."

Nadia's mouth pursed. "I understand. I want to see you at the dance tomorrow. There are some nice young men I want you to meet."

Cassandra's face went still, and she stared at Nadia, her expression cool and distant.

There she goes again, Angela thought. Nadia knew she and Cassandra were in a committed relationship, yet she refused to accept that it was more than a phase Angela was going through. She put her hands on her hips. "Nana, we've been through this..."

Nadia waved her hand. "Never mind. Come to the party for me, then. I love you, Angel."

Angela sighed and went over to peck Nadia on the cheek. "Me too."

Cassandra was already on her feet. She stared for a moment at Nadia then turned and went to the door.

"Uncle Michael, I'll talk to you later." Angela went over to Michael's chair and bent to hug him.

Her great-uncle looked sadly at Cassandra. "Will you give me a hug too?"

Cassandra quick-stepped over to where Michael was sitting and one-armed his shoulders. She glanced at Nadia again, then she and Angela hurried back to the car and left.

Angela drove pensively back across the Bay Bridge. Michael this, Michael that. Nadia had always been in charge of the family. She had even bossed her older brother, Angela's grandfather George—something that no one else had dared to do. Angela remembered the heated family discussions in Nadia's warm kitchen. All the shouting had made Angela hide under her bed when she was little, and she had been intimidated by her great-aunt's flashing eyes and scowl.

As Angela grew older, she came to realize that Nadia loved the entire family and all the Roma. Even when her great-aunt had pushed the clans to cast her out, declaring her marimé, Angela had understood that she had done so for the sake of the community. When, last year, Nadia had been instrumental in lifting Angela's banishment, it had been for similar reasons. Now that she and her great-aunt were getting along, it was important to her that Cassandra felt welcome, as well.

"Hey, Cassie," Angela said, glancing at Cassandra. "Love you."

Cassandra stopped staring out the window long enough to smile at Angela. "Love you, too."

CHAPTER FIVE
TO DANCE AT DEATH'S DOOR

An Angel spreads her hallowed wings

To seek the hellish nightmare thing

That holds him fast to nightmare task,

That binds his soul to battle's king.

"Stop your vehicle." The loudspeaker-amplified voice cut the night air. Simon felt an adrenaline surge. He glanced at his buddy and nodded, raising his weapon. The oncoming headlights did not slow.

"I repeat, stop your vehicle, or we'll open fire."

The car accelerated with a roar, and Simon felt himself tense as he lifted the rifle to take aim. Suddenly his head swam with vertigo, and he blinked, shaking his head as he awoke within the dream. Simon pulled his finger away from the trigger guard and lowered the weapon. Once again, he walked away from the checkpoint, into darkness.

Simon froze, hearing a faint thumping sound. He whirled, becoming more awake. He remembered the soldiers that, in previous dreams, would come to get him. But no one approached. The thumping grew louder, more insistent, matching his heartbeat. Absurdly, he was reminded of the club music he had danced to before he lost the use of his legs.

Abruptly, the walls of darkness around him collapsed as if he were on a flimsy movie set. He stood in a large stone chamber, his breath rasping as it echoed. Green and dark-red light streamed down from stained-glass windows far above, illuminating a tall woman who stood before him. She wore elaborate brocade robes in an archaic, formal style and a tall, conical headdress. He felt the wind go out of him, and his legs trembled. Though he had never seen her before, it was as if she had been in his dream all along, waiting for him.

"My... my Lady." The words spilled out from a place deep within him and echoed in the room, and Simon fell to his knees. She extended a long, six-fingered hand for him to kiss. He reached out to take it, but it had become an insubstantial mirage. Looking up, he saw that she was motionless, frozen in the act of reaching toward him. Simon looked around at the room in the dim light. He stood, feeling his heart trip-hammering in his chest.

With an explosive roar, the wall to his left collapsed, and a group of marines broke into the place. They stormed through the billowing dust, flashlights glaring from their rifle mounts.

He backed away. "Stay away from me. Stay away!" He should have kept the rifle, though part of him knew it would have made no difference in what was to come. The soldiers cut off any hope of escape as they neared him. Looming behind them was General Iron Star, his glowing eyes pinning Simon down like a bug.

"Lady! Help me!" Simon shouted. The room dissolved, leaving Simon surrounded by his abductors. He was grappled from behind, his arms held to his sides. "Lady!"

"That is not permitted." Iron Star spoke in a grating, repulsive voice. He gestured at the checkpoint, and the soldiers hauled Simon to where his rifle lay on the ground. The car was about ten yards from the checkpoint, clouds of dust hanging suspended in the air behind it.

"No. No! Lady!" Simon screamed, struggling fiercely. "Help!"

Simon's strength ran out of his limbs when he saw the face. It was that of a young woman, seemingly suspended in midair beyond the checkpoint. Though far away, her features were vivid. Short black hair, high cheekbones, exotic dark eyes. The most beautiful woman he had ever seen. And she saw him! Her eyes widened with shock, and her lips moved as if she were speaking, though he could hear nothing.

Iron Star picked up the rifle and shoved it into aiming position against Simon's cheek. He nearly broke Simon's trigger finger slapping his hand into position. The young woman's face faded, the car roared into life, and Simon pulled the trigger with another howl of anguish.

Angela got out of the car and ran her hands down her sides, pressing down the ruffled skirt and straightening her lace-up corset. Cassandra stretched and yawned then wriggled to settle her vinyl pants on her hips. They looked each other over.

"Ready?"

Cassandra nodded. "Yeah."

Stepping carefully to avoid splashing her granny boots in a puddle, Angela strolled across the street to the club, holding hands with Cassandra. With the lighting nearly nonexistent at the entrance, all Angela could see were several shadowy forms clustered outside the door, laughing, talking, and smoking.

One of them turned and waved. "Hey, Cassie. Angela."

"Hey, Janet. You made it." Cassandra smiled. "Where's Joe?"

"He's out of town." Janet gestured at another woman with her lit cigarette. "You guys, this is my cousin Martina."

They exchanged greetings. Angela searched the other shadowy forms for her best friend, without success. She glanced at Janet. "Have you seen Eric?"

"I saw him dancing half an hour ago."

"Great. I was hoping he'd make it."

"Can I bum a smoke?" Cassandra asked.

Janet shook out a clove, and Cassandra took it, lighting from the glowing tip of Janet's cigarette.

Angela suppressed a shiver. The aroma of clove cigarettes still tempted her. It had only been a few months since she'd quit. Seeking a distraction, she began to sway to the thumping rhythm from the club. "Cassie, I'm going to go find Eric."

"Sure. I'll be there in a minute."

As Angela opened the door, the music slammed into her. She smiled, diving into the strobe-lit darkness. Reaching between swaying bodies, she parted the crowd, scanning for the platinum hair of her business partner. She searched for several minutes without finding him, gradually losing herself to the rhythm.

She felt a touch on her shoulder and turned. Cassandra, illuminated by the flashes, was smiling mischievously at Angela. They began dancing together, Angela's body moving in tight synchrony with Cassandra's. Their gazes locked, and Cassandra's inner voice, always present under the surface of Angela's awareness, rose into a wordless singing. Her lower belly tightened while her dance movements became more sensuous and provocative, her hips rocking in time to the music.

—*Let's play*— Cassandra's voice echoed in her mind.

Angela's lips quirked into a half smile. Her girlfriend wanted to dance in the Otherworld again, and though it was risky, she relented. Raising her right hand high to touch empty air, fingers twirling to the rhythm, Angela evoked her dream-walking talent.

The walls of the club dissolved, replaced by the shadowy silhouettes of trees against a star-dusted sky as they entered an in-between place, neither earth nor Otherworld. The forms of the other dancers were ghostly, indistinct. Angela and Cassandra put their hands on each other's hips, their faces inches apart. Looking past Cassandra, Angela noticed that the dancers had assumed nonhuman shapes with animal heads and human bodies that shifted form and size from moment to moment. No two visits to the Otherworld were ever quite the same, and this was especially true when the two of them made these random excursions.

They moved gracefully amongst the theriomorphic dancers while the strobing scenery marked time to the rhythm of the music, trees becoming walls and then trees again. A light grew in both Angela and Cassandra, as if they were illuminated by an invisible source. They moved closer together, almost but not quite embracing.

Angela inhaled her lover's scent, and her pulse quickened. Cassandra smiled, her eyes glittering, and she glanced down, pulling Angela closer. Their hips pressed together, and Angela's belly grew warm. She lowered her hands to Cassandra's waist and tightened her fingers.

The temptation to make love to Cassandra grew in that place. Angela took a quick, steadying breath. It was dangerous. And exciting. What if she lost control of her talent and they were ejected back onto the dance floor? She grinned. She had always known that she was a little bit of an exhibitionist.

Reading her mind, Cassandra drew her close, and they kissed, tongues flicking delicately between warm, soft lips. The kiss drew a shiver up Angela's spine as her hands massaged the small of Cassandra's back. She drew her fingers up as Cassandra's arms encircled her shoulders to pull her head down, deepening the kiss. Cassandra lifted a leg, wrapped it behind Angela's hips, and began to rub herself against Angela's thigh. Cassandra's presence in her mind changed, becoming more primal as it dropped below the threshold of awareness and accelerated her arousal.

Angela dipped her face into the hollow of Cassandra's throat, kissing and licking. Cassandra moaned, lowered her leg, and pulled Angela down on top of her as they lay on the grass. The shadowy dancers moved all around them, oblivious. Angela lowered her hands to Cassandra's abdomen then pushed her fingers up under her shirt as they hungrily kissed. She began stroking the undersides of her girlfriend's breasts. Cassandra lifted her right leg and wrapped it over Angela's hips, and they thrust against each other's thighs with increasing urgency.

A tingling grew in Angela's center as they moved, amplified by her connection with Cassandra. An electric shiver ran up her spine, and she gasped, her legs trembling. The tingling spread as she flexed her hips. Her breath accelerated, and another wave of sensation rushed from the base of her spine all the way into her fingertips. Her nerves caught fire, and she cried out as she climaxed. Dimly, she heard Cassandra's own voice, a high-pitched keening, in that hot, liquid moment of timelessness.

Angela realized she was lying half on, half off of Cassandra, their arms and legs intertwined, as her awareness of herself descended from those heights of ecstasy. She lifted her head. Their noses touched as they looked into each other's eyes and smiled. Angela held her breath as she held onto that moment of timelessness, but the distant beat of the music drew her back into the Otherworldly reality. She pushed herself up on one arm. Shadowy, oblivious forms moved all around them. They sat up, still embracing, and Cassandra put her head on Angela's shoulder.

"Lady! Help me!"

The distorted shout penetrated the thump of the music. Cassandra looked up sharply, her eyes wide.

"Lady!"

They scrambled to their feet. The dancers around them faded away, along with the club music. The nighttime meadow was silent as they fully entered the Otherworld.

"Did you hear that?"

Angela shook her head. "I heard something. I don't know."

"Someone called out a name. Sounded like 'lady.'"

"I hear stuff like that sometimes. It's usually just one of the animals crying out. You know how this place is."

Cassandra put her hand out. "Wait."

"Help..." The voice was faint.

"There it is again," Cassandra whispered.

They waited a moment longer, but there was no further sound aside from the anonymous rustlings of the forest around them.

Cassandra made as if to push away from Angela. "Someone needs our help."

"Hang on, Cassie. If we go chasing that voice, we'll get lost. This is a random meadow, not yours or mine." Angela had no idea where in the Otherworld this place was. She had first found it while dancing with Cassandra several months ago and assumed that, like all such meadows in the Forest of Souls, it corresponded to the mind of someone at the club. However, she was mystified that it was always night there. The meadow of an awake mind was always day-lit.

Cassandra stiffened and stared at something amid the trees. Angela turned to look. There was a mist rising up from the ground. There was the suggestion of a face suspended in it, twisted in fear, though Angela could not clearly make out the features. Cassandra's breath hissed, and she disengaged from Angela to move slowly toward it.

Angela put a cautionary hand on her shoulder. "Cassie. You know what happened the last time you went wandering here."

Cassandra stopped and shivered. The mist had vanished, and she glanced at Angela. "I saw something. It looked like a man in pain right there." She pointed at the spot.

Angela felt as if she were standing at the edge of an abyss as electrical chills spidered all over her body. The unknown pressed down on her from the darkness, and for one breathless, terrifying moment, she was once again trapped in self-imposed exile here, guarding the Soul Thief. She found herself muttering a charm she had used to ward off the fear and anguish brought by that solitude. Angela wrenched her gaze away from where the mist had appeared and, reaching for Cassandra, drew her close once again.

"Let's get out of here." Cassandra's eyes were wide and shining in the starlight, her eagerness gone.

Angela nodded, lost in memory. That voice had cried out "Lady," which was a title she had held in her previous lifetime when she had led her people to the earth so long ago. Could it have been a revenant from that other time, reawakened by her reckless exercise of power? She regretted the impulse that had brought them here.

Cassandra nuzzled Angela under the chin and hugged her tightly, sensitive to her mood. Angela sighed and exerted her dream-walking talent. The club and its occupants reappeared around them with a deafening thump. The music shocked her ears after the silence of the forest at night, and Angela looked around to get her bearings. A familiar thatch of white hair moved in the crowd nearby.

Leading Cassandra, Angela pressed through the crowd to where Eric was dancing. "Eric!" She waved, catching his attention. He mouthed something inaudible, gesturing toward the wall, and they went to one of the lighted alcoves at the perimeter of the room.

"Angela! Cassie!" Eric beamed, hugging them both.

Cassandra smirked. "Hey, Eric. How's hunting?"

Eric grinned. "The odds are good, but the goods are odd."

Both women laughed. Angela mimed tipping a shot glass.

"Want something to drink?"

Eric nodded. "I'd love to. My usual."

"Let me get the drinks." Cassandra disappeared into the swirling crowd.

"Are you okay?" Angela peered at Eric, noticing new lines around his eyes. He was working too hard despite her remonstrations.

He rocked a hand. "Meh. Shit happens."

She put a hand on his shoulder and gave him her best sultry look. "He is going to miss you."

"Never mind him." He dismissed his ex with a wave of a hand. "I'm just glad you're here. It's been weeks!"

"Yeah." Angela shook her head. "I need to do this more often. It's so hard to get away, though."

It was later than Angela's usual bedtime, and she wanted to be rested for Nadia's party the next day. Eric, Angela, and Cassandra emerged from the club, talking loudly and laughing, and walked the gauntlet of smokers at the entrance.

"So, see you at eight tomorrow?" Unlike Angela, Eric was able to stay out partying and still get up early.

"Yeah." She sighed and looked at Cassandra. "Ready, hon?"

"Yeah, sure."

Angela scrutinized Cassandra's face. Cassandra grinned and playfully shoved her shoulder.

"Where'd you guys park?" Eric asked.

Angela pointed.

"That's where I'm parked too." Eric accompanied them as they walked toward Angela's car.

Angela glanced at him. "So, how'd you do tonight?"

Eric cracked his knuckles. "I got three phone numbers and one guy who wanted to do it in the bathroom." He grinned merrily at them both. "Don't worry about ol' Eric."

WAR IN HEAVEN: THE FLUX

BATTLEFIELD NEAR *Bald Eagle*

There were countless battalions of angels in formation on the great, featureless plain while air squadrons soared overhead. Huge insectile war engines, snake-like arcs of electrical force crawling over their armor, aimed their blackened muzzles at a smudge on the horizon. In the sky hovered the image of a gigantic scimitar marked with a crescent and star. Iron Star stared, feeling the electric tension that preceded a storm or a battle. It was impossible to see any details, but he knew the enemy well enough to guess that they had brought a force twice the size of his own. Otherwise, they would not have dared to venture forth.

His helmet, which he never removed when on the battlefield, magnified the sound of his breath as he stepped back into the mobile command post to confer with his commanders. His rust-red armor clanked as he took a seat at the table over which they were conferring.

"Shaken Fist and an ally are believed to accompany Silver Scimitar here." Swagger Stick, a seasoned command veteran, pointed at a curved line depicting the right flank of Bald Eagle's army.

Shaken Fist, an ancient foe, sought at all times to foment division within Egregores and pursue their proliferation rather than consolidation. In keeping with his philosophy, he was not a true Egregore, rooted in the living minds of the underworld. Instead, he was a loose aggregation of angels and other spirits, coalesced into a constantly changing, monstrous entity. Little more was known of his origins, much to Iron Star's frustration.

"Have we rooted out the remnants of insurrection?" Iron Star asked. His ever-present rage pulsed in his ears as he contemplated the damage done by the separatists within his own ranks. Their efforts to split Bald Eagle into smaller factions were an outrage to his orderly nature.

"Three spies from Shaken Fist have been executed."

Before Iron Star could reply, an angel burst into the room, stopped, and saluted. Iron Star regarded the intruder. "At ease. What is it, soldier?"

The angel, a genderless servitor, relaxed its salute. "The Root Hexagon. There's an intrusion. Looks like a flux surrounding it."

"There's a lot of battle flak right now. Could be anything."

"We're sure it's something new, sir."

Iron Star turned to his commanders. "Wait for me here. I must attend to this."

He rose and followed the angel out of the post, and they stepped through the rippling cloud of a portal nearby and emerged at the lip of the Crater. Iron Star and the angel climbed down and approached the Root Hexagon. There was, indeed, a shimmering veil of force that circled the crystalline form. Sparks and smoke arose where it touched the bubbling pool. Faces could be glimpsed in the smoke, prominent among them being that of a woman with dark, unruly hair, her brow creased in concern, and a younger woman, short haired, dark eyed.

Iron Star stared at the flux for a moment. He had not seen

anything like it before so near the Root Hexagon. It resembled a portal, though the nature of the Root Hexagon normally prevented one from opening anywhere within the Crater. One thing was clear, though: it did not belong at the heart of Bald Eagle's power.

He signaled to the angel, who reached behind its shoulder and unlimbered a standard-issue dissolution gun. The angel took aim and pressed the trigger. Nothing happened for a moment, and then a curl of smoke rose from the apparatus. The angel looked at it, frowning, then dropped it to the ground, where it disintegrated into the soil.

"It appears to be invulnerable to ordinary weapons." Iron Star crossed his arms. "We must study this thing. It's interfering with the Root Hexagon." He paused, thinking. "If possible, send a probe into the flux to gather intel. Report back to me with any conclusions, no later than four turnings from now."

The angel nodded. Iron Star turned to stride back up the slope. Partway up, he looked back at the flux, which was already stronger. "This is not acceptable."

CHAPTER SIX
SOMETHING NEW, SOMETHING OLD

"Coming below?" Angela asked.

Cassandra shook her head and waved a paperback. "Nah. I'm not sleepy."

Angela climbed below decks on the dark, silent sailboat, leaving the companionway hatch open. She walked with dragging steps toward the master cabin, shedding clothes as she went. She flipped on the cabin light and swept cast-off clothing from earlier in the evening onto the floor, grumbling. Pulling back the covers, she got into bed then fumbled for the light switch by the headboard.

Although she was exhausted, sleep eluded her, and she turned over restlessly several times. The slight ringing of lines slapping spars, usually unnoticed, was like a hammer, rhythmically pounding out the passing moments. She opened her eyes once to stare at the pearlescent glow leaking around the curtains from the moonlight outside then closed her eyes with a sigh.

Ring, slap, ring. Each chime of rope against aluminum spars echoed, becoming weirdly distorted, and the sounds began to blur together. Then the ringing gave way to the song of night insects, and a breeze tickled the hair on her head. The fog of sleep in her mind lifted, and when she opened her eyes again, she groaned. Not again.

Angela sat up, her palms resting on damp grass in her meadow in the Otherworld. The sky brightened as if the sun had been switched on, revealing wisps of torn, cottony clouds in an achingly blue sky. Wearing nothing but her cotton briefs, she shivered in the moist morning breeze. Angela got to her feet and surveyed the scene around her.

"What now?" Her voice had more irritation in it than she had intended.

There was no answering voice or portent. She walked over to a small, tidy cabin that, years before, she had built at the edge of the forest. Going in, she pulled on a serviceable pair of pants and a shirt then retrieved a tall walking staff from behind the door.

Going out and closing the cabin door, she tried again. "Who's calling me at this hour?"

There was a faint song, a tuneful humming in a deep voice. Angela smiled, feeling warmth in her heart. "Granddad!"

She walked toward the sound, her tiredness forgotten. Materializing out of the darkness under the trees was the broad-shouldered, wild-bearded form of George, dressed in his favorite red-checkered shirt and a pair of Levis. He looked so substantial and real that she had to remind herself that this was his oversoul.

"Angel! I can see that you are here." His voice was, as always, reassuringly solid, but his eyes stared past her, fixed on some distant point. Sometimes it took a while for him to "arrive" from wherever it was that oversouls lived.

She closed the distance between them but didn't hug him just yet. She waited, smiling, until his eyes focused on her.

"Ah, okay. I am here now." He grinned and spread his arms to hug her, and she laughed when he lifted her off her feet and set her down again.

"Did you call me here?" Angela asked.

"I did. There is something I must tell you, and something I must show you. Come. Follow me."

He led Angela to the edge of the clearing. They reached a path and walked along it, George leading the way.

"What is it?" Her grandfather always had a good reason for calling her into the Otherworld.

"You will see." He resumed humming. It was a haunting melody, and as they walked, the trees morphed from the deciduous variety that surrounded her meadow into tall conifers. The light shifted as well, as if the sun were traveling swiftly in the sky. Then they emerged from the forest to stand at the edge of a clearing that she knew well. Ahead, beyond a gentle rise, a cliff's edge dropped steeply to boulders far below at the edge of an endless ocean. She had visited this place many times since her first dream-walk had led her here. She always learned something new about herself when she did; the ocean represented the limits of her understanding

"Come see this," George said, motioning her to follow him. They climbed the slope and then stood, bracing against the constant offshore wind, and watched the crashing waves receding to the horizon. George pointed downward, and Angela leaned carefully to peer in that direction.

Far below, hundreds of animals thronged the narrow beach at the foot of the cliff At first it was unclear what the animals were doing. She shaded her eyes and squinted. The scene leaped into focus, and she gasped.

A magnificently antlered buck was on his hind legs amidst

the churning horde of creatures, his front hooves windmilling as he dueled with another, smaller deer. Both stumbled to one side as a lumbering brown beast, a bear for God's sake, lunged at them, swinging a massive paw. Two wolves leaped, bringing the bear down.

"They're fighting!" She realized that the tiny dots swirling in the air below were birds. Specifically, they were birds of prey, because one stooped on another. Both dots corkscrewed downward to vanish into the heaving ocean beyond the strand.

"Yes. That is what they are doing. Can you tell me why they fight?"

The sight of animals warring was unnatural, even for this place. Angela looked at George, confused. Then light dawned. "This is a test. I get it."

George nodded.

"When I was in training, you showed me that the animals are our instinctual nature," she continued.

George raised a finger. "Ah."

"I mean, they embody our instinctual nature."

He nodded. "Go on."

She peered down again. "But why is there a huge crowd of them? I mean, this isn't right. That's not anyone's meadow. Why are the animals gathering there?"

George was silent.

Angela thought for a moment. "If those are the incarnations of our instincts, that's too many for any one person."

George smiled encouragingly.

"Wait a minute." She snapped her fingers, guessing the answer to the riddle. "That's it. They didn't come from just one person."

"I think you know now." George nodded.

Angela remembered the spot that she and Cassandra had found while dancing at the Rings, crowded with animal-headed, shadowy forms. This was no meadow, but she guessed it was similar to that night-shrouded place. "That's a crowd. A crowd of people."

"Almost right," he said. "That is an angry mob mind. Many people, bound together in purpose by a common foe. But their instincts are at war with each other."

"Okay. These creatures are drawing strength from the deeper unconscious, which the ocean embodies. But I thought that a mob was more together, more cohesive than that."

"They are, but their instincts fight. Can you tell me why?"

Angela knew part of the answer. She turned to face George, her mind calm once again. "Because at heart, we are peaceable." Then she felt the rest of the answer click into place in her mind, and her voice rose. "But a mob, especially a violent mob, drives us against our instinct to get along."

George nodded, smiling broadly. "Remember what you have learned here. We gather together for many reasons. Families, friends, communities. Nations. Religions. Our minds join, creating a new thing, called an Egregore, that has a life of its own. Some of these gatherings result in something like that below, particularly if they are bound by hate rather than love. Look again." He pointed down

Angela peered, and the rocky beach far below was empty. She saw nothing but waves, advancing and receding on that lonely strand. She moved closer to the cliff's edge, trying to find where the animals went.

Suddenly, she felt a sharp blow between her shoulder blades, and she cried out in alarm. The earth, sky, and ocean tilted around her as she lost her balance. Her vision tunneled until all she could see was a spot on a boulder directly below. Time slowed down, and certain fatalistic peace came over her as she plunged toward that ocean-washed patch of granite. Then, with a wrench, she felt herself dragged back to stand, gasping and shaking, at the cliff's edge.

When she could get her breath again, she whirled on her grandfather. "You pushed me! What the hell was that about? I could've been killed!"

George gazed placidly back at her. "Angel, I did nothing. You did everything."

"Bullshit! I felt you hit me in the back. I was falling." She doubled over, a wave of nausea washing over her, and retched on the grass. She coughed and spat then wiped her face with a handful of grass and stood once again, glaring at George.

"I am sorry. I know how much that hurt," he said calmly. "But I did not touch you. It was your Guardian spirit who pushed your vision. All I did was bring you to an appointment with your destiny."

Her mind spinning, Angela's stare faltered. Her grandfather's oversoul never lied to her. So, whatever had happened had been necessary. Up until now, her Guardian spirit had been an abstraction, a cipher that represented her intuition. The fact that this spirit could affect her in such a direct way was a revelation.

Angela walked several paces away and sat. George sat next to her and waited while she wiped again with another handful of grass to clean her face. Tossing the grass away, she studied his face, so much like the face of the man who raised her from childhood and yet so different. The eyes set his oversoul apart from the grandfather she'd grown up with. She found herself mesmerized by the agelessness of them and shook herself. George nodded as if guessing her train of thought.

"So, when you say the spirit 'pushed my vision,' what do you mean?" she asked.

He chuckled. "I think you already know the answer. Think on what you saw when you thought you were falling."

That was just like him, never answering her questions without asking another. Angela concentrated, remembering every detail of the terrifying experience. The element that stood out was the odd tunnel vision, when it seemed as if she were falling toward the rocks at the base of the cliff. She glanced back at George.

"I think that something happened to my eyesight when it, uh, pushed me. I felt as if I were leaving my body." She shuddered.

"Almost right. Your vision traveled. You see this place"—he swept his arm to encompass all that surrounded them—"in ways that none of us saw in life. You have the eyes of death, my sister would say. You see the way that the spirits of the dead see. But your vision is still confined to this one level. The Otherworld has many levels within it, as you know. Some are higher; some are lower. There will come a time when you must be able to see into those other levels."

She looked down at her hands, turning them over to study

their backs and palms. He had told her years ago that his training required that he be able to see his own hands clearly with his second sight before he could move on into more advanced work. She, however, had been born with a talent that, according to her far memories of an earlier incarnation, represented the fruition of millennia of study and training. Yet limits to her strange gift remained.

She looked back at him. "So, does this mean that I can see more than I did before?"

"Yes," George answered, his smile broadening.

"Can I see your home? Where oversouls live?"

"Not yet." He pushed himself back to his feet and reached down to help her up. "But you will. You will."

They walked together back to the forest edge. Angela jammed her hands into her pockets, her mind racing. She was full of questions, but he would let her discover the answers on her own. That was the way he taught her.

As they returned the way they'd come on the forest path, she thought back on her previous lifetime. She had developed many complex uses for her talent. The tricks that she and Cassandra used arose from some of those techniques, enriched by her studies with George. But this method of opening the vision was new.

They arrived at her meadow, and Angela turned to regard her grandfather's oversoul. "I remember most of my previous life. But why can't I remember who you were in the old world?"

He winked. "Someday you will. But for now, you must return to your sleep. Much work awaits you." His smile faded. "Much work, Angel. Your power awakens many sleeping things."

"What do you mean?"

"I mean that many things that have slept these ages past are remembering the old world, both here and on earth. You must seek your people, Lady."

"Granddad. What are you talking—?" Angela reached over to grasp his arm. "Wait. What did you just call me?"

"Sleep, my Angel. You will know more soon."

His form grew brighter and filled Angela's vision. Then, out of nowhere, an image flashed into her mind of her old world, torn by war. Her ancient, wise culture, destroyed. That image burned itself into her heart before the relief of black oblivion dissolved her awareness.

The thump of her paperback falling to the deck awoke Cassandra. She stood to stretch and yawn before retrieving it to mark her place then went below decks.

She found the trail of Angela's clothing on the way to the master cabin. Grinning sleepily, she picked up the discarded garments on her way to bed. To avoid waking her girlfriend, Cassandra stopped herself from switching on the overhead light. Feeling her way around the bed, she deposited the clothes in a single heap, shucked her own somewhat clammy clothing, and crawled under the blanket.

Reaching out to touch Angela, she hesitated. Some premonition stopped her, a sixth sense that she had grown accustomed to. Angela was on a dream-walk. Having realized this, Cassandra could detect a whiff of the strange aroma that sometimes clung to her girlfriend, like wet soil after a lightning storm. She heard a high keening sound at the edge of audibility as if her ears were ringing. Knowing that to touch Angela while she was dream-walking was to court disaster, Cassandra instead tucked the blanket around her girlfriend's recumbent form and curled up under the top sheet.

As occasionally happened after a night of strenuous dancing, she couldn't fall asleep. She turned over, seeking a more comfortable position. Then, between one moment and the next, she was hovering, bodiless, in a vast darkness.

A man stood in a slump-shouldered posture. He was dressed in a formal uniform, as befitted his high station in the Council. It should have been comforting to her to see the brightly colored tunic, high, conical hat and pleated kilt. Instead, he looked simply gaudy, overdressed, as if a common thief had put on the robes of an emperor. His face, somehow familiar, had a pleading expression beneath the hat, and he held his arms out in entreaty.

"Forgive me," he said. The words echoed and distorted, acting like a key to unlock her memories. She had seen this man in dreams all her life.

CHAPTER SEVEN
MEETING STRANGERS

Rise up, she says, and take command

To lead us all with steady hand

And liberate our frozen hearts

From endless toil at war's demand.

JANELLE, THE floor manager, was at her desk, an officious smirk on her face. Cassandra sat uncomfortably in the chair in front of the desk.

Janelle steepled her fingers. "I've been getting reports that you aren't getting along with your coworkers. Can you explain this to me?"

Cassandra shook her head. That bitch wasn't getting anything out of her. "I don't know what you're talking about."

"Look, Cassie. Can I call you that, Cassie?"

No, Cassandra said silently.

After a short pause, Janelle continued, leaning forward. "I have a business to run, and I can't afford any troublemakers on my staff. I'm giving you the opportunity to provide your side of the story."

Cassandra looked at Janelle—at the store uniform and at the expression on her boss's face. *This bitch thinks she can scare me. She has no idea who she's dealing with.* But Cassandra kept her expression bland, neutral. She wanted to keep her job.

Deciding to take the offensive, Cassandra sat forward.

"Who's been talking shit about me?"

Janelle's synthetic smile disappeared. "I can't tell you that. My policy is that employees can file complaints. When I've heard from all sides, I'll call a meeting, and everyone can talk it over. So, I'm asking again. Do you feel that you are not getting along with your coworkers?"

Cassandra thought about all the annoying coworkers who'd been disrespecting her, crossing her boundaries. She had a right to draw a line around herself, to make a circle of safety. So she just shook her head without speaking. Janelle was the worst offender, but she'd never see it Cassandra's way.

"Cassie?" Janelle sighed. "Because you're still in your probationary period, I'm afraid I'll have to let you go. I had hoped you would cooperate with me, but I can see that we're just not a good fit for you."

"What?" Cassandra leaped to her feet. "Bullshit! This isn't about me, and you know it. You just think I'm a lying, thieving gypsy. I've heard you joking about me! You bitch!"

The manager's face grew red, and her mouth opened, but she appeared unable to speak.

Cassandra pointed at her and glared. "You have no idea who you're fucking with."

With that, she spun on her heel and stormed out, slamming the door behind her.

Cassandra touched her clove cigarette to her lips. She took a luxurious drag, watching the tourists gawk at the clipper ships. The warm sun and cool breeze were intoxicating, and she basked, her mind empty. Her eyes tracked a tan, athletic, blond woman jogging past. A pair of skateboarders careened between the pedestrians.

After she had left NutriMart, she had driven aimlessly in Berkeley to cool off. North on Telegraph toward the university then a U-turn back south. Right on Ashby. North on Fulton all the way to University Avenue. By the time she arrived at the entrance ramp to 580, she had managed to put her rage behind her. With nothing else to do and unwilling to bother Angela at work, Cassandra had decided to drive over the Bay Bridge to hang out in Maritime National Park for the rest of the beautiful June afternoon.

She ground her cigarette out on the cylindrical ashtray and flicked the butt into the waste receptacle underneath. A black convertible passed by, its premium stereo thumping. The sound reminded her of the club music from the night before. Angela rarely went to the Rings to dance since she was busy with the clinic. Last night's Otherworld play and the subsequent lovemaking had been a treat.

She thought about that strange voice she had heard and the face in the mist.

—*Help.*—

There had been a strange familiarity to it.

—*Help me.*—

It was odd how the voice had echoed. She could almost hear it again. The traffic sounds faded.

—*Lady.*—

Cassandra saw the face and part of his torso in her mind. He was pleading, his hands outstretched in entreaty, but he was not as panicky as he had been the first time. She felt a tug somewhere in her midsection, and she stood. Turning slowly in place, she felt the tug intensify, and she began walking. Her visual field narrowed so that everyone who passed came into focus and then disappeared as they walked by.

—*I won't kill them.*—

She continued along Beach Street then turned right onto the crosswalk at Larkin. A rising babble of voices washed over her mind, and the faces of the other pedestrians acquired hallucinatory intensity. Cassandra reached into her pocket and pinched her fingers together. The voices receded, along with the faint tugging sensation and the vividness of the scenery. She stopped, uncertain. Then she saw a café ahead and, realizing she was ravenous, headed purposefully toward it.

As small as Julian's Café was, Cassandra was almost alone when she went in. She glanced at the "Seat Yourself" sign by the entrance, took a seat at a small table, and tossed her pack on the floor by her chair.

Someone handed her a menu. Then she shook the fog out of her head and took out her cell phone to check her messages. Glancing at the screen, she realized that she had left it turned off.

"Dammit." She checked her voicemail. There were two messages, one from Angela and one from Janet. She touched the list entry for Angela's message and held the phone to her ear. She sighed. It was a reminder about the birthday party at Nadia's. Nadia didn't like her, but nothing she said would convince Angela of that.

"Five-ish. There'll be dancing, I promise. Love ya. Bye." Angela's voice always tightened Cassandra's throat with longing, and she knew she would crawl on broken glass if her girlfriend asked, but the birthday party was going to be hellish. Noting that her battery was almost dead, Cassandra turned the phone back off as a waiter approached the table. She ordered a sandwich and coffee then read her book while she waited. It occurred to her to reply to Angela's message, but she told herself there was plenty of time before the party started.

Twenty minutes later, lunch finished, she paid her tab and started for the door. As she opened it, she nearly collided with a wheelchair-bound man coming in. She glanced at his face and froze. Dark hair, lean, pale face, colorless eyes. The man from her vision was real. As he saw her, he stopped.

"Sorry! I..." Cassandra stepped to one side.

The man began to wheel through the door and stopped again, a puzzled frown on his face. "Thanks. Don't I know you from somewhere?"

Cassandra caught herself backing away and froze. She had to know if he was really the man who had called out to her. She closed the door and faced him. "In your dreams." She felt heat rise to her face. "I didn't mean it like that."

They stared at each other for three seconds, blocking the doorway.

"I'm sure I recognize you from somewhere," the man said. "I'm sorry. I'm terrible with names."

"Oh. I'm Cassandra. Cassie to my friends."

"Hi Cassie. I'm Simon." He stuck his hand out, and she touched it and then jerked hers away as if stung. A woman came up behind him and cleared her throat.

He grinned at Cassandra and gestured. "Why don't we find a

table and let this lady through?"

Cassandra nodded, and they went to sit where there was good clearance for his wheelchair. The waiter approached them as Cassandra plunked into her seat.

She glanced up. "I already ate, but I could use a latté."

Simon took a menu. Then he lifted an eyebrow at her. "So... where do I know you from?"

Cassandra shrugged. "NutriMart, maybe? Do you go dancing... oh, shit. Sorry."

He chuckled. "I don't shop there. And dancing is a little awkward. I'm always running over someone's feet."

They both laughed. Cassandra felt the tension in her shoulders ease somewhat. "Yeah, I recognize you too. Just can't say where from." *Won't say*, she added silently. She paused as she got one of her telepathic "news flashes." "But I remember that you don't live around here. Right?"

"Right. I'm visiting a friend in the City. I live in Oakland."

The waiter took their orders and left.

"My girlfriend and I live in Alameda." It was best to let him know where he stood with her. Guys always got the wrong idea when she talked to them.

Simon's eyes tightened for a moment, but he said nothing.

"Actually we live on a sailboat at Bayside Marina in Alameda."

He sat forward. "That's pretty cool. I used to want to go sailing. Never really got around to it."

Cassandra's eyes widened as another flash came. "You were in Iraq."

Simon's face darkened. "Apparently, you remember a lot

more about me than I do about you."

"Look, I didn't mean to—"

Simon raised a hand. "Don't worry about it. I'm just not used to forgetting a pretty face."

"Huh. Sure. Whatever." A charmer. She looked around, momentarily at a loss. There was an awkward pause. "So what do you do?"

"I'm a computer programmer. It's good work when you can get it."

"I bet. I thought about getting into that. I need to go to college first."

"Focus on web design. That's where the money is."

Cassandra drummed her fingers then tugged at an earring. This wasn't going anywhere. "Look. I don't actually know you. But I think you were in trouble last night. I heard you calling for help. What's going on?"

His face hardened. "I don't know what you're talking about."

"You called out. You said, 'Lady.'"

Simon's mouth opened, and his face went pale. Cassandra waited.

"How could you know that?" he blurted. "That was a nightmare!"

On an impulse, Cassandra tried projecting a thought. —*I'm a telepath, Simon.*—

He jumped, jarring the table and spilling some of his coffee. "Holy shit!"

Several of the other diners turned to stare. Simon, his eyes wide as he stared at Cassandra, took no notice.

Cassandra leaned forward. "Like I said, I saw you last night."

"It's these dreams." His voice faltered. "Nightmares. I've been having them for years, but they got really bad about a year ago." Now his face was drawn. "So, you know I was stationed in Iraq. Marine Corps. I was on a fast track to sergeant, thinking about officer school. But then my unit was deployed to Iraq..."

Cassandra lost her nerve, feeling the riptide of Simon's emotions now that she had reached out mentally to him. This wasn't going well at all. She stood. "I'm sorry. I gotta go."

Simon put his hand out. "Please stay. Look, I don't think I know you either, but something tells me I need to."

She sat back down slowly, her pulse quickening.

He continued. "I was having one of my nightmares. This is going to sound crazy, but something or someone is controlling my dreams."

Cassandra nodded. Now they were getting somewhere. "That's not so crazy."

He stared at her, his mouth open, then shook his head. "I've had these nightmares for a while." He hastily added, "Oh, I've been to therapy. I've got my meds." He shook a pocket. Then his eyes became distant, introspective. "I was a guard at a checkpoint in Baghdad. I did something bad..."

"Go on," Cassandra tried to keep the impatience out of her voice. This guy had a story all right.

"Look, I really don't know who you are, and I'm not sure why I want to open up to you. Maybe I'm just lonely." Simon chuckled. "I don't run into telepaths every day." He glanced around as if to reassure himself of the reality of their surroundings.

"Well, I don't run into guys who saw me in their nightmares, either."

Simon sighed heavily. "Like I was saying, I did something at that checkpoint, and it gave me PTSD. So I've been coping with that, forcing myself to stop the nightmares. But lately, these really creepy guys show up in my dream. They grab me, hold me down, put the gun in my hands, and make me shoot." He stopped.

"Shit." Cassandra felt a shiver run up her spine.

"Yeah. I had another one last night." He sat forward a bit. "That nightmare was a little different. See, there was this lady. The dream stopped when I... when I stopped it. And then she was in front of me. Somehow, I knew I needed to ask her forgiveness. Then those bastards showed up and took me away. Back to the checkpoint." He thumped the table repetitively, lightly. "And then somehow..." He looked at Cassandra, eyes wide. "I saw you there."

Cassandra smiled grimly. "That's because I was there."

Simon trembled, pulling his hand across his hair and down his face, and he started breathing faster. "Oh shit. Oh shit. This is crazy. I'm having another episode."

"Stop. Simon, look at me."

He swallowed, his hand covering his mouth, and looked at her.

"You're not crazy," she said. "I'm not crazy. I'm a telepath, and I saw you while you were having a nightmare. I didn't give you that nightmare or anything. So calm down, okay?"

He remained silent and unmoving. Just staring.

She smiled, trying to defuse the tension. "So let's cut the bullshit and try to pretend that the world is weirder than either of us can possibly imagine. Okay?"

After a moment, Simon nodded. "Okay. Okay. I know it is. I've seen some weird shit too, you know. You're not going to believe this, but I can go out of my body any time I want."

"I believe it."

He stared at Cassandra for a moment then blinked. "Okay. Well, Alice, let's take a tour of Wonderland."

She rolled her eyes.

"So here's the deal," he continued. "In Baghdad seven years and four months ago, I was on patrol at a checkpoint. When we saw a car approaching fast, we had to act. I mean, there were car bombers everywhere. So finally, we had to fire on them." He swallowed, his hand trembling. "You know, it's been years, I've been to therapy, and it's still really hard to talk about this."

Cassandra kept her mouth shut, though she was once again struggling with the intensity of emotion radiating from this wounded man across the table from her. She braced herself and nodded encouragement.

"I shot a mother and her two daughters." He was talking fast, his words spilling over each other. "I didn't know who it was. It could've been someone with a bomb. It could've been someone with guns ready to shoot us all. But instead it was just someone who didn't know who we were, and so now..." He stopped.

Cassandra pinched her fingers together surreptitiously, shutting off the pain, and sagged with relief. Sometime during his recitation, the waiter had brought their orders, and she sipped her latté to conceal her reaction.

"Every few nights I relive that." Simon stared at nothing

now. "But later when I learned how to get out of my body, I also learned how to stop the dream. Used to be when I stopped it, I could just walk away. About a year ago, that changed. Now, when I go to sleep, or try to go out of my body, I end up at the checkpoint. And if I try to leave, those guys show up."

"Tell me about them."

He glanced at her. "They look like Marines in desert kit. But the light's weird—weirder than usual for a dream, anyway. And behind them is a really scary dude. Way taller than me, more like basketball-player tall, but built like a quarterback. Wears a general's uniform, but his eyes are glowing white."

They both shivered.

"I've started to call him Iron Star." Simon picked at his food. "Not sure why. The name just came to me. So, last night, the dream changed. I can't remember the details, but there was this really tall woman. The Lady. I felt like I should know her, and I thought she was going to save me. So, when the General was pushing me down to shoot those people, I yelled out for the Lady." He looked at Cassandra. "That must be what you heard. And saw."

Cassandra nodded slowly. "I think I can help. Iron Star's probably a part of your mind that wants you to keep reliving that. Maybe I can talk to it."

"Nuh-uh. If this nightmare gets in your head, it'll fuck you up. I don't want that on my conscience, too." He pushed down on the grips of his chair and shifted in his seat. "Cassie, I've had to learn how to live with some nasty shit."

"Me too, Simon. I lived on the streets for five years." She closed her mouth firmly.

"No shit. Five years ago I was on patrol when my APV drove over an IED. Boom." He gestured at his legs. "That's when I learned how to get out. One minute I was lying there, knocked out on a morphine drip, and suddenly I was bobbing near the ceiling."

"Cool. I'd like to know how to do that." The five-years thing was probably just a coincidence, Cassandra told herself.

Simon shook his head. "You don't want to learn that way. Trust me. Look, I know you want to help, but there's other stuff that came back home with me that you probably don't want in your head. Like, I used to get in a lot of fights."

Cassandra frowned. Anyone who would pick on a guy in a wheelchair was a real prick. She opened her mouth to say so when he interrupted.

"Not fistfights. Arguments. It seemed as if everything I said pissed someone off. I drove away a lot of friends, lost some clients. Then one of my buddies from the war told me about an anger management class." He chuckled. "Turned out that it wasn't real helpful. But I figured there wasn't anything to lose. While I was in that class getting my ear chewed off, I met a woman."

Cassandra raised an eyebrow.

He grinned. "At the time, I was curious about Buddhism. It sounded like a good way to develop inner peace. When I mentioned that in class, she told me she was a member of a group that melded meditative practices with western polytheism."

"You mean like multiple gods?"

"Exactly."

"I read a lot of mythology books when I was a kid. Loved 'em."

Simon nodded. "It turns out that there's a modern movement to restore the religion of ancient Greece. You know, altars to Zeus, Poseidon, Ares. Ritual. Prayers. That's what I'm doing these days when I'm not designing websites."

An odd thrill ran down her spine. It felt as if something or someone was calling to her. Cassandra finished her latté and set her cup down. "Did it help? I mean, do you still get into lots of arguments?"

Simon stopped eating and stared at her. "If I still had that problem, we wouldn't be having this conversation. I'm serious. Every time I talked to someone, it went badly. Yeah, I think that my spirituality really helped me get a grip on myself. Guess which god I worship these days?" He looked down and took another bite.

"Zeus? Or... Apollo?" She liked Apollo. Sun god, played music. He'd be entertaining. She had a serious boner for Artemis the Huntress. But she doubted that Simon worshipped the Virgin.

He shook his head. "Nope. Ares. Turns out that if you want to control yourself and stop fights, he's the one who can help the most. I light incense to him every Tuesday. That's his holy day."

Cassandra leaned back in her chair and crossed her arms. This guy was serious. "Crazy. So, can anyone join this religion?"

"They took me, didn't they? If you're interested, you could come to one of our meetings. The next one's on the second

Tuesday in July. You'd be my guest."

Cassandra shrugged, pretending a lack of interest. "Maybe."

"You know something?" Simon eyed Cassandra. "I think you'd like Aphrodite."

She laughed. "Yeah, right. I'm not the romantic type. A love goddess seems kinda mushy to me."

"No, I'm serious. She's mysterious. Powerful. Works behind the scenes."

"Hm." Cassandra glanced out the window at the afternoon sunlight. "I don't know."

WAR IN HEAVEN: ROOT HEXAGON

ROOT HEXAGON, Bald Eagle

Iron Star and two attendant angels were tending the Root Hexagon, tuning its power flows. He held a barbed-and-hooked tenacity staff so that one end touched the Root Hexagon. The angels stood to either side of the crystal, their hands held out toward each other. The flickering light of a data stream danced between them. Visible in this flow of information were images from a military checkpoint scene showing a careening vehicle riddled with bullet holes. That was replaced by an image of an explosion that threw one man aside and killed several others. Still another image, a close-in shot of a woman's agonized face as a group of men raped her, evanesced between the working angels. He viewed all of this dispassionately. The needs of Bald Eagle required sacrifice.

"In your dreams!"

The shout echoed from the Crater walls, breaking the attendants' concentration. Two enemy angels, armed with glowing spears, leaped over the lip of the crater opposite Iron Star, landed gracefully, and raced toward them. Iron Star dropped the staff, drew his sword, and ran to intercept them. The attendants lowered their hands and turned sluggishly, having been completely absorbed in their work.

An attendant angel collapsed with an agonized cry as one of the enemy thrust its spear entirely through its body. Iron Star charged the enemy, shouting a deafening battle cry. His sword moved in a vicious sweep, tearing through two adversaries at once. He whirled, his weapon clanging and showering him with sparks. He beat aside another angel's spear and skewered his attacker.

A scream of tormented air and the throb of lively martial music announced the opening of a portal nearby. Iron Star turned to see more attackers pouring over the Crater's edge. Racing toward the Root Hexagon, the dark-eyed, black-haired newcomers brandished short, stabbing swords and axes. They immediately set upon the power cables, hacking with their weapons.

"Warrior angels, to me!" Iron Star shouted, desperation lending power to his voice. "Protect the Root Hexagon!"

He glanced over to where the remaining attendant was heavily embattled. It was wounded, electrical discharges arcing from its side to the ground. The enemy dropped its spear and grappled the attendant, and there was a searing flash as the attendant was absorbed by its attacker.

Iron Star raised his sword as three assailants set upon him. He parried their attacks and dispatched them with ruthless efficiency.

Another angel howled in pain near the Root Hexagon. One of the spear wielders had skewered a member of the dark-eyed faction. The wounded angel locked gazes with Iron Star then collapsed into a gelatinous pile of disorganized matter. Iron Star knew better than to be grateful to the spear wielder, however. Both factions sought to disrupt the Root Hexagon in their own ways. He bounded toward the enemy, a ululating cry on his lips, batted aside the spear, and decapitated the angel.

Another shout of defiance announced the arrival of a dozen

reinforcements. Bald Eagle's angels poured over the lip of the crater behind Iron Star. He spared a glance at the Root Hexagon. It was glowing far more dimly than before. Seeing a new crack in the crystal, he growled.

With renewed vigor, he swung his deadly sword, and with his help, the forces of Bald Eagle drove the enemy back. Finally, forced away from the Root Hexagon, the foemen turned as one and scrambled out of the crater. Iron Star had sent more than one back with poisoned wounds inflicted by his weapon. With any luck, the poison would spread amongst the enemy angels and weaken their masters.

He turned to survey the Crater, the sword in his hand dripping with ichor. Iron Star's forces had taken heavy losses from the enemy's wild, determined assault. He scrutinized the damage to the Root Hexagon. Its integrity had been breached, and he guessed that at least one of the enemy had penetrated it despite its isolation within the pool. It was remotely possible that an enemy had actually sabotaged the keystone, though he dismissed that terrible possibility as being unlikely. They would need to destroy his projection first. He believed he would know if that had happened.

An angel approached Iron Star and saluted. "They were infiltrators from several enemy Egregores. One of those was our ancient foe, Serpent Lion. It appears that he has a renewed interest in the Root Hexagon. Another attacker, Dark Eyes, stepped in as well, even though he's an enemy of Serpent Lion. We do not know yet how they managed to penetrate so far into Bald Eagle."

Iron Star swore. "Serpent Lion and Dark Eyes." He wiped his

sword on a shapeless heap of cloth lying near his feet—all that remained of the enemy angels that had attacked. "This could be related to the power drop we experienced recently. Double the guard. Inform me immediately if you see any more interference. I leave you in command while I report this to Bald Eagle." He slammed his sword into its scabbard and stalked toward the palace.

While the other Egregores had been troublesome for Bald Eagle, Dark Eyes required special attention. He had been fighting a desperate battle to disrupt the Root Hexagon ever since its capture by Bald Eagle. The initial assault by Serpent Lion had probably opened the portal for Dark Eyes to attack. However, it should be possible to fan the flames of their mutual hatred.

War on Earth

The woman at the grocery store turned to her friend. "I heard they're sending our boys back to Iraq."

"No! Not again..." Her friend's hand flew to her mouth.

—

"We're marching on the Federal building," Rafe said at lunch. "Someone's gotta stop this."

His two friends nodded, frowning. Roma should stick together when times got tough.

—

"More Roma are gonna die in *gadje* wars." The old woman shrugged. "What can we do?"

—

"That stuff in the Middle East is none of our..."

—

"... none of our business..."

—

"Big business..."

—

"Yeah."

Oakland He

Monday, June 2, 2014

Protestors March on Federa

About a hundred rallied Monday afternoon in front of the Oakland Federal Building, protesting U.S. involvement in the Iraqi conflict. Several protestors spoke to the media, claiming that military intervention in the Middle East could precipitate a global conflict. Two arrests were made when several Romani marchers chained themselves to the doors.

Ren
foll
imp

The
that
rela
the

CHAPTER EIGHT
NADIA'S HOUSE

While ancient foes trade bitter blows

That echo in the worlds below

The earthly pawns do play their games

To reinforce the status quo.

NADIA WAS highly regarded in the Roma community, which was already predisposed to celebrating virtually any occasion. Her birthday party was, therefore, a blowout. Because she had insisted that everyone wear what she called traditional attire and celebrate with music, they took the excuse to wear flashy clothes and show off the best dance steps.

A fiddler, two guitarists, and an accordion player were playing lively tunes, and a large contingent of dancers swirled near the bonfire, Angela among them. Light flashed from sparkling jewelry, the long skirts of the women fluttered and billowed as they spun, and the men's vests, dark pants, and brightly decorated shirts bestowed a dazzling array of colors to the Romani throng, boisterous with drink and song.

Angela skipped away from the dancers to take a break. Her body tingled from the endorphin rush, and she could feel sweat cooling on her face as she plunked down in a chair away from the fire.

One of her cousins, a heavyset, bearded man sitting next to her, touched her shoulder. "Where's Cassandra?"

Angela looked at him and shrugged, masking a surge of frustration. "She couldn't make it."

"Too bad. The music's great tonight."

Angela nodded. She had gotten Cassandra's voicemail how many times now? Obviously, she had blown off Nadia's invitation yet again.

The tune changed, and Angela looked back at the dancers, thoughts of her errant girlfriend temporarily driven away. She shot to her feet as one of her favorite songs kicked off. "C'mon. I love this tune."

She reached over to tug at his hand, but then she paused, feeling a powerful sense of being watched. She turned to look, her heart sinking and her enthusiasm losing some of its sparkle. Nadia beckoned from her seat away from the fire. Angela hesitated, debating whether to ignore her great-aunt, but then she let go of her cousin's hand reluctantly and waved vaguely toward the bonfire. "Go ahead. Nana wants to talk to me."

Her cousin grinned and trotted back into the dancing fray. Angela went over to where Nadia was sitting in a lawn chair.

"Are you having fun?" her great-aunt asked.

"I am. You throw the best birthday parties."

"I'm glad to hear it. I wish Cassandra could have come."

"Well, you know." Angela shrugged. "Sometimes she gets distracted. I'm sure she'll have some reason waiting for me when I get back."

Nadia reached up and put her hand on Angela's arm. "I wanted to talk to you while everyone's busy."

Angela crouched, but Nadia shook her head. "Pull up a

chair."

Angela found another lawn chair, moved it closer to Nadia, and perched on the edge of the seat.

"I had a vision of you last night," Nadia continued. "Were you doing anything... special?"

Angela nodded, though inwardly she squirmed. "Cassie and I sometimes play a little bit when we dance. We've worked out some interesting techniques."

"I thought so. You know how I feel about playing with power, so I won't repeat myself. But my vision had nothing to do with dancing." She cleared her throat and picked up a glass from the table next to her. She sipped from it and set it down. "You were dressed in armor that glowed in all the colors of the rainbow. You had weapons, and you looked ready to go to war."

"No way." Angela pursed her lips. "You know how I feel about war."

"Yes, I know. It was that Great War you've told me about, wasn't it? That would make a pacifist out of me, too."

"It's not just the old War." Angela glanced toward the fire then back at Nadia. "I've been treating patients with PTSD, and none of my clinical training prepared me for the reality. I have more in common with the vets than I thought."

"PTSD?"

"Post-traumatic stress disorder. They used to call it shell shock."

"Ah, right." Nadia shook her head. "I had a cousin in Vietnam who came back a broken man."

"Well, these boys—they're mostly boys—came back from Iraq. Sounds like we're repeating a lesson we didn't learn."

"Yes. But back to the vision." Nadia shifted in her chair. "You were at War. Angela, please listen to me."

Angela stopped herself from glancing at the fire again and focused her attention on her great-aunt.

"You need training," Nadia continued. "Yes, you have more power than any of us. And yes, you remember things you learned from very long ago. But this is the here and now, and you are human. You are Roma."

Angela shook her head. "Nana, I know what you're saying, and you're probably right. But this just isn't a good time. Between the clinic and the new patients and Cassie, I just don't have the energy. When Granddad was teaching me, I would be wiped out for a week sometimes."

Nadia's eyes narrowed. "You're going to his oversoul for instruction. You also know how I feel about that."

"That's none of your concern, Nana."

Nadia shrugged. "Be that as it may, your power isn't going to wait. And my vision tells me that soon you will be forced to choose your path. I want you to know that you don't need to do it alone."

Angela could not simply outright refuse Nadia after all her great-aunt had done to receive both her and Cassandra back into the community.

Angela placed a hand on her great-aunt's shoulder. "Nana, I really can't promise anything. But I will see if there's a way for Eric to cover for me one day a month."

Nadia nodded. "Thank you, Angela. This means a lot to me."

"Thank you for caring for us."

Nadia made a shooing motion. "Now. Go dance. I hear

another tune starting."

Angela pecked Nadia on the cheek and went back to the dance circle.

Late that night, after the party, her cousin Martha visited Nadia for a prescription. When she was ready to leave, Martha stood by the door, clutching a small paper bag with both hands.

Standing on aching feet, Nadia leaned on her cane. "You know what to do."

"A pinch in his coffee in the morning and a teaspoon with his meal at night."

Nadia nodded. "And be sure to add a little sugar. It can be bitter. Call me in a week. Sooner, if things turn around quicker than that."

Martha smiled, her plain features beautified by the expression. "Good night, cousin. And happy birthday."

"Thank you. Good night to you, too."

Martha left, closing the door after herself. Nadia returned to her chair and lowered herself into it with a grunt. She glanced in the direction of the hallway. "Michael! Martha's gone."

There was a moment of silence, and then he opened the door and shuffled down the hall to the living room. "That's the third one tonight. The spirits must be anxious."

"What would you know about spirits?" She paused. "No, it was man trouble. We can lay that at the feet of the gadje and their evil ways." Nadia proffered her empty teacup. "Now be a good brother and make us some tea."

Michael took her cup to the kitchen and got one out of the cabinet for himself. While he made tea, Nadia brooded.

Angela's relationship with Cassandra was controversial in the community among those who knew of it. Her dream-walking talent was both a boon and a curse, depending on whether the Roma considered it a gift from Del or sorcery from Beng. And her status in the Roma community was still recovering from the ban of marimé that had only been lifted late the previous year.

There were no easy solutions. Nadia reluctantly concluded that she needed to talk to her brother about the girl. Michael was a wise man for all that he lacked anything of the Gift or the Sight. He was also closer to his great niece than Nadia, much to her chagrin.

"I need your advice on a matter to do with Angela and Cassandra." She tried to keep all inflection out of her voice. "It came to a head at the party."

Michael glanced at her and lifted an eyebrow. "Angela looked like she was having fun. But I didn't see Cassandra anywhere."

"She never showed up. I wouldn't want to be in her shoes when Angela sees her again." Nadia chuckled.

"You don't like Cassandra, do you?" Michael frowned.

Nadia returned his look for a moment, contemplating how much to tell him. Well, if she wanted his advice, she had better be forthright. "Cassandra is a wild child. She was homeless for the last five or so years. It's not her fault, but I don't think she's a good influence on Angela. You know."

He nodded. "There's that. But they're in love. You've seen them together."

"Angela just hasn't found the right man yet. She's got a touch of the wild in her, too. Her momma was a hippie gadjo after all."

The kettle began whistling. Michael poured the tea and brought two cups and saucers back into the living room. He gave her one and went to his own chair, grunting as he sat. He glanced at Nadia. "Why don't you leave Angela be? She's had a hard year."

"If it was just Angela, I would." Nadia set her cup aside. "You know I care about her. But you know what she is. And what she can do."

"Yes, I do. Nadia, she's deep, like George was. I think you need to trust her more." He sipped his tea and regarded her over the steaming cup.

Nadia blew across the top of the cup to cool it then took a sip. He had a point, and after all, she had asked his opinion. She settled farther back in her chair. "It's not just her I'm worried about. Michael, our community is in trouble."

"Trouble?" He frowned. "More than the usual trouble?"

"There's an old story that our momma told me. It was about a Rom boy who decided to go to the city to make his fortune. His daddy took him aside and made him memorize this spell." She paused for dramatic effect. "Turn, turn, turn away. I will never go astray."

Nadia sipped her tea and continued. "He told his boy to close his eyes and use this charm whenever a gadjo wanted to show him tempting trinkets or lure him away from the laws of his people." She paused.

Michael nodded his understanding. He must have heard stories like this one.

She cleared her throat. "Well, he went to the city. Sure

enough, along comes a prostitute. He saw her, shut his eyes, and made the spell until she went away. Later he met a man who wanted to take his horse and cart and give him a car. He shut his eyes and said the spell until the man grumbled and went away. But each time he saw a temptation, it took him a little longer to shut his eyes, a little longer to say the spell. Soon, he stopped saying the spell, and then he kept his eyes open, and snap! He was trapped by the gadje. Left the ways of the Roma and became a vagabond and wasted his days and died unhappy."

She sipped more tea and watched her brother. Michael waited, unspeaking. He was, she knew, aware that she had a point to make in telling the story. Nadia sighed. "This is happening to us."

He rolled his eyes. "That is not news, Nadia. Everywhere we go, the gadje tempt us. We have to live in their world, so we grow and change. That is how life is."

Nadia waved irritably. "No, no, no. I know all that. I'm saying that in the last few years, we have been losing families, whole families. They turn their backs on the rest of the Roma and disappear into the world of the unclean ones. Some of us..."

She put her teacup down again, feeling her anger rise. "Some of us have gone and joined the military. Rom boys fighting for the gadje. Dying for them too. What are we going to do about it?" She smacked her thigh in frustration.

"Nadia," Michael said gently. "I know that already. It's not news. Our people have fought in wars for a very long time."

She stared at him. "You don't understand. Since last year, eighteen Roma families have just disappeared. Gone. Moved away, left no way to reach them, no explanation, and no contact with anyone on the road."

It was his turn to stare. "Eighteen? That can't be right. There was a big bunch of us at your party this evening."

"Yes, and I am thankful for them. But they are our clan. Two of my cousin's daughters came to me. I cannot tell you what they had to say, but I can tell you that we are losing people. Something is tempting them away from the Roma. And I believe Angela can stop it. But how can I convince her to help?" She lifted both hands then dropped them.

"Ah, I see now." Michael set his cup down. "You think this is something from the Otherworld coming to steal us away. You want her to go there, find it, and stop it. Like when she fought the Soul Thief."

Nadia's breath caught in her tightening throat. That battle had taken the life of their brother. Not trusting herself to speak, she nodded.

"Nadia, why don't you just tell her what you told me?"

She spread her hands again. "It's not that simple. She needs to gain the trust of these families. Otherwise, they will not let her go into their meadows to find this thing that is weakening us. How are they going to trust a lesbian psychiatrist half Romani with their souls?"

Michael's lips pressed together in a grim line. "So this is really about Cassandra. Nadia, this is not something you will be able to change Angela's mind about. She'll walk away from all of us again if we meddle in her life."

"I can't believe that. Surely she—"

"Nadia, listen to me. Angela came to me a couple of months

ago to talk about Cassandra. She wanted my approval. I am not comfortable with the homosexual life, but she had a light in her eyes I have not seen in many years."

He turned in his chair to face her. "If Angela helps us, she'll do it on her own terms. She is older and wiser than all of us put together, Nadia. You've heard some of her stories. She led all of her people to this world." He shook a fist, suddenly animated. "She killed the Soul Thief. She saved us all. And she can do it again. Please, just talk to her. Tell her what you know. Also tell her your fears. Trust her." He stopped, staring fiercely at her.

Nadia looked down at her hands. He was sensible, true, but he failed to see the bigger picture. She would have to keep chipping away at his misguided opinion. Sighing deeply, she looked back up. "Maybe you're right. But it's not going to last. One day she will meet a man, and he will melt her heart. You'll see."

WAR IN HEAVEN: SERPENT LION AND DARK EYES

"Leave." The woman lounging on the Lion Throne waved an imperious hand. Her attendant angels were naturally reluctant to depart, delaying as long as possible to drink in the sight of her. Several of them—nude, male, and beautiful—were the last to leave. She relented and shifted form, allowing them a glimpse of her—his—male body. Swooning, they departed.

He sighed as the last of his angels drew the hanging curtain across the doorway. Serpent Lion surveyed his throne room. It was the embodiment of luxury, the floor a mélange of rich color carpeted with soft, embroidered cushions and thick rugs. The walls were concealed by hangings, lanterns, and tapestries. The air was thick with scents both musky and sweet. Yet to his practiced eye, something was amiss, and he examined the details more closely, shifting back to female form out of an eons-long habit.

Then Serpent Lion saw it. Where there should have been a soft cushion, there was instead a large stone—patterned skillfully, to be sure, but hardly comfortable. In the instant that she identified it, it erupted with a roar. She leaped up off the throne. A geyser of stones and other debris exploded outward, coating all surfaces and filling the air with choking dust.

"Guards! To me!" Serpent Lion shouted.

Two of her attendants hurried into the room, waving their hands and coughing. They stood at attention, their faces twitching and their eyes watering.

"At ease."

At that, both attendants sneezed. They recovered themselves apologetically.

Serpent Lion nodded. "This is the work of Dark Eyes, without a doubt. You must gather a contingent to counter attack. Better yet, send one of my warrior angels to breach their defenses. The coward sought to destroy many of our number with that weapon, and I must teach him never to penetrate this far into my realm again."

The guards saluted, glancing wide-eyed at the still-smoking crater where the rock had exploded. They turned to leave.

"Wait," Serpent Lion said, raising a hand. "There is another matter. The Root Hexagon is vulnerable to us now. If you can damage that blasphemous artifact as well, so much the better."

CHAPTER NINE
LOVE AND STRIFE

Then with a sigh she turns once more

To lift her shield, a dismal chore

And save herself from cunning jabs

That seek her secret fragile core.

IT WAS one in the morning when Angela finally returned home, and there was no sign of Cassandra there, either. She felt a hollowness in the pit of her stomach as she debated whether to call Janet. Finally, she dialed Cassandra's friend, but Janet had not seen Cassandra that afternoon after she had been fired.

The news of Cassandra's firing filled Angela with new dread. Why hadn't her girlfriend called or come by the office? Angela contacted the local hospitals. Nothing. The police department took her information and reported no incidents involving anyone matching Cassandra's description.

Angela tried to reach out to her link with Cassandra. Though, to her relief, the sense of her girlfriend's presence was strong, there was no response. Finally, reduced to impotent waiting, Angela changed into sweats and a T-shirt and settled in the salon to read.

Two pages into her novel, Angela realized that she had just reread the same sentence three times. Aside from the reading light overhead, all other interior lights were dim. She glanced at the clock. Two in the morning.

Boots clumped on the deck. The companionway slats were raised, and Cassandra descended into the salon. She was halfway down when she saw Angela, paused, then finished her descent.

"Where were you? I called you. Three times." Angela put down her book. "Then I called everyone else."

Cassandra stood at the foot of the companionway ladder, hands by her side. She stared at Angela for a moment. "I know."

Angela slapped the cushion next to her. "What the hell, Cassie?"

"Maybe I didn't feel like answering. Sometimes I'm busy, you know?"

"What do you mean, busy? You said you were going to the party!"

Cassandra stalked over to the sink, ran some water, and washed her hands, scrubbing vigorously, not looking at Angela. "Something came up."

"Is that it?" Angela felt the heat in her face. "You don't answer your phone, and you don't show up or anything? Sometimes you can be so fucking selfish."

Cassandra turned around, wiping her hands on her pants. "I was going to come home and meet you. But then I met this guy."

"Excuse me?"

Cassandra flinched. "Not that. Jeez, you know me better than that. We started talking, and I lost track of time."

Angela threw up her hands. "You let me down, Cassie. Again. Look, I know you're still dealing with a lot, but can you at least try to follow through?"

Cassandra dropped into the settee across from Angela. "He was interesting! He's in a wheelchair because of the war. I want to help."

Angela snorted. "Help with what, Doctor?"

"Look, I see you helping people all the time. Maybe I feel like doing something with my telepathy besides figuring out what my customers at the checkout want." Cassandra twisted her hands together then looked Angela in the face. "Besides, I'm sorry, but I don't like Nadia very much."

Angela froze, glaring. "You ungrateful... Nadia's been nothing but nice to you."

Cassandra barked a laugh. "She says she likes me, but she doesn't. Remember? I'm a telepath. I know what she thinks of me."

"Goddammit. At least she's trying, which is more than I can say for you. You've blown her off four times in a row now, and I think you owe her an apology."

"Fuck Nadia. She can go ice skating in hell!" Cassandra shot to her feet and stomped out.

Angela sat in shock for a moment. Then she took a deep, shuddering breath and stood slowly. Cassandra had thrown tantrums before, storming out to go dance at the Rings or prowl the marina before skulking back to the boat. They always had amazing makeup sex afterward, but it still hurt.

She poured herself a stiff shot of whiskey and went out to sit in the cockpit on a deck chair. She sipped thoughtfully, her eyes tracking the blinking lights of an airliner far overhead. She idly wondered where they were going. A sunny island paradise, perhaps. Or maybe a raucous, electrifying city like New York. Somewhere else, anyway.

Angela picked at a tooth. At times like this, the temptation to drop everything and disappear into the Otherworld for a while was strong. At least there it was warm, and no one argued with her. She let out another sigh as her stomach knotted again. No, here was where she lived and here was where she would fulfill herself.

Nevertheless, the fights always took a lot out of her, thanks to her telepathic bond with Cassandra. Not to mention the fact that they shared a previous lifetime together. Images from that other life, an eon past, floated in her mind's eye. There, too, the relationship had been volatile, but her partner, the Chancellor, had been more mature, both physically and emotionally. True, Angela had not been through the kinds of trauma that lives spent on earth could inflict. Such experiences could build up a kind of shell around a soul, resulting in buried complexes that could take many lifetimes to unravel.

She tipped the last of the whiskey back and felt it burn its way down her throat. With a sigh, she set the shot glass down on the binnacle and made her way back below to sleep.

Cassandra danced out her frustration at the Rings. The strobing lights, body-shaking beats, and dim bodies were psychotropic. Cassandra enjoyed riding the mental tide of the collective mind that formed there. She prowled, circulating amongst the others. The eyes of other dancers would drop rather than meet her stare, perhaps sensing their vulnerability to her secret power. She felt a catlike satisfaction when that happened.

As she moved, she tuned into the limbic minds of the dancers, synchronizing her movements with theirs and drawing inspiration from their interpretations of the music. She picked individuals whose grace was most appealing and partnered with them, regardless of their physical proximity to her. She imagined herself weaving the massed minds together, as if she were a spider casting its web.

Her thoughts turned to Simon. Cassandra admired his serenity and courage, and though she would not admit this to anyone, she sought to emulate him. They were connected somehow, like soul twins, life after life spiraling down millennia of shared history.

Maybe he would like to dance. The thought of giving the wounded soldier some enjoyment made her smile. Lifting her hands, she wove a series of gestures that felt right, somehow, while reaching out with her mind in his direction. What she was doing was risky, especially in this crowded venue, but Cassandra didn't care.

More clearly than she had ever experienced before, she had a vision. Simon was lying awake in bed. He had been trying to sleep but dreaded dreaming, so he had drunk quite a lot of wine to sedate himself. Unfortunately, the sulfates in the merlot were having the opposite effect.

His body jerked as he became aware of her. He looked around the dark bedroom, confusion washing over him.

—*Cassie?*—

His voice echoed in her mind, overlaying the music. The thumping receded from her awareness as the link intensified.

—*Hi, Simon.*—

—*What...? How...?*—

—*What did I tell you? I'm a telepath, man. C'mon, let's dance.*—

—*Whaddya mean? I'm not going out now.*—

She could feel his irritation.

—*No, right now. Just relax and open your mind.*—

There was a silence, and then she could feel new impressions of him lying in his bed. She turned her attention to his limbs, particularly the numbness in his legs, and as she had sometimes done with Angela, she projected an impression, a sensory gestalt.

—*Dance, Simon.*—

—*Holy...*—

A surge of desire shook him.

—*Just let it happen.*—

Now Cassandra began to dance as if she had a partner. This was what she missed when she went dancing alone. The sense of two bodies moving as one intoxicated her. Cassandra's talent allowed Angela to play with her Otherworld abilities without losing her body sense in the physical, and now it allowed a man who had lost use of his legs to experience graceful movement again.

Simon's throat constricted as a wave of painful joy washed across his mind, erasing the last five years of suffering. Losing awareness of his bed, his darkened apartment, and his pain, he gave himself up to the movement and the beats.

Angela dreamed of her past life as the Lady of Light. She walked with her closest advisor, discussing the war being waged against her people. The uncrowded boulevard was quiet, and she bent to inhale from a scent fountain before continuing her stroll.

"He's everywhere. His engineers are everywhere, fighting and conquering," her advisor said. His ornate mustache drooped as he twisted his hands together. "Our people are divided like never before—"

She raised a hand. "I know. I've been paying attention." She fell silent as they walked, her mind replaying the shouts of "strength to the strong" and "chosen people." It was a contagious madness.

A passerby nodded a greeting, and she smiled. It had not reached the capitol, anyway. She frowned and turned to her advisor, feeling a sudden urgency. "We are beset by storm. By war. Go home and be with your family while you still can."

The scene whirled away, and she was standing in a councilor's chamber, bent over a map display. "Here." She pointed. "We can halt his progress here, though it will cost us." She looked up into the troubled gaze of her old friend, the Minister of Culture.

"We will lose everything up to that point, Lady." He shook his head. "Maybe we have already lost everything else."

"Do not give up! I have found an infection, a traveling disease spreading throughout the Forest of Souls." She passed a hand over her face and rubbed her eyes. "I believe I know the cause, too."

Having discovered the machinations of her dead lover, the Soul Thief, who had crossed over into the Otherworld to poison the minds of her people, she had also discovered the key to defeating their enemy.

Fragmentary images of her interminable journey in the Otherworld replayed in her mind. Many times, she had dueled with the bizarre denizens who carried the mind virus that the Soul Thief had unleashed. More often, she would swing a massive scythe to destroy the choking vines in the dense undergrowth surrounding the meadows of those infected.

One mind was impervious to her aid. The virus had turned one of her closest friends against her, a man who came to style himself as the "General." That man had nearly destroyed her world. Over the ensuing years, the General's followers had turned on him, one by one, until finally he was isolated, captured, and brought in chains to be judged at the Council tribunal.

He was in shackles, dressed in a prisoner's drab garment, and his head hung as she questioned him in the Council chamber. Her heart broke all over again as she tore down his rationalizations and forced him to face the fact that he had been coerced, blinded by anger.

Angela surfaced from her troubling dreams of conflict and destruction. For some reason, she thought of the animals fighting on that lonely Otherworld beach. Could it be that the Soul Thief had found a way to manipulate Egregores? She vowed to ask her grandfather's oversoul about that the next time she went to visit him. As to the content of the dream, no doubt it had been brought to her mind by both George's lesson and by her vision of the General earlier that day.

There was a muffled thump from above and an awkward slide of panels. Then she heard the tap of shoes on the ladder, soft footsteps in the passageway, and the rustle of clothing. Cassandra climbed into bed quietly, and Angela felt the mattress dip. A moment later, a hand touched Angela's side, restoring peace to her heart. She shifted her body, thoughts of intimacy briefly arising, but the fog of sleep overtook her. They curled up together, and Angela drifted into calm oblivion.

WAR IN HEAVEN: THE LION'S ROAR

REALM OF Dark Eyes

It was night at the perimeter of Dark Eyes's realm. Three guardian angels were playing a dice game near a campfire, throwing and laughing uproariously. One of them, the youngest, was taking the brunt of their gambling and had already lost much of his apparel in wagers.

A twig snapped, and three heads swiveled to peer into the night shrouded forest beyond the border. Seeing a movement, the senior guardian leaped up to grasp his weapons, and the others followed suit. Someone approached. The form was indistinct, but as it neared, their weapons lowered, and they gaped. An impossibly beautiful woman, nude, a violet shimmering aura delicately wrapping her body, stepped into the light of the fire beyond the border.

"You..." The youngest guardian licked dry lips. "Halt. State your name and business."

The newcomer stopped just outside the perimeter and, without speaking, spread her legs slightly and raised her arms. The invitation was unmistakable. All three guardian angels swayed in her direction, but the nearly naked one swayed farthest. Before the other two could stop him, he staggered forward across the border of Dark Eyes's realm.

Without seeming to cross the intervening space, the woman was on top of him. The guardians raised their weapons and shouted, preparing to leap to his defense, but before they could do so, both the young guardian and his seductress vanished.

The senior guardian's mental fog lifted, and he swore. "That came from Serpent Lion!"

Root Hexagon, Bald Eagle

Iron Star's commander, along with a sizable guard contingent, stood watch over the Root Hexagon. The crack in the great crystal was wider, allowing a thin, electric-blue stream of liquid to spill into the corrosive pool. However, he was satisfied that no enemy could penetrate again without his knowledge.

From nowhere, a lightning-like bolt of pure force struck the Root Hexagon with an ear-splitting crack. Sparks showered over everyone in the Crater. The air was filled with the shouts of his alarmed guards. Their weapons were up instantly, waiting for the expected attack. But none came.

After a tense moment, the commander approached the pool for a closer look at the damage. The crack gaped, a sizzling hell mouth drooling life force and raising yellow, stinking clouds from the coolant. Iron Star would arrive shortly, alerted by the automatic alarms, so the commander inspected the flaw closely for his report. Something moved rhythmically within the crystal. He peered at it, recoiled in shock, then leaned closer.

A beautiful, dark-haired man was engaged in coitus with an equally beautiful woman. Their lovemaking was generating stress flaws in the crystal even as he watched.

CHAPTER TEN
THE LONG ARM OF WAR

Yet ever do the mighty strive

To seek the heights lest hellward dive

For power's sake they bend the world

Insuring they alone survive.

THE SHADES were drawn in Simon's apartment. He was sleep deprived from dancing the previous night, so he napped in his wheelchair in front of the TV, which was still switched on.

He surfaced briefly from sweet oblivion, hearing shouting from somewhere far away. His sleepy mind reached for the sound.

Simon opened his eyes, alert once again. The rest of the soldiers on duty were at their stations as the vehicle approached the checkpoint. The nightmare replayed itself, a scripted horror story he could not escape.

At the key moment when he would fire upon the car he awoke within the dream. Simon pulled his finger away from the trigger guard and set the rifle down. Everything slowed to a crawl, and he turned to walk away from the checkpoint. Then his buddy stood to bar his way. The man's face had changed to something robotic and alien, its features inhuman in their perfect regularity. The man reached for him, and Simon jerked away. Then two pairs of hands grasped Simon from behind. He struggled, but his strength drained rapidly as he panicked, and the hands forced him back to his position near the abandoned rifle.

General Iron Star strode up to him from the darkness and waved peremptorily at the other soldiers. "You know what to do. Make sure he doesn't escape." The huge man folded his arms and watched impassively as one of the soldiers thrust the rifle into his hands, and another one held him fast.

"Cassie!" He screamed her name in desperation.

It was June, and the farmer's market at the marina was open. Vendors crowded a large, roped-off section of the parking lot with their stalls and canopies. The scent of flowers and the aroma of baked bread mingled with the salt air blowing off the bay while customers strolled with their cloth bags and woven baskets.

Cassandra had enjoyed shopping there on her Tuesdays off, but now she could go any day she wanted. There was something satisfying about choosing organic produce and taking it home for the week's meals. The morning after her meeting with Simon and the subsequent fight with Angela, she felt a need for that satisfaction.

The day was cool, the way she liked it, with gray clouds rolling in from the ocean and a stiff breeze kicking up. She scooped a bunch of snap peas from a produce box, dropped them in a plastic bag, and deposited it in a cloth sack slung over her arm. As befitting her recent decision to blend in with her fellow shoppers, she was dressed in what she called her "unscary" clothes.

Reaching for a fat artichoke perched atop a pile across the

table, she knocked an asparagus bunch onto the asphalt in front of a fellow shopper.

"Oops, sorry." She smiled apologetically, bent, and picked up the bunch. She examined it then dropped it in her bag. Her mind was occupied with thoughts of Simon's intriguing problem, alternating with worries about how to smooth things over with Angela.

Her cell phone chirped the ringtone for Angela, but Cassandra decided to ignore it. She would call back after she thought of a way to make her girlfriend understand what was going on.

She moved to the next table in the stall, searching and choosing.

—Cassie!—

Cassandra's hand jerked, and the entire pile of artichokes tumbled over onto the ground. She took a breath, rapidly gathered them, and put them back on the table with a muttered apology. She set her cloth bag down on the ground under the table and sidled out of the stall to walk a few feet away into the sunlight.

Her surroundings blurred, and then she was there. The speeding car. The soldiers. The shouting. Her stomach twisted.

—Simon!— Her telepathic voice echoed in that dream space. She reached out to touch his mind, but it was blank with panic, and he was unable to respond.

She shouted again. —Simon! It's Cassie! Open up to me.—

A huge man, standing near Simon, turned and stared at Cassandra as Simon fired on the car. She froze, a shock of terror washing through her that made her legs weak. Iron Star.

She gasped, and the contact with Simon vanished.

The first thing she noticed was the sound of shouting men. At first it seemed like a continuation of the vision. Then she regained her sense of the physical world, and she turned to see that a fistfight had broken out at the next stall. Two men were holding a third, who struggled and kicked.

"Asshole! He tried to steal my money!" shouted the stall keeper.

Cassandra backed away. A passerby jostled her as he muscled his way through the crowd to help restrain the thief. She realized that she had narrowly avoided being swept into the scuffle. At that moment, several security patrolmen came forward and cuffed the miscreant.

"What a jerk, huh?"

Cassandra turned her head. The woman standing next to her glared at the thief. Her eyes were fierce, and she breathed heavily as if she had been fighting as well. Violence rumbled in the back of her mind—violence and a hunger for vengeance. Cassandra shuddered, paid for her produce, and left as quickly as she could.

WAR IN HEAVEN: DIAMOND ANGEL

Iron Star stood at attention on a dais in his audience chamber, a vast red-and-orange hall with colonnades marching along either wall. Between the pillars hung swords, spears, nets, and axes, as well as pellet-throwing guns and beam weapons. Before him, one end of a large, horizontal, tornado-like vortex flashed with fitful lightning. The vortex was flanked by two pillars, each carved with the symbols of Bald Eagle's might: a pyramid topped with an eye, the S sign of the Great Dollar, and most prominently, an eagle clutching arrows in one claw and an olive branch in the other. There was a faint image of an eagle's head visible in the vortex. The General noted that the visage of his master was noticeably dimmer, no doubt because of the recent power losses. It was a sign of troubled times that Bald Eagle could not send an avatar to meet him but instead needed the gateway to commune.

"The Root Hexagon continues to provide our forces with both power and intelligence," Iron Star said. "However, there have been a number of fluctuations lately, and they have attracted a nuisance element. One of these is a flux that I call Diamond Angel. I believe this flux has opened a path for Serpent Lion and, by extension, Dark Eyes. Both factions have attacked and damaged the artifact."

There was silence, then Bald Eagle's rumbling voice filled the air. "Diamond Angel may be a simple flux to your eyes, but I see a form of ancient power intruding from the lower worlds. It may have alliances with both of our enemies and perhaps with Shaken Fist, as well."

"Then I must choose between tending to the Root Hexagon myself and investigating Diamond Angel."

"Such a choice is guided by the context in which it is made." Bald eagle paused. "The war with Silver Scimitar has escalated. An entire army of angels was born, resulting from his attack on Golden Star, and Silver Scimitar is ready to turn that force against us."

This was unwelcome news. The threat of the new army could tip the scales against Bald Eagle and overrun much of his territory.

Bald Eagle continued. "The war between Red and Blue Eagles, fought against my will, has recently escalated as a result of Shaken Fist's subversion. Our survival depends on the extra power that the Root Hexagon provides to me. This Diamond Angel that threatens our artifact draws strength from ancient sources and is a greater danger than it appears. Concentrate your energies to defeat that one, and both Dark Eyes and Serpent Lion will fail. Do not, however, abandon your post as War Leader."

Iron Star raised a hand then closed it in a fist. "I shall dispatch my most trusted lieutenant to act on my behalf while I fulfill your orders. He will monitor my image within the Root Hexagon and take whatever action is needed to ensure against power loss."

CHAPTER ELEVEN
WILL'S WAY

IT WAS impossible to be depressed when greeted by the Bay Area's mild June weather. Angela parked her Prius across the street from her clinic, got out, and set the car alarm. Before crossing the street, she studied the front entrance. Her clinic.

When she was a rising young psychiatrist, fast-tracked for the position of chief administrator at Franklin Psychiatric Hospital in San Francisco, she had been ambitious. Her dreams had usually centered on the large office occupied by Dr. Josef Lindquist. She would imagine that it was her office, instead, with her feet planted under that desk and her plans governing the operations of the aging facility. She'd had plans, indeed, to make Franklin a household name for high-quality mental health care on the west coast.

That all had changed last year. Now her dreams centered on the building before her. Its brick facade, a faux-modern abomination designed in the seventies, featured large, curtained windows whose brown, peeling frames begged for someone—anyone—to repaint them. The windows in the currently unused upstairs rooms were blank. Someday, those rooms would house the majority of the treatment facility, providing cutting-edge care to underprivileged patients in the East Bay Area. For now, she was content to use the ground floor for her and Eric's few clients.

Starting across the deserted four-lane cracked-asphalt street, she dodged a plastic sack swept by the wind then walked up to the entrance and touched the frosted glass panel with the name

Brooklyn Basin Mental Health Clinic etched into it. That had been one of the first things she had done to the place, even before the interior remodeling work.

By this time, Eric should have already opened the clinic. She pushed the door open, shoving hard against the sticky spot, then stopped partway through the doorway. Someone was already seated in the waiting room. The man was brown-haired and lean, and his skin was pocked as if he had suffered severe acne. He was dressed reasonably well, though his clothes were a bit shabby. She practiced her smile and came the rest of the way in, tugging the door shut behind her.

The newcomer rose from his seat as she approached and held out his hand. He had stunning halitosis whose odor had permeated the room, forcing her to breathe shallowly.

She shook his hand. "Good morning. Are you Mr. Longsmith?"

"Yes. Call me Will. Sorry I'm early. The bus was ahead of schedule. Dr. Weiser told me I could wait here."

"No problem." She went to the admission counter, picked up a form and a pen, and handed them to him. "Do you mind filling this out while I set my things down?"

"No. Sorry."

She went behind the admission counter and logged herself into the system. When she'd finished, she looked up. "Will? Why don't you come on in?"

Longsmith came through the inner door. Angela took his form, dropping it on the desk, then led him to one of the treatment rooms. His records indicated that he suffered from PTSD as a result of wartime trauma during a tour in Iraq. He was one of the first spillover patients from the local VA facility to be referred to her clinic.

After she led him to one of the treatment rooms, Angela washed her hands and retrieved her tablet from her office before returning to begin the session.

"Thank you for waiting." She took a seat to one side of the desk and set the tablet down. Longsmith sat on the edge of the couch, his body stiff as if he were ready to bolt, but his face remained placid and detached. His eyes were steady albeit unfocused.

"Okay. What I'm going to do is start by asking a few simple questions." She paused and tapped the screen. "First, for the record, are you currently using any mind-altering substances?"

"Nope."

"Thank you. And are you currently in treatment with another therapist?"

"I was seeing Dr. Jacobs at the VA hospital till two weeks ago. Then he got sick. Liver cancer."

"Yes, I heard about that. Very sad."

"Yeah, it sucks." Longsmith fidgeted. "Look, can we cut to the chase?"

Angela nodded and tapped again on the screen, scrolling ahead to the free-form notepad. "Of course. Go ahead. You're in charge of your treatment here."

He clenched his hands and looked down at them. "Doc, I was using meth." He glanced at her then back down at his hands. "I went to rehab about three months ago, and I've been clean and sober for two weeks."

Angela took some notes. Methamphetamine addiction,

already a challenge, was especially difficult for patients like Bill to kick because the drug was often used to self-medicate for the emotional numbness that accompanied PTSD. "Go on."

"Doc, I'm afraid I'm gonna hurt someone. Sometimes I feel like I'm back there in Iraq." He paused, breathing heavily, tapping his heels on the floor. Angela waited, placing her hands flat on the desk in front of her.

Longsmith got to his feet. "I don't want anyone else to die. I don't wanna hurt anyone. But the government's sending boys to die, and I wanna stop them."

He started pacing. Angela remained seated behind her desk and watched him closely. Obviously, he had bottled up a lot of anguish, and her role was simply to be a pair of sympathetic ears. However, her instincts told her that his outburst hid deeper issues, and she wanted to draw those out.

He continued. "I wanna clear my head, Doc. Take another shot of meth." He turned, his face sagging. "But I know it's gonna kill me. I don't know what to do. You gotta help me." He collapsed on the couch and buried his face in his hands. He groaned and started sobbing.

Soon his shoulders were quaking, and he howled his agony, doubled over and beating his fists on the front of the couch. He stopped suddenly and turned his red, bloated, tear-streaked face to her.

"It's okay, Will," Angela said. "Let it out. We'll get you through this."

He put his face in his hands, dissolving into tears. Angela placed a box of tissues on the corner of the desk near where he was sitting.

Something flickered in the room. Her first thought was that a mouse had gotten in, but then she realized that the light in the room was changing subtly. New, starker shadows were being cast from a source of light above as if daylight shone through the ceiling. Angela suppressed a gasp. The Otherworld was intruding.

The ceiling became translucent, revealing a brilliant blue sky above. It was preternaturally vivid, with gigantic, dramatic clouds, tinged oddly red as if by a second—setting—sun. And far up, above the clouds, there were great, shining beings, dressed in baroque armor and other costumes. They fought a fierce, silent battle. Angela had never in all of her experiences of the Otherworld seen anything like this. The vision persisted for what felt like an eternity but was probably only a minute, and then earthly reality abruptly reasserted itself. Her ears popped.

Longsmith continued sobbing quietly. There was a faint burning odor in the air, and as if from far away, the cries of soldiers in battle swelled in volume. Then the odor and the faint sounds vanished.

He blew his nose on a tissue and wiped his face then looked at Angela, his shoulders hunched. "I don't know what came over me. I never cried like that before. I'm sorry." He blew his nose again.

Angela spent the next half hour listening to Longsmith's story, elicited between sobbing jags. He had lost his best friend while on patrol, ambushed by Iraqi insurgents. The emotional scars left behind had driven him to drug use and then petty crime to support his habit. After serving a brief sentence for burglarizing a health-food store, he had decided to clean up his act. So far, his PTSD had been resistant to treatment, but Angela hoped that she could use dream-walking to make a difference for him.

"Look, Doc, I gotta run. I know I've got some more time coming, but..." He peered at her, his mouth downturned at the corners. "God, I'm so tired of crying."

"It's okay. It often happens to people when they've been traumatized." Angela reached into a desk drawer and pulled out her scrip pad. "Let me write you a prescription." She scribbled on it and tore one off. "This'll help you sleep. Let's put together a plan, okay? I'd like to see you again next Tuesday. Same time?"

"Sure, Doc." He took the scrip and stood.

Angela rose to her feet. "The pharmacy down the street will fill the prescription for you."

"Okay. Look, I'm sorry about that..."

She raised her hand. "Don't apologize. I'm sure we can get through this together. Go get some rest, okay?"

"Okay."

They shook hands, and he left. Angela jotted down a few more notes then set the tablet down. The Otherworld intrusion during Will's outburst had shaken her. The vision of those gigantic beings battling had made her feel as if she were an ant beneath the heel of uncaring titans. She believed that there were no coincidences when it came to the Otherworld, so there had to be a reason for what she'd seen.

Her mind returned to the fight she'd had with Cassandra the previous evening. She had not slept well afterward, so it was possible that she was especially vulnerable to events in the Otherworld. Maybe Longsmith's inner turmoil had dragged her into his mind, where she saw things relevant to her own personal quest. That was as good a theory as any.

The thought of Cassandra brought a lump to her throat. Angela needed to clear the air between them, preferably face-to-face. Opening the mail program on her tablet, she composed a message.

Hey, Cassie. I hope you're having a great day. I'm sorry I blew up at you yesterday. If you're up to it, I'd love to talk about it. Love you, Angela.

Angela had two more appointments that afternoon. One was a VA patient who needed to be evaluated for a return to active duty, and the other was a client on her third of five scheduled office visits who had presented with an eating disorder.

After writing up the last of her reports and waiting another hour, Angela decided that Cassandra was not going to reply to the text message. The odd Otherworld intrusion during Will's session was eating at Angela. It represented a potential threat to her control of her talent. She needed guidance from George.

Angela informed Eric that she was going home, not wanting to stay at the clinic during a solo excursion to the Otherworld. Once she arrived home, Angela went below. She doffed her backpack and retired to the master cabin to lie down. Reaching to pull the curtains, her hand halted as her gaze rested on the painting hanging above the headboard. It was the Roger Charles piece that the artist himself had given her the previous year, depicting a strange, six-fingered woman standing on a hill overlooking a bountiful valley. It was breathtaking, an image of her own past life somehow captured by an artist's feverish mind. She shivered at the chill of memories intruding from that long-ago time.

She was preparing to seek advice from an oversoul as she'd done in that other lifetime. She lay down on the bed, touching her forehead and then her clavicle, and she launched herself into the Otherworld.

Her meadow was peaceful and sunlit, and she breathed in great lungfuls of air fragrant with the perfume of blooming lilacs and wild roses. Beneath the brilliant blue sky, artfully decorated with ideally fluffy white clouds, the kelly-green wild grasses gave off their own rich aroma. Black oak and big-leaf maples surrounded her on all sides, their leaves applauding the wind with a gentle susurration.

Invigorated by her surroundings, Angela went to her cabin with a jaunty strut to retrieve her walking staff. After hefting it and surveying the meadow once more, she started for the edge of the forest to search for a path, as they had a tendency to move around. She found one quickly, as her years of self-work had cleared the underbrush of repressed emotion.

Humming to herself, she strolled along the path, feeling her lingering tension melt away. Despite the potential for supernatural danger here, she still trusted the Otherworld more than physical reality.

Realizing that time was of the essence, Angela told herself she had done enough sightseeing. Time to find her grandfather. She muttered under her breath in a singsong voice, "Granddad. George. Hello."

She poked her staff into the humus as she walked and kicked aside a pile of leaves. A movement caught her attention high up. Shading her eyes, she peered into the tangle of tree branches. A huge Nuttall's woodpecker rested on one of the limbs above the trail ahead. The bird looked calmly back down at her. Then someone, somewhere, laughed warmly. Recognizing George's voice, her heart skipped a beat.

"Granddad?"

The bird blurred, shifting its shape. Now a man sat on the branch, dressed in colorful beaded clothes. He resembled a much younger George. Before she could greet him, he vanished.

"That was weird." Angela had encountered many bizarre beings in the Otherworld, both animal and human, but this was the first time she had seen a younger version of her grandfather. She continued her stroll, and she watched all around her for more portents. He would show himself when he was ready.

Ahead of her, obscured by the shifting shadows of trees, a man, or perhaps a woman, stood in the path. Angela slowed her pace. As she approached the stranger, she was able to make out more details. It was indeed a woman. She had honey-blond hair, shoulder length, and wore an expensive-looking, high-waisted green dress.

Angela stopped walking. "Hello?"

"Angela." The woman had a lovely contralto voice. "Don't you recognize me?"

Angela racked her brain. She would have remembered someone so striking. "I'm sorry. I don't."

"I'm your old friend. Your old teacher. You used to call me George."

Angela peered at her dubiously. "Ah, I don't mean to be discourteous, but you look nothing like my granddad."

The stranger beckoned with a graceful gesture. "Follow me, please."

She turned to continue along the path in the direction that Angela had been going, and Angela followed her through the forest. Soon they arrived at a clearing. As the woman entered, her body smoothly shifted to the bearlike, balding form of her grandfather. He turned and awaited Angela.

She approached him hesitantly. "Granddad? What was that all about?"

"Everything changes, my Angel." His face was radiant with that familiar smile that always used to soothe her doubts. "All things pass, sooner or later." He scrutinized her with narrowed eyes. "Ah, good. You have brought your body with you. That will make this easier."

Angela opened her mouth to ask him what he meant, but he raised a hand. "We don't have much time to talk. I need to show you something. Please, come over here."

She obliged, absentmindedly noting that the accent he had had on earth was virtually gone. He took her arm in a soft grasp and pointed with his other hand. "Now, look at that tree. Look at the roots, then let your eyes go up until you see the crown."

Angela studied the tall conifer that stood out against the skyline. Most of the trees surrounding the meadows in the Forest of Souls were deciduous, though she did not know why.

Her gaze traveled up the tree, and the daylight dimmed as if a cloud were passing overhead. At the crown a mist appeared, and she stared at it for a moment. Nothing happened. She started to turn to George to ask what she was looking for.

"Don't look away," he cautioned.

She stared at the treetop and gasped. The sky split like a curtain, revealing a battlefield. The sky there was black with red, violently churning clouds. Many warriors, dressed in all forms of battle gear from all the ages, were silently engaged in brutal combat below that sky.

Dark-haired, dark-eyed fighters, resembling Romani folk, faced off against fair-haired and light-skinned warriors, while larger people, some half again as tall as the rest, directed the battle. Swords rose and fell, splitting skulls and chopping limbs. Rifles sprayed dazzling thunderbolts that destroyed whatever they touched. There was no blood, though. As the warriors fell, they dissolved into shapeless masses. The ground was littered with the debris of war.

Then, as if the sound were suddenly switched on, the air was rent with the cacophony of battle. Bellowing cries, shouts of agony, and a continuous rumble of explosions shattered the peace of the Forest.

Angela raised her voice over the noise. "Granddad. What the hell is this? I've never seen war here before."

"This is not really here," George shouted back. "There are many levels in the Otherworld. What you see is a much higher one than where we are now. But this war belongs to you and to your people, my Angel, no matter where it is. It is a battle between cultures, between ideologies, between Egregores—or group-mind beings—like the one I showed you. It is fought by warrior angels who serve those great masters, such as you see there. Now that you can perceive other levels, I wanted you to see this."

Angela reluctantly turned away from the scene and stared at George. "What do you mean, this war belongs to us?" The sounds of warfare faded. She resisted the temptation to look back at the treetop, keeping her eyes on her grandfather.

"Just that, my granddaughter... my student. This war has been fought since the beginning of time. But now your incarnation brings many changes to earth's people. Creatures who slept for ages are awake, and there are some who would use the newly awakened for their own ends."

"I knew that being born on earth would bring completion to some things." She glanced at the now-silent tree. "The end of the Soul Thief being the most important. But how can a war be mine? I fought my last battle!"

George shook his head. "Not your last battle, no. You have hardly fought at all, my Angel." His form began to fade.

"Wait!" Angela raised a hand. "When I saw you at first you were a woman. What does that—?"

But he was gone. George had been more forthright when she first started coming to see him, but now he was behaving like the other oversouls, speaking in riddles and shape-shifting. While she understood, intellectually, that change in the Otherworld was inevitable, that didn't mean she had to like it.

Angela needed more answers from him, so she sat on the grass, cross-legged, to watch the flight of birds and listen to the rustle of the underbrush, seeking omens. None were forthcoming. Peace had been restored to the Otherworld, but now it was an undesirable peace, concealing mysteries.

Finally, running out of patience, she stood and walked back toward her meadow.

CHAPTER TWELVE
COINCIDENCES

The trap they set for Angel's feet

Would douse her light, her love defeat;

Then once again the Child will fight

To stoke the flames and feed war's heat.

CASSANDRA KNEW Simon was waiting for her before she opened the door to go into Julian's Café, so she scanned the tables, zeroed in on his, and in her best casual walk, made her way there and plunked into a chair.

"Hey, Cassie. Thanks for calling me." His face was lined and pale, but his eyes were warm with gratitude.

Cassandra mumbled a greeting. Now that she was face-to-face with Simon again, and they shared some intimate history, she couldn't meet his eyes. Even though she had only danced with him psychically, the contact between them had been intense. The fact that he was male only made it worse.

Simon proffered his menu. "Want to order something?"

She took the menu and stared at it, unable to decide, unable to even read it. Her head was full of voices, but unfortunately, they were all her own. "You had another nightmare today, didn't you?" She did not look up at him.

"Yeah," he said, his voice rough. "I tried to fight. I think... you heard me call you, didn't you?"

"Yep."

She put the menu down, and the waiter appeared. Ignoring him, she leaned forward on her elbows. "Listen. I know someone, and I think she can help you. She's a psychiatrist."

Simon shook his head in a spasmodic movement. "Nuh-uh. I've seen enough shrinks to last me a while."

"She's not just a shrink."

The waiter cleared his throat. "Can I take your order, or do you need a few more minutes?"

"Just a couple of minutes," Cassandra replied without looking up. She studied Simon's face, noting the new lines around his eyes and the tension in his neck. The waiter disappeared from her peripheral vision. "Look, I don't know if I can help you. I thought I could, but there was a fight at the market right then. I almost got dragged into it."

"Holy crap." Simon said. "You're okay, right?" When she nodded, he continued. "That's a relief. But... what does that have to do with my nightmare?"

"Nothing. Everything. I don't know." She looked away from his face, which had hardened, accentuating the shadows under his eyes.

Simon put his hands on the table to push away. "I'd better go."

Cassandra reached out. "No. Wait. My friend. She understands this stuff better than I do."

"I already said I've seen enough shrinks." He sighed. "I'd rather just talk to you. I don't know where you got your power. But you can see what I'm seeing, and maybe you can see what or who these people really are." His voice was pleading now. "Are they parts of my own mind, forcing me to relive that night? Are they ghosts, haunting me?"

Cassandra stared at him for a moment. She shivered, thinking about how close the violence at the market had been to her. If only Simon would come to his senses and seek professional help. But his mind was made up, and in a rare moment of clarity, she decided to choose discretion over confrontation.

She shrugged. "Hell, maybe the fistfight was just a coincidence. Oakland can be pretty rough sometimes. Okay. If you aren't going to see my friend, maybe I can sort of tag along next time. Someplace safe. At least I can tell you what I find out."

"Wait." Simon's brow furrowed. "You don't actually live through what I'm experiencing, do you?"

"Hell no. I just see it, like I'm watching a movie."

Simon grunted. "Good. It's kind of bloody. Cassie, I'm really sorry you had to see that." His voice cracked on the last word, and his shoulders heaved as he started sobbing. He put his head down on his arms.

Cassandra looked away from his public display of grief and glanced around, but no one else was paying attention to him. She stared down at her hands while he sobbed, and silently willed him to pull himself together. Right now she was seriously jonesing for a smoke.

After a moment, he blew his nose and dried his eyes with a napkin. "Sorry about that. I don't usually let myself go. I'm just really tired."

"Don't mention it." Really don't, she echoed mentally. She reflected that she was probably not cut out for therapeutic work, after all, if it meant watching people fall apart like that.

Cassandra spent the early afternoon shopping for comfort food then caught a movie. After that, there was an interview that didn't go well, but she hadn't wanted the job that badly anyway. Angela would understand—or so Cassandra hoped.

The night was cool but humid when she returned to the boat. The dead-fish aroma of the bay tickled her nostrils, and she sneezed. Cassandra clomped over to the companionway. Then, remembering her boots, she shucked them and wiggled her sweaty toes. The slats had been removed, so Angela was already home. Time to have that little talk. Cassandra paused, took a deep breath, and gathered her wits.

"Angela?" There was no answer. She started down the ladder into the darkened interior and found that the salon was empty. "Angela? Are you here?"

The boat was silent but for the slapping of water against the sides. She looked for Angela in the master cabin, but it was empty, too. Maybe Angela was at the marina store getting some whiskey. Cassandra's stomach rumbled, and she returned to the galley to grab a granola bar out of the cabinet. Dropping her backpack on the dinette table, she settled on the settee with her paperback and waited. Soon she was engrossed in a midnight chase through Paris with the heroine of her novel.

—*Cassie!*—

Simon's voice echoed in her mind along with the sound of other men shouting. An electrical jolt of adrenaline rushed up her spine.

"Simon!" Cassandra leaped up, dropping her book and the

snack. Simon was having the nightmare again. This was her chance to help with something meaningful.

She hurried to the master cabin, formulating a plan as she went. She would pull him out of the nightmare with her telepathy. It was the only way she could think of to assist her friend.

Cassandra lay down on the bed. Folding her hands on her belly, she closed her eyes. "Simon. Simon. Simon..." She sent her mind questing for the panicked soldier.

Simon was waiting for the car, his rifle at his shoulder, while the shouts from the megaphone rang out. As the car reached the crucial position in its headlong rush toward the checkpoint, he once again put the gun down and glanced around anxiously. The man next to him immediately turned and grabbed him by the shoulders.

"Cassie!" he shouted. He broke the man's hold and lashed out with his fist, but the man blocked Simon's punch easily and put him in an arm lock. General Iron Star approached from the shadows. Simon began struggling again, and the General slapped him hard.

—Simon!—

Hearing Cassandra's voice, he looked around wildly, thinking in his confused state that she was nearby.

—Picture my face. Concentrate on me.—

The voice was in his mind. He visualized her face, but then Iron Star picked up Simon's rifle and forced it into his hands. He yelled Cassandra's name again.

Cassandra heard Simon's yell, but she could not complete her connection with him. Frantic, she searched for Angela's mind. Between the two of them, they could break through into wherever Simon was and help him. But there was still no sense of her presence.

"Angela!" she yelled out loud, uncaring of what the neighbors might think.

Angela had just returned to her meadow and was heading for the cabin to put her staff away when she heard Cassandra's mental scream.

—Angela!—

She froze then closed her eyes. "Cassie! Cassie, where are you?"

—I'm at the boat! Help us!—

Angela's pulse raced as she scanned the clearing rapidly, searching for a path back to the boat. She froze suddenly when Cassandra's words registered. "Us?"

Across from her, a gray mist boiled up out of the ground, rapidly growing into a column of colossal height. Churning shadows projected upon that cloud sharpened to reveal a violent scene. Several soldiers were subduing a frantic soldier, whose inarticulate shouts rang out in the still air. One of his captors, a colossal, powerfully built man wearing a general's uniform, was forcing a rifle into his hands.

The captive soldier looked up then sagged in the men's grasp when he saw Angela. His form wavered, indistinct within the cloud, but his wide-eyed face registered shock.

—Angela!—

It was Cassandra again.

—*Help him! He's my friend.*—

Angela strode forward quickly and extended her staff to him. "Grab it! C'mon!" she shouted.

He wrenched an arm free and reached, straining, for the staff. As his hand neared it, his form suddenly sharpened. He touched the staff. There was a snap and a flash of light, and he stumbled free. For a moment, the large officer's face came into focus as well, and he locked stares with Angela. An unexpected wave of terror washed over her. His eyes glowed! They narrowed as he opened his mouth to shout, but then the mist vanished, taking the scene and the terrifying man with it.

The soldier's body wavered in and out of focus as he grasped the staff. He groaned and collapsed to the ground. Angela reached out cautiously to shake him by the shoulder, but her fingers found no purchase in the cold, misty substance of his body. He jerked as her fingers passed through him and released his grip.

"Sorry." She straightened to give him space to recover, leaning on her staff.

He pushed himself to his feet and peered myopically at his surroundings. "Where am I?" His voice sounded muffled.

"You're in the Otherworld. I'm Angela. Who are you?"

—*Angela, this is Simon.*—

"Cassie?" Simon looked around until his eyes focused on the staff. Following its length, he squinted at Angela. He stuck out his hand in greeting, but Angela turned away.

"Thank you for rescuing me." He looked around again, lowering his hand. "Cassie?"

"She's not here. But she's got a mind link to... to both of us, it seems." Angela stepped back a bit and looked him over with narrowed eyes. "So, you're Cassie's new friend?"

His mouth tightened. "Friend, yes. You're her girlfriend, right?"

She nodded. At least he knew that much.

Simon shook his head. "Look, let's not get off on the wrong foot, okay? Cassie's been helping me with my nightmares. That's all."

Nightmares? Then why hadn't Cassandra referred him to her immediately? Angela shook off a sudden sense of déjà vu. "Okay. Nightmares are my specialty."

She inspected his somewhat insubstantial form, which, though it had sharpened since he arrived, was still somewhat translucent. "You look like a ghost." She remembered that her grandfather had once told her about how he and the other chovihanos could leave their bodies and explore other levels of the Otherworld. "You can go out of your body, can't you?"

Simon nodded.

"So what was that all about? Who was that guy with the headlights for eyes?" He had seemed oddly familiar.

"I call him Iron Star. Otherwise, I don't know who he is. But when I try to stop the nightmare, he shows up with his men, and they force me to relive it. To shoot some people." He shuddered, looking down at his feet.

Based on his visible symptoms, Angela suspected that he suffered from PTSD. The large soldier probably represented an aspect of his trauma that he relived over and over. She wanted to learn more, but this was not the time to ask questions. First, she needed to get him back to his body. Unlike her or the Romani chovihanos, he probably lacked the skill to find his way back safely from the Otherworld.

"Okay. I don't know how you fit in with what's going on, but I don't believe in coincidences. Not anymore." Angela beckoned. "Follow me."

She turned and strode toward the path where she had earlier left the meadow. She glanced over her shoulder. Simon hurried to catch up, half walking and half floating. They entered the forest, and Angela began humming a pathfinder song of power to help her locate Simon's meadow.

To her surprise, the path opened up to the windswept escarpment above the ocean where George had shown her the Egregore—where her spirit Guardian had "pushed" her vision. The pathfinder song was not infallible, after all. She took in her surroundings, looking for hints as to what had gone wrong, but there was nothing evident. The clouds overhead were thicker, hiding a wan sun and lending a chill to the ocean-scented air, but there was nothing abnormal about it.

Time for plan B, apparently, only she had no idea what plan B was, aside from following her instincts. She turned and motioned for Simon to come closer. "Now, what I want you to do is think about home. Think about where your physical body is. Close your eyes."

He did so, and his translucent body began to blur at the edges. Angela reached toward him with her staff, following that intuitive urge. Everything around her began to glow more brightly, becoming indistinct, as she felt her talent take hold.

"I hope this works," she muttered.

The scene changed. For a moment, she and Simon were surrounded by trees as if they had been transported to a mind meadow. But before the scene could solidify, it was swept away by darkness.

WAR IN HEAVEN: TRAPS

Iron Star's Workshop, Bald Eagle

The air in the cavernous workshop was cluttered with glowing orbs and geometric solids, some of which were shedding sparks. These objects were floating in midair. Some of them were in motion, traveling along glowing lines of light to merge with other forms.

Iron Star stood on one of the geometric solids. In his right hand he held a Condition Calibrator, a complex device festooned with levers and spiked knobs. He was tinkering with a dissolution bomb, a much more powerful weapon than the dissolution gun. Resting on a pedestal, the trap resembled a head-sized, faceted quartz crystal, but extended into many more than the normal three dimensions. He crooked a finger, and an angel materialized by his side.

"Set this trap by the Root Hexagon," he said. "Attach it to the primary avenue of approach from below. That appears to be the weakness that Diamond Angel is using. Report to me when this is done."

He handed the object to the angel, who disappeared in a burst of orange light. Iron Star laid down the tool and swept his hand in an arc before him, creating a portal. He stepped through and, arriving in his chamber, strode to his chair. His lieutenant approached from the red shadows at the perimeter of the room. Iron Star waved the angel forward. "Speak."

"There has been another power loss in the Root Hexagon despite the image that you placed within it. We have seen signs that our ancient enemy Dark Eyes has taken a hand. We did not see any sign of Serpent Lion, though."

"No doubt the power loss is the work of Diamond Angel. That enemy will discover the folly of its actions soon enough. For now, though, deploy a strike force into Dark Eyes's territory. That miscreant has been assisting Diamond Angel." He waved a hand peremptorily. "Send troops from Bald Eagle to weaken Dark Eyes's defensive perimeter. If he is busy rebuilding that, he will lose interest in the Root Hexagon." Iron Star paused, considering. "And use poison. I recall that it is quite effective against Dark Eyes's people. It worked well against Serpent Lion."

The angel nodded and disappeared. Iron Star leaned on the arm of the chair and rested his chin on his fist, contemplating the deep connections between Dark Eyes, Serpent Lion, and Diamond Angel. More disturbing, he saw a similar connection between Diamond Angel and himself, as Bald Eagle had hinted at.

Realm of Dark Eyes

Fierce Hands, a female warrior angel serving Serpent Lion, approached the perimeter to Dark Eyes's realm, searching for another guardian to entrap. Once she'd absorbed the guardian's psyche, the resulting power would enable her to attack the Root Hexagon again.

The sound of crashing underbrush made her freeze. To her left, perhaps twenty paces away, a small detachment wearing the livery of Bald Eagle had arrived. A towering commanding angel led them. Fierce Hands watched as they brought their powerful weapons to bear on the invisible perimeter force field.

A bone-rattling hum filled the air as powerful beams lanced out to strike the field. Angels from Dark Eyes poured out of the woods within the perimeter, raising their own weapons. Soon the night was crisscrossed with energy-weapon fire and filled with the screams of dying angels.

Fierce Hands, seeing a weakness in the field near where she waited, crept forward, hoping to remain unnoticed. She raised her own weapon, a Spear of Desire, and lashed out at the perimeter. With a crackling snap an opening appeared. Just as she'd hoped, she was able to piggyback on Bald Eagle's assault. Her spear alone would not have succeeded. Crouching, nearly doubled over, she breached the perimeter then sped toward the darkened woods beyond as Bald Eagle's forces, with a tremendous shout, broke through a portion of the perimeter.

Her core warm with the anticipation of finding a high-ranking commander to grapple, she dodged swiftly between the trees. Suddenly, an electric blue blaze consumed her world, and she was gone.

War on Earth

The man tipped his beer bottle. "You said it, buddy. Our women need to be put in their places." He took a swig.

—

The pastor nodded to the young woman. "I mean that authority flows from God, through man."

—

"You can take your authority and shove it," she yelled at her boyfriend. "Who..."

—

"Who're you calling?" he demanded. "Put the damn phone down."

"My mother." His wife glared. "I'm moving out. You can..."

—

"Cook your own damn..."

—

"Go to..."

—

"... hell."

CHAPTER THIRTEEN
BITTERNESS

THE WEDNESDAY evening service at the Methodist church had been less than satisfying for Nadia. The pastor had been all fired up as he talked about the flow of authority from God. Something about what he said had bothered her, though she couldn't put her finger on it.

As she and Michael made their way back home, she gripped the armrest tightly. Cars always made her nervous. They were giant metal boxes careening in all directions, soulless and pitiless. Oakland traffic was the worst. She picked at her starched blouse. The thing was wretched and uncomfortable, but she would never be seen in anything less than her best at church.

"The Carters were there today." Michael drove carefully, and at the next intersection, he signaled for a right turn. "Robert said they're on their way back south."

Nadia shifted uncomfortably in the passenger seat. She had a long-standing feud with the matriarch of that extended family. It went back decades, but she was sure if she put her mind to it, she could remember the original reason for their animosity.

"Yes," she said irritably. "Emma was ridiculously overdressed. And she brought the twins. She should not have done that."

Michael grinned and shook his head. "Well, I thought they were good boys today," he said. "They fought just once, and the pastor only had to tell them to be quiet twice." He chuckled.

Nadia sniffed. "Be that as it may. They were ridiculous." Her brother had never taken the feud seriously. He had no idea. She lapsed into silence, her mind turning to more important matters. How could she broach the subject of Angela? Finally, she gave up searching for diplomacy. "I have reconsidered talking to Angela about our problem. Things are going from bad to worse. Did you see how empty that church was?"

"Nadia, we are supposed to be nomads. Our own family has settled down, but most of our people keep moving. What did you expect?"

"I am aware of that," Nadia snapped. "But there are always at least a dozen families in the area at any one time. Today I saw three. Three Roma families in that church."

"So, our people aren't steady churchgoers. I don't see how that's a sign of terrible things." He swerved to avoid a badly parked truck, forcing Nadia to clutch the safety handle above the door.

"Michael, I can see something dark over our people. Something that makes us abandon our Romani heritage. It weakens our families. It destroys our values. It steals our souls." With that pronouncement, she released the safety handle and placed her folded hands in her lap once again.

Michael slowed to turn, negotiating a pedestrian-filled corner. "There you go again. The Soul Thief is dead, and Angela said there were no more like him. I think you're seeing things that aren't there."

Nadia turned, shocked into speechlessness. Her mouth opened then shut. Finally, she took a deep breath. "Some nerve you got! How dare you question my Sight!"

Michael shrugged, avoiding her stare. "Well, someone's got

to. You think you are God or something, controlling people's lives. You are a human just like—"

"I most certainly do not! My Sight is a gift from God! When you question it, you question—"

Michael thumped the wheel, making her jump. He glanced at her, and his face was twisted in anger. She held her breath, shocked into silence.

"You interfering old biddy! You see your visions, you meddle with other people's affairs, you plot and scheme like a fat old spider, and you treat us all like we're nothing but your tools."

He glared at her for a moment longer than it was safe, glanced back at the road, and slammed on his brakes, narrowly avoiding a collision. *"Du te dracu!"* he shouted.

Nadia shrieked and straight-armed the dashboard. Then, when it looked as though they weren't going to be smashed into bits by the other cars, she lowered her hands once more. As his words sank in, her fear gave way to desolation.

She felt dizzy and weak. Her brother had always been supportive of her and had championed her amongst the Roma as a faultless seer. Now he called her a sorceress, a witch, poisoning her own people. As she thought about this, hot anger burned away the sadness. How dare he say that to her?

Meanwhile, as if nothing terrible had just happened, he drove carefully though he refused to look at Nadia. She seethed. The coward.

Finally, she turned on him. "You will take all that back. I serve our community, and I have served our people most of my life. This is the only way I know to serve, as a chovihani. I will be damned if I let you lecture me and call me a witch or worse."

"You have let your power go to your head. I see you jerking strings and messing with people's heads. You have no respect for them. No respect for me!"

"Well, maybe if you did something worth my respect, I'd change my mind."

The instant she said that, Nadia clapped her hand to her mouth. Michael's face went white then beet red. He actually growled.

"Fuck you dead, Nadia! I'm leaving you. You can rot in your goddamned chair without me."

His words hit her like thrown bricks. She gasped, her heart racing. Despite herself, hot tears gather behind her eyes, and pain stabbed briefly in her chest. She could not speak for a moment. She had endured far worse from others, giving as well as she took, but she had never been shouted at like that by her younger brother. George, yes—he and she had fought like cats —but Michael had always been so devoted to her.

A black wave of despair threatened to overwhelm her. She surreptitiously wiped her eyes. Michael was staring straight ahead, mouth set, his shoulders hunched. She had no idea how to respond without making it worse.

They passed the rest of the drive in stony silence.

Michael had dropped her off at the house and muttered something about going out. She suspected he had gone to a bar somewhere. His explosion at her and the subsequent fight had left her drained, though, and she couldn't bring herself to care where he was.

Sometimes a chovihani needed counseling, too. Sitting in her chair, she dialed her phone. "Andrea? It's me, Nadia."

"Nadia! How are you?"

"I could be better, but I can't complain. How are you these days? And Jordan?"

Andrea chuckled. "We are all fine, though I bet Jordan is hitting the sauce again."

"It's going around." She sighed. "Do you have a few minutes? I think I can complain, to tell you the honest truth."

"You have my permission."

Nadia cleared her throat. "We're under attack."

"Hang on a minute. I need to sit down." There was a pause. "Start at the start. What do you mean?"

Nadia slowed her breathing, trying to calm her voice. She'd had no idea she was so worked up. "Michael and I just had a huge fight. In fact, it's the worst one we've ever had. You know how close we are. Were."

"Oh, Nadia. I'm so sorry. What did he do this time?"

Nadia chuckled now, ruefully. "It's not just him. We both got into it. For a little while I really hated him. My brother!"

"Go on."

Nadia crossed her legs. "I have realized that we're fighting because we're under attack. There is a darkness that's driving our families apart."

Andrea actually tutted. "Now, aren't you reading a bit much into this? I haven't seen a single thing that tells me of a darkness. I haven't seen anything amiss since the Soul Thief died."

Nadia squirmed, uncrossing her legs, but she could not get comfortable in her chair. "This is different. Andie, you need to ask your Guardian to show you this thing. Right now. It'll know."

"Okay." She sounded dubious. There was a muffled thump and then silence on the line. After several minutes, she came back. "Nadia?" Andrea's voice was rounded by fear. "Why didn't you tell me about this sooner?"

"Because I just learned about it. Anyway, the same darkness that's driving our families apart is affecting me and Michael. I just don't know how it got in. My Guardian should have taken care of it."

"Yes." Andrea fell silent.

A memory surfaced from earlier in the day. Nadia had to choose her words carefully as Andrea was a devout churchgoer as well as a powerful chovihani. "At church, the pastor said something. Something about authority proceeding from God to man to woman."

Andrea grunted but said nothing.

"Well, that pastor's no Rom." Nadia recrossed her legs the other way and rested her elbow on the arm of her chair. "He does not understand that each of us has a role in society, and within those roles, we have the say-so."

"Yes, you have a point. But the Good Book says..."

"Never mind what the Good Book says!"

Andrea gasped. Nadia pressed on, no longer cautious. "This is about our people. Nobody really knows what everything in the Bible means anyway. But what I do know is that this is where the gadje are driving their wedge. They are destroying our people with words. Can't you see that?"

"Maybe the pastor was right, or maybe he was wrong. But what does that have to do with—"

"Everything. Those words were a worm, and words just like it ate up Michael's Romani soul. He is nothing but a sorry old drunk now."

"What are you needing, then, Nadia?" Andrea's voice was quiet. "What about your sons? Did you call them?"

Nadia sighed, feeling old and vulnerable. "They're on the other side of the country, and I don't want to bother them with chovihani problems. Andrea, I need to know I'm not alone. Angela's fighting it, too. I can feel it. I've been dreaming about her again. Her and war. Something is happening. There's a war in heaven, Andrea, and I'm fighting blind. Will you help me?"

There was but the barest hint of hesitation. "Yes. I will go to my spirits and find out what I can do to help. Should I call you tomorrow?"

"Please do. Thank you, Andrea." Nadia hung up. She looked around her empty living room and felt a premonitory chill. Someday, she would be alone for good.

CHAPTER FOURTEEN
STRANGE JOURNEYS

Bald Eagle soars above the sun

Believing that the battle's won,

Yet ancient magic will prevail

And finish that which was begun.

ANGELA STOOD in pitch darkness. As her eyes adjusted, she saw that she was standing in a room, though it was still far too dark to see more than the dimmest of shapes. She remained still, afraid to move for fear of colliding with something. "Simon?"

There was a muffled thump from her right followed by indistinct swearing that sounded like his voice coming from another room. The only reasonable approach, she decided, was to act as if it were perfectly normal for her to materialize in someone else's home and to explain herself as honestly as she could.

"Simon? It's me, Angela, from the meadow." She was able to keep her voice steady with effort.

There was more muffled cursing, then a door opened. The accompanying light revealed that she was in a living room. She moved to a clear spot in the center in case she needed to run for her life. There was another loud thump, the door opened farther with a jerk, and Simon emerged. To her surprise, he was sitting in a wheelchair. He saw Angela and stopped, mouth gaping.

"How in the hell...?"

She raised both hands in a peaceful gesture. "I followed you here."

"Whaddya mean, you followed me? Are you a burglar?" He wheeled backward, disappearing into the room.

"No! Wait! I'm Angela. Cassie's girlfriend."

He came back out with a pistol. She raised her hands further and froze, suddenly aware of the sweat cooling on her forehead and her heartbeat in her throat. He rolled into the living room.

"I don't know how the hell you got in here, but you'd better get out. Now." He motioned with the gun toward what she guessed was the front door.

She began sidling in that direction. "Simon," Angela said in a calming voice. "Don't you recognize me?"

Simon frowned. "I... uh. You look like the woman in my dream. But that's impossible. Dreams don't walk through locked doors." He raised his gun. "Nice and slow, now. Just turn around and walk out."

—*Simon!*—

Cassandra's voice echoed in Angela's head.

Simon jumped as if stung and looked around at the room. "Cassie?"

—*Simon, what the fuck are you doing, pointing a gun at Angela?*—

She sounded exasperated.

Simon blinked at Angela. Then he quickly lowered his gun. "But... how...?"

Angela's hands were still raised. "I have a special talent, Simon. I don't know how to explain."

With the gun now pointing at the floor, Simon's hand visibly shook. "I can't believe..." His voice trailed off with a gasp as he dropped the pistol and slumped in his chair.

Angela hurried over, stepping carefully around the fallen weapon. She checked his pulse then went to the kitchen sink that was visible from the living room and, after hunting a bit, found a cup. She filled it with water, returned to crouch by Simon's side, and dribbled some into his mouth. "Simon. Wake up. You're in shock."

He coughed, and she took the cup away. His eyes opened, blinking rapidly. Then, seeing her face, they opened wider. "Lady? Oh my God."

Angela rocked back on her heels. "No one's called me that for a very long time. Who are you?"

He rubbed his face, silently trembling.

"You must be chilled. Hang on; I'll get something to warm you." She went into the lit room, a bedroom, which was orderly and sparsely furnished. There was a blanket at the foot of the bed, and she brought it back to the other room. She met Simon as he was rolling toward her, and she held the blanket out to him

Simon took it gratefully, shivering, and looked up at her. "For a second there you looked like someone in my dream." He looked around the room, still clearly dazed.

Angela took a seat on the couch. "I get told that a lot. Look, just take some deep breaths and try not to think about what just happened."

He stared at her and then nodded. After a moment, color returned to his face. He reached over to a floor lamp, switched it on, and scrutinized Angela carefully. "Okay. Please tell me what the hell is going on here."

"Okay." Angela adjusted her position on the arm of the sofa and rested her hands on her thighs. "Let's start over. I'm Angela, Cassie's girlfriend. You're Simon, and you just had a nightmare."

"Yeah. What I want to know is why you were there. And how did you get in here? My door is always locked and dead-bolted."

"First answer." She paused, wondering how much to reveal. Well, if Cassandra had already confided in him, she could too. "I have a talent. I can bodily enter other people's minds, even become part of their dreams." She looked at the room and sighed. Her scientific mind hated to admit it, but her talent had definite supernatural elements to it. "And for the second question, I can travel from one physical place to another through this realm of the mind. We call it the Otherworld. Yeah, I know. Real creative name."

Simon's lips twitched up at the corners. "You know, I'm not completely ignorant. I know there are unseen things in the world." He waved a hand. "Powers that can control our actions. I have other friends besides Cassie who can do pretty crazy stuff. But there's no one anywhere who can do what you say you just did."

"I'm pretty unique that way." She sighed. "If it's any consolation, I spent most of my life thinking that it was just some form of telepathy. But last year changed my mind. Long story. Ask Cassie about it sometime. So let's get down to it. Maybe we can learn more about the big man with the eyes. Tell me about this nightmare."

"Okay. I don't know if Cassie told you anything about him."

Angela shook her head. She opened her mouth and hesitated. Could this have something to do with what her grandfather had shown her? There appeared to be a warfare theme to her recent excursions in the Otherworld. "Cassie didn't tell me anything. Only that she met someone." Her voice came out a little harsher than she intended.

Simon squinted at her and shook his head. "I get it. Relax. Like I said, you got nothing to worry about between me and her. Anyway, about five years ago..."

Angela jumped as if stung. Five years?

"What is it?" He stared at her.

She waved her hand. "Nothing. Go ahead."

Simon looked at her curiously then shrugged. "About five years ago, I was stationed in Baghdad. I was part of a guard detail, and we were manning a checkpoint. Keeping the bomb-throwers out, you know? Anyway, one night—" He grunted and frowned and then, in an unsteady voice, related the nightmare.

Angela watched him, saying nothing though her heart went out to him despite her initial misgivings. This was a man in hell.

He cleared his throat. "So, ever since then, I've had nightmares. You know. Standard PTSD crap." His voice had returned to normal. "A few months after the incident, I was on patrol, and our carrier ran over an IED. Boom. Body parts everywhere. I was thrown clear, and then I passed out. When I came to in the hospital, they told me I wouldn't walk again." He gestured to his chair. "So here I am. But get this. While I was in the hospital on drip, I'd wake up sometimes, floating up near the ceiling, looking down at my body. And ever since then, I can just pop out. Pretty much whenever I want." He stopped.

"Go on," Angela said.

"You believe me. Good. Saves us some time. But I guess this is pretty small potatoes for you."

Angela waved dismissively. "No. Nothing's small potatoes to me. So, about the nightmare?"

"Yeah. Anyway, I can control the nightmare. When I'm there, I can wake up in the dream and stop it. So far, so good. But a few months ago, something changed. Every time I had the nightmare, it seemed harder to stop. And then these guys would show up. They looked like our guys, but they'd fight me. Force me to go on with the nightmare. I could fight 'em off for a while, but they got real persistent. Then Iron Star started to show up."

He shuddered again and wiped his mouth. "You said you saw him. Well, he's scarier in person, let me tell you. He handles me like I'm a kid. Just pushes that gun into my hands, clamps my hands on it, and makes me shoot those people. Over and over. Every time I have the nightmare."

Angela picked her teeth with a fingernail. "Simon, would you be willing to come see me at my office?"

"Your office?" He grinned at her, evidently nervous. "That's right, Cassie said you were a shrink."

"She's right. I am."

His grin vanished. "No offense, but I've seen enough doctors to last a lifetime."

Angela got up, walked over to the window, and looked out. "You've seen what I can do. I can help you with your nightmares. We can go to their source, in your memories and emotions, and put a stop to them." She remained standing by the window to give Simon time to consider what she said.

"I don't know. I can't see how you can fight off those dudes."

"I don't need to. We would work at a different level. More symbolic, I'd say, except that these symbols are real in their own way. We won't confront your nightmares directly. I won't make you relive that. But I can't promise it won't hurt." She turned around and looked Simon in the eyes.

His looked vaguely upward. "Cassie? Can you hear me?"

—Do it. She's a healer, what we call a chovihani. She can work miracles. She helped me.—

Angela was impressed. Even though Cassandra had been an extraordinary receive-only telepath when they'd first met, Angela had helped her learn how to send messages, as well, and her skills were improving daily.

Simon nodded and looked at Angela again. "Okay, Doc. When do we start?"

All business now, Angela looked around. Her eyes widened when she took in the room's contents. It looked as if she were in an armory. Every wall had weapons of some form mounted on it—swords, guns, knives, spears. She even noticed a pair of Argentinian bolas in a glass case.

She tore her eyes away from the display and glanced at Simon. "I'll let you know as soon as I get back to the office. Do you have something I can write with? I left my backpack at home."

Simon rolled over to the coffee table and retrieved a pad and pen from a stack of papers. She took them and started to scribble some notes on what she had seen so far.

"This is just too weird." Simon's voice was low. "God. You could just go anywhere in the world, can't you?"

"Only to where there are people," Angela replied absentmindedly. "Can't go to the deep desert or to the moon."

She tore off the sheet, folded it, and stuck it in her pocket. Then she put on her most reassuring smile. "Actually, it's not like teleportation. I usually have to walk, and sometimes I need to go farther than I did tonight. Showing up here was odd, even for me. I'm not sure if I could do that again." She tilted her head back to look up into the air. "Cassie? Can you come pick me up?"

—*I got the address out of Simon's mind. You're in north Berkeley. Be right there.*—

Simon chuckled and shook his head. "You two are something else."

WAR IN HEAVEN: PROGENITOR

EGREGORE SPACE, Somewhere in the Upper Reaches of the Overworld

There was a vast plain, which, if seen by human eyes, would be shrouded in thick darkness as the human mind could not begin to comprehend it in its true form. But for the great Egregore Bald Eagle, the place was both his secret home and the true arena where the ceaseless war of the Egregores was fought. The plain was crowded with all manner of fantastical, shifting forms, some resembling earthly animals and others abstract geometric shapes. Joining them all were barely visible threads of light, pulsating as they conveyed the angels of thought between the Egregores.

The Egregore of the United States of America perched upon his symbolic pyramid in his true form. He bore his battle scars proudly. Though he was young, he had already fought and devoured many other Egregores, incorporating their essence and bolstering his unstable power.

He was flanked by smaller versions of himself, one with red-tinted feathers and the other colored blue. Those raptors, connected by numerous threads of angelic communication, eyed each other fiercely. They were enemy Egregores, though each was spawned from within him. Their presence was a constant, revolting reminder that he was vulnerable to division and even destruction. Thus, he remained ever vigilant.

Recently, a new thing had formed near Bald Eagle, an extrusion resembling a woman, created from the substance of the plain. The Egregore had been watching this new development with alarm. While many other such proto-Egregores came and went, making the plain appear sometimes as if it were gently boiling, this one appeared to have an extra spark of power in it. Its stability indicated that it might even be a self-generated, permanent entity, a type of creation that had not been spawned before in Bald Eagle's living memory.

Bald Eagle stared at it then leaped off the pyramid to fly at the intruder. The new thing shrank away from him, but then it rallied its strength and stood firmly, rebuffing his threat with an aura of confident power. Bald Eagle returned to his perch, dissatisfied. To his dismay, threads of light now joined Bald Eagle to the new creature, whom Iron Star had dubbed Diamond Angel. He searched himself for clues as to how those connections had been established. There. They ran directly to the Root Hexagon, buried deep within his body.

A possibility occurred to Bald Eagle: the new creature might catalyze the creation of yet another division within the Egregore. He glanced at the two entities flanking him on their own pyramids, each of whom embodied much of his old vitality, now gone. The prospect of more divisions terrified Bald Eagle. He had always sought to consolidate power and resist the efforts of the separatists—Shaken Fist and the others —thereby emulating the Roman Eagle, upon whom he had based his own shape. Even more dangerous to him, however, were the indications, visible now, that Diamond Angel threatened the existence of all other Egregores.

Mindful of this possibility, Bald Eagle examined the core of his identity enshrined within the Constitution of the United States. Though it had been shaken recently, it remained solid, and he relaxed.

A pulse of light blazed forth from Diamond Angel and entered Bald Eagle's breast. He croaked in alarm. That was no mere angelic invader. The light was a direct attack, using raw power. Calling upon the defenses he had acquired from the Soul Thief, Bald Eagle deflected Diamond Angel's blaze, but the effort wearied the Egregore.

He shifted uncomfortably, drawing life force from the underworld, and his thoughts grew red with anger. Diamond Angel would pay for this offense to his dignity. As he sharpened his rapacious gaze, the constant stream of angels from him increased in volume, chipping away at other Egregores in his vicinity. He would need all the vitality he could steal to overcome this new foe.

CHAPTER FIFTEEN

THE HEALER AT BAY

Oh bitter woe! the trap is set

To bind the new angelic threat,

And so it is that Light is chained

Another lien on battle's debt.

THE NEXT day, Simon arrived at one in the afternoon for his appointment. Angela prepared the treatment room for him while he filled out his new patient paperwork, arranging cushions on the couch after wiping it down with odor-free disinfectant.

"Simon? Come on in—through that door there." She held the door open, indicating the treatment room, and he wheeled through the short hallway and entered.

Angela shut the door after them and went to lean over the desk with his forms. "Let's see." She flipped through the pages, scanning quickly. "Simon Fenway. Is that...?"

"No relation. I'm not even into baseball." He drummed his fingers on the wheels of his chair.

"Ah. Says here you moved to Oakland two years ago. Did you come out here to be closer to your family?"

He shook his head. "Nope. I was looking for work and got a lead. Actually I had several, but something told me Oakland was the right choice."

"Mm hm." She finished reading and looked up with a bright

smile. "Tell me about yourself. Your goals, your ideals. What makes Simon Fenway get up in the morning?" She picked up a tablet and stylus.

He told her about his childhood dreams of becoming a warrior for justice, righting wrongs in the world, and displaying a superhero's courage. He recalled his idols, both fictional and real—Superman, Mandela, Gandhi. He recounted his successes: the time he asked for his first date; the night he faced down a friend's abusive father, who towered over him but could not confront him; his admission of fault to cover for that friend later. He told her about his failures, too: fistfights when he should have walked away; angry words that cost him friendships; the abandonment of cherished ideals. He skirted the more recent events of his life—his tour of duty in Iraq, the checkpoint, and the bomb. Throughout his recitation, Angela smiled, nodded, probed gently with questions, and took notes. Finally, she lowered the tablet and gestured.

"Please lie on the couch there."

He frowned. "I can't sit in my chair?"

"No. You're probably going to go into deep trance while I'm working. It's even possible that you'll come with me to the Otherworld, though not all patients do."

He rolled to the couch and began levering himself out of the chair. His expression was troubled. "How in the heck is that supposed to work? I mean, you're sort of going into my mind, right? So, how can I go there too?"

Angela shrugged. "I'm actually not sure. There's a lot of mystery in this. I've spent a long time learning to dream-walk, but there's just no way to make sense of it in modern terms."

He finished pulling himself onto the couch with his powerful arms.

"Okay." Angela pulled up the chair next to the couch and sat. "What I want you to do is just relax and don't bother trying to control your thoughts. Let them wander. What I'm going to do is sit beside you in my chair and touch your forehead."

Simon regarded her, frowning. "That's it?"

Angela grinned. "Yep. Usually, I induce a light hypnotic trance first. I don't want my clients to freak out about the dream-walking, but you already know what I'm going to do, so there's no point in doing that extra stuff."

"Got it."

"One more thing," she said. "Don't try to touch me. I can touch your head, but that's it."

"Why? Will you burst into flame?" His chuckle sounded forced.

"No, but you might." She raised a hand. "Sorry, that was tasteless. It's just not a good idea to touch me. Okay?"

"But you touch me, right? What's the difference?"

"If I initiate the touch, I can incorporate it into my work. If something stimulates my body while I'm away, it's like a backlash of some kind occurs." She glanced at Cassandra, whose face was blank. "Cassie can tell you more about it."

"Okay. Let's do it," he said.

She reached over and touched his forehead. The room blurred, and the scene of a meadow overlaid it as Angela transitioned, feeling the familiar dropping sensation in her stomach.

Angela stood near the center of the clearing and surveyed the scene. The Otherworld sky was overcast, and the trees swayed in the turbulent wind. The meadow itself was rough and weed-choked. Large mounds of grass were scattered all around, and there was brackish water pooled in several places. Simon was nowhere to be seen, though she had not blocked his access to the Otherworld as she customarily did for gadjo clients.

She sighed then sniffed the air and gagged as a stray current wafted the fetid odor of death into her nostrils. That was the usual sign of a long-standing repression. This wasn't going to be easy, though she hadn't really expected it to be.

Angela explored, walking in a rough, spiraling path that would cover the most ground and end at the forest's edge. That was where she expected to find the most trouble. She skirted several of the pools, noting that they were situated close to where she had started at the center of the clearing. He had a lot of bottled-up emotion that would take a great deal of work to clear up.

As she searched for the source of the odor, she peered at the hummocks and thick clumps of grass. Angela stopped and nudged one with her toe. It was a soldier's helmet, wound tightly by the coarse sedge, representing a tightly held memory that needed to be released. The other mounds probably hid similar artifacts. *Let's stay focused*, she told herself. *We can look at the smaller problems later.* She continued searching.

There was cluster of especially large, grassy humps near the verge of the forest ahead. Approaching it, Angela noticed that the smell was getting stronger. She covered her mouth with her hand. There was a cloud of flies over the humps, and she suppressed another gag reflex when she saw the partially stripped bones of a hand protruding from one of the mounds. She looked for a fallen branch for prodding the mound and found one nearby.

She cautiously pushed at the largest hump with the stick. Suddenly, the ground shook with a low rumble, and the wind whipped the tops of the trees with an almost human howl. She pulled the stick back. The shaking continued, and Angela had trouble keeping her balance.

"I'm sorry, Simon. This isn't going to be easy." Angela began levering up on the mound, revealing more of a badly decomposed human body. It was small and could have been a woman or boy.

Angela jumped as a deer crashed through the thick underbrush, charging at her. Angela backed hurriedly away, and the deer trotted up to stand between her and the mound. The earthquake diminished as the wind died down. But the deer snarled in an undeerlike fashion, revealing gleaming fangs.

It had been years since Angela had seen creatures like this. "Aw, crap. Not one of you guys. What did I do the last time?" She snapped her fingers. "Right."

She walked away from the fanged deer toward one of the stagnant pools. Reaching the water, she found a soggy branch that was half-submerged. She pulled it out and carried it back toward the deer. It dripped with slime.

The stagnant pools represented repressed emotion, blocked and toxic. The stick, impregnated with the emotions of the pool, could bring them to bear on the instinctive defenses expressed by the deer.

The ground began to shake again, and the wind picked up as she neared the deer. A branch struck the ground with a loud thud nearby. The deer began to growl, its lips quivering, and its eyes tracked the stick as she held it up. With a rapid flip she tossed the stick at the deer. It tried to dodge but failed. As the stick struck the animal, it screamed, shuddered, and limped away.

Something crackled from far above. Angela looked up and dived out of the way. A gigantic falling branch landed with a crash where she had been standing. Something thrashed in the underbrush. A large brown bear skidded to a halt and reared up, roaring a challenge and revealing a mouthful of yellow fangs. It must have weighed at least a thousand pounds.

"Shit! You're just not gonna let me near that, are you?" She came up in a crouch and backed away from the bear, which appeared to be content to stand guard. Angela looked around the area again. The stagnant pools of emotion, the mounds of half-buried memories, and the terrible weather were too much to take on right then.

Putting some distance between her and the bear guarding the mounds, she scanned the ground near the center of the meadow. After a moment, she found a patch of barely visible linoleum floor and stepped on it. The patch spread as she walked until the clinic reappeared around her.

Simon was a picture of misery as he wept, shuddering and curled in a fetal position on the couch. Angela retrieved a box of tissues from her desk, took a seat in her chair by his side, and waited quietly. After a few minutes, he had calmed enough to struggle upright, his useless legs dangling over the edge of the couch. He wiped at his wet face, his bloodshot, swollen eyes staring into a private abyss. She handed him a tissue. He hesitated then dried his eyes and blew his nose.

"Simon," she said. "Take your time. I know that was rough."

"God. Damn." He was breathing heavily, but he nodded.

"Okay? This is going to take a little longer than I expected. You've got a lot of buried trauma and blocked emotion to work through."

"That was really, really hard. I'm..." He shook his head, his Adam's apple bobbing repeatedly as he swallowed.

"I understand. I'd like to pick this back up soon if that's okay with you. However, you'll need some rest. I'm giving you some B12 vitamin supplements. I've found that they really help you recover from dream-walking fatigue. Would you be willing to come back tomorrow for another session?"

He nodded.

Cassandra was lying on the bed in the sailboat's master cabin. Her eyes were closed. Angela's voice still echoed in her head, along with Simon's wordless agony.

After a moment, Cassandra's eyes opened, and she sat up, hugging her knees. Her face was wet with tears. The magnitude of his suffering was overwhelming, more than she had ever thought possible.

Angela was writing up Simon's case report when Eric rapped on the doorjamb. She glanced in his direction, pushing the keyboard away. "C'mon in."

Eric threw himself in the chair across the desk from her. "The suits are being a pain in the ass. Again."

"What?"

"Sac town's tightening their tutus." He picked up a pencil and started flipping it. "Our rep said they don't know when or even if we'll get the money to hire staff."

Angela threw up her hands. "Dammit! I thought we were through with all that. When I talked to them just the other day, they told me it would come through in a week or so."

"I know." Flip. Catch. "They're playing dirty politics with the DMH budget again, and this time they're dipping their sticky fingers into the grants program."

She got up from the desk. "Is there someone else we can talk to?"

Eric shook his head. "I don't think so, hon." Seeing the expression on her face, he relented. "Well, maybe." He gestured with the pencil. "I'll take another stab at the bureaucrats. But Angela, there's something else."

"What?"

"I heard a rumor that someone doesn't want us taking PTSD patients. One of my friends at the club told me he heard that some vets were angry. Said they were being handed off to the fags. I think that means us." He rolled his eyes.

Angela sighed and stared out the window, her hands in her pockets. "Looks like it's going to be a while before we get to have a clinic." She turned around. "How's your client load?"

"Well, it's raining patients, regardless of the hypothetical homophobic vets. There's all kinds of business for me as a therapist, and at least we can still get paid for our own VA patients." Flip. Catch.

"Yeah." She paused and looked more closely at the shadows under Eric's eyes. "How're you doing? Personally, not professionally."

"Well, you know we marched at UN Plaza in the City, right? The media showed up and asked Bobbie about our stance on the war with ISIL—"

She interrupted, shaking her head. "No, I mean, really personally."

He looked away for a moment. Flip. Catch. "I'm not sleeping much lately." He glanced back at her. "You know, it's been a while since I've seen my own therapist. So, yeah, I know. I'll make an appointment with her." He dropped the pencil in a cup on her desk and cracked his knuckles.

She studied his face. Something was bothering him. But if he didn't want to talk about it, Angela wasn't going to press him. "Take care of yourself, Eric. And as for the bureaucrats, let me know if anything changes, okay?"

"Sure." Eric got up. It was his turn to study her face. "Angel, honey? We should both go out soon. I think we've been under a lot of stress lately."

Angela smiled. "Soon. Yeah."

He saluted ironically and left.

Angela's phone rang. She retrieved it from under a pile of papers and answered it. "Hello?"

"Angela, dear?"

"Oh, hi, Nana."

There was a crackle, then Nadia spoke, her voice high and agitated. "Angela, someone's trying to frighten us. The *muskers.*

They raided Dan's trailer."

"Poor Dan! Is he okay?"

"They took him away," Nadia snapped.

"Why? Dan's harmless."

Angela heard a voice in the background. "They can't just do that. We've got rights!" It sounded like her cousin Riley.

"Riley?" Nadia's voice was somewhat muted as she replied to him. "You should know better. The cops don't care about us." Then her voice was louder again. "His neighbors complained about the music. Usually the cops show up, warn him, and he turns the stereo down. Not this time."

"Lawyers!" Riley was shouting again. "We need lawyers. There's got to be something we can do."

"Will you calm down?" Nadia shouted back. Then to Angela, she said, "I had a vision, Angela. Something is hunting us. Dan was just in the way, but I'm afraid it wants you. You need to watch yourself."

"Nana, Dan's got a green card, right?"

"Not anymore, he doesn't."

Angela rubbed her face. "Are you sure this isn't just someone trying to get back at him? He can be hard to deal with sometimes."

There was silence on the line.

"Never mind. Sorry I asked. Nana, I promise I'll be careful. Please let me know if there's anything I can do to help."

"I will do that, dear. Call me tomorrow, please." Nadia hung up.

Angela set the phone down, propped her chin in her hand, and stared into nowhere. Her instincts told her that something was going on in the Otherworld, but maybe she was just being paranoid. It could simply be one of those bursts of random bad luck that occasionally happened. She hoped she was simply projecting her own difficulties on the world.

WAR IN HEAVEN: ISOLATION

The commanding angel guarding the Root Hexagon saw a misty vortex appear high above the crater near the great crystal. His body began to fray a bit at the edges, and he struggled briefly with the temptation to lay down his arms and surrender. Regaining his composure, he observed the flux, waiting.

The swirling mist pulsed, coalescing into the form of a radiantly beautiful woman with six-fingered hands and a long-boned face. Diamond Angel. Her eyes were focused on the Root Hexagon, and hovering near the artifact, she appeared to be seeking a way into its heart. As she descended slowly toward it, she neared the dissolution bomb. Sparks crackled on the crater floor nearby. Then, with an explosive snap, a huge discharge of energy enveloped her. She threw her head back and howled silently.

"Iron Star!" The commander's shout echoed.

General Iron Star appeared at the lip of the crater, his hands on his hips, and his head lifted proudly as he glared at his foe. His hands dropped when, with unexpected strength, Diamond Angel pulled herself free of the trap. The General reached into a pouch by his side, took out another, smaller object, and hurled it at the intruder. There was a flash, and a net of pearlescent strands of light enveloped her.

The commander grinned. It was an isolation trap, a device intended to restrain an enemy rather than destroy it. Diamond

Angel struggled but was unable to free herself. She glared wildly in all directions, then her eyes settled on Iron Star. He swayed at the lip of the crater, and the commander rushed to his side to prevent a nasty fall. But Iron Star regained his balance, raising a hand before his face in self-defense.

With a flash of brilliant light, Diamond Angel vanished. Iron Star gestured, and two angels—in the livery of Bald Eagle's dour ally, Gray Suit—appeared by his side. He lifted a hand from which two threads of barely visible light hung, glimmering.

"You will take control of the isolation trap which I have deployed on Diamond Angel. Report to me if there is any problem. In the meantime, use it however you see fit."

The angels nodded. Each took a thread and departed. Iron Star crossed his arms and stared in silence at where his enemy had been suspended above the Root Hexagon. The commander, for his part, felt growing admiration for Diamond Angel, as he did for all creatures possessing great power. This was a worthy foe.

War on Earth

"Heard about the new clinic that's opening up?" His buddy shrugged, and he continued. "Well..."

—

The pool player shifted his grip on the stick. "I heard the doctors are all gays."

—

"You won't catch me going in there." He passed the bottle.

—

"Something's gotta be done."

—

"Someone's got to..."

—

"I'll do it."

CHAPTER SIXTEEN
THE WARRIOR PRAYS

A lifted hand, a plaintive cry,

A warrior prays, his fear defied,

And granted is that sacred plea

Though he'll not hear the god's reply.

"LORD ARES Obrimos, grant me strength." Simon sat in his wheelchair before the altar of his god, his arms raised in supplication. He visualized the form of his god, seated on a great throne behind the altar in His palace, wearing bronze armor and crowned with a golden helm. "I offer You incense. I offer You the weapons of war." Lowering one hand, he indicated the smoking burner on the altar and the short, leaf-bladed sword, unsheathed, lying next to it.

He lowered the other arm and bowed his head. "Today my courage failed me. My shame at what I did to those people..." He stopped for a moment, overcome again. "I need Your strength, mighty one. As a warrior and servant of justice, I ask for Your strength to overcome my greatest enemy: my fear."

He sprinkled another pinch of incense, closed his eyes, and bowed his head once again, silently awaiting any omen or whisper of insight. He would not be disappointed if none came. That's what he told himself, anyway. Ares helped those who helped themselves.

WAR IN HEAVEN: THE PRAYER

The air rumbled with the ceaseless sound of distant explosions in the large, dim, red-lit hall. Hung with weapons, vehicles, trophies, and other mementos of every conflict that had ever been fought between conscious beings, this hall was nevertheless empty of any living soul but one.

Tiny within the vastness, an angel of Ares stood at attention.

"You will go forth and guide her to the foot of my throne," Ares's voice boomed.

The angel bowed deeply then turned on one heel and strode toward where a swirling in the air announced the presence of a portal. The angel vanished within it.

There was a huge sigh. "Beloved Aphrodite, please do not interfere."

CHAPTER SEVENTEEN
SHATTERED GLASS

ANGELA WAITED at her desk for Simon. He was already half an hour late for his appointment, and she glanced at the clock with a frown. She knew that clients could get cold feet for a variety of reasons, but the dream-walking demonstration may have driven him away for good.

Perhaps it was because Simon was the first gadjo dream-walking client who knew about her talent. The Roma understood that their tribal shamans, the chovihanos and chovihanis, were blessed—or cursed—with extraordinary abilities. Her dream-walking was legendary even amongst that elite circle, but the Roma took it in stride as they did all such paranormal phenomena.

Anglea had learned to prevent gadje patients from accompanying her when she went over. She completed the deception by calling her work hypnotherapy. Until yesterday, she had not considered exposing that paranormal ability to a non-Romani. The risks were too great, to her and to them. If Simon were indiscreet, the fame or notoriety that might result could be damaging to her career. It could also cost Angela her license or get her sued for malpractice.

To take her mind off of those concerns, she threw herself into her chores, cleaning out a huge backlog of paperwork and applying the finishing touches to an article she planned to submit to an upcoming conference.

Glancing at the clock two hours later, she picked up the phone and dialed, trying to reach Simon for the fourth time.

She got his voicemail again. "Simon? This is Dr. Cooper. Please call me back as soon as you can." She hung up.

The wind tossed the leaves in the trees with an oceanic susurrus, and there were secretive rustlings from the animals that lived in the forest. Angela poked aside a fallen branch with her staff and took a deep lungful of the clean air. The path was well worn, and though none of the paths remained the same from visit to visit, this one seemed familiar.

By that afternoon, Angela had given up on Simon. Whatever his problems were, he represented an intractable puzzle, and she knew only one person whom she could turn to for answers. After notifying Eric that she would be in her office and not to disturb her, a familiar routine by that time, she had entered the Otherworld.

"Granddad? George?" She walked away from her meadow, deeper into the forest. Sunlight dappled the duff and flashed in her eyes, making it difficult for her to see into the shadows.

The sound of humming floated down from above then vanished. Angela stopped and looked up into the canopy but saw nothing there. "Who is it?"

The humming began again, coming from another direction. She glanced that way, leaning on her staff. The source of the sound circled, and she stopped trying to track it.

"Angel." A young voice drifted on the wind.

She looked up again. Sitting on the branch of a gnarled oak nearly overhead was a girl, perhaps eight years old. She had blond, curly hair and a cherubic smile.

"Really?" Angela muttered. Then, more loudly, she asked,

"Are you George?"

The girl giggled. "No, silly. I'm his oversoul."

She clambered down from the tree like a monkey and walked over to stand in the path in front of Angela. She spread her hands. "I know. I look really different, don't I? I'm preparing for a new life on earth."

"I hate to say it, but I need proof. You could be a trickster after all. Change back to George's shape if you're really him."

"We don't have much time, Angel," the girl said. With a sudden movement, she grabbed Angela's wrist. In her mind's eye, Angela saw a rapid-cut replay of George's life as her grandfather. Scenes from his childhood were followed by visions of her parents and then of herself as a child on his knee as he told one of his stories. She saw him at work, building a boat, swinging a mallet. There was a flash of him with her in the Otherworld, exploring its wonders. She began breathing more rapidly and felt a lump in her throat as her eyes stung. The visions stopped when the girl removed her hand.

A moment passed before Angela could speak again. "Granddad. But I thought you would always be here. Nadia's oversoul is here."

The girl shrugged. "After my soul is born again, I'll be back here to watch over my new life." She reached out fondly and placed a hand on Angela's staff. "You can come see me then." Then the girl became businesslike. "Now, I need to tell you something very important. Listen to me, my Angel."

Angela wiped away a tear and stood quietly, awaiting her teacher's instruction. George continued in a singsong voice.

"Ancient poison twists the heart,

Ancient warrior plays his part,
Angel finds a reborn king,
Fitting heir of everything.
Hero breaks the racial curse,
But things still go from bad to worse,
Till love prevails on killing field,
And war no more his weapons wields."

With that, the girl giggled, twirled in place, and vanished in a burst of light. Angela stepped back involuntarily. "Granddad? George? Where are you?" She looked all around her at the suddenly dark, empty forest.

A voice whispered on the wind. "Look for me in newborn eyes." Then there was silence. Angela heaved a shaky sigh, her chest constricted with grief, her vision blurred. She felt as if he had died all over again. Though he had promised he would be back, she knew it wouldn't be as her grandfather but rather as an enigmatic oversoul, filled with riddles.

A shout followed by the crash of metal shattered the silence, sending a shock through her body and making her heart race. She whirled to face it and hurried back along the path. Skidding to a stop, she caught a glimpse of men fighting near the left edge of the clearing. The vision faded along with the sounds of combat as she stared.

"What the hell is going on?"

Her meadow was quiet once again. The conflict had happened at the base of a tall pine identical to the one that George had pointed out on her earlier excursion, but this was in her own meadow. Angela allowed her gaze to travel up it. A mist coalesced at the top, and another scene appeared in it. She saw a vast military formation with rank upon rank of soldiers of all sorts. There was no sound, only images. Walking alongside the soldiers, his hand waving as he chivvied them, was a large man dressed in archaic red armor. Iron Star.

Someone approached him with a document. He read it and handed it back. The scene seemed to rotate on an invisible axis to reveal a gigantic shining golden star hovering in the sky several miles away. Behind it, the sky to the left glowed blood red while that to the right shone white.

The golden star rippled as if seen underwater, then sparks cascaded off its edges as it disintegrated. A gigantic silver curved sword, imprinted with a crescent moon and star, materialized in its place, blood-red light dripping from its edge. A brilliant flash of red filled the sky, and the scene disappeared.

Angela threw up her free hand in exasperation, grasping her staff more firmly. "Granddad, I wish you'd tell me what's going on."

Nothing more happened. She sighed, returned her walking staff to the cabin, then hunted for a patch of floor. Finding one, she returned to her office in the clinic.

Angela went to her desk, opened her laptop, and entered the search terms "war," "golden star," "silver scimitar," and "moon and star" on her web browser. Nothing came up. She spent a few moments racking her brain. The scimitar resembled the symbol for Islam, so she added that to the search. After a few more minutes of drilling and refining, she found a news report concerning the Middle Eastern conflict. She clicked the link.

Her breath hissed when she saw a flag displaying a golden

star upon a bisected background, red on the left and white on the right. The report included an article link, and she opened it in a new window. It was the flag of the Yezidis, a minority religion that had existed in the region for centuries.

She turned back to the news report, which confirmed her suspicion. The sword, moon, and star were symbols for Islam, and under that banner flew the flags of a dozen war-torn nations in the Middle East. Within those nations, a new, dangerous enemy—ISIL—had arisen, which intended to establish a sovereign nation over all Islam and stamp out the presence of the West once and for all. She read the article with growing agitation. One phrase leaped out at her.

"ISIL is responsible for genocide against Yezidi Kurds in Iraq."

She closed the laptop and stared at nothing. What connection did this genocide in Iraq have with her meadow in the Otherworld? Evidently there were larger movements behind the scenes in the Otherworld, and her work with Simon had peeled back a metaphorical corner of the world to reveal them.

Suddenly, there was a crash of shattering glass. Angela leaped to her feet, her heart racing. Running feet pounded in the corridor outside her office as she hurried to the door.

"Asshole!" Eric's shout was like that of the soldiers in the Otherworld, and she froze for an instant. Then Angela unlocked her office door and flung it open. "Eric?"

"Angela, you need to see this."

He was standing in the corridor by the open door to the waiting room. Scintillating reflections from broken glass covered the floor. She looked at the front windows. One of them was shattered, fragments still clinging to the window frame. "My window!"

"There was a bang and then a crash," he gasped. "I ran out. Heard someone peeling off. They smashed the front window. Maybe they shot it out."

She went to stand by his side in the doorway, reluctant to walk on the glass shards that covered the floor in the waiting area. Angela examined the window frame where small pieces of glass still clung like jagged teeth. She felt a chill down her spine. Her vision of war had been followed by vandalism.

"Shotgun, maybe," she muttered. She craned her neck to peer at the wall next to the doorway but saw no sign of damage. She scanned the floor, searching for clues. Suddenly she hurled herself at Eric. "Get down!"

They dropped to the floor in a tangle of limbs. Angela held her breath, her mind emptied by the adrenaline rush. Nothing happened. She let her breath out and looked at what had frightened her. An unexploded grenade rested on the carpet in a bed of glass. She motioned back down the hall. "Back away. Hurry! Crawl!"

The two of them disengaged and awkwardly crawled away until they got to the fire exit. Angela pushed it open, triggering the alarm. They ran outside.

"What...?" Eric gasped.

"Grenade."

"Holy shit!"

"They must've gotten it from military surplus somewhere." Angela's cold panic gave way to shuddering relief. "I don't know why it didn't go off, but we're lucky to be alive."

Eric and Angela stood in front of the clinic with one of the police officers who had arrived as a result of the 9-1-1 call. There was police tape strung around part of the sidewalk in front of the building, and beyond that milled a crowd of gawkers.

"We've secured the ordnance. You're really lucky its components were old and rusted solid. Otherwise, it would have gone off." The officer gestured at the gaping window. "You're going to want to get that boarded up right away."

Angela nodded. "Thank you. Yeah, we'll do that tonight."

Hugging himself and shivering, Eric stared at the tread marks on the sidewalk made by a small bomb-disposal robot that had removed the grenade. "Who would want to do something like this to us?"

"Who knows?" The officer scratched his face. "Town's full of whackos. It's been a long day."

Angela glanced at him. "What do you mean?"

He let out a long-suffering sigh. "We've had three calls for vandalism, though this is the first grenade I've seen in a long time. There were also two fires, probably arson. And altercations all over town. If I were you, I'd go home today."

"After I get those boards up, I'm going to do just that," Angela said with a curt nod. "Thanks again."

"Just doing our job, ma'am." He touched the brim of his hat and left.

Angela put her hand on Eric's shoulder. "I think we'd better lie low for a couple of days. That nut job might try again."

Eric rubbed his face. "I'll call my patients and reschedule. I need to keep working, though. Any suggestions?"

"No idea. I'll think about it. If you get any good ideas, call me whenever you want, okay? In the meantime..." She hugged him. "Get some rest. I'm so sorry this happened."

"Hey, it's not your fault." He returned the hug briefly, then they resumed staring at the broken window.

"I don't know about that," Angela muttered.

CHAPTER EIGHTEEN
SAILING

THE SAILING on the bay was choppy but otherwise pleasant beneath a clear blue sky. A stiffening westerly breeze keep the sailboat heeled at a twenty-degree angle, propelling it at hull speed. Cassandra sat on the binnacle under the wheelhouse canopy, a clove cigarette dangling from her lips. She kept one hand behind her on the wheel while the other lazily grasped the line that controlled the position of the mainsheet traveler. The traveler, a pulley mounted on a horizontal track, provided a mobile attachment point for the mainsail boom. By tugging on the line in her hand, she could control the sail's angle relative to the wind.

Fortunately for Simon, the sailboat had been built wheelchair-accessible with lockdown points. He peered through the spray-spattered windscreen as the boat smacked into the chop.

Cassandra puffed on her unfiltered smoke and glanced at Simon. "So. Wanna talk about it now?"

Simon sighed. "No, but apparently you're not going to leave me alone till I do."

Cassandra grinned. "Exactly."

There was an uncomfortable pause, then Simon sighed. "It started like an old-fashioned session with me on a couch, shrink on a chair—except she put the chair right next to me. First, she told me to relax. Then she reached out and touched my forehead." He rubbed his face. "I felt this weird falling sensation in my stomach, but nothing else happened for a few minutes. She just sat there, eyes closed, her fingers touching my head. Then..." He grunted and stopped.

"Then?"

He licked his lips. "It was like a shot to the gut. All the grief and guilt just... just came up. Then suddenly, I was full of rage. No reason. Then she got up and backed a couple of paces away toward the center of the room. That's when I just lost it. I couldn't stop crying."

Cassandra puffed on her clove and studied the waves. She tugged on the traveler to adjust the mainsail when the trailing edge started flapping with a shift in the wind. They were making good headway on an upwind tack.

"I curled up in a ball." His voice was steady again. "A minute later she started talking to me. Obviously she was back from doing whatever she'd done. Man, it really hurt." He looked at her. "I'm not going through that again. I'm just going to keep fighting in the nightmares. Maybe I can win if I keep fighting Iron Star. But not if I have to go through another session with Angela."

"She told you it wouldn't be easy."

His fists clenched briefly. "Yeah. I know. But I thought she was going after the nightmares. I didn't agree to go digging up emotions from the past."

"But that's how this stuff works." Cassandra adjusted the wheel as the wind shifted direction slightly. "We all have an emotional history. She just knows how to find it. I don't know why you're giving up, is all."

He smacked his chair. "I'm not giving up! But I gotta choose my battles, Cassie. In the Corps, we learned that sometimes the enemy's position is stronger than yours and to not throw yourself at impossible odds. If I'm an emotional wreck, I'll be in no shape to deal with the nightmares."

He was probably right, but the nightmares were slowly killing him. There were circles under his eyes, he had lost a lot of weight, and his hands sometimes shook. Her telepathic talent gave her glimpses into his befogged and tattered mind, which was even more disturbing than his outward deterioration.

However, he was also an adult, so she decided to give him some more time. She pointed through the windscreen "Treasure Island. Let's go around the south side."

Simon looked at Cassandra rather than at the island. "Look, I'm sorry your friend can't help me. I really appreciate you trying. No hard feelings, I hope."

Cassandra returned his stare, keeping a poker face to hide her strong feelings. "When Angela met me, I had a family and a home. I told you about that and about the fire. Look, I spent five years being hunted by that thing, that Soul Thief. I was completely overwhelmed. I couldn't think. I barely survived on my animal instincts, and I still don't remember big chunks of those five years of my life. She brought me back from that. She helped me deal with the fire. And she destroyed the Soul Thief. I think you're making big a mistake in cutting her off."

Simon looked down. "I've made my decision."

Silence descended once again.

Several hours later, the chop was rough on the bay as the sailboat headed back toward Alameda and the marina. Cassandra had already taken the main sail down, by two reef points, to expose less canvas to the wind, and was considering running with just the jib. She normally enjoyed this kind of sailing, when there was tension between the boat and the elements and when the risks associated with sailing began to rise. For the moment, though, she was preoccupied with Simon's stubbornness.

"Look. I know it's a lot to ask. But Angela knows how much it hurt. I know she'll find a way to help without taking you down so hard." She glanced sidelong at Simon and, seeing his frozen expression, shook her head. She turned her attention back to the sailing, peering at the buoys as she approached them. Then, as if torn by the wind, the horizon peeled back. Cassandra drew a shuddering breath when she saw what lay beyond.

Countless soldiers marched in formation in an eerie silence. They wore a bewildering array of uniforms and bore unidentifiable weapons of many shapes and sizes. In the foreground, a large man wore elaborate red armor. Nothing could be seen of his face except for glowing eyes and a cruel slit of a mouth. He waved his hands in apparent agitation as he marched alongside the formation. He extended an arm and pointed at one soldier. There was a flash of light. When the flash faded, that soldier was gone.

Someone handed him a large, square object. He examined it and handed it back. Then, beyond all the ranked soldiers, a gigantic golden star appeared, hovering in the sky. The air behind it, to the left, glowed blood red while that on the right shone white. The image rippled and began to fade in a shower of sparks. A gigantic silvery curved sword materialized over it.

The symbols disappeared with a brilliant flash of light.

At that moment, Cassandra heard Angela's voice shout something unintelligible. The scene collapsed, restoring her view of the water ahead.

"Holy crap..." she gasped.

Simon mumbled something, but when she glanced in his direction he was staring at his hands, oblivious to her distress.

"All right," she muttered. "I don't know what's going on, but it's getting personal."

She set the autopilot on the wheel and walked over to stand directly in front of Simon. She put her hands on the arms of his chair. "Hey. Asshole."

He glared up at her. "What the fuck did you call me?"

"You're being an asshole, Simon, and you know it." She met his stare without flinching.

"You've got no right to talk to me that way." His voice was low, dangerous.

Cassandra stood up straight and crossed her arms, one leg braced against the bulkhead to help her keep her balance. "I think Angela just tried to help you again, and all you can do is sit there like a lump. I agreed to take you sailing if you would consider going back to her."

"I considered it, and I refuse."

"You think you're the only one with PTSD?" She tapped herself on the chest. "I was haunted by a demon for five years, pal. I was completely insane, and she brought me back. Yeah, it hurt, but look at me now." She reached out and shook his chair. "She can do that for you, too. You gotta give her another chance."

Simon stared silently at her, and his mouth compressed. Then his attention shifted to something behind her. "You might want to steer."

She turned around and saw a buoy several hundred feet ahead. She quickly unlocked the wheel and adjusted her course. While Cassandra steered, she brooded about Simon's stubbornness and worried about what was happening to Angela.

CHAPTER NINETEEN
AT DOCK

LATER THAT day, after she and Eric boarded up the broken window, Angela drove back home to the marina. When she arrived at her slip, though, the boat was gone. While Cassandra often enjoyed, as she put it, "taking the house for a spin," she had always checked with Angela first. Coming home to find it missing jolted Angela badly.

Angela took out her phone and dialed. The call went directly to voicemail. Cassandra had turned her phone off again. "Cassie? Call me back. Please. Just let me know you're okay."

She hung up and stared into the empty space, her mind a confused welter. Then a movement caught her eye. She glanced at the breakwater and breathed a heartfelt sigh of relief upon seeing her boat's welcome silhouette against the afternoon sun, heading for the marina entrance.

Angela paced, waiting for the boat to arrive. It was under engine power already, and both sails had been furled. The wind must have been much stronger on the Bay. She readied the docking lines and, shading her eyes, watched for Cassandra. As the boat neared, Angela could discern her girlfriend at the helm. Something or someone was in the cockpit with her, but they were too far out to see clearly.

The engine revved in reverse as the boat drifted toward dock. Cassandra went onto the deck and dropped the bumpers. She did not look directly at Angela, but when Angela threw her a docking line, she tied the boat fast.

"I called. Why don't you ever pick up?" Then Angela saw

Simon in the wheelhouse. Heat rose in her face. Simon had blown off his appointment, and evidently Cassandra was party to that. And what kind of fool took a wheelchair-bound man sailing?

She glared at Cassandra. "He had an appointment today! I waited an hour! Then we had a bomb scare, and all this time you were playing with your new friend?"

Cassandra's glance in return was cool and distant. "He wasn't going to go to see you anyway." She prepared the ramp for Simon to roll across from the dive platform, at the rear of the boat, to the dock.

"And so you decided to help him avoid therapy."

Simon spoke up. "Angela. It's not her fault."

Angela turned her glare on Simon. "She knows better than to interfere with one of my patients. Stay out of this."

"I will not." He unlocked his chair and began rolling toward the ramp. "Cassie was trying to talk me into seeing you. She spent the last three hours yakking my ears off about how you were a miracle worker and stuff."

Angela crossed her arms, glowering. Cassandra shouldn't have gone off without telling her.

"So... I'm sorry." Simon rolled across to shore. "I couldn't handle what happened at the clinic. But I think she won the argument, anyway."

Cassandra stared at him. "What?" Then her eyes widened as she turned and looked at Angela again. "Bomb scare?"

Angela waved her off. "I'll tell you about it in a minute."

"Angela." Simon rolled over to her. "If you're still willing, I'd like to try again."

"I don't know. I'm still angry about Cassie just running off with the boat like this." She turned to Cassandra. "What's with the cell phone? Why couldn't you just call and tell me what you were up to?"

"I was going to call." Cassandra looked away. "I forgot to charge my phone again. And then I was trying to get this guy to go back for another try." She turned back to Angela. "What's this about a bomb?"

"Okay." Angela sighed. It sounded as though she owed Cassandra an apology for blowing up at her. The tension began to drain out of her shoulders. She bent to help tie off the boat. "Cassie, someone threw a grenade through our window."

"Holy shit," said Cassandra. At almost the same moment, Simon asked, "Who did it?"

Angela answered Simon. "I don't know. It didn't go off, but the fire department and police were there. The place is closed down for a while."

"But why would anyone do that?" Cassandra came over to crouch next to Angela.

"Beats me." Angela stood. "I had just gotten back from a dream-walk where I saw something really weird. Then—"

Cassandra pointed her finger at Angela. "Let me guess. A big battle scene, some kind of giant golden star with red and white behind it, and then a huge sword and some other stuff."

"You saw that?" Angela recapped what she had learned. "So, the Yezidis are getting wiped out."

Cassandra nodded. "Yeah, it really sucks. But what's that got to do with us here?"

"I don't know." Angela turned to where Simon was waiting.

"Whatever it is, it seems to be connected to you. Can we do the work at your place? The clinic's shut down for now."

He loosened his shoulders and gave her a thin smile. "That's fine with me."

CHAPTER TWENTY
THE MEDIUM

An ally joins the raging fight

To rid the world of ancient blight,

Yet stronger still is angry god

Defending vice with armored might.

THE SOUND of sipping tea and the sibilance of indrawn breath dampened by the fragrant liquid passing through her lips were a comfort to Nadia. She needed comforting. The earth felt hollow under her feet as if she would fall through at any moment. She set the cup down and regarded her visitor.

Andrea was comfortably stout, dressed in one of her faded flowery dresses. If it weren't for her dark Romani eyes, she would have passed for every gadjo grandmother alive. She even wore reading glasses around her neck, which Nadia decided looked silly.

Andrea had pulled up a kitchen chair rather than take Michael's seat or sit across the room on the couch. She picked up her own tea from the side table next to Nadia and took a sip.

"Michael's gone to stay with Marko," Nadia said. "You remember Marko, Catarina's oldest?"

"Yes. He's a wild boy." Andrea chortled. "Michael's gonna be holding an aching head every morning."

"He already does." She set her teacup down. "Andrea, I've

tried to see him, but my Sight is failing. I don't know why. I asked you to come over to help me do a spirit working."

"I'll get the space ready." Andrea nodded, all business. She got up and went into the kitchen.

"Don't bother with the salt. I've set rock salt all around."

"Good. Is the bonfire ready?"

"No bonfire." At Andrea's surprised expression, Nadia scowled. "Neighbors complained, and we nearly got a ticket from the fire department. So..." Her face sagged, and she sighed. "We compromise. Fetch me the incense sticks on the sill there. And the holder."

Andrea returned with the requested items, shaking her head but saying nothing.

"Thank you." Soon pungent smoke curled lazily toward the ceiling. Turning back to face Andrea, Nadia put her hands on her thighs.

"I've got the wand." Andrea pulled a decorated, ribbon-festooned wand out of her handbag and flourished it. "Where's the drum?"

Another thing she could not use was a drum—drat it all. "No drumming. Neighbors complained." Nadia shrugged.

"Really?"

"Really." Nadia closed her eyes and began mumbling a chant in Romani to call the spirits.

"Spirits, angels, hear our call,

I speak my spell, attend us now,

Bring us wisdom."

As she muttered, she heard a rustle and relaxed, knowing that Andrea was gesturing to the four directions, to the sky, and to the earth. Knowing what would happen next, Nadia still jumped when she felt the wand touch her knee. A mild electric shock ran through her legs, and they quivered for a moment.

The repeated chant drew her mind into its circular pattern, and she heard her blood singing in her ears. A comfortable, floating sensation came over her as she entered into a light trance. Her lips moved automatically, and her awareness of the chant faded, replaced by a vibration that shook her body. The drumbeat of her heart whisked her away to the world of the spirits.

Her first impression was of bright light that illuminated the room. However, it seemed as if the light were somehow inside her head rather than outside. She no longer heard or felt the chant, and she no longer cared. She was there. She spoke firmly in her mind.

—*Who's there? Tell me who you are, or my Guardian will make you go away.*—

There was a blank stillness that felt oppressive, heavy.

Then, as if they had been present but below the threshold of hearing, the words became clear. —*Who disturbs me?*—

The floating sensation of trance deepened. She replied. —*Look at me. My name's written on my forehead, spirit.*—

There was a long, drawn-out hiss. —*Nadia. I know of you. What is your desire, sorceress?*—

Nadia prepared herself. No matter how many times she had done it, she had never become entirely comfortable with the work of trance mediumship.

—*Speak through me to the woman named Andrea. Come into my body.*—

There was a pause, and then the white-light sensation intensified. Nadia's awareness frayed into nothing.

Nadia's awareness returned piecemeal, beginning with her sense of hearing. A vast booming sound resolved into Andrea's voice.

"Nadia. Nadia. Wake up. Easy there."

Nadia's temples exploded with a throbbing headache. This was the part she hated the most. She imagined this was what Michael woke up to after a night of binge drinking and wondered, not for the first time, why he didn't just stop.

She took a breath and opened her gummy eyes. Rubbing them with leaden fingers, she groaned. "Water."

Bless her, Andrea was ready. She lifted a glass, and Nadia took it, sipping at first then drinking deeply. Her throat was raw as if she had been screaming. Maybe she had been. "Did you get everything?"

Andrea held up a single sheet of paper torn from the notebook. "I hardly got anything. Something big is going down in the Otherworld. The spirits are clamming up."

Nadia's head throbbed. She settled back and closed her eyes for a moment to try to ease the pounding headache. Nothing, no pain relievers or other remedies, would make it go away more quickly. She opened her eyes again and looked at Andrea. "Okay. Let's hear it."

Andrea pulled up her reading glasses from around her neck and peered at the paper. She frowned. "You—I mean the spirit —said this." She pointed at the paper and cleared her throat. "The Eagle tears you with iron claws." She glanced at Nadia, a worried expression warring with puzzlement.

"Go on," Nadia said. "Maybe the whole thing will make sense."

Andrea resumed reading. "The dreamer holds the key to power."

Nadia was puzzled. Dreamer? "I don't know. Maybe it's Angela. Go on."

"Then there's some mumble mumble. I couldn't catch it all, Nadia! Then you got all glittery eyed. You—the spirit—said, 'An angel wakes at the touch of war.' That has to mean Angela."

Nadia grunted. "Then who's the dreamer?" She scratched her chin. "I was right. There is a war in heaven, Andrea. And we're right in the middle of it."

WAR IN HEAVEN: ANOTHER ATTACK

Root Hexagon, Bald Eagle

Two angels stood guard near the Root Hexagon, facing outward, while others were arrayed at the perimeter of the crater. The commander of the team was stationed at the edge of the pool, monitoring the crystalline power source as it continued to pump energy in a steady pulsation along the connecting cables.

Another angel appeared at the lip of the crater between two at the perimeter. The two nearer the pool immediately raised their weapons, alert to danger. The commander prepared to reach for his own weapon. However, the new arrival wore the livery of Bald Eagle and calmly descended into the crater. Its movements were soothing in their familiarity, and the guards returned to attention, having dismissed its presence from their minds as they watched for intruders from other Egregores.

The commander monitoring the flow glanced again at the newcomer and felt a shudder of recognition. Something was wrong with its appearance. Perhaps its color was subtly wrong, but he could not determine this without a closer examination, and the work of monitoring power flows was all consuming. The newcomer assumed a guard position, and the commander resumed his work.

The intruder burst with a deafening roar, knocking the commander to his knees. Brilliant shards of all colors scattered about the crater. Where each shard landed, an enemy angel materialized, weapon ready. The commander got to his feet.

There was no sign of the guards who were nearest the explosion.

"Iron Star!" With that shout, the commander unsheathed a many-bladed sword glowing with power. He rushed to engage the dark-eyed attackers. Others of his surviving cohort were already struggling with the enemy.

Iron Star materialized near the Root Hexagon and, with an irritated growl, leaped into the fray. Powerful swipes of his iron claw-like weapon dispatched several of the enemy immediately. Those that remained concentrated their efforts on him. The commander collapsed, exhausted, and watched the battle. A shimmer in the air near the Root Hexagon betrayed the presence of Diamond Angel. Bands of force entangling it proved that the entity was still enmeshed in the isolation trap.

Iron Star's wily foe stabbed at him skillfully with its sword, forcing him to retreat a few steps. Then, with renewed vigor, Iron Star beat his enemy back, dispatching him. More of Bald Eagle's defenders appeared, and the remaining attackers retreated hastily. Diamond Angel began to fade, apparently unable to remain in proximity to the Root Hexagon now that the Dark Eyes contingent was in retreat.

The enemy portal was nowhere near the crater, preventing a speedy escape. Iron Star exulted. This was his chance to put a stop to Dark Eyes's interference. "After them!"

Growling racial slurs, several of the defending angels leaped over the edge of the crater, Iron Star following. They sprinted among towering organic shapes and geometric solids, vaulting piles of debris and the detritus of warfare. Soon Iron Star had pulled ahead of the rest of his warrior angels as they raced along the avenues of Bald Eagle.

Frustratingly, the enemy angels stayed just ahead of Iron Star's contingent. They rounded a corner, and the portal came into view on the outskirts of the Mothers' District. Iron Star and his band redoubled their efforts and nearly caught up with their foes. They hurled themselves through the portal after the enemy.

The landscape blurred around them. Iron Star felt a tug in the center of his being as he departed the realm of Bald Eagle. The sky had darkened, and the landscape was not nearly so cluttered with the features of a complex Egregore. Wild grass and low shrubbery, rather than pavement, made the footing treacherous as Iron Star led his force in pursuit. The chase continued through a lightly forested area under glowering clouds. The smells of fresh rain and ozone permeated the air.

Ahead, the contingent from Dark Eyes entered a clearing dotted with cyclopean statues, weathered by the passing eons. Iron Star, having pulled ahead of his fellow warriors, dodged around a monument carved in the form of an old woman bent over a staff. The next moment, he was sailing backward, and he landed on his back, stunned. He had slammed into a barrier of some sort. Iron Star looked up. That old woman was no statue but a Guardian possessing great power. He had never penetrated this far into Dark Eyes's territory before.

The angels who were running with him were scattered on the ground. Two of them rapidly decomposed as he watched. The rest of the warriors staggered to their feet, groaning. Iron Star got up, aching all over, and hefted his sword. Raising it over his head, he charged the statue with a howl of anger. But before his weapon could connect, there was a flash of light. More of Dark Eyes's angels, radiant with power in their own territory, appeared between him and the Guardian. They were armed with massive, weighted nets, and they flung these at his squadron. He managed to dodge the attack, but a number of his angels weren't so lucky. Several of them, trapped in the netting, began to dissolve in fitful sparks.

Iron Star slashed with his sword, but the netting was too tough to hack through. He backed up, gauging his losses. "Fall back. Fall back now!"

The remainder of his force, those who were not trapped by the nets, joined him. He raised his sword in an ironic salute to the old woman Guardian then opened his own portal to home.

War on Earth

"Freedom begins at home, man." The speaker waved his hand. "Don't get distracted."

—

"The media's lying to us." She waved an angry fist. "We gotta get our own house in order."

—

"There's one way to do that." He shared a scowl with his friends. "Kick out the no-good..."

—

"Kick out the filthy immigrants!"

—

"... taking all our jobs..."

—

"Filth."

CHAPTER TWENTY-ONE
THE NEIGHBORS

LATER THAT afternoon, after Andrea had left, several members of Nadia's extended family had come by to help with chores. Afterward, they laid the table for an impromptu potluck, something Nadia loved. Children were playing and yelling in the yard, and several of the men had brought guitars and were playing a lively tune. Of course, there was plenty of dancing.

Nadia was ensconced in a lawn chair. The outdoor table by her side was laden with tea and a crumb-covered plate. Despite her worries, she was content.

She turned her head at the sound of crunching gravel next door. Nadia's neighbors, an older gadjo couple, had returned home in their ancient Cadillac luxu-beater. They were a withdrawn, surly pair of retirees who had made no secret of their dislike for her Romani family. Nadia kept a sharp eye on them as they emerged from their car.

Two of the running children were playing close to the hedge her neighbors maintained on their property line. That could spell trouble. She waved at them. "You kids get away from there!"

The children ignored her. Nadia looked around for their parents, annoyed. She loved children at play, but she dreaded another confrontation with the neighbors.

There was a crackle, followed by laughter, quickly stifled. One of the kids had fallen into the hedge and had broken several branches. The gadjo woman, Gladine, shouted, "My hedge!" Her face was twisted in an ugly grimace, and she stalked toward where the children watched her, transfixed.

"You filthy gypsy animals! Look what you did to my hedge!"

The children scattered. Gladine turned to her husband. "Bob, call the police. I've had it with these... these gypsies!"

One of her cousins put his hands on his hips. "Hey! Who're you calling filthy?" Several of the Romani adults had stopped what they were doing and stared in open animosity at the couple.

The woman jumped then put her hands on her hips, her face red. She pointed at him. "I'm calling you filthy, you animal! Lazy, good-for-nothing gypsies can't keep your filthy children out of my hedge!"

The man stepped toward her, his fists clenched. Gladine recoiled in shock. "Bob!"

Bob came around the car. He was not usually a fast-moving man, but he made good time. He was scowling too. "I'm calling the cops. They'll throw all of you in jail. You set foot on my property, and I'll shoot you dead!"

This had gone far enough. Nadia heaved herself to her feet, cane in one hand. "You will do no such thing, Robert Strong."

Bob's head snapped around, and he glared at Nadia. Before he could respond, she pointed a long, steady finger in Gladine's direction.

"Now, you will take back what you said about our children. They are just being kids. I know you have grandkids. Are they animals, too?"

Gladine's eyes bulged. "How dare you compare our grandchildren to yours? We are hard-working Americans. You are nothing but gypsies!"

She spat the last word like a curse. Nadia placed both hands on her cane and leveled a stare at the gadjo woman. "You ought to be ashamed of yourself, Gladine Strong. You go to church every Sunday. What kind of Christian condemns someone like that?"

Gladine's mouth opened and closed, but then she rallied. "Well, you people would test the patience of the Lord himself." She waved her hand angrily. "Look at this place! It's always a mess. And you all stink to heaven. Not you, Nadia. The kids and the men."

"Well, you can hold your nose, then. These men worked hard today, Gladine. Instead of taking showers, they came straight over to help me with my messy place 'cause I'm crippled." She glanced at one of her cousins, who gave her a thumbs-up. "They love their kids and their wives, too, so they brought them. This is what family means, or did you forget that? And because they all came over, they brought food to share."

Gladine dipped her head, and her shoulders rose like a turtle.

Nadia continued. "But we're proud people, Gladine Strong. I'm telling you these things so you understand, not for your pity. We came from a very old race, an old part of the world, and we brought our culture with us. Since we left our original home, we have been hounded all over creation, but we have never given up who we are." She pointed a finger at the two of them again. "And we never will! I might not have your approval, but I will have your respect for me and my family."

Bob Strong shook his head and walked toward the house. Gladine, deflated, turned to go in, muttering to herself. A "got a lot of nerve" floated back to where Nadia stood.

Someone started clapping slowly as the neighbors disappeared into their house. Soon the entire Roma clan was hooting and yelling Nadia's praise. The men stood a little taller, and the kids screeched their joy and formed an impromptu dancing circle.

The women drifted closer as Nadia took her seat once again, their heads lifted just a little bit higher. One of them smiled at Nadia. "Cousin, that was a powerful speech. Made me proud to be Romani."

Nadia glanced up at her. "Every word of it is true. Never forget who you are."

CHAPTER TWENTY-TWO
NIGHTMARE'S COST

And thus is eldritch artifact

Renewed in strength, a primal pact

Affirmed once more for cruel strife,

To keep the realm of War intact.

SIMON OPENED his apartment door and went in, followed by Angela and Cassandra. He flipped on the light. "Can I get either of you something to drink? I'm nuking some water for tea."

"Just water," said Cassandra.

Angela nodded. "Same for me, thanks."

He rolled into the kitchen. "Water coming up." There was an electronic beeping in the kitchen followed by the sound of a running microwave.

Angela stepped over to the window, drew the curtain aside, and peered out at the street, feeling a nagging sense of unease. The bright afternoon sun was flimsy, as if it were a thin film that could be torn at any moment to reveal uncaring gods at war. She shook herself. That kind of thinking could lead to fatalism, and she knew life was more complicated than that.

Cassandra stood by her side. "You think someone's gonna throw another grenade?"

"No. Not at all." Angela drew the curtain shut and prowled restlessly. Suddenly Cassandra was in her arms.

"God, I'm sorry. So glad you're okay." Cassandra's voice was muffled against Angela's shoulder. They held each other, and Cassandra was the one who trembled.

"Me too, love."

They kissed. Angela heard a throat-clearing noise, and they turned to see Simon bringing in a tray with a pitcher of water, two glasses, and a cup with steam rising out of it.

"Here you go." He positioned himself by the couch. "So... same as last time, Doc?"

"Yeah." Angela and Cassandra disengaged. "Go ahead and drink your tea. I need a moment to prepare." She scooted a chair to sit by Simon while he pulled himself onto the couch. Cassandra sat in a kitchen chair, bent forward with her elbows braced on her knees.

While Simon sat up and sipped his tea, Angela dug into her backpack and pulled out a vitamin bottle. "I've been over there a lot lately, so I need to take a B-12 vitamin supplement. I suggest you do the same." She handed Simon a capsule, took one herself, then sat back to compose herself while he finished his tea.

"So, why're we seeing these visions?" Cassandra rubbed her face.

"I don't know, and I'd like to find out," Angela replied. "But I think the first thing to do is work with what we do know. Wouldn't you agree, Simon?"

He nodded. "Sure sounds like some kind of connection. Maybe I'm picking up on this war situation, and you're seeing that?"

"Maybe so." She turned to Cassandra. "I didn't tell you, but I visited George."

Cassandra snorted. "You did? I thought you weren't doing that anymore. You're gonna piss off Nadia if she hears about it."

"She already knows, and at this point I don't give a tiny spherical crap."

Cassandra snorted then grinned.

"Who's George?" Simon asked.

Angela paused. "He's my dead grandfather's oversoul." He didn't blink, so she gave him the short explanation.

"Do I have an oversoul too?" he asked with a lifted eyebrow.

"I'm sure you do. We all do."

Simon set his cup down then lay back within Angela's reach. "Okay. I'm ready."

Angela nodded. "Let's go." She reached out and touched his forehead, willing that he be allowed to accompany her if possible.

The apartment dissolved around her to reveal the day-lit meadow she had visited before. Angela once again stood near the center, but this time Simon was with her. His stare was vacant at first, and his mouth was slightly open, but then his eyes focused and grew wide. "My God." He goggled at his surroundings, at the ground, then at Angela.

She smiled. "You came along. Good. That should help."

He staggered suddenly, and she got an arm under his shoulders. He looked down at his legs. "I can walk!"

"Good. I was hoping you could. Sometimes a patient's body image carries over to this place, wounds and all."

His face was a study in wonder, and his breath was coming

faster. Angela felt his body quiver.

"I'm guessing you could walk when you were out of the body, right?" she asked.

"Yeah, but this is different. I feel... real." He held his breath then let it out, and his stance became firm.

Angela withdrew a little and looked him up and down. "Well, I'm pretty sure you're still out of your body, but this place is different than the astral plane or whatever it is that you go to." She bent, picked a stalk of wild grass, and showed it to him. "The plants and animals here are real and alive. But they're also symbols." When he shook his head, she continued. "It's really hard to explain, so I'm not going to try. Let's get started, okay?"

He nodded, and they began walking toward the perimeter.

"Over here is where I found those bodies." She pointed at the clump by the edge of the forest. She noticed that Simon was a little behind. He probably needed some time to adjust to all of the changes. Stepping carefully over the deeper areas of standing water, he grunted and frowned but continued walking steadily. He was bearing up well under the pressure of the stagnant emotions that such pools always triggered.

Soon they neared the two large hummocks. The sickly odor of death filled the air, and as before, Angela had to suppress her gag reflex.

"Phew." Simon covered his mouth and nose with one hand. "I know what that smell is."

Angela stopped walking. "Now, even though you're here in person, you're still going to react strongly to what we do. So, this time I'm going to go very slowly when I tamper with these bodies. We still need to get some information, and it's going to be there, hidden by those mounds."

She continued walking, leading him over to where the hand bones protruded. "Look at this." She glanced up at him.

He looked at the bones, and the color went out of his face. Simon gulped. "It's her." His voice cracked, and he wiped angrily at his face. "I don't know why this is so hard. I've seen her body in my nightmares hundreds of times."

"It's because here everything is magnified. We're getting at the root of your psyche. It's not just a memory. In a way, this is that actual woman, at least as far as your mind is concerned. So it's going to hit you just as hard as it did when you..."

"Yeah." Simon hunkered down, breathing heavily, and put his head in his hands.

Angela discreetly covered her mouth and nose. "Take your time."

After a moment he nodded. He glanced up at her, and his face was open, vulnerable, in a way that she knew she would never see in the physical world.

"Okay. I need a stick." Angela searched the ground, kicking aside piles of leaves. "I want to try to uncover this a little bit." Finally finding one several yards away, she returned to his side and handed it to him. He took it in one shaking hand and let the tip fall to the ground while he took several shallow breaths. Then, lifting his shirt to cover his mouth and taking a deeper lungful of air, he reached out to poke the mound.

Simon cried out and dropped the stick. He hunched on himself, groaning and shuddering. Angela waited patiently. He was doing better than she had expected. After a moment, he reached out and picked up the stick.

He managed to poke the matting partly off the dead arm, and then he scrambled backward. "Oh God. Oh God. Oh God."

Angela followed quietly as he fetched up against a tree and curled into a fetal position.

"There's no hiding from the emotions here. Every time you try, though, it gets easier." She reached out and touched his shoulder.

Simon flinched and raised a stony, expressionless face. "It's too hard."

"Okay. Let's take an indirect approach." She crouched next to him. "If you could talk to that woman today, what would you say?"

"I'd tell her I wish I could take it all back," he said, his voice flat. "Give her her life back, her children back. Give my life instead."

"Then do that. Talk to her body. Imagine that she can hear you. Maybe she will. The dead do come here, too."

He looked at her, incredulous. "You're shitting me."

"I shit you not. I've been visiting my dead grandfather for months now." She looked around, feeling for a moment as if she were being watched, but saw no sign of anyone else.

"So... is she gonna show up?" His voice rose a little.

Angela thought for a moment. Given Simon's current state, it was probably better to reassure him. Maybe telling him about the dead was a mistake. "I doubt it. I don't think they stay very long. My dead grandfather moved on, and he's probably reincarnated by now."

"I'm just about done being wowed. Nothing's gonna surprise me. I swear." He got to his feet. "Okay. Let's do this."

They returned to the mound. He was breathing deeply and steadily despite the odor.

"Now, kneel like you're praying." Angela stepped back a bit to give him room.

Simon kneeled awkwardly then looked up at her, a question in his eyes.

She gestured at the mound. "Tell her what you told me."

He looked at the mound then closed his eyes and cleared his throat. "I found out who you were, Maisa Assani. They didn't want to tell me, but I found out anyway. I took everything away from you, that night. I took your life, and your kids' lives." He paused. "There's no way I can make up for that. And if I could give mine instead, I would. But I can't. I..." He stopped.

"You can do it," said Angela.

He took a deep breath and coughed. Recovering his composure, he continued. "I am so, so sorry. I never saw what they did with your body. You should've been buried with honors. You were trying to get your kids to safety, and here we were, robbing you of that chance. I just wish..." He buried his face in his hands and shuddered.

Suddenly the ground began shaking, accompanied by a low rumbling that was rhythmic and insistent, as of far-off explosions. Angela looked around for the cause. Simon appeared to be oblivious in his suffering.

She saw a flash of movement above. She shaded her eyes, peered up into the sky, and gasped. "Simon? You need to see this."

He turned his face to her then to where she was pointing. "Shit. Oh, shit."

A scene was building in the now red-tinted clouds, depicting bloody warfare. Clearly visible, Iron Star hacked at winged soldiers, who crumpled and dissolved beneath his relentless attack. The punctuated rumbling kept time with his swinging weapon. Suddenly, Simon was on his feet. He backed away from the scene. Then his body began to fade. He looked at her hopelessly and vanished.

"Well. That's never happened before." Angela felt a flutter in her belly. She looked around the quiet meadow, at the ominous mounds and dark forest eaves, and shivered. Resisting the urge to leave, she paused for a moment, thinking.

While her grandfather had helped her to learn how to use her gift, her recovered memories of past incarnations remained the source of her deepest understanding of dream-walking. She dug into those memories of an unimaginably distant past when she used her power for healing and for learning.

When someone came with her into a meadow, that meant that the person's consciousness was attuned to hers. Her talent for assembling a coherent reality carried over to them, allowing them to create a body image as well as perceive the meadow and its contents. That connection had never been broken before. Somehow, the vision of war she and Simon had seen was connected to an interfering force. It was isolating Simon and preventing Angela from helping him resolve his trauma. She racked her brain, trying to remember whether she had ever seen or heard of anything like this before, but she drew a blank.

Upon Angela's return, she found Simon on the living room

floor, vomiting, while Cassandra stood helplessly nearby. Speculation on the vision of war had to wait until she got Simon settled and the mess cleaned up.

After swabbing up the carpet and laying down an old towel on the damp area, Angela and Cassandra conferred quietly on the other side of the room while Simon dozed.

"We tried to work through his guilt, but he withdrew into himself at a critical moment." Angela glanced at Simon. "Then when he saw the vision of war in the sky, he just faded away without my having to bring him back. I've never seen that happen. Did you see anything?"

"As soon as you guys started the session, you just disappeared." Cassandra's face, paler than usual, was drawn and beaded with sweat. "I blinked, and poof. It freaked me out." Her voice shook.

"I hate to say it, but we've got to go back." Angela tried to keep her own anxiety out of her voice. "This thing's escalating, and we're not going to find answers here."

Cassandra shivered. She glanced at Simon and then looked quickly away. "I'm trying to shut him out, but I keep seeing flashes of that battle you saw in the sky."

Angela touched Cassandra's hand. She had not seen her girlfriend so afflicted by the thoughts of others in months. Evidently, Simon's distress was able to overcome Cassandra's hard-won mental barriers.

Then a thought occurred to her. "Cassie, what if we link up when you follow Simon into his nightmare?"

Cassandra frowned. "What do you mean?"

"You know. Like what we do at the Rings. When you reach

out with your mind, I believe you're touching the Egregore, the group mind, of the club itself." At Cassandra's confused expression, Angela shrugged. "It's something George showed me. I'm pretty sure that's why we end up in that half-meadow together. You're part of that, so you can come with me there. I don't know why it's always night, though. Maybe the group never becomes self-conscious." As she said this, she realized that they had probably given everyone in the club a boost in libido when they had made love in the meadow. She suppressed an inappropriate grin.

"Can't we just do this tomorrow? Simon's wiped out." Cassandra looked over at Simon.

Angela shook her head. "If we wait, he's going to just get a lot worse." She stretched then walked over to where Simon was resting and touched his shoulder.

He started and looked blearily up at her.

"Hey. We're going to try something different."

"Leave me alone," he mumbled.

"I'm sorry, Simon. That won't do you any good. Those creatures are coming after you." She crouched. "I want to come along with you into your dream."

His eyes opened wide, and he struggled to sit up straighter. "What? Are you insane?"

"No. Evidently we can't do this my way, so we're going to do it yours. Or at least try to. I've never dream-walked this way before, but it's worth a shot."

He rubbed the back of his neck, wincing. "You don't know what it's like. We're soldiers. You're a shrink. Those guys'll take you out."

"I'm not going to die there," Angela said. "And you don't know everything about me." Such as the fact that she had learned hand-to-hand fighting and how to use beam weapons while his prehistoric ancestors were still braining each other with chipped stones. "Listen, we don't have much time. You need your rest, and I have a hunch they're coming for you tonight. So, Cassie's going to link up with you first. Then you can just fall asleep, like you're about to do anyway."

He shrugged, evidently too tired to argue. "Whatever. It's your funeral."

He pulled himself into his chair by the couch, waving off Angela's offer of assistance. She signaled for Cassandra to follow them into Simon's bedroom. He rolled up to the bed, levered himself onto it, and closed his eyes.

Cassandra, standing by the bed, touched his shoulder. "Hey, buddy. I'm here."

He nodded, not looking up. Cassandra lowered her head for a moment then grunted softly. She looked up at Angela, her gaze unfocused, as she swayed.

Angela went out to the kitchen and came back with two chairs. They took their seats by Simon's bedside and waited. Soon, Simon's breathing slowed and deepened.

After five minutes or so, Cassandra glanced at Angela again and nodded.

"I hope this works, Cassie. I think you'll be able to see everything through your link." Angela closed her eyes, raised her left hand, and touched the air.

At first, nothing happened, and her heart sank at the prospect of another failure. But then there was a flash of confusing lights and movement. Like an old-fashioned movie reel, the vision blinked in and out of her mind more rapidly. Then, with no other warning, Angela felt a nauseating dropping sensation far deeper than what she experienced when going to a meadow. She swallowed, breathed deeply, and opened her eyes.

Shouts and running feet shattered the silence. Angela winced. She looked around her, taking in her surroundings. She saw no sign of Cassandra, but there were more soldiers than she had expected, and she dropped into a crouch behind a stack of sandbags. Most of the soldiers, but not all, were carrying assault rifles. Keeping still to avoid attracting attention, she resisted the urge to scratch at the nape of her neck. The omnipresent sand, as fine as baking powder, trickled down past her T-shirt collar and irritated her skin.

Then she saw Simon, in desert kit, standing to one side of a makeshift barrier at the checkpoint. Angela remained where she was, grateful to be ignored by the other soldiers. Just as he had described, car headlights flared as the vehicle approached. A megaphone-amplified voice called for it to halt. Flashlights waved, followed by warning shots. The car accelerated with a roar, and she tensed.

At that moment, Simon put his gun down, and the action froze. Everything was grainy and poorly focused, as if she were in a video that someone had paused. Angela watched carefully, remembering that this was when he said that Iron Star would show up. Seeking a better position, Angela crab walked across the dimly lit pavement to within a few feet of the checkpoint.

When one of the soldiers jerked into motion, Simon decked

him with a roundhouse punch. Another blank-faced soldier reached to grapple him. Rising from her crouch, Angela kicked the soldier hard in the lower back. His rifle fell with a clatter, and she scooped it up, holding it more like a club than a gun.

She whirled so that Simon and she were back-to-back. The soldiers surrounding them moved slowly as if drugged.

"Pick up a gun," Angela gasped.

"No," he grunted.

One of the enemy, a young, husky woman, lunged for Angela. Using the stolen gun like a quarterstaff, Angela dealt a powerful blow to the robotic soldier's head. As she fell, the soldier shouted, "Shock and awe!"

Angela glanced back as Simon fended off another attack, but he moved slowly as if he were dazed or mildly paralyzed. More soldiers approached, faces blank and hands outstretched. Soon Angela was busy fending off the zombie-like soldiers attacking her and could spare Simon no more attention. She smacked hands and jabbed at faces. Like the first woman, the soldiers shouted slogans as she struck.

"There's no I in team!"

"Iraqi freedom!"

"Mission accomplished!"

"Shut up!" Angela kicked her nearest assailant in the abdomen, doubling him over. She swung the rifle sharply upward and was rewarded with a solid crack. He went down silently.

She felt her throat close spasmodically as memories of the long-ago War fought by her people overlaid the fighting here. Instead of blank-faced soldiers, she saw the bodies of her own people, possessed by her Enemy. She hesitated more than once before striking, but the attackers' reflexes were not much faster than Simon's. Had they been professional soldiers, not nightmarish automatons, they would have long since overcome her.

"Lady!" Simon's agonized shout made her whip around. The soldiers were forcing his rifle back in his hand. Then she was once again defending herself from her attackers. A gigantic shadow heralded the arrival of Iron Star.

"When two or more are gathered, there I am," he grated in a repulsive voice. Apparently, that was a command. Two of the soldiers facing her linked arms and, in a nightmarish blur, merged into a single, larger man. Two more did this, and she found herself facing eight-foot-tall, powerfully built soldiers.

For a moment she panicked. The monsters would crush her. But then she remembered that this was like any other lucid dream. She could control it. Angela concentrated, and the rifle in her hands lengthened, becoming her walking staff. As she hefted it, preparing to strike, all of her memories as a dream-walking chovihani returned in a rush. She had never used the staff to fight, only to heal and to explore. She lowered it for a moment. Why was she at war with these dream creatures? She should have been healing Simon instead.

The gigantic soldiers crouched and prepared to rush her. She panicked. From deep within her ancestral instincts, she pulled up a word of power. "Sakhu!" she shouted.

The word echoed in rumbling thunder against the now-overcast sky, and with two sweeps of the staff, she knocked the two large men aside.

Her hands glowed faintly with a white aura. Iron Star approached, wearing red armor rather than the general's uniform he had worn in Simon's dream before. He idly swung a gigantic axe in one gauntleted hand as he glared at her with white-hot eyes. Angela backed away warily and saw that the two of them were surrounded by a ring of men. To one side, several soldiers were holding Simon by the arms, forcing him to watch the impromptu death match.

"We are the few," Iron Star rumbled. "The proud. The separatists who use strife to conquer us must be defeated. Tell me, Lady. Who the hell are you?"

Angela remained silent, refusing to give away any information that would help this creature.

He looked her over once more then, in a sudden movement, lifted the axe aloft. She raised her staff to deflect the blow. Iron Star swung the axe in a vicious arc to bury its head in the ground. A gigantic crack in the earth opened, knocking her off her feet. She rolled and rose in a crouch, bringing her staff up, but the expected follow-up blow never fell. She spun as she heard the roar of the automobile along with the tearing-cloth sound of automatic weapon fire and a scream of anguish.

The world around her faded as Iron Star turned and walked into misty darkness along with all of the soldiers. Simon huddled nearby, groaning and sobbing, his still-smoking rifle discarded at his feet. She walked over to him, and he lifted his tear-streaked face to her.

"Just leave me alone. You can't do anything for me."

For a moment, Angela stared angrily at the sky, willing that the enemy return so she could exact vengeance for Simon's pain. Then the rest of the scenery whirled and disintegrated as she awakened, slumped in her chair.

Simon was curled up in fetal position on the bed. Cassandra had a hand on his shoulder, awkwardly patting him, but he reached up and pushed her away. Her shoulders slumped.

Seeing Angela awake, Cassandra came and stood by her chair. "I'm sorry, Angela. I couldn't follow you. It was like I was too heavy or something. Anyway, you just sat there for a few minutes, then he screamed and woke up. It didn't work, did it?"

"No." Angela passed a hand over her face. "This Iron Star is something else. We couldn't beat him."

"Go away." Simon's voice was muffled.

"Simon..." Cassandra reached out a hand.

He lifted his head. "Get out of my house!"

Angela and Cassandra were still sitting on the couch in Simon's living room. Angela could not bring herself to leave yet, and Cassandra seemed to want to stay as well. Ignoring them, Simon had remained in his bedroom, the door locked.

Angela could almost feel the powdery sand still trickling down her neck. What she needed was a shower and a four-hour nap. What she got instead was a quiet conference with Cassandra.

"There's more to this creature than I expected," Angela said. "A repressed complex could not do what he did." She hunched over, fighting the urge to scratch her neck. "Iron Star. I wonder why Simon named him that."

Cassandra's eyes narrowed as she stared at Simon's locked bedroom door. "The nightmare's gonna kill him, Angela. He can't keep losing sleep like this. I know. I've been there."

"I don't think so. He's got something they want, and making him relive this nightmare seems to give it to them. They're going to milk him as long as they can." Angela sat straighter. "What's weird is that these soldiers and this Iron Star kept shouting slogans when I hit them. It was like they were advertising something. Or like they were robots, repeating programmed messages."

She felt her jaw clench and forced her mouth to relax. The mystery had deepened unexpectedly, and they were no closer to solving it than when they had started. Angela wanted to go back and shake some answers out of Iron Star.

Somewhere outside, a siren yowled. An anonymous thump resounded in the apartment building. Cassandra sighed and cracked her knuckles.

Something in Angela snapped. Feeling an urgent need to do something useful, she got to her feet and picked up her backpack. "Let's go."

Cassandra stopped staring at Simon's door and frowned at Angela. "So we're just gonna give up?"

"No, but he threw us out, and I have to respect his wishes." She lifted an eyebrow and studied her girlfriend. "You have feelings for him."

Cassandra levered herself off of the couch and stood, jamming her hands into her pockets. "Well. Sorta. I mean, he's like... he reminds me of my brother."

That was unexpected, though Angela suspected it wasn't the whole story. She put a sympathetic hand on Cassandra's shoulder. "I'm sorry."

Cassandra tilted her head to touch the back of Angela's hand with her cheek. "I miss the little jerk, you know." She heaved another sigh. "Okay. Let's get outta here."

WAR IN HEAVEN: RENEWED STRENGTH

ROOT HEXAGON, Bald Eagle

Iron Star and his remaining troops were arrayed around the crater, staring down into the Root Hexagon. It glowed with renewed vigor and had successfully withstood another attack from within the keystone. There had been a hint of Diamond Angel's presence, but the isolation trap had done its work well, and her aura had quickly dissipated.

"Full power is restored for now." Iron Star almost smiled. "Our retaliation against Dark Eyes, though unsuccessful, will deter them for a while. I'm not as worried about them as I am about Diamond Angel."

He turned to one of the spy angels whom he had originally sent into the flux. "Do you have any further intel on the enemy?"

The angel held out a recording stone from which sparks crackled and snapped. "Yes, sir. As we have surmised, it appears to be a revenant Egregore from the old world of the Progenitors." The nameless angel saluted Iron Star with its free hand. "Here's more on the most recent conflict within the Root Hexagon, sir. Your image escalated its resistance, as it was programmed to do, but was only able to extract a small amount of information during combat."

It handed Iron Star the device. He grasped the stone, and the information it contained spooled across his sensorium. He scanned the data with growing unease.

"So." Iron Star paused for a moment. "We appear to share a

common origin, she and I." He fell silent, reflecting on the new information. He was not aware of their paths having ever crossed, but perhaps Diamond Angel had simply avoided him.

What he did know was that Diamond Angel harkened from the world that gave birth to him, the same world on which the God whom he served also arose to power. Furthermore, she had a strong connection with the God's opponent who had been working tirelessly to undermine His plan.

What Iron Star did not understand was how anyone, no matter how powerful, could have penetrated so deeply into the Root Hexagon, bypassing all the safeguards surrounding it. There was a mystery there, and Iron Star hated mysteries.

Coming out of his reverie, he nodded approval. "Very well. You are relieved. Return to your home and await further orders."

The angel gave a salute and vanished. Iron Star faced the Root Hexagon again, pondering his next move.

CHAPTER TWENTY-THREE
DELEGATION

THERE WAS a knock at Nadia's door. She awakened from an impromptu post-dinner nap with a start. "Michael! Someone's at the door. I don't know who it is." Then memory returned with an ache. Michael was gone. Grumbling, she pushed herself out of her chair, grabbed her cane, and hobbled to the door, her knees clicking painfully.

"Who is it?" she called.

"It's me, Nadia. Andrei."

She pulled the door open with her free hand. Her second cousin once removed, a middle-aged man with a long, flowing mustache and thick wavy hair, stood there. A grin flickered on his face then vanished.

"Come in, come in." She stood aside as he entered, then shut the door.

He went over to the couch and plunked down in it. "Nadia, you're looking younger than ever."

Nadia shook her head. "No, I'm not, and you know it, cousin." She hobbled over to her chair and suppressed a grunt as she sat. "There's tea fixings in the kitchen. Be a dear and make some for yourself and for an old woman, won't you? Here's my cup."

Andrei hopped up, took her cup and saucer, and went into the kitchen. "Nadia, I've got trouble, and I need your help." Dishes clattered, water filled the kettle. Bags went into teacups.

"What kind of trouble?"

"It's Joanna. My daughter. Do you remember her?" The kettle

clanked on the stove.

Nadia nodded. She knew everyone in the family. "Your youngest. Yes. She's eighteen now, isn't she?"

"Yes. And unmarried. She has turned away every boy she's met."

Oh no—don't let her be like Cassandra. But Nadia kept her thoughts to herself.

"It isn't that she doesn't like men," Andrei continued, as if reading her mind. "She is a lusty gal. Drives me and the missus crazy. But she's been having nightmares."

"Nightmares?"

"Yes. She wakes up screaming. Scares the crap out of us, too. Last night she told me she'd had a nightmare about her latest crush. Stefan, I think his name is. She said in the dream he was a soldier, and he came after her with a gun." The kettle started whistling. Andrei took it off the heat and poured the tea.

"Sounds like a typical teenage girl's dream to me. Like Angela would say, sometimes a gun is not just a gun."

Andrei did not reply immediately. He didn't laugh, either. Usually Andrei was ready with a nasty joke or two. He came back in with the teacups and placed one on her side table before returning to the couch to sit.

"It's not always a gun. Sometimes the boys are killing each other too. But it's always war." He looked at her, a haunted expression on his face. "I think she's got the Sight. My wife tells me that Joanna gets premonitions. Sees ghosts. Is there anything we can do?"

"Of course." Nadia nodded firmly. For some reason, the Ancestor's words about the Eagle's iron claws came to mind.

"Bring her here tomorrow afternoon."

His expression became even more miserable. "Nadia, please don't get mad. Joanna is scared of you. I told her to come to you herself, but then she started hollering about how you were going to kill her."

Nadia sat back in her chair. "Well, that's just ridiculous. Who put that in her head?"

"Not me." He sat back, his hand to his chest. "And not her mother. We know the good you do for us all."

She thought for a moment. This could be a good way to steer Angela back to the family. "Okay. I think I will call Angela and ask her to help."

He exhaled and smiled, his eyes tired. "I was hoping you'd say that. We've heard about Angela's dream-walking. If anyone can help, it's her. Joanna idolizes her."

"Well, then. It's settled."

CHAPTER TWENTY-FOUR
A DARK DREAM

ON THE way back home, Angela's phone rang, and she peered at the display. It was Nadia. She touched a button on the car's console to answer it. "Hi, Nana."

"That's right, it's your great-aunt." The connection was poor, and her voice sounded choppy. "I haven't heard from you since the party."

"I've been really busy. What's up?"

"One of your cousins needs your help. She needs a dream-walker's help."

Angela glanced at Cassandra—who was staring moodily out the window—then back at the road. She suppressed a yawn. It was ten at night. "Can you call me in half an hour? I'm on my way home."

"This will only take a moment." Nadia's voice sounded clipped and harsh, and Angela suspected that this was not solely because of the connection. "A cousin of mine's daughter hasn't slept in weeks. She's had horrible nightmares. I was hoping you could help her tonight."

"Nana, I just got back from working in the Otherworld. I'm exhausted."

"Angela, she's quite weak from lack of sleep. But never mind. You've got to keep your strength. Can you go see her tomorrow morning?"

Angela sighed. Then the word clicked. "Nightmares? What kind?"

"War. Terrible, terrible war."

Angela tensed. Coming on the heels of her failure with Simon, this could not be a coincidence. "Okay. I'll go see her tomorrow morning. Where's she live?"

Nadia gave her an address, then they said their goodbyes and hung up. Angela glanced at Cassandra again. "Something tells me this is related to what we're doing."

Cassandra didn't react but continued staring out the window, her face leaning slightly on the glass.

"Hey." Angela reached out and touched her on the shoulder. "You okay?"

"Yeah."

Her voice was inflectionless, but Angela suspected that she was masking her sadness. Angela brushed her hand down along Cassandra's arm. They twined fingers and drove the rest of the way home in silence.

The next morning, Angela drove alone to Joanna's home. Cassandra had remained in bed, blissfully asleep. Fortunately, Angela's relatives didn't live far from Alameda, and soon she pulled into an apartment parking lot. She nosed the Prius into one of the guest slots, got out, and after a few minutes searching, found the apartment.

The door opened almost immediately after her knock.

Andrei greeted her with a haggard smile. "Dr. Cooper? Please come in."

"Please call me Angela." Angela entered. "You're family."

He led her to one of the bedrooms and tapped lightly on the door then opened it a crack. "Joanna? Angela Cooper's here."

"Come in." The girl's voice was quiet.

Joanna, a rather thin girl with long, straight black hair wearing jeans and a T-shirt, sat on the edge of the bed. She indicated a desk chair, and Angela took it, setting her backpack down by her side. She looked around. The walls were plastered with pop-star posters and heaps of clothes covered the floor. In other words, it was a typical teenager's bedroom. But the air reeked of sweat and tension.

"I'm going to let you work," Andrei said. "Can I get you something to drink?"

"Water?" Angela nodded her thanks as he left, then turned to Joanna. "Do you know how this works?"

Joanna nodded, fidgeting. "Nana told me you touch my forehead and then I fall asleep and have a dream?" Her voice rose uncertainly.

"That's basically it. So, tell me about your nightmares."

Joanna shivered and glanced down at her feet. Angela noticed shadows under her eyes. Joanna's shoulders drooped, but her hands never stopped moving, twining and untwining.

"There's this dark forest. I'm standing there, and I'm lost. Then there's crashing sounds, shouting voices." She swallowed. "Right in front of me, two men come out and fight. One of 'em looks like a boy I know." She glanced up at Angela then back down at her feet. "The other one is a really big man. He cuts the boy's head off with a sword. Then he sees me, raises the sword, and comes at me."

She paused as Andrei came back to deliver Angela's water, then continued. "I wake up screaming. Every night for the last four nights. No one gets any sleep, me included. If I go back to sleep, I have another nightmare." She swallowed. "I'm starting to see things when I'm awake too. Animals. Weird people."

"That's an indication of acute sleep deprivation." Angela sipped her water and considered what little she knew. Joanna didn't come from a violent household, and there was no evidence of video games anywhere in the room to feed such nightmares. She shook herself. The day was passing quickly, and it was time to get started. "Okay. Go ahead and lie down on your bed and cross your hands and feet."

The girl lay down and stretched out. She scooted her weight to center herself on the bed then lay still, crossing her hands and feet as requested.

Angela lowered her voice. "This won't hurt at all. You'll just drift off. It's like hypnosis but deeper."

Joanna nodded and closed her eyes. She breathed in, then out with a sigh. Angela reached out and touched her forehead.

The room dissolved, replaced by a day-lit Forest meadow. Joanna had come with Angela and was standing by her side. The girl looked around her, eyes wide, and staggered a bit on the uneven ground.

"Hi," said Angela. "This place is real for you right now. Relax." She helped the girl get her balance. "When you're awake, it's just a symbolic place. Look around. Take your time."

Joanna gasped and shrank back against Angela. "This is the Forest!"

That was interesting. While her patients sometimes dreamed of Forests, they rarely recognized their own meadow. Almost none of them had any Second Sight, and of those few, none had ever been trained to see the Otherworld the way Angela did. "Really? Joanna, do you get premonitions? Hear voices? See visions, sometimes?"

The girl hesitated then nodded.

"Okay, it all makes sense now. You're psychic, and that's a good thing. It'll make this easier, believe it or not." Angela gestured at the edge of the woods. "The first thing we need to do is to show you that you have nothing to fear. There are no warriors in the forest. Those are dream images."

Joanna needed to be tugged a bit as Angela led her toward the dark eave of the forest. The meadow itself was remarkably tidy, and though the woods were dark, they were not overcrowded with underbrush. "Joanna, how's your home life?"

"It's good."

"You love your family? How about school?"

"Yeah." Joanna's voice quivered. Angela glanced back and saw the girl staring at the forest.

"It's so dark," Joanna murmured.

"That represents your unconscious mind. All the stuff we learn about ourselves comes out of that darkness." She reached out and, grasping Joanna's hand, drew the girl to stand beside her. "Now, what I want you to do is concentrate on your dream images. Don't worry. I'm right here."

The girl looked at Angela then closed her eyes.

Looking back at the dark forest, Angela saw a movement. As it approached, it resolved into the form of a large cat, perhaps a lynx, slinking in and out of the shadows, its eyes glinting with reflected light. She squeezed Joanna's hand. "Now. Open your eyes, and don't jump!"

The girl gasped and jerked in Angela's grasp. She began trembling.

"This is your fear," said Angela in soothing tones. "Just let it come. I've got you. Hold on."

Joanna clasped Angela's hand so tight it hurt, but Angela said nothing, unwilling to distract the girl. The lynx neared the two, its belly low to the ground and its ears flattened against its head.

"Put out the back of your hand. Please. It won't hurt you if you show it you're not scared."

Joanna hesitated then held out the back of her hand. The lynx craned its neck, ears pricking forward, and sniffed delicately at it. Joanna yelped and jerked her hand back. The creature's ears flattened again as it bared its teeth with a growl.

"Hush," said Angela. "Don't do that. It won't hurt you, but you can't show any fear. Put your hand out again. Slowly."

Joanna reached out with a trembling hand. The lynx sniffed then closed its eyes and rubbed its head against her fingers. Her mouth dropped open. "It's so soft!"

Joanna began scratching delicately. The lynx's eyes half closed, and it began to purr with a muted rumble. Joanna stroked it between the ears. Then, releasing Angela's hand, she kneeled. The lynx lowered its head and rubbed against her chest. Joanna hugged the big cat, crying.

"That's how you conquer fear," said Angela. "You make it your ally. Fear shows you something you need to know. You should always confront it and never run away."

Joanna looked up, eyes shining. "Thank you."

Angela shook her head, smiling. "You did all the work. I just brought you here so you could."

Giving the girl a few minutes more to make her

acquaintance with the lynx, Angela scanned the tidy meadow, searching for further clues regarding her nightmares. There was no obvious reason why this teenager would have such horrific wartime nightmares, unless she was picking up on other people's troubles. Angela touched the girl's shoulder. "Joanna, I need to ask you something."

"Sure." She sounded relaxed, even happy.

"Those warriors. Can you tell me more about their appearance?"

"Well, the one who died looked like a boy I know, which made it even scarier. He, um, has black hair and eyes. The other one was a big man, taller than anybody I've ever seen, and he had glowing eyes. He was wearing red armor, like a knight, and his helmet covered his face. Except for those eyes."

Angela felt a shiver go up her spine, and a breeze tossed the tops of the trees for a moment. "Iron Star," she muttered.

"What?" Joanna frowned.

"Nothing. Joanna, do you know someone named Simon? Simon Fenway?"

"No. Why?" Now the girl's brow was creased with worry.

"It's not important," Angela lied. She regarded the meadow again. Somehow Joanna was picking up on what was happening to Simon. Or, as she had begun to suspect, Simon's nightmares were an indication of a real threat from the Otherworld. For now, the most important thing was to help Joanna put up protection.

Joanna stood, one hand resting on the lynx's head. "I'm friends with my fear now. Does this mean I won't have any more nightmares?"

Angela shook her head. "Not exactly. But you won't be afraid anymore. If you want the nightmares to stop bothering you completely, this is what I want you to do." Her voice shifted into the smooth cadences of hypnotic induction. Angela intended to take advantage of Joanna's highly suggestible state while in the Otherworld. "The next time you have one of those nightmares, you're going to wake up in the middle of it."

Joanna nodded, and Angela continued. "Just hold one hand up and tell these soldiers in a firm voice to leave. They don't really belong here, after all. You're just picking up on problems other people are having."

"You mean Simon Fenway?"

Angela smiled. Joanna was a sharp kid. "Yeah. I'm helping him with his nightmares too." She ran her fingers through her hair. Angela was starting to run out of steam. "I think you're going to be just fine, and you know you can call me if you have any more trouble. We need to get back."

CHAPTER TWENTY-FIVE
HAUNTED BY THE PAST

But Diamond Angel stands apart

To gaze upon the Eagle's heart;

Then swiftly does she send her spies

His secret lore to her impart.

THE NEXT morning, Angela called her great-aunt to tell her about what she had seen in Joanna's meadow. She began speaking rapidly as soon as Nadia answered the phone, feeling a sudden urgency.

"Angela, dear, slow down. Who or what is an iron star?"

Angela was in the boat's cockpit, staring at nothing. She heard clattering in the background, over the phone, and suspected that Nadia was cooking. "It's a who. Iron Star is a creature who lives in a part of the Otherworld I never knew about. He fights. All the time, it seems. And now he's targeting us. We've been helping a soldier with his nightmares. Iron Star's been tormenting Simon for a while. And now Iron Star's showing up in Joanna's nightmares, too."

"The eagle's iron claws. And the dreamer!"

"What?"

"I went to the spirits, and that's what they told me. Something about iron claws and that a dreamer held the key to power. I was thinking the dreamer was Joanna, but maybe it's your soldier instead." She paused then spoke more slowly.

"There is a plot, Angela. A plot against our people. Maybe these are hungry *mulos*, or a curse. I don't know."

"It's not just our people," Angela said. "Simon, the soldier, is a gadjo, and he's taking a lot of horrible abuse from this... whatever it is. Maybe it's a hungry ghost. I don't know. But I've got a hunch it's something different, something new."

"Could the Soul Thief have anything to do with this?"

"No. He's long gone." Memories of that terrible conflict arose in Angela's mind. "I saw to that. You know I did."

"I mean, maybe this—this Tin Star—is something he left behind."

"Not Tin Star. Iron Star." Angela's her breath caught, and she felt a flutter in her stomach. She had not considered that the presence of Iron Star might be related to last year's struggle, but knowing the power of the Soul Thief, it was possible. She considered what she knew of that ancient enemy, her old lover and would-be destroyer. "Maybe he did leave Iron Star behind. But I never saw any hint of it. If he'd had something like that up his sleeve back then, he'd have used it."

There was another pause. Then Nadia continued. "My neighbors gave me some trouble, and I had to shout at them. A bunch of family were visiting that day, and they liked what I said. Said it gave them backbone. Then I had to stop a fight between the boys the next day. Did I tell you? Something's gotten into people. They just can't stop fighting over the most ridiculous things."

Angela heard sipping on the other end of the line. Her stomach rumbled as she thought about Nadia's cooking. "Well, please let me know if you hear about any more nightmares involving war, okay?"

"I will." She cleared her throat. "Angela, I know you're busy. But there's a lot you need to learn, starting with how to deal with the hungry mulos and how to lay them to rest. How to work with the spirit world. I can teach you that. And better than the ghost of your grandfather."

Angela sighed. *Here we go again.* "I know. I know. I promise, I'll find some time soon. As soon as I can, okay?"

"Very well, dear. Give my love to Cassandra and Eric."

"I'll do that. Give Michael a big hug for me, okay? Love you. Bye." She hung up and closed her eyes to concentrate, remembering all she could of the many powers of the Soul Thief and the Great War he had caused. Pressure mounted within her as if her prior incarnation as the Lady of Light were seeking dominance. She fought down the temptation to give in and allow those old habits of thought to take over. The most poignant memories centered on the Chancellor, who'd been reborn over many lifetimes to become Cassandra.

As if hearing her thoughts, Cassandra came up from where she had been lurking below decks. Angela glanced at her. "Cassie, remember the stories I told you about the War our people fought?"

"Yeah."

"I'm afraid we're not through fighting it."

"You said that was a long time ago."

"It seems like only yesterday to me. I spent the last umpteen-zillion years in the Otherworld, watching... him, but that was more like a long dream. I remember the lifetime before that time very well when he destroyed our world."

Cassandra eyes widened. "But he's dead! Worse than dead." She hugged herself.

"Yes, he is. But I'm still worried about us. Our world. And the legacy of the older world that he reawakened." *Or that I may have reawakened*, she added silently.

After further discussion, Angela and Cassandra decided they needed to try to enlist Simon's help. He offered the only reliable way that Angela could use to contact Iron Star, and they needed to learn more about their new enemy. Angela had a sense that time was running out, though she could not put her finger on why.

Now they were outside his apartment, and Angela rapped on the door. Cassandra stood beside her. Angela smelled something pungent, an aroma that she could not identify. The odor reminded her of incense, but if it was, it was not one she would ever burn.

"Simon? It's us, Angela and Cassie." Angela glanced at Cassandra, who was staring at the door. "Simon? I know you're home. I heard you moving. Cassie can hear you thinking."

There was a thump. "Go away." Simon's voice was muffled.

"I'm not gonna do that. This is bigger than you, bigger than us. We need to talk."

"I said, go away!" His voice was louder. It sounded as though he was in the living room. "You can't help me. Neither can Cassie."

Cassandra rolled her eyes and snorted.

"I don't think we were going about it the right way," Angela continued. "Simon! Please, let us in."

There was silence. Cassandra looked at Angela. "He doesn't want us to get hurt. He's got no idea what you—what we—can do."

Angela stared at the door, willing Simon to open it. "Look, I know you're worried about us. But this isn't just about us. There's a war going on, and we're all in it. Together."

There was more silence, followed by another muffled thump. They waited.

Cassandra jerked her head at the street. "C'mon. That asshole's not gonna let us in."

Angela hesitated, but she heard disgust in Cassandra's voice and trusted her insight. She threw up a hand. "Dammit!"

On the way back to the boat, Angela's hands-free unit chirped with Eric's ringtone. She pressed the talk button. "Hey, Eric."

"Hi, Angel. Can you come over to the clinic?"

"What's wrong?"

"I don't want to talk about it over the phone." Angela thought he sounded unusually tense. "There's something urgent I need to go over with you in person."

"Why can't we do it over the phone?"

"I can't tell you why over the phone. That's why I want to meet you here."

Now Angela and Cassandra stared at each other for a moment, eyebrows simultaneously raised.

"Hey, man. Don't panic, I'll come over. Just give me a little time. I'm having a rough day." Angela shrugged.

"I'm really sorry. It's kind of stressful all around, huh?"

Angela stretched her arms against the steering wheel,

working out a knot in her shoulder that was starting to accumulate tension. "Yeah. Okay, Cassie, do you want to go back to the boat or come with me?"

"Take me with you." Cassandra spoke in a flat voice, but her eyes were alight with curiosity.

"Okay. Eric, Cassie and I are coming right over."

"See you in a few." He hung up without his customary cheery goodbye.

Angela pushed the off button thoughtfully. "He seems really wound up."

WAR IN HEAVEN: INDIVIDUATION

WITHIN THE Unclaimed Overworld

Diamond Angel explored the vast gray realm of the Overworld beyond the territories claimed by Egregores. Constrained by the isolation trap, she had been unable to venture anywhere near Bald Eagle. Exploration of the Egregores' realm was her sole remaining option if she wanted to establish herself here.

She followed her instincts. She had no guide, no path through the endlessly complex layers of the Otherworld. Each step she took opened an entire vista of higher geometries, unfolding like an enormous fractal chrysanthemum.

Turning another five-dimensional corner, her world exploded with light. She halted, blinded in all her senses for a moment, and raised her hands defensively.

"Don't be afraid." The voice was strong, calm, reassuring.

"Who or what are you?" She concentrated her forces in her belly, preparing to unleash a killing bolt of energy.

"I am a friend." In that same calm voice, the visitor explained that he had come from a secret ally. He was an angel, he said, and he brought knowledge.

Diamond Angel relaxed, composed herself, and listened. The angel explained that the Root Hexagon was a fragment intruding from an even more rarefied region, one occupied by gods to whom the Egregores were but children at play. The artifact's power, though corrupted, was still tremendously helpful to Bald Eagle in that it was able to capture and replay every kind of imaginable energetic pattern.

"Follow me," the angel said.

Setting aside her reservations, Diamond Angel accompanied her benefactor along one of the turnings she had abandoned in her exploration. She felt a sudden constriction and then burst through.

She stood on an endless blank white plain. Arrayed around her were small statues taking the form of various animals and geometric solids. Diamond Angel looked for the angel, but it had vanished. Extending her senses, she probed the new realm and discovered that it was a secret place that gave her a unique perspective on the Egregores. Each of the statues was connected to an Egregore. Through them, she could gain the insights she needed.

Nearby was a statue of a bald eagle perched on a pyramid. It sparkled with activity, and as she focused her attention, Diamond Angel felt an itching, prickling sensation in her core. Disregarding her discomfort, she gathered her strength. This was her best chance to safely study her foe.

Diamond Angel pushed a hand into her solar plexus and pulled out a large dollop of glowing, mucus-like substance. She dashed eight gobbets of it on the ground around her. Each rose up into the form of a larva, a vaguely humanoid, mindless creature that served as an extension of her will. She lacked the resources, as yet, to create an independent, conscious angel that had the power to retrieve knowledge from an Egregore. The eight larvae would have to serve, infused as they were with the vitality of her alien viewpoint.

With a sweep of her hand at Bald Eagle, she sent the larvae

flying like arrows. As they neared the statue, they shrank then vanished. Satisfied, she waited for the results of her probe.

An indeterminate amount of time later, two of the creatures returned. She opened her arms, and they flashed as they merged with her solar plexus. None were able to penetrate the realm of Bald Eagle. Her resources were limited, and without aid, Diamond Angel was unable to proceed with her original plan.

Sparks flashed in the periphery of her vision to the right, and she peered in that direction, shading her eyes against the uniform whiteness. The sparks resolved into the forms of two angels, appearing in the somber suit-and-tie garb that signified their membership in the Egregore Gray Suit. They held thin strands of reddish light, which reached toward her and vanished before they entered her aura. She tensed, worried that the two angels had power over her. Raising both hands, she flung bolts of force at them. But it was merely a vision, and the angels weren't truly present. The images faded.

Another movement nearby caught her attention. Two of the statues, one depicting an exotic woman and the other a handsome man, had emitted threads of blue light in her direction. She perceived that those two were offering alliance in the realm of the Egregores. One named itself Serpent Lion and the other Dark Eyes. An angry veil shimmered between them. They were enemies to each other, which would complicate any alliance they offered.

Allies were fickle amongst the Egregores, but she could have used any assistance offered to her, so Diamond Angel opened herself to them. However, when their helpful threads neared her form, they were blocked by red flashes of light, similar to the veil. Gray Suit again. Although Diamond Angel was not by nature a vengeful creature, she contemplated revenge for her drab opponent and its ally Bald Eagle.

Composing herself once again, Diamond Angel prepared to establish her own realm.

War on Earth

The navy vet sat up, sweat pouring off of him. His nightmare clung to him like a shroud, and for a moment he forgot that he was home. "Whaddya want..."

—

"Go back home, I ain't got none." The homeless woman, an army vet, swatted at the translucent things hovering by her face. "No!"

—

"Get away from me!" he shrieked. The orderly held him down with difficulty. "Dammit!"

—

"We're almost outta Abilify. Crap. Gettin' distracted again. But..."

—

"I served my country. Shit happens. Service..."

—

"Service demands a willing..."

—

"... sacrifice."

CHAPTER TWENTY-SIX
A REUNION

(An ally meanwhile mends the wall

That serves to keep his woodland hall

Safe from all who would destroy

His mystic race beyond recall).

NADIA BROODED. The book she had been reading had done nothing to ease her tension. Now it lay facedown on her side table. Her empty teacup next to it mocked her indecision. Michael was still angry with her; she could feel his anger like an open, pulsing wound. The knowledge that some of that wrath was fueled by a virulent impulse sent by the enemy did little to help her mood. The unknown foe, human or not, appeared to be a smooth-talking bastard, influencing minds with words and images.

She needed to contact Michael and reconcile with him. Their feud was undermining her position as an honored *puro dai* more effectively than if she had simply rolled over. Of course, she appreciated everything he had done for her over the years. She wished that he had said something rather than stewing in his own juices and then exploding at her as he did. Maybe it was worse because George had died.

Nadia shuddered. Angela had defied her by seeking her grandfather out, but she could do nothing to restrain her great-niece until she began proper training.

But never mind that right now. Time to swallow her ego and try to reach Michael. She picked up her phone and dialed his cell number. The phone rang five times and went to voicemail.

"This is Michael. Leave a message, and I'll forget to call you back. Okay?" It beeped.

"Michael, this is your sister. I am sorry for saying what I did." Nadia sighed. "It was wrong of me to do so. Please come back home. We all need you. I need you."

She paused, not certain if she needed to say something else, then hung up. She stared at the wall, wracked with memories.

Nadia stood outside her old trailer home beneath a gigantic full moon, watching as someone approached. At first she could not make out who it was or even if it was a person; its size grew and shrank in the silvery illumination that filled the yard and suffused the air. As the figure neared, however, she saw that it was a beautiful man. He had dark eyes, black hair, and aquiline features. Evidently Roma, he lifted an empty hand in greeting.

In her dream, Nadia stood stock-still as he stopped about three feet from where she stood. His presence was a radiant warmth. This was no mere dream figure but a spirit of great power. For a moment he was silent. He would speak in his own time if speaking was in his nature.

"My Nadia. Seer, sorceress, and one of my greatest servants."

She lifted her chin. "My service is to my people, spirit."

His smile was a thing of beauty. "Your people are within me, as I am in all of them, so when you serve them, you serve me."

The Ancestor! She had not recognized him. The shock almost awakened her from the dream. She mastered her emotions and settled back into the curious half-awake state of lucidity. "As you say. You are welcome, of course."

The Ancestor quietly searched her face. Then he turned and pointed behind him. "I bring you a vision as a reward for your fine work on my behalf."

She looked toward where he pointed to, and gasped. A great storm was boiling up from behind the horizon, red lightning flickering within the clouds. A gigantic, half-formed face appeared. Its knitted brows and fierce, white-hot glowing eyes seemed to strip Nadia's soul bare.

Walking swiftly from that direction, Cassandra's slight figure drew near. The girl appeared to be unaware of the cloud behind her as well as of Nadia and the spirit. Cassandra strode toward Nadia, her hands jammed into her pockets. A flickering cloud of darkness shrouded her body, resembling the invisibility spell that George and Angela both practiced. It did nothing to deter the intent stare of the monstrous entity in the cloud.

Suddenly, a bolt of red lightning struck the girl. She cried out and tumbled to the ground. Nadia tried to rush forward to her aid. The Ancestor blocked her with an outstretched arm.

"Don't go near her," he said. "I can't protect you from him if you do."

"But she's hurt!"

"This will come to pass, and no one can stop it." The spirit's face was calm, placid. "But you can warn Angela for me so he cannot hurt her, too. Will you do that?"

Nadia stared at the prone form of Cassandra then looked back at the Ancestor, torn between the instinctive urge to help and the command of the spirit. "Will Cassandra survive?"

He nodded. "She's very strong. Yes. But I cannot say the same for Angela. She has made herself vulnerable to him." He nodded in the direction of the storm. "I can't reach her anymore. Angela is her own person, beyond all of us. But the enemy has her in his sights. Warn her, and help her when you can. Beware the gadje in your world, for they are the instruments of his will. Their words are his weapons, and they often act on his behalf."

He stepped forward a pace and reached out to touch Nadia's arm. "Now wake up. Wake up."

His voice echoed, distorting, and Nadia felt the world quake. She struggled toward wakefulness. A hand was on her shoulder, the voice murmuring in her ear. Nadia opened her eyes. Michael stood over her, gently shaking her.

"Nadia, wake up. I'm here. You were having a nightmare."

She stared up at him, then she felt the remnants of her hard-held anger at him disappear. "Oh, Michael."

He bent and hugged his sister, and her tears wet his shoulder.

Nadia and Michael were back in their accustomed chairs, and all was right with the world. The comforting tea had been made and was being drunk, and their discussion was amiable.

"So, you say there is a spirit that made us quarrel?" Michael asked again.

Nadia hid her sigh, resigned to explaining for the third time. Michael was having difficulty grasping these concepts because he lacked a chovihano's subtle skills and understanding. "Yes. This Iron Man, Tin Star, whatever his name is. He is a no-good, meddling mulo or something. Anyway, he is speaking through the mouths of the gadje and working through his tools, the police. This much the Ancestor told me."

Michael scratched his chin. He had decided to shave his beard. It had never looked good on him. "What can we do? If the Ancestor says to stay away, should you try to fight this mulo?"

"I cannot fight him. But we can all help Angela."

Michael lifted an eyebrow.

"And Cassandra too," she continued. "She is one of our own, and she has a great power as well." *Even though it's not proper for her to be with Angela*, she thought. But she prudently decided not to go on another rant.

Michael thumped his chair, making her jump. "Then let us do this thing. My brother would say so."

Nadia nodded. "I will call a gathering of the chovihanis."

Michael's jaw dropped. "Can you do that?"

"When times are this dark, yes. But we have to do this quickly. Angela almost died last year because we didn't help her. Not again."

WAR IN HEAVEN: RECONSTRUCTION

REALM OF Dark Eyes

"Reinforce the fortifications here and here." Dark Eyes's finger stabbed at the air, indicating the floating image mapping his realm's perimeter. "Meanwhile, I will strengthen the Guardian."

His attendant angels scattered to busy themselves with the work of reconstruction. Satisfied, he spread his arms, opened a portal, and stepped through.

CHAPTER TWENTY-SEVEN
THE MEME

Though empty are her hands that day

For Eagle leads her spies astray;

Bestirs she then to make anew

An angel, thus his lies betray.

WHEN THEY arrived at the clinic, Angela parked hastily, and they approached the front entrance. Cassandra had assumed the hard, streetwise face from her pre-Angela days and glanced around warily. Angela stared at the boarded-up windows and sighed. She had known that opening a clinic in this location might be risky, but that didn't make the reality of grenades and broken glass any easier to swallow. She unlocked the door, and they entered the admitting room.

Eric was pacing but halted mid-step after she came in. His normally insouciant expression was gone, replaced by that of a man at bay, something that she had never seen in all the years she had known him. "Thank God you're here. It's DMH, Angela."

He led them to her office, shut the door and, once inside, resumed pacing, his steps rapid and small, his shoulders hunched, saying nothing.

"What about them?" Angela asked.

He stopped and flung a hand up in the air. "They're not only yanking the funding. They're demanding we return the benefits payouts for the patients we've treated."

Cassandra gasped. "They can't do that!"

"Yes, they can." Angela saw a crumpled piece of paper in Eric's other hand. He waved it at Cassandra. "They cited irregularities in the filings and said we may be charged with fraud."

Angela felt as if all the air had been sucked out of the room. Reality had just taken a surreal turn. She drifted over to a chair and absentmindedly took a seat. "Oh, shit."

Eric resumed pacing. "One of my friends at the hospital warned me to watch out for this kind of crap from Sac town. Said that we'd get caught in the middle of a bureaucratic feud, but I didn't want to believe him."

Abruptly, Angela's world snapped into focus. This was something she understood. Heat rose to her cheeks as she stared at Eric. "Are there any additional details on that memo?"

Eric shook his head. "No, it's just a single-page notice. When I called, my liaison wouldn't explain further. Said we'd be getting the rest of the paperwork in the mail. But he said we might want to consider filing Chapter 13 if we don't want to lose the clinic altogether."

Angela smacked the desk. "Like hell! We followed their goddamn rules to the letter. Our lawyers made sure of that. Let me talk to those bastards."

Eric put a hand to his face then rubbed downward before releasing his chin. "Angela, they could take everything, and we'd both be finished as psychiatrists if this got out." He stared at her, lines creasing his face. "God, all the money you've invested, the proceeds from the condo. Out the window."

"That won't happen, Eric."

He looked at her. "Dammit. How do you know that? This is the government we're talking about."

Angela stood, resolve flooding her. "No, this is a bunch of bureaucrats. I know how to deal with those."

"What the hell do you think I've been doing all this time?"

Seeing the fright in Eric's face and voice, Angela's anger evaporated, giving way to pity. She raised a placating hand. "Eric. Relax, please. We're on the same side."

The lines on Eric's face deepened, and he nodded. Angela could feel the exhaustion emanating from him.

"You're right, hon." His sigh was high, sad. "We can't let strife divide us. We've got to win."

Angela stared at him, recognition dawning. She recalled a huge armored figure saying the same thing. "Iron Star!"

"Who? What?"

"Never mind. Eric, remember when the regulators wanted to shut Franklin down? They cited the uncontrolled biohazard conditions there, as well as numerous health-code violations."

He nodded. "Yeah. I remember. It seemed impossible. There were about fifty malpractice suits on top of plain old civil lawsuits." He chuckled, a little life coming back into his face. "You marched in there and..."

"And I told them that San Francisco needed us more than ever thanks to what went down. I showed them our new protocols and the signed contracts with the VA and about a dozen corporate contracts for human resources support. Not only did we get the hospital out of trouble..."

"It turned a huge profit three months after the disaster. I

know. I was there."

"So." She grinned at Eric. "I don't think a few paper pushers are gonna stop us. Listen, why don't you go home and get away from all this, okay? You'll feel better in the morning, I promise. Can you meet me here tomorrow?"

Eric nodded. "Sure." He came over to her and hugged her. "I'm sorry, hon."

"Me too. We'll get through this."

Eric exchanged hugs with Cassandra, as well, and left.

After closing the door, Angela practically ran into her office, Cassandra trailing after.

"What? What is it?" Cassandra asked.

Angela didn't answer but instead flipped open her laptop and entered the password twice before getting it right. She fired up the browser. "Something Eric said reminded me of one of the things Iron Star said during our fight." She spoke rapidly while she alternately clicked the mouse and typed. "It was as if Iron Star spoke through Eric, somehow. Let's see. Aha!" She pointed dramatically at the screen.

Cassandra bent to read. "What's this about?"

Angela read the document summary with growing excitement. Then, glancing up, she locked stares with Cassandra, whose eyes widened. Angela pointed at the document. "This is a white paper discussing the use of the science of memetics, the study of memes, in clinical psychology. You know what memes are, right?"

"You mean like LOLcats?"

"Well, sort of. Those are internet memes. I'm talking about something bigger."

Cassandra shook her head uncertainly then bent to read what was on the laptop display.

Angela continued. "A meme is an idea, something which conveys cultural thought. Like, shaking hands is a meme. It tells the other person you're unarmed and friendly. Slogans are memes. They reinforce the norms of a culture or subgroup. But memes can make people do terrible things, like what Iron Star's doing to Simon."

"What do memes have to do with anything? We're fighting a real enemy, not cultural ideas."

Angela shook her head. This was familiar territory for her, but Cassandra was still new to it. "The Otherworld is full of real things that represent ideas. I deal with them all the time. That last girl, Joanna, had fear that gave her nightmares. In the Otherworld, her fear came in the form of a lynx."

Cassandra snapped her fingers. "And you think this Iron Star and his soldiers are memes."

"Something like that. Granddad warned me about these creatures—these 'angels' and the Egregores they serve. I think that, somehow, they're causing trouble for a lot of people in this world. That might explain why I heard the soldiers shouting trite slogans and why Iron Star sounded like a recruiting poster. I think Iron Star and his Egregore are threatened by what we're trying to do with Simon. I don't know why, yet. But I think I'd like to try an experiment."

Her ideas took shape rapidly in her mind, driven more by intuition than by logic. "According to this paper, memes are transmitted from person to person like viruses. But they're viruses of the mind. Maybe this is why I keep seeing traces of

Iron Star in other people's nightmares. It might be how we can fight him, too. I'm going to need your help."

An hour later, Angela was still seated at her desk, typing furiously at the keyboard. Cassandra sat in another chair, peering over Angela's shoulder.

"Okay," Angela said. "That's the tenth Facebook account I've created so far. Let's hook into the friend networks from the other ones."

Cassandra pointed at the screen. "Don't forget to approve the friend requests in the other accounts."

"Right." Angela's fingers flew. "Now. Time to paste our little meme." She posted the text then copied it to the Twitter accounts they had also set up.

Angela was proud of her new slogan: "You don't owe your dreams to Uncle Sam. So why keep fighting his wars in them?" It was short enough for Twitter, and it conveyed a message that she hoped would spread among PTSD sufferers who were fighting Iron Star and his minions. She had made sure to send a copy to Simon's e-mail and Facebook accounts, of course, as he was the primary target for her work.

She tapped a key triumphantly and beamed at Cassandra.

Cassandra nodded, her lips turned up slightly, but her face was otherwise expressionless. "Cool. How about pics? Got any headshots? All those accounts look fake without them."

Angela's smile faded. "I didn't think about that."

With Cassandra's help, she located enough photos in public domain collections to supply the accounts she had created. Finally, she opened her personal album, located a shot she had used for a recent article, and dragged it over to the browser.

"Not my favorite look, but at least it's professional." She clicked the mouse and sighed.

Cassandra touched her shoulder. "Angela, I've got an idea. You're gonna think I'm nuts."

Angela raised an eyebrow at her. "Too late."

Cassandra playfully punched her. "Seriously. I can track the meme."

Angela shook her head. "Track it? What do you mean?"

"I can hit the streets," Cassandra continued, "and pick up the thoughts of anyone who reads this."

This wasn't one of the good ideas. "I don't see why. This is going out on the Internet. Memes don't have a physical location. It's in the Otherworld that we'll see an actual meme angel, if I'm right." Angela stood and stretched. "Besides, it's way too dangerous. Remember the grenade? If Iron Star is behind that, he could hunt you down. If I'm right, what appears as a dangerous entity in the Otherworld can translate into violence in this one."

"But I want to help."

"You've already helped so much. I'm no expert in social networking. We've launched a meme thanks to you." She kissed Cassandra on the forehead then smiled. "Hey, Cassie. Let's go celebrate."

WAR IN HEAVEN: A NEW ANGEL

Diamond Angel had established her realm in the Overworld, taking over a depopulated area once belonging to a now-dead Egregore. She was buttressed in her efforts by the indirect support of Serpent Lion and Dark Eyes, despite the isolation trap, as well as by her own considerable power. In addition, her new advisor, the strange angel she had met, had formally allied himself with her.

Building a palace to consolidate her power, she patterned the edifice after the ancient designs of the prehuman culture of her old world, with mosaic tile walls inset with stained glass windows, elaborate groined arches, and tall, fluted columns. She planned to fill the near-empty halls with a store of knowledge as her power grew.

Her body now had sufficient vitality to create an independent servant to send into Bald Eagle to gather knowledge and disrupt her enemy's access to the Root Hexagon. She exerted her will. Her vision blurred momentarily, and when it cleared, a new angel stood before her throne. Her servant was armed for war, but it was nearly doubled over, glowing fiercely from the fires of its birth.

"Speak your name, angel." Her command rang out, echoing from the surrounding walls.

The creature straightened slowly from its crouch, shaking its head and groaning. Its body, limned with light, was somewhat indistinct at the edges, but the glow rapidly diminished, and its outlines sharpened. It—no, he—lifted his head and looked steadily at Diamond Angel. He bore a strong resemblance to her.

"I am called Prescription, my creator." His voice was a pleasant baritone.

"Prescription, you will infiltrate Bald Eagle, using your staff." She indicated a staff, which had just appeared by his side, sparking with energy. He grasped it.

She continued. "You will gain influence in that realm. You will locate the controller for the isolation trap that Iron Star used on me and which Gray Suit now controls. Steal it and disarm it. I will send an army of larvae with you. Failing that, you will continue to attempt to create division between Bald Eagle and its bureaucratic ally, Gray Suit."

The angel nodded. Diamond Angel gestured at a wall, and an opening appeared. Beyond it lay the abstract forms and decaying relics of the outskirts of Bald Eagle. The angel strode through the opening, which closed after him.

Her advisor, silent during those proceedings, nodded encouragement when she glanced at him. "Beautiful work, my Lady."

"And the others?"

"Defectors from Serpent Lion and Dark Eyes are, even now, marching to your support."

"I cannot be entirely comfortable with them. If they have betrayed their masters, they will betray me."

He clasped his hands behind his back and paced. "This is the first lesson of power, my Lady. When a tool comes to hand that fits your purpose, you use it but never become attached to it.

And when it fails you, discard it."

She mused on this advice. Her own nature had always been that of peacekeeper and civilizer, but since arriving in the Overworld, she had adopted warlike traits. The first lesson of power had already taken root within her, and not for the first time, she wondered at the consequences. In the darker corners of her mind, she feared she might have been ensnared by a secret, cunning web spun by others.

He cleared his throat, pausing before her throne. "Is there anything further you require of me, Lady?"

Distracted from her reverie, she sat up straighter. "Do you still intend to return to your own realm?"

He smiled. "You have already grown in power beyond any assistance I might offer you, and I believe you will accomplish your high goals. I shall return to my people with a great store of knowledge thanks to your wisdom."

She inclined her head in acknowledgment, comforted by his reassurances, and he vanished.

War on Earth

"You don't owe your dreams to Uncle Sam. So why keep fighting his wars?" The question was rhetorical by now.

—

"Hey, I don't want these nightmares either." The old man shrugged. "Whaddya gonna do?"

—

"Therapy, man. They owe you." Her gaze was intense. "You don't owe them..."

—

"Owe them my dreams? Hell no..."

—

"I own my own.."

—

"...my own dreams."

Mr. Longsmith's Living Room

Will Longsmith gnawed on a stick of jerky and watched a report on the Iraq situation. He listened to the news with growing agitation. He started pounding his fist on the arm of his easy chair. Finally, he swore and dug out his smart phone. He poked the Facebook app open to message one of his buddies, but something caught his eye. One of his vet friends had reposted a slogan, something about not owing his dreams to the government.

"Damn straight," he muttered. Maybe he should see that therapist again. Dr. Cooper. She was the first one to take him at face value. And she didn't freak out and try to prescribe more pills when he broke down. She deserved another shot.

His Facebook message forgotten, he dialed her office number and left a message, asking to see her the next day.

CHAPTER TWENTY-EIGHT
BRIEF SUCCESS

But ere her agent's task is done

And freedom for herself is won

The Warlord brings an army foul

To strike his blow, then homeward run.

EARLY THE next morning, a Saturday, Angela played a message from Will Longsmith. He sounded agitated, claiming that he'd had a breakthrough. Although the clinic was closed for repairs, she called him back and told him to come on over right away.

When he arrived, Angela noticed that he had done something about his halitosis. *Thank God.* She welcomed him and asked him to recline on the couch. The session began.

"It's like, I don't owe my dreams to the Army. So, I knew I should come back for another session." He glanced at Angela.

She returned his glance impassively, concealing her excitement. Her meme was already spreading much faster than she had expected.

"You did the right thing," she said. "Here's what I'd like to do, but only if you're comfortable with it. I'd like to hypnotize you. Have you ever been hypnotized before?"

He shook his head. "No. Everyone I've been to wants to push pills. No offense."

"None taken. Why don't you lie back and relax, and we'll get you started."

Will reclined, though the tightness around his eyes betrayed his nervousness. "Are you gonna make me look at a swinging watch?"

Angela smiled reassuringly. "Not at all. I'm simply going to help you get into a state of relaxation. You might not even notice that you're hypnotized."

She proceeded to lead Longsmith through a standard induction procedure. Soon his face slackened, and his eyes began to flutter.

"Now. I am going to lightly touch your forehead. You need to concentrate on the sensation. That's all."

There was no reaction. He was already in a trance, so Angela reached out to touch his forehead. She transitioned smoothly to his meadow and looked around. Stagnant pools choked with brambles formed an intimidating labyrinth. The tattered trees swayed in an ominous wind. The sky, a swiftly changing tapestry of dramatic clouds, churned darkly overhead. She was alone, and she paused to think.

So, I know he's been affected by my meme. How am I going to see if it's real? What does a meme angel look like? A soldier?

Angela looked for a tall tree, hoping that perhaps there would be a gateway in his meadow to what she believed was the world of memes. However, none of the trees looked suitable. They were all scrawny scrub oaks, draped with moss and gray with lichen. Angela picked her way around the meadow, exploring.

She heard a sudden cracking sound, coming from the forest eave. She stopped. Something thrashed in the underbrush. Skirting a stagnant pond, she approached it. It appeared to be a deer with a crippled leg. As she neared it, it snarled, revealing fangs, and she jumped.

"Good grief. You guys are everywhere." Angela crouched and stared at the deer, an idea taking shape in her mind. After a moment, it calmed, eyeing her warily. Guided by her chovihani instincts, she waited. Something flickered in her peripheral vision.

These creatures were guardians of traumatic memory. If her meme was helping Longsmith, maybe it had done this. Carefully avoiding its fangs, she reached out to touch the broken leg at the hoof. The creature screamed in pain, and she jerked her hand back. Now that she had touched the creature, perhaps she could establish rapport with her creation if it had done this to the deer.

Angela stood and closed her eyes, concentrating on the words of her meme. The faint sounds of combat became audible. She nodded and opened her eyes. Above the trees to her right, an image flickered, resembling an old-fashioned newsreel. Two warriors, armed with swords, traded furious blows. Though she could not say how, she recognized one of them. It was her meme, her angel.

She turned back to the deer. The sounds of swordplay faded. "He's the one who did this to you. Be grateful you're not dead." With that, she walked around the animal into the forest. Just beyond, in the darkness, someone or something small huddled on the ground. As she approached, he looked up at her. A younger version of Longsmith, he sobbed quietly, his eyes red with weeping.

She stopped a short distance away, her stance open and

relaxed. "Hi. I'm Angela. Who're you?"

"I'm Willy," he choked out.

"You're a long way from home, Willy. Can I help you?"

The wretched man nodded. "They killed my friend." He pointed to a dark pile of forest detritus nearby. Angela stared at it, and gradually the pattern of leaves and bracken resolved into the sketchy form of a dead man, spattered with blood. Then the form shattered, becoming a pile of debris once again.

She nodded at Willy, understanding. "I'm sure your friend would want you to remember him by living a good life. Willy, the past is done."

He looked at her, his chin trembling, but his sobbing stopped.

"It's time to let go," she whispered.

The lines around his eyes smoothed, and after a quiet moment, he reached a hand up to her. She touched it, and he vanished. A powerful wind swept through the meadow, and a patch of sunlight appeared as the clouds began to part. Then, with unnatural swiftness, the sun dropped out of sight between the rapidly darkening trees.

Angela returned to the center of the meadow. Looking around her, she saw fewer stagnant pools—a sign of the emotional release that had occurred. Hurriedly, she hunted for tiles in the fading light, returning to the treatment room.

Longsmith was lying on the couch asleep.

"Mr. Longsmith? Will?" she said in a gentle voice.

He stirred and opened his eyes to look at her. His face looked younger than it had when he'd arrived. "Dr. Cooper? I must've passed out."

"No, you just fell asleep. You did some very difficult work today. How do you feel?"

He paused, then wonder suffused his expression. "I feel great!"

"That's great news." She stood, smiling.

He swung his legs off the couch and stretched. He reached out to shake her hand. "Thank you so much, doctor."

"You're welcome. I'll give you a call and set a follow-up appointment, okay?"

"Sounds good." He left the room, his steps light, and walked out the front door into the California sunshine.

Later that afternoon, while Angela was catching up on one of her professional periodicals, she heard a tap on the door. She looked up and saw Eric in the doorway.

"Hey." She put the magazine down. "What's up?"

He came in and sprawled on one of her office chairs. "Can I ask you a favor?"

She steepled her fingers. "Sure. Anything."

Eric rubbed his nose and didn't speak at first. Then he glanced up at her. "I set that appointment with my usual therapist, but it's not till next week. Could we have a session?"

Angela had been expecting something of the sort, given the stress he was under. Eric had been one of the numerous people she had treated the previous autumn at Franklin. Since then, he had come to her on several occasions.

She glanced at the clock on her laptop and shut the lid. "How about now?"

Eric nodded, relief evident on his face. "Can we do it in

here?"

"I don't see why not." She went over and closed the door. Even though no one else was in the building, the evidence of privacy would be reassuring.

Returning to her desk, she took out her pad and stylus then started a recorder app. "Okay. Why don't you tell me about it?"

Eric sat back and stared up at the ceiling. "It's these nightmares, Angela. I've gone round and round with them, trying to analyze their meaning. But I keep drawing blanks. I wake up two, maybe three times a night. I know I'm losing REM sleep." He glanced at her. "They're really weird."

"Okay. You know I can handle weird."

"All right. I'm back at Franklin, only we're having a dance party in the third floor rec room. By 'we,' I mean all my friends from the Rings and the other clubs. No one from the hospital. Anyway, the music's loud, the lights are flashing. Then suddenly everything stops. The lights come up a little, and the room has been redecorated. It's really wild. I can't describe the colors." He smiled a little. "But they're gorgeous.

"Anyway, my friends turn to me, and that's when I notice that they all have wings. You know, like angels, or maybe fairies." He laughed. "Yeah. But then there's this huge crash, and one of the walls explodes. There's sparks everywhere. Suddenly my friends are fighting. There are these military types with guns, and they're shooting everywhere. I don't know why, but I'm not worried. It's like I'm invisible."

He shifted uncomfortably. Angela glanced up from her note taking. "At your own pace, Eric. Take your time."

"Thanks. Anyway, my friends are dying all around me. It's

horrible. But there's no blood. That's what struck me as weird at the time. When someone dies, they just collapse in a pile of sludge. Then they vanish. But then my friends pull out these big spears and start stabbing the soldiers. One of the soldiers, a really big guy with glowing eyes, glares at me and comes at me. That's when I wake up. I think I screamed because my throat was raw." His voice was steady, but when he looked at Angela again, his eyes were pleading. "Can you help? I take tranquilizers, and they help, but you know there's no restful sleep when you use them."

Angela set the pad down and thumped it with her pencil. Maybe it was time for a follow-up dream-walk.

She got up and walked around to his side of the desk. "Eric, I'd like to do another hypnotic session. Is that okay?"

He breathed a quick sigh. "Hell, yeah. I was hoping we could do that."

"Good. You know the drill. Relax and close your eyes."

He did so, and she reached out and touched his forehead. The room blurred as she sank into the Otherworld.

His day-lit meadow was tidy, thanks to the extensive work she had done a few months back. Alone, of course, she glanced around for any clues to the nightmares. Seeing nothing obvious, she began walking the perimeter, planning a spiraling search path toward the meadow's center.

It wasn't until she was close to the opposite side of the meadow that she saw it. Near where she had entered was a new tree, a conifer.

"Well, look at you." She trudged over to the center of the meadow. "I wonder." Perhaps this tree was a symbol of something her grandfather helped awaken in her. But why hadn't it shown up in Longsmith's meadow?

Letting her gaze travel lazily up the trunk, she saw a mist gather near its top. Her heartbeat quickened as movement flickered in the mist. Then a thunderous explosion rent the air.

Men fought on a battlefield, just as in her own meadow. But whereas in hers they had been dark-haired men resembling Roma, these were fair complexioned and almost unnaturally beautiful in an androgynous way. The warfare was just as ugly, though, and ear-splittingly loud. Screams mingled with meaty smacks as soldiers butchered each other, their lives erased by the hundreds with careless brutality.

She watched for a few minutes more, but finally she turned away, nauseated by the violence. The sounds faded as she withdrew her attention. Eric deserved an explanation, but she wasn't about to tell him about seeing meme angels at war—if that was what they were. George's explanation had been somewhat cryptic.

About to return to the office, Angela paused. Why hadn't she take Eric into her confidence? If he'd gotten mixed up in whatever was going on with that strange meme war, he might be endangered in the same way as Simon. He did, after all, go through a period of trauma recovery, so he might be vulnerable to whatever was afflicting PTSD sufferers. She gave the question due consideration. She knew she could trust him. That wasn't the issue.

What she worried about the most was his mental flexibility. He was, after all, conventionally trained, and though he was a brilliant Jungian psychiatrist, he would probably be unhinged by the direct experience of the supernatural. Angela had grown up with it, and her Romani relatives had their own vocabulary for what she saw almost daily.

Her rationalizations were a little thin, but she could not make such a momentous decision on Eric's behalf right then. With a sigh, less enlightened than before and more uncertain of herself, she found her path back to the office.

She was standing to one side of Eric's chair. She walked back around to her own chair and sat, swiveling back and forth, while Eric regained his normal awareness.

His eyes fluttered, and he opened them to stare at her. "Man, I feel like I just slept for hours. So, what did you find out?"

Angela grimaced. "I'm afraid I don't know. About all I can say is that it's probably related to last year, and that I want to see you again. In the meantime, hang in there." His face fell, and she raised a hand. "It won't be more than a couple of days, I promise. I just need to do a bit of research so I'm better prepared next time."

WAR IN HEAVEN: IRON STAR ATTACKS

Iron Star rode his chariot, a rare thing for him to do. Surrounded by his strike force, he sped above the terrain of Bald Eagle toward a gateway that opened into Diamond Angel's realm. Her most recent attack on the Root Hexagon had been devastating, and if it weren't for his timely intervention, she would have plumbed its innermost secrets and, by implication, those of Bald Eagle himself. Her emissary, a new, powerful angel, had been wounded grievously but had not been destroyed before he escaped.

The beasts drawing his chariot howled as they accelerated. Iron Star counted on the element of surprise such an attack would give him. He had a specific objective in mind and did not want a protracted war with Diamond Angel.

Peering over the chariot's windscreen, he raised a hand then thrust it forward as the squadron entered the gate. Almost immediately, powerful forces buffeted him. The alien spaces surrounding the enemy realm were filled with turbulence and dimensional incongruities caused by the isolation trap as well as by Diamond Angel's own alien origins.

Several of the flying angels accompanying him disintegrated in blinding flashes, unable to weather the changes forced upon them by the new realm. The rest continued, heading toward a shining palace ahead. Diamond Angel had gathered a disquieting amount of power in a short time.

Hordes of anonymous angels burst out from orifices in the

building—defectors, serving Diamond Angel. They were ground forces, though, and his squadron decimated their ranks. The defectors hurled spears of light at his angels, striking several of them. However, most of his fighters were able to bring their weapons to bear on the defenders. Vast explosions rocked the edifice, blasting away at its fundamental structure.

Iron Star aimed his craft at the main entrance, landed with a bone-jarring thump, and leaped off. He paused to survey the defending phalanx that had gathered between him and the palace. He hefted his sword, and his battle cry echoed from the castle walls. Running across the intervening space, he was a whirlwind of destruction, leaving a trail of decomposing carcasses as he approached the gate. With a mighty heave of his sword, he split one of the doors and pulled it apart.

As he crossed the threshold, something punched him, hard. He staggered but remained upright. His ears rang and his limbs tingled, but his armor protected him from the attack. More angels poured out of the shadows to engage him.

Raising his sword in a high overhand grip, he attacked them, dispatching two and sending the rest fleeing. He strode toward where Diamond Angel was waiting, her staff raised before her. When they were within striking distance, they began circling one another, their weapons moving as they sought weaknesses in each other's defenses.

There, a vulnerability: she was weakened by sentimentality. Without hesitation, Iron Star struck at an opening and was rewarded by a scream of pain as she fell to a knee. Flame spilled forth from a wound in her side.

"Cassie!"

He ignored her strange cry and raised his weapon high. She rallied, twisting her staff and striking a powerful blow. His armor protected him from its crushing force. He hurtled through the air to land in a heap by the door.

Iron Star picked himself up, shaken by her strength. She was mightier than he in her own palace. He was lucky to get a strike in.

The fighting sounds outside grew fainter. Fearing that his forces were being driven back, he retreated, escaping the palace. Iron Star climbed aboard his vehicle and took off. His remaining squadron members followed him back to Bald Eagle. He predicted she would retaliate soon and seal her own doom. He derived some small satisfaction from that.

War on Earth

"Nobody's watching, man. Just do it." He mimed an overhand blow for his reluctant friend. "Like this..."

—

"You bump into her." There was the flash of a knife. "I'll get the backpack..."

—

"That ho got some back, bro. I'm gettin' me some."

—

"That bitch got some money."

—

"I'm gonna ride that..."

Lakeshore Drive by Lake Merritt, Oakland

Cassandra drove in rush-hour traffic, her thumbs tapping

the steering wheel to the rhythm of the music on the stereo. The little skeleton swung on the rearview mirror as she turned a corner. Her mind was preoccupied with thoughts of what to do with her day when she heard a voice in her head.

—*owe your dreams to Uncle Sam*—

She slammed on the brakes and narrowly avoided getting rear-ended. The car passed her on the left, honking. Cassandra started looking for a parking spot, driving slowly until she found one.

She climbed out of her car and locked it then turned carefully in place until she felt an inner nudge. She stared at an apartment building across the street. With part of her mind, she tuned into the thoughts of passing cars and pedestrians. Cassandra wove her way across the street.

Pause. A car passed. Four steps, angle left. Another car, horn blaring, whipped by. She reached the other side.

With most of her attention, she began tracking the mental "tone" of the meme that she and Angela had crafted. Another voice echoed in her mind.

—*fighting his wars*—

Now on the sidewalk near the apartments, she began walking toward the new voice. Cassandra shivered suddenly, feeling a sense of menace. The shadows around her darkened, and she heard a different voice.

—*bitch got some money*—

She pretended to see an imaginary person and waved, standing on tiptoe. No one was nearby. She quickened her pace and decided to broadcast a protective thought.

—*I'm not here. You need to look away. Keep going. Don't bother me*

—

Relaxing and seeing no sign of pursuit, she opened herself once again and resumed her walk. At first, there was mental silence. But then she heard a faint babble of voices. It grew louder and more discordant. She reached into her pocket and pinched her fingers together. The voices stopped.

More carefully, Cassandra opened her mind just a little bit. The massed thoughts of Oakland were like a bellowing storm, but she managed to hold them back. After a moment, she heard another voice.

—*why keep fighting*—

She looked up. That had come from an upper-story apartment. She felt her heart swell with the accomplishment. Cassandra stopped walking, oriented herself, and listened for more traces. Angela was going to want to know how well the meme had spread. Cassandra would tell her in a few minutes. This work required complete concentration.

—*gonna ride that*—

She tensed. Her broadcast should have taken care of all such threats. She looked at her watch, feigning concern. She resumed walking more quickly. She heard footsteps behind her, accelerating. She broadcast another thought.

—*I'm not worth it. Cops are coming*—

The sound of pursuit continued. She glanced in a window to one side and saw a reflection of a man who was half walking, half running to catch up to her. She gasped—a thin almost-screech—and an electric shiver ran down her spine. Her legs were weak, but she broke into a run. Her mind filled with a cacophony of voices. The blaring shattered all remnants of concentration. Her heart raced as she dodged into the street to get away.

—*Cassie!*—

Tires screeched. She turned her head to see flaring headlights and a white face. Cassandra felt an enormous jolt, followed by red darkness.

CHAPTER TWENTY-NINE
VENGEANCE IS MINE

Then liberation comes to those

Whose poison'd minds had no repose;

Their dreams reclaimed, they waken then

To live again and war oppose.

ALL HOSPITALS smelled the same, and Angela had never gotten used to the antiseptic odor. It was the aroma of help, fear, and sickness. She strode to the nurse's station.

One of the duty nurses smiled. "Can I help you?"

"I'm looking for a patient named Cassandra Grey."

The nurse tapped on her keyboard. "Room 304. Down the hall—"

"Thanks. I've been here before."

Angela hurried down the corridor, ran up the stairs to the third floor, and flung open the door to the corridor. Turning left, she sprinted then slowed to a rapid walk to catch her breath as she approached the room. Barely glancing inside before entering, she rushed over to Cassandra's bedside. Her leg was in a cast, and her head was bandaged.

"Oh my God, Cassie." Angela leaned over the bed carefully and hugged Cassandra. Her injured girlfriend's scent erased all thought. After a moment, Angela straightened, still holding Cassandra's hand.

With her free hand, Cassie gestured at her broken leg.

"Looks like the hunter got me."

"Cassie, what happened?" Angela pulled up a chair and sat.

Cassandra grimaced. "I was on the way home when I picked up a piece of our meme."

"What do you mean?" A chill ran down Angela's spine. "What exactly were you doing?"

"That's what I'm trying to tell you. I heard someone's thoughts, and they were thinking about your meme."

Angela choked. "Cassie? Didn't we talk about that?" Before her girlfriend could reply, she waved her hand. "Never mind. I'm just glad you're alive." She took a steadying breath. "So you can track it after all."

"Well, I'm not sure. Maybe it was bait. Anyway, I parked the car." Cassandra's eyes widened. "Did you...?"

"Yeah, Eric'll drive it back to the marina. Go on."

"So I got out and started walking. Lake Merritt's usually pretty safe in the afternoon, so I wasn't worried. But then I started picking up threats." Her face tightened, drawing lines across her young forehead. "First there was someone thinking about robbing me. So I pretended to wave to somebody."

Blood pounded in Angela's ears. No one touched her Cassandra. She didn't trust herself to speak, so she nodded for Cassandra to continue.

"Then, it was like I was being followed. Got a creepy premonition. I picked up some guy thinking about raping me, only maybe it was just some random dude. I don't know anymore. Thing is, I was putting up my 'do not disturb' vibe after I heard the mugger, so no one should've bothered me."

"The hunter." Angela's voice was clipped, and her throat

tightened with anger.

"Yeah. So, then this guy started following me. I saw his reflection in a window and panicked. Kinda lost control. Ran out into the street. I swear that car wasn't there just a second before, and then boom. Out like a light. Woke up in the ER." Her brow wrinkled again. "There was something..."

The room's details became unnaturally vivid, and Angela's body quivered. She restrained the urge to leap up and start punching someone. Starting with that bastard Iron Star. She squeezed Cassandra's hand and let go. "He's gone too far."

"Angela." Cassandra put her hand up, palm out. "Don't go after him. If he can do this to me, he'll kill you."

"Cassie, he's going to come after me anyway. The least I can do is save him the trouble and take his fucking ass out. Time to use this power I've got."

"There's no way I'm letting you do this." Cassandra's stare pinned Angela down. "You need me to get to Iron Star through Simon's nightmare, and I'm not going to take you to the other side like this. Just..." She lifted her hand again, this time palm up. "Just stop, okay? When I get out of here, then we'll get back on his trail. Okay?"

Angela lowered her eyes. Cassandra was right, of course, but everything in Angela rebelled against common sense. An atavistic impulse within her pushed her to go to battle with the warmonger. But it was true that Angela had no way to get to that dream world without Cassandra—no way that either of them knew of, anyway.

With great difficulty, Angela brought her emotions under control and forced a smile. This wouldn't fool Cassandra, but

Angela desperately needed to change the subject. "Cassie, Eric's coming by a little later. I'll stay till he gets here, though. So, how's the food?"

Cassandra stared at her for a moment longer, face smoothing. Then she stuck her finger toward her mouth and made a gagging face.

Angela grinned. "This might cheer you up. I was on the way home with these when Eric called about you." She dug in her backpack and pulled out a box of chocolates.

"Awesome." Cassandra's face lit up as she took the box and opened it. She took out one of them and popped it in her mouth. "Mmm, cherry." She grinned at Angela, chocolate bits between her teeth.

Angela laughed. "Hey, Cassie. Maybe now you'll have more time for your poetry. Someday I'd love to hear your readings at a slam."

Cassandra blushed. "Um, well. Someday. Thanks."

"The doc told me you'd be in a wheelchair for a while." Seeing Cassandra frown, Angela raised a hand. "It's okay. We can set you up with an outdoor bed in the cockpit if you're up to it. I'll rig a ceramic heater, and you'll have the sleeping bag."

"You know how I feel about sleeping outside." Cassandra's mouth was set.

Angela already had a fallback plan. "Well, Eric said he'd be glad to put you up if you'd like."

"I guess that's okay." She winced as she shifted her weight in the bed. "You can stay over too, right?"

"Sure, hon. Whatever you want."

As Angela was leaving the hospital, Nadia's ringtone chimed from her pocket. She took out her phone. "Yes."

"Angela? This is your great-aunt."

Angela sighed. "I'm sorry, Nana. I've got a lot on my mind."

"Is Cassandra all right? I just heard the news from your friend Eric."

Angela filled Nadia in on what had happened, hearing what sounded like genuine concern in her great-aunt's voice.

"I saw it," Nadia said.

"What?"

"I saw what happened to Cassie."

"How? Were you watching over her?" Angela heard the incredulity in her own voice.

"I had a vision sent by the Ancestor himself. By the way, your young lady is very noisy, Angela. I can hear her thinking way out here."

"I thought she had that under control."

"Well, for most people she does, but remember that I'm sensitive. Anyway, in the vision I saw something dangerous stalking her."

Angela reached her car and stood by the door. "She says it was a rapist."

"Nobody human was after her." Nadia sounded impatient. "Anybody she saw was just a puppet. It was that creature, Tin Claw or whatever his name is. He was chasing her." Her voice turned steely. "Listen to me. Right now you're in danger. I don't know what sort of creature this Tin Claw is, but he's got you in his sights."

Angela got in the Prius. "You know I can't let him get away

with this. I'm going after him."

"Angela! He's very dangerous. Worse than the Soul Thief ever was."

Angela plugged the phone into the hands-free unit and started the car. "And so am I. Dangerous, that is. Please do me a favor and don't get involved. You saw what Iron Star can do. He's got the power to reach into our world and persuade people to do things—through what they read and what they see. I need to find him and stop him."

"Too late. I'm already involved. Apparently, we all are." Nadia paused. "Well, you never do listen to me. Just be careful. And Angela," Nadia said, her voice warmer, "I'm going to keep an eye out for you. I know you don't want my help, but it's there if you need it."

Her words lifted Angela's heart unexpectedly. Nadia defended her clan with an iron will. It was good to have that will on her side. "I love you, Nana. I'll call you when I can."

"You do that, dear."

Angela stood in her Otherworld meadow, staff in hand. She stared, frustrated, at the tall conifer. No visions of war or of her enemy manifested. She closed her eyes again and concentrated but to no avail.

"Granddad? Are you here? Anywhere?" She'd started calling for him as soon as she had arrived, with no answer, no hint that he even existed in the Otherworld. She had hiked into the forest as far as she dared go, skirting other meadows, and had found nothing unusual. There was no sign of her enemy, of her mentor, or of Nadia's oversoul, who sometimes haunted this region.

"Dammit." Angela waited several more fruitless minutes then stashed her staff in the cabin and returned home.

WAR IN HEAVEN: PRESCRIPTION DELIVERS

ROOT HEXAGON, Bald Eagle

The commander of the guard at the Root Hexagon watched for an attack, yet when one came, it still took him by surprise.

He heard a loud crack followed by shouts of alarm. He whirled to face the Root Hexagon in time to see one of his men tumbling into the pool at the base of the artifact. The other angels had their weapons out and were scattering to the perimeter of the crater.

He collared one of them. "What happened?"

The angel was breathless. "I don't know. My partner was scanning the sky near the pool, and then his head exploded. Something flew by so fast I couldn't see it. It struck the crystal there. It may be a new type of angel, but I can't be sure."

The commander peered toward where the angel pointed. He could just make out a crack that had not been there before. Iron Star was going to be furious.

He shook his head and turned back to his subordinate. "Lieutenant, stand your men down. Whatever did that is long gone. I will need to report this to Iron Star when he returns from his mission."

Franklin Psychiatric Hospital, San Francisco

"Nurse, this patient is ready to check out." Dr. Weatheridge flipped the chart shut. "She has responded excellently to the EMDR work you've done with her. Very commendable."

"Actually, I think we can thank Facebook." Seeing his

confusion, Nurse Delaney continued. "She told me she saw a posting telling her she didn't owe her dreams to anyone. So why relive the past in them, right? Anyway, she said that was what helped her let go of the need to punish that burglar."

He lifted an eyebrow. "That's one for the books. Social media as therapy."

CHAPTER THIRTY

THE OVERWORLD

Emboldened by her victory

The Angel uses strategy

To hurl the Warlord from his perch

To rise in noble majesty.

ANGELA RETURNED to normal awareness lying in bed. She swung her legs off and stalked to the kitchen, muttering angrily to herself. She had not eaten since morning, so she nuked something from the freezer.

Waiting for the microwave to finish, she jumped when her phone rang. She dashed back to the master cabin to retrieve it, whacking her elbow painfully on the way. She picked up, wincing. "Ow! Simon?"

"Yeah. Cassie just called and told me she was in an accident."

"I don't think it was an accident."

"Me neither. Listen. I'm sorry I've been a complete asshole."

She walked back to the galley, nursing her elbow, and took a plate out of the cupboard. "You quit on us, Simon. I understand, though, and I'm glad you called."

"I still feel responsible. It was my monster that got her, wasn't it?" He didn't wait for her reply. "I want to do something to make up for it. I want to help."

She took the hot burrito out of the microwave and poured a dollop of sauce on it before taking it to the dinette. "I hope you're ready to fight. Really fight. It's going to be harder than anything we did before."

"Somehow, my nightmare went after my friends. I don't owe my dreams to anyone. Not Uncle Sam. And not to this creature."

Angela smiled, relief washing through her. "That's my meme talking." Then she froze as an idea pushed into her mind.

"What?"

"Just a sec." A superstitious fear of jinxing the notion made Angela reluctant to speak. "Listen. I've got to fill you in on a few things. Cassie and I did an experiment. Do you know what memes are?"

"What, like the funny pictures you see on Facebook?"

"Um, yeah, sort of. Anyway, I think Iron Star is the Otherworld equivalent of a meme. I've been doing some reading on memetics as a treatment protocol..."

"Angela?"

"Sorry, I'm babbling. So, Cassie and I created a new meme, and what you just said came from us. About owing your dreams. Cassie went chasing after it in the minds of people in this town, and Iron Star did something that made her run into traffic."

"Son of a bitch. It's my fault."

"No! Iron Star isn't your thing. He's something else. He's been around a long time, I bet. As long as there've been people with PTSD anyway. Simon, I tried to find Iron Star just a few minutes ago using dream-walking. No dice. But maybe I can use my meme to get to him. Are you up for some nightmare work right now? I know it's really late."

"I can't sleep anyway."

"Neither can I."

The hospital room was dark and quiet. Cassandra remembered the nurse adjusting her morphine drip and the ensuing warm blanket of pleasurable darkness. She also remembered waking up, her head stuffed with cotton, calling out to Angela and apologizing for not being able to help her go after Iron Star. When she awoke again, however, her head was clear, and she felt energetic and free of pain. When she opened her eyes, Cassandra found that she could see everything clearly. Someone must have left the light on, though the illumination was oddly uniform and sourceless.

She sat up easily and swung her legs off the bed. For some reason, her feet felt as if they were wrapped in cotton: pleasantly numb, slightly rigid. She could barely sense that there was a surface under her at all.

It was time to go help Angela. On her way to the door, something made Cassandra pause and turn. A small form lay on her bed, and for a moment she wondered who had snuck in and taken her spot. Then the realization rolled into her mind. She was out of her body.

At first she thought that she was dead. She should have felt horrified, but her mind seemed to be working very slowly, albeit with great clarity, and she felt no worries. Then it occurred to her that she was doing what Simon did. Immediately, Cassandra thought of Angela again.

The world dissolved into whiteness, and she felt a pulling sensation in her solar plexus. When the light faded, she was standing in the living room at Simon's place. The room was dim, though crowded with the same eerie illumination she'd seen at the hospital. She looked around herself. There was Simon in his chair, apparently dozing. Her eyes lit on Angela. She was stretched out on the couch.

"Hey, you guys. I'm here." Her voice crowded in her ears, as if she were talking in a barrel.

No one reacted. She was not about to let that stop her. Cassandra concentrated, reaching into herself to that secret place where she could communicate with other minds. She mind-shouted, —*Angela!*—

Angela's eyes flew open. "Cassie?" she whispered, turning her head and scanning the room.

—*Yeah. I'm out of my body. Like what Simon does.*—

Angela sat up carefully to avoid waking Simon. "You're here? In the apartment?" She glanced around again, obviously not seeing Cassandra in her astral form.

Cassandra crossed her arms and waited for Angela to catch up with what was going on. A moment later, Angela nodded.

"I can't seem to follow Simon," Angela murmured. She rubbed her face. "I've been trying. I went to his meadow to look for my meme. But it never showed up." She leaned forward, her elbows on her knees. "Cassie, that creature is coming after all of us. The war in Iraq? It's his fault. I know it. And I'm the only one who's ever fought him and had a chance of beating him. Please. Can you help me? Us?"

Someone somewhere was shouting, but the sound was faint. There were gunshots. Suddenly Cassandra knew what she needed to do. —*I'll help you. Just think of me.*—

Angela lay back, a tiny smile on her face. Cassandra looked

at Simon, feeling a similar expression on her own face as she reached out mentally to contact him.

The room abruptly faded to black. Men shouted. Boots tramped. It was a chilly night. There was the floodlit checkpoint, the guard station, the running men, and the oncoming headlights. Angela stood by her side.

Looking down, Cassandra saw that both she and Angela were dressed in battle fatigues, like the soldiers. She touched Angela's arm, making the older woman jump. Angela turned to her, face white with shock.

"Cassie? My God, what're you doing here? I thought you were staying behind."

"Does it matter?" Cassandra glanced around, a nervous fluttering in the pit of her stomach. "I'm here. So let me—"

Angela took Cassandra's hands in her own. "Cassie. You've got to go back. Remember, this guy almost killed you."

Cassandra pulled out of Angela's grasp. She looked around. At first she could not make sense of the confusion, but then she saw him. Simon stood nearby, lit by the flood lamps that starkly illuminated the checkpoint under the strange red sky. He stood in a firing stance, his rifle at his shoulder, muzzle pointed down but ready. She and Angela stood near one of several piles of bricks and other rubble about twenty feet away.

"Angela, I want to help. We don't have much time." She shook Angela by the shoulder, gently. "Stop worrying about me. I can take care of myself."

An engine roared. Cassandra saw the approaching headlights, and though she knew what was going to happen next, her heartbeat accelerated. She pointed at Simon. Angela shook her head then stared in his direction.

"Simon!" Angela shouted without bothering to conceal their presence.

He swiveled in place, ready to fire. But then he lowered his rifle. "You made it! How?" Then, seeing Cassandra, his jaw dropped. "Cassie?"

"No time for questions," Cassandra said. "Let's do this."

Nodding, Simon laid his rifle down. The scene froze, and the nearby soldiers turned their heads and began walking toward him.

Cassandra picked up a brick, aimed, and beaned one of the soldiers. He dropped like a sack of potatoes. The others turned sluggishly, and heartened by their slow reactions, Cassandra backed away, staying out of their reach. Someone screamed. Angela clubbed a soldier down with the butt of a rifle. She spun to deal a blow to another coming from behind.

Cassandra noticed Simon and gasped. She ran over to tug at one of the soldiers who were struggling with him. Then Iron Star strode from the shadows, gigantic and implacable. Cassandra felt a chill emanating from him, and her own energy was sapped by his presence.

Iron Star glared at both Angela and Cassandra. "My enemy," he growled. "Leave now, or you will be destroyed."

"Fuck off, Iron Star." Angela put the rifle to her shoulder, aimed, and fired. A small hole appeared in Iron Star's flak jacket. He pulled a large knife out of a sheath at his belt and crouched, menacing them both. Angela backed up, circling away from Cassandra. Ignoring the younger woman, Iron Star tracked Angela's movement, waving his knife. His crouch deepened as he prepared to attack.

Cassandra saw her opening, and she leaped onto his back. He roared and reached around with a massive arm in an attempt to claw her off of him. She clung tightly. Unable to dislodge her, he bellowed with rage. Then the world around her vanished into a white roar, and her awareness shredded with it.

Iron Star and Cassandra vanished as Angela watched in horror. "Cassie! No!"

She looked wildly around at the soldiers, who were now passive. Simon, too, was staring at where Iron Star had disappeared. Then inspiration struck Angela. Those soldiers appeared to be projections of some kind, extensions of Iron Star's will. She would follow her enemy by using one of them as a conduit.

She approached a fallen soldier, whom she saw was still breathing, and reached out and touched his forehead. The checkpoint dissolved around her.

Simon felt his heart sink. "Cassie? Angela?"

The soldiers who had been forcing him had vanished as well. Then reality stuttered as if it were a movie whose reel was jammed, and his eyes opened in the dim living room.

"Oh, shit."

WAR IN HEAVEN: RETALIATION

REALM OF *Diamond Angel*

Diamond Angel grimaced in pain. Waves of force, emanating from her own energy body, beat on the interior walls of her gigantic palace. She got to her feet, moaning in anguish. An underworld creature was coming through from within her. Someone or something had given the creature new weapons, granting it the power to enter the Overworld. The stress from this, as well as from the wound she had suffered at Iron Star's hand, drove spikes of pain into every part of her.

She staggered toward an opening that had appeared in her palace wall. Beyond it loomed the Root Hexagon. Thanks to the underworld intrusion, Diamond Angel had unprecedented direct access to her enemy's stronghold. She passed through the opening as her awareness submerged under the weight of a more primitive consciousness. Too late, she realized that she had left her staff behind. With her last conscious thought, she prayed to whatever gods were listening that the intruder would be strong enough to defeat Iron Star.

CHAPTER THIRTY-ONE
AN ANGEL GOES TO WAR

Then Eagle comes with offer bold

To grant the Angel throne of gold

Wherein she may with ceaseless will

Uphold the law within his fold.

ROOT HEXAGON, *Bald Eagle*

At first, Angela could make no sense of her perceptions. She was embedded within a vast, geometrical form, an infinitely complex network of rust-red, slate-blue, and dingy-white shapes. Her sense of her own body was gone, and it required a tremendous effort of will for her to think at all. But ancient instincts took over. Training from countless lifetimes, which had helped her assemble her perceptions in other realities, came to the fore. With a massive jolt, the world crashed into shape around her.

She sneezed. An acrid, penetrating odor reminded her of a laboratory experiment gone wrong. She coughed and reflexively covered her mouth and nose. She looked at her feet. She was standing on a reddish, sand-covered surface like that of a desert in the American southwest. Then she looked up and around her.

Angela stood on the debris-strewn floor of a large crater, the ridged walls rising well above her line of sight. At its center, half-submerged in a bubbling pool of putrescent yellow liquid, a towering, crystalline boulder glowed in a shifting spectrum of colors. It looked like raw quartz. Cables of some sort wrapped the crystal and snaked across the floor of the crater to disappear over its lip. A large, indistinct form stood near the pool, something smaller at its feet, but the glow of the crystal confused her vision.

She glanced up at red clouds scudding across a turbulent sky. The perspective was wrong. Then something dragged her gaze back to the center of the crater as her wits returned with a rush.

Iron Star stood over the crumpled form of Cassandra. Angela's vision tunneled, and she heard someone screaming. Her thighs bunched as she ran at the gigantic form of her enemy. Streamers of light swirled from all directions toward her. She seemed to be flying, and as she neared Iron Star, her peripheral vision began to glow.

Iron Star pulled out a huge sword, braced himself, and swung. Its arc dragged a swath of red light behind it. He moved slowly, though, and she ducked easily under the swing of the sword and continued forward to tackle her much larger opponent. When she hit him, he was not an immovable bulk as expected. Instead, he felt massless, and she drove him several yards across the crater floor, away from the pool.

Something snapped, and Angela was hovering, bodiless, over a battlefield. The roar of combat filled the air along with the stink of fear. Men, covered head to toe with mud, fought with swords. Some wore archaic armor while others fought nearly naked. Blades smacked into flesh with a spray of blood, fingers gouged eyes, and everywhere was the chaos of death.

Then she was back in the crater, her arms wrapped around Iron Star's bulky form. She heard a clang, and then both his hands were pushing on her, trying to pry her off of him as they struggled and staggered across the crater floor.

Another snap. A Native American chief howled a challenge, whirling his axe aloft. Then with a vicious downward arc, he split the skull of an enemy. Blood and brains spattered his face.

Snap. Iron Star shoved Angela away. She grabbed his arm, twisted it, and pushed his elbow out and down. Using her body weight, she forced him down on one knee.

Snap. Now she was in another battlefield with men in blue coats fighting a ragtag mob. Most had knives out, and they fought in close quarters. There was no shouting, just grunts and groans when blades were slammed home in flesh. The sound of gunfire split the air. Two men directly in Angela's view dropped, one with half his face gone and the other with a spray of blood from his throat. One man nearby, on a horse, was pulled down and gutted by two other men.

Snap. Iron Star heaved, and Angela was thrown to the ground. Sparks filled her vision, and the crater floor shuddered. She rolled back to her feet and squared off against him. He had his sword again, and he circled warily. His helmetless face held an expression of angry respect. Cassandra was nowhere to be seen.

He feinted a blow with the sword then stabbed at her throat. Unable to dodge, she expected an agonizing deathblow. But the tip of the sword stopped mere inches away with a brilliant flash of light. A sound, as of a crowd shouting, filled the air. She leaped back out of range and noticed that the tip of the sword glowed white-hot. Iron Star stared at it for a split second in disbelief.

Angela reached back over her shoulder and pulled her staff out of thin air. Flames crawled along the shaft of her weapon. Iron Star's eyes widened. There was no escape as she backed him up to the edge of the bubbling pool.

Angela whirled the staff overhead with a scream and smacked the sword aside with it. There was another brilliant flash.

Snap. Smoke was everywhere, and the stink of cordite filled her nostrils. A commander ordered his men to attack, and they screamed and ran, bayonetted rifles raised. A vast rattling sound, and the soldiers were mowed down.

Snap. Iron Star's sword whirled away, falling into the pool. A cascade of sparks erupted as it dissolved. Angela's staff counter-spun and struck his midriff. There was another flash.

Snap. A helicopter hovered over a field, and the last of a group of soldiers leaped aboard as it began to lift off. With a deep roar, it exploded in a ball of flame.

Snap. Iron Star doubled over. Angela's staff caught him under the chin, and the force of the blow lifted him off his feet and hurled him into the pool. With a hoarse bellow, amid a fountain of pyrotechnic light, he disappeared beneath the noxious liquid.

The ground rumbled again. Angela staggered, falling to one knee. A smothering wave of exhaustion fell on her, and she bowed her head. The sound of her breath filled her ears. When she looked up again, a bizarre assemblage of winged beings was surrounding her. Wildly varying in height, they were clothed in vividly colored light. Cassandra was nowhere to be found. Her ears rang, and her heart clenched, but the creatures each bent a knee, in unison, and bowed to her, arms outspread.

Angela rose to her feet, holding her staff warily before her. "Who are you?" Her voice echoed as if doubled.

Wings rustled, and they replied, "We are the servants of Bald Eagle. Now we have been sent to serve you, if you in turn agree to serve our master."

Angela staggered. Her vision narrowed, and she heard a high-pitched whine that drowned all other sounds. There was a momentary taste of iron in her mouth, and then Angela's awareness dissolved into endless white light.

WAR IN HEAVEN: THE WAR LEADER

ROOT HEXAGON, Bald Eagle

Diamond Angel returned to awareness within the crater. Cassandra's astral body, nearby on the crater floor, had begun to disintegrate. On an impulse, she took it within her own energy body, saving it from destruction, but the effort exhausted her. When she looked up, she was surrounded by enemy angels. She tensed, expecting another fight, but they bent their knees in unison and bowed to her, arms outspread.

She slowly rose to her feet, holding the staff, which she had been able to summon from her palace during the fight. "Who are you?" She heard odd cadences in her own voice.

The wings of the warriors rustled, then they replied. "We are the servants of Bald Eagle. Now we have been sent to serve you, if you in turn agree to serve our master."

Diamond Angel surveyed the troops, focusing her attention while further submerging Angela's consciousness. It appeared that Bald Eagle so highly valued having a war leader that it was extending this office to her.

She regarded the Root Hexagon, pulsing with light and power in the center of the pool that had destroyed her foe. Bald Eagle had been her enemy, but she was tempted by what she saw. There was tremendous potential to accomplish her goals by serving the great Egregore and using its tools for her own ends. Believing that she could leave Bald Eagle later if she disagreed with the terms of service, she decided to explore this opportunity.

She turned to one of the angels. "Bring me to your master."

The angel saluted smartly, turned on its heel, and marched across the crater floor to clamber toward the lip. She followed, climbing easily, her honor guard falling into step behind her. They crossed over the crater's edge and descended to an avenue that led to an enormous structure, the center of Bald Eagle's power.

They arrived at the entrance, whose great door swung open automatically. Together they made their way through echoing halls. Rounding a corner, Diamond Angel saw a large, horizontally spinning vortex silently hovering over the floor. A shape was dimly visible in its center. As she neared, she was able to make out a pyramid with an eye on one face. The eye was surrounded by feathers as if it belonged to a gigantic raptor. Bald Eagle.

The angel led her to a spot before one end of the vortex where a plinth was mounted upon a dais. Diamond Angel moved to stand on the dais, and an understanding of how to position herself entered her mind. After laying down her staff, she placed her hands upon the surface before her, and she felt a stirring of forces within her.

She felt, more than heard, a voice all around her.

"You have defeated the old General, War Leader. Yours is the power to command mine armies and conquer mine enemies. This is destined. This is your fate as it has been foretold by the God."

The air grew reddish as if seen through a filter. A powerful Presence entered the room, and Diamond Angel suppressed the urge to drop to her knees. With an effort, she addressed

Bald Eagle. "Why do you believe that I shall acquiesce to your authority? I am not a part of your world."

To her mind, in the unspoken voice of the Presence, came new knowledge so potent that it bowed her head with its weight. If there had been actual words to hear, they would have been earsplitting.

—You have opposed me for an eon. I was nearly banished from your world until the great Progenitor reawakened war amongst your people. But you destroyed his power, costing me much. Then you redeemed yourself by carrying both me and my beloved opponent into this new world. Every Egregore, every daemon, every spirit here owes you for that courageous act. Serve Bald Eagle as war leader, and you serve your destiny as well.—

There was no gainsaying that persuasive power, and she nodded her head in acquiescence. Immediately, a newfound strength poured into her from the plinth. She lifted her head and gazed into the eyes of an eagle-headed man, clothed in radiant power, who stood before the slowly turning vortex.

He approached the dais and reached out for her hand. Drawing her close to him, he enveloped her with that radiance. Though she retained her identity, her senses and her body were submerged within his vaster self in ecstatic surrender, and she gave herself wholly to Bald Eagle.

CHAPTER THIRTY-TWO
WAR'S AFTERMATH

As water takes the vessel's form

The Angel does to war conform;

To smite the foes of Hungry Lord

Her armies ride the raging storm.

SIMON'S APARTMENT

Simon's apartment was dark, as usual, and Angela banged her shin on the coffee table before she could find a light. Seeing that Simon was asleep in his chair, she resisted the urge to wake him and left quietly. Her head still swam from when she had awakened on the couch. By the time she got back to the car, her mind had cleared, but something was wrong.

Once in the car, she glanced at the dashboard clock and saw that it was four in the morning. She would go see Cassandra later. First, she needed sleep.

Traffic was unusually congested for that time of night. A belligerent driver cut her off while changing lanes, and she honked her horn.

"Who let the assholes out of the bars?" Her shout was startlingly loud in the confines of her Toyota. She honked again for what seemed to be the hundredth time as yet another jacked-up pickup truck cut her off. Then a movement caught her eye. Headlights behind her swerved suddenly, followed by the muted bang of a collision. It was too difficult to turn around, though, and she didn't feel up to being a witness.

When she finally returned to the boat, she wearily clambered aboard, opened the companionway hatch, and descended the ladder. Making her way to the master salon, she peeled off her clothes, collapsed on the bed, and drifted into troubled sleep.

WAR IN HEAVEN: DIAMOND ANGEL RETURNS

DIAMOND ANGEL's Palace, Bald Eagle

Diamond Angel returned to self-awareness within the throne room in her palace. She extended her senses and discovered that her seat of power had relocated to Bald Eagle's realm. Climbing into her throne, she felt great strength pulsing within her. The consciousness of Angela, independent but submerged, stirred within her, as well, feeding on that strength Like a nagging memory, the disembodied awareness of Cassandra pushed against the constraints Diamond Angel had placed on it.

Her energy body quivered again. Diamond Angel focused her attention and opened a portal deep within herself, where the gravitational pull of the Underworld was strongest. Taking careful aim, she hurled both Cassandra and Angela into that place and allowed the portal to slam shut. She settled back in her chair, at ease once again, and gestured. An angel materialized before her throne.

"Send one embassy to Dark Eyes and another to Serpent Lion. Tell them that I decline their offers of alliance and that I am now War Leader for Bald Eagle."

The angel raised a fist in salute and vanished.

Her new work began immediately. Diamond Angel was taken up, in vision, to a place far above Bald Eagle to gaze upon the battlefield. Countless rectangular stains on the blank ground far below resolved into legions of winged, armed warrior angels. They had been assembled to attack Silver

Scimitar, whose phalanxes were visible ahead in the empty regions adjacent to Bald Eagle's territory.

Gigantic war engines already under Diamond Angel's command fired blazing bolts of light at the enemy. The enemy retaliated with mighty weapons that sprayed fountains of glowing fluid that dissolved the warriors of Bald Eagle where they stood. Those weapons bore the mark of Shaken Fist, the leader of the separatists, and their power was overwhelming. Dissension within her ranks broke out wherever Shaken Fist attacked, magnifying the natural strife that existed between the angels.

It was her nature to consolidate rather than to divide, so the ideological roots of Shaken Fist were monstrous in her eyes. Reluctantly, she decided that her long-term goals would, indeed, be best served by waging war in the battlefields below. She closed her inner eye and rested for a moment on her throne before taking the decisive next step.

Parapet, Bald Eagle

Diamond Angel stood upon a wind-swept parapet. She had abandoned the shape of her former self and had chosen to appear as a winged woman dressed in a high, elaborately spiked helm and ruby-red scintillating armor. Her face was completely covered but for her eyes. She surveyed her vast armies below and raised a gauntleted fist. Her voice, powerfully amplified, rang out across the realm.

"Armies of Bald Eagle! This day we go forth to fight, and perhaps defeat, the forces of Silver Scimitar as well as our separatist enemy, Shaken Fist. Along the way we shall destroy the traitors within our realm, Serpent Lion and Dark Eyes. Many of you might not return from this fight. For those who do not, I salute you for your courage and strength. Know this: I shall fight beside you, for as War Leader, I understand that no battle can truly be fought without unreserved commitment."

A ground-shaking shout rose from far below. She smiled, pride filling her. Turning her head, she studied the flanks of her massed armies, where she expected to see new arrivals. "We will have allies. Their strength, added to ours, will help ensure our victory."

She pointed dramatically. "Bulldog!"

There was a far-off boom and flash of light as the way was opened for the massed armies of Bulldog. A huge, translucent image of a ferocious dog hovered over the angelic troops. The quartered flag, red on blue with white borders, was evident everywhere in that army as it merged with hers.

"Rooster!"

Another explosive sound shook the air, accompanied by the arrival of that ally. Just as with Bald Eagle, the colors blue, white, and red predominated.

"And Golden Eagle!"

The final allies arrived with a more muted rumble. There was a muttering roar from the massed ranks of her own armies. There had been bad blood between them and the forces of Golden Eagle ever since the last Great War. For a moment, a broken swastika was visible, flickering above the ranks of Golden Eagle before being obliterated by their current standard.

Diamond Angel turned to one of the angels standing nearby.

"Bring me the new weapons." Serpent Lion and Dark Eyes had given those weapons to Angela. Their power had enabled her to enter the Overworld, but now the weapons had fallen into Diamond Angel's hands. They would allow her to penetrate deeply into enemy territory, or so she hoped.

The angel nodded and hurried off. Diamond Angel turned back to the parapet and raised her arms in a gesture of invocation. Far above, the great form of Bald Eagle materialized. Diamond Angel basked in the mighty shout of acclaim from the massed armies.

The angel returned with a wrapped bundle. She opened it and pulled out a spear and sword, both encrusted with numerous medallions of arcane power. Strapping the sword in a scabbard to her side, she lifted the spear, which was modeled after that said to be carried by the God of Battles himself. With an imperious gesture, she opened a portal and stepped through, emerging beside her war chariot at the head of the armies. She turned and surveyed them.

She spoke to one of the angels by her side. "Give me the lines of communication."

The angel came forward with threads of glistening light, and Diamond Angel took them up. Faces and forms flickered in her mind's eye as lesser angels shuttled back and forth between her and the armies.

She climbed up into the chariot and took up the reins. Lifting her spear, she urged the chariot into the air. Leading her armies toward a vast, cloud-rimmed portal ahead, Diamond Angel charged at the massed forces of Silver Scimitar, Shaken Fist, and her other lesser foes.

In a single, world-shaking movement, the armies of Bald Eagle advanced on the enemy.

Diamond Angel's chariot was hurtling toward the enemy when an agonizing, electrifying net of force wrapped her body. She screamed, more in anger than in pain. Hauling on the reins, she came to a halt. Her armies continue their advance. She signaled to each of her lieutenants that they should take over command.

Wheeling around, she headed back toward her palace, seething with rage. The isolation trap was responsible for the setback, and she was determined to locate the angels that maintained it. She would punish them for remaining loyal to their old master. With an angry gesture, she opened a portal to her palace.

War on Earth

"God is on our side in this war. They serve the Evil One, not..."

—

"This isn't about God; it's about us. I'm speaking..."

—

"That's blasphemy! How dare you? You must..."

—

"I'm stayin' home, man. They can..."

—

"They can mind their own..."

—

"Just mind your own business."

Angela's Sailboat

Angela sat bolt upright, a shout ringing in her ears. She looked around the empty cabin, breathing heavily and bathed in sweat. Overly vivid images of the dreamlike fight with Iron Star crowded her mind, and the air crackled with the energy of war.

She lay awake for what felt like hours as the morning wore on, but weariness finally overcame her adrenaline surge, and her consciousness collapsed back into a fragmentary nightmare.

Simon's Apartment

"I'm sorry, Mr. Fenway, but only family members may visit Cassandra Grey on Sundays."

Simon moved the phone to his other ear. "Can you at least tell me how she's doing?"

"I'm sorry, sir. It's against the law for us to communicate personal medical information over the phone."

"Dammit." Simon took a calming breath. "When can I come visit?"

"Our visiting hours for non-family members are from ten in the morning until nine at night, Monday through Saturday."

"Okay, thanks." He hung up. Neither Cassandra nor Angela was returning his calls, and he didn't know anyone else who could reach them.

He tried to take his mind off his concerns by working, but after he crashed his client's website for the fourth time in a row, he gave it up. Frustrated and anxious, he finally got in his car and drove to Ghirardelli Square to brood and, perhaps, lose himself in the crowds.

The Oaklan

Sunday, June 8, 2014

Air Attack on Syria

WASHINGTON - The U.S. military led an air assault on ISIL strongholds in Syria today, escalating the war on the militant organization. A statement by the Department of Defense confirmed 18 air strikes were carried out on ISIL targets.

CHAPTER THIRTY-THREE
THE CONVOCATION

Then warring Angel trips a snare

Which holds her back from battle's glare

Then vengeful scheming fills her heart

That furtive traitors should beware.

MICHAEL WAS sleeping off a bender at home, so Andrea offered to take Nadia for an emergency errand. They were on their way to an all-night food mart to pick up some crackers for tea.

"So I told him to leave her be." Andrea shook her head. "She already told him no, and that was that, I said."

Nadia, in the passenger seat, was only half listening. Something was boiling away in the Otherworld. She should have been seeking a vision instead of going on this foolish errand.

"Nadia?" Andrea glanced at her. "What do you think?"

Nadia shook herself. "I'm sorry, I was somewhere else. So Lilya is interested in the Connor boy instead?"

Andrea nodded. "Yes. He..." Her voice trailed off. The car began to drift into the other lane.

"Andrea!" Nadia screamed and grabbed for the wheel.

Andrea slammed on the brakes. Tires screeched from behind, followed by honking. A car pulled around them, the driver making obscene gestures. Andrea sat, shaking and staring out the windshield. After a moment, she resumed driving, turning right into a parking lot. She stopped the car, turned off the engine, and slumped, her face white as a sheet.

Nadia waited for her own heartbeat to slow then touched Andrea's shoulder. "What's wrong? What happened back there? Did you see something?"

Andrea turned to Nadia, her mouth open, her eyes bugging out. Nadia had only a moment in which to react. Like lightning leaping from one tree to the next, the vision overcame her. All she could see was a roaring flame, though she could feel no heat. The thundering voice of the flame shaped itself into words that shook her.

"The Angel has defeated War's minion. The Angel has become the slave of War. Praise War."

Suddenly the flame disappeared, replaced by a vision of a fire-crowned, winged angel wielding a red, bloody sword. Though her face shone too brightly to make out the features, Nadia somehow knew it was Angela.

The vision vanished, and the ordinary world returned. Nadia gasped with the shock of its departure. Her heart was racing, and sweat poured off of her. She matched stares with Andrea.

"You saw it, too." Andrea's voice shook.

Nadia could only nod. Something terrible had happened to Angela.

The gathering of chovihanis was an excuse for a party, naturally. No one was taking it too seriously, even though the eight or nine chovihanis in the area had all agreed to meet due to the extraordinary circumstances. After all, nothing was all that solemn with the Romani. Nadia approved. The spirit of the

Roma must never bow to darkness. Andrea couldn't make it, though, as she had fallen ill.

While the children shrieked and played, while the neighbors' curtains twitched, and while the rest of the adults played lively music and danced on the other side of the yard, a circle of elderly Roma passed around a bottle of whiskey and talked.

The woman currently holding the bottle was the youngest chovihani present. Florica was Angela's childhood friend as well as a cousin and had taken up the discipline of the chovihani after a dream-walk that Angela had done for her. She was dedicated to the art, but sometimes she was braver than she was smart.

"I say we hex him," Florica said, shaking the bottle. "Give that spirit a beating. I got strong allies. Nobody hurts Angela if I got any say."

There were grunts of approval and nodding heads. She took a swig and passed the bottle to her left. The older woman who took it, a stick-thin Roma named Kishi with skin like worn shoe leather, took a big swig and set it in her lap to gesture with both hands. "And I say find out who called this spirit and hex her! Somebody pissed off the spirits. Somebody called this Tin Man."

She picked up the bottle and drank again. It was a liquor talking stick. Kishi passed it to Nadia, who was seated to her left. Nadia took the bottle, examined the level critically, then drank. The liquor burned its way down her throat, and she suppressed a cough with iron determination. She didn't normally touch the stuff, but this was ritual.

She set the bottle on the table next to her lawn chair and

pulled herself upright. She looked around the circle. "The Ancestor told me not to fight Tin Star. I aimed to follow that advice, but it doesn't matter now. I'll tell you why in a minute. Make no mistake; I am going to help Angela every way I can. But I learned she got dragged into some kind of fight, and now she's a slave to war, whatever that means."

The fierceness was draining away from a few faces, replaced by puzzled frowns. But Nadia could tell that others were ready to argue the point with her. She decided to play her trump card. "Angela beat Tin Star already anyway. That's what I learned."

The women gasped and muttered.

She continued. "So all our planning to fight is for nothing. We got to find a way to free Angela now. Nobody can beat war. It's everywhere. So let's work an unbinding."

She raised the bottle in a salute to the others, who all nodded. A couple of the older women, her longtime compatriots and occasional sparring partners, scowled and gave her sidelong glances, but there was no arguing with the facts. She passed the bottle to her left and schooled her expression. No need to be smug.

The next woman, Lucretia, took a long drink. Somebody muttered, "Save some for us," but no one had a serious complaint. She was respected for her deep Sight, and she had many friends amongst the wood elves.

"My allies done told me that we are already a-fighting." Lucretia's voice rose. "Them spirits from the gadjes already come against us once. I felt it. We all felt it. But now we gotta back off. I don't like it. Not one bit. But..." She nodded tipsily at

Nadia. "Nadia here talks to the Ancestor better'n the rest of us. And so I say we follow along. I can unbind just about anything. Remember Jaelle's young 'un?"

They all nodded wearily. This was an old story that she never got tired of retelling.

"He was asleep in that coma, and we all thought he was a goner." She waved a finger dramatically. "I went to his bedside, and I shook him good and hard. I told his soul get back in him right this minute. And you know what? He did. I unbound him from his wandering. I did."

She nodded decisively and passed the nearly empty bottle somewhat reluctantly to her left. When the liquor ran out, the discussion would be over. Sure enough, the next one in line took a look, tossed off the last of the whiskey, and upended the bottle.

"Good," Nadia said. "Let's do it. Who wants to make the poppet?"

Kishi and Florica both raised their hands. Florica deferred to the older woman. Kishi bent to retrieve her bag from beside her chair, rummaged in it, and pulled out a candle and some string. She got out a knife and carved a name on the candle then wrapped it up with the string. The others watched, talking quietly to each other.

"Nadia," Lucretia said. "Got another bottle of that there whiskey? I'm powerful thirsty."

"I got one in the house." Nadia turned to yell at the men. "Michael! Fetch me that bottle of whiskey out of the cupboard, will you?"

Michael looked back at her and beamed. "My pleasure."

Nadia turned back as Michael shuffled toward the house. Kishi flourished the candle, now tied with so much string it was barely visible. Nadia noted that a red ribbon was wound in the string. Kishi knew her stuff.

"Okay," Nadia said. "Pass it around and fill it with your thoughts of our Angela."

The poppet was passed from hand to hand. They muttered, gestured, and grimaced dramatically. When it was Nadia's turn, she closed her eyes and remembered happy times with Angela, particularly the most recent ones. She put her irritation and impatience out of her mind, concentrating on the good and the power of her great-niece. Then an inspiration struck her, and she silently thanked the Ancestor.

Nadia held one hand over the poppet and muttered the Romani charm to turn away gadje poison. "Turn, turn, turn away. I will never go astray."

Satisfied, she passed the poppet to her left. Lucretia stared at it, her expression sober and dignified. The poppet eventually returned to Kishi.

"Now, who'll do the cutting?" Nadia asked

This time only one hand was raised. "I'll do it."

Nadia smiled. "Florica, thank you."

Kishi gave the poppet to the young chovihani, and Florica pulled out a small knife from her bag. She tested the edge then sat at attention and waited.

"We know what to do." Nadia looked around the circle. "Let's free our Angela."

The women closed their eyes, all except for Nadia, and soon a muttering chant arose from everyone in the circle. The incantation rose in volume, and soon they swayed in their chairs. Someone pulled out a small drum and began tapping on it, lending rhythm to the chant.

Nadia closed her eyes and visualized Angela, bound by red cords, seeing her as the sword-bearing angel. The vision became stronger and then leaped into brilliant, flaring color. Her eyes flew open.

"*Ekh... duj... trin!*" Nadia shouted.

The women all shrieked the last word. Florica cut the string with one swipe. There was silence, heavy, expectant.

A wind howled suddenly, whipping around the circle. Florica fell backward with a gurgling scream. The poppet flew to one side.

An electric jolt convulsed Nadia, and her vision flashed red. A clamp seemed to squeeze her heart. She thought, *This is it. I'm going to die.* But after what seemed an eternity, the pressure eased, and she could gasp for breath.

One of the women leaped to her feet, her chair falling in her haste. She rushed over to where Florica lay, groaning. Several others rose to assist.

Nadia put a hand to her chest and waited for her heart to stop pounding. Looking around, she didn't notice anyone else in trouble.

"I'm... I'm all right. Help me up." Florica got to her feet, stumbling a bit. Someone righted her chair, and she took her seat unsteadily.

"*Te feril ame o Del!*" Nadia exclaimed.

The women all looked at her, a circle of white faces. Nadia focused on Florica. "What happened?"

"I saw her," Florica said, her voice trembling. "I saw Angela. And I saw something else. It was a really big eagle. It ate her right up, and then it flew at me. Oh, Nadia!"

Everyone started talking at once. Nadia glanced toward where the non-chovihani Roma were clustered, talking excitedly about something or other. None of them appeared to have noticed what happened. She raised her voice to get their attention. "Roma! Hear me! Hear me."

The babbling both in the circle and outside of it died down. Nadia waited until she had gotten their full attention.

"We couldn't do it." She threw up her hands. "Something has our Angela, and it's bigger than we are."

The chovihanis nodded, muttering in agreement, while the others remained silent, clinging to each other or frowning.

She continued, looking at everyone in turn. "We need to watch. Ask our spirit allies for help. Find a way." She swallowed, her throat suddenly dry. "You all go home now. I don't know about my sisters, but this thing nearly killed me. We got to use our Romani cunning and wit to find a way. I will ask the Ancestor for help."

WAR IN HEAVEN: COMMUNION

Unable to fight on the battle front, hampered by the isolation trap, Diamond Angel decided to commune with the Root Hexagon while she waited for her angels to apprehend the traitors. She opened a portal from within her throne room and stepped through. Standing in the crater near the crystalline artifact, she stared into its depths. A familiar face appeared.

"Old friend, what secrets do you yield to my new enemies? What hell world do you haunt now?" asked Diamond Angel.

She reached out a hand toward it then jerked back, suddenly conscious of her peril. Touching the Root Hexagon would be agonizing and might even trigger her dissolution. However, she was able to observe the images playing within it that offered fleeting glimpses of the Underworld. In nearly every scene, there was an aged woman with fierce, dark eyes. This was the Wise Old Woman, an oversoul and servant of Dark Eyes.

An alarm suddenly blared. Diamond Angel climbed out of the crater to see a skirmish nearby. Two groups of angels, one from Serpent Lion and one from Dark Eyes, were attacking. Their shouts and those of Bald Eagle's defenders rang out along with the sound of weapons and the anguished screams of the fallen. On the heels of her vision, it appeared that this was a coordinated action between the Wise Woman and Dark Eyes, which Serpent Lion appeared to be using to its own advantage.

"I must enter this battle." Diamond Angel, War Leader and

scion of primal wisdom, pointed both hands at the ground and dissolved into it.

Region near Root Hexagon, Bald Eagle

A group of spearmen from Serpent Lion, accompanied by sword-wielding, dark-eyed angels, charged Bald Eagle's battalion. They clashed, and several shield-bearers went down, dissolving as they died. The spearmen dropped their weapons and drew short swords, likely borrowed from Dark Eyes. They hacked and slashed with deadly effectiveness.

The ground shuddered, and everyone staggered. A brilliant light emanated from newly formed cracks at their feet. Several enemy angels burst into flame, screaming as a dancing wall of coruscating light formed, rooted in the cracks. A grating sound arose, causing the others to drop weapons and grasp their heads. The defenders stepped forward quickly and dispatched their foes.

Diamond Angel materialized. She gestured distastefully at the piles of decaying debris that were all that was left of her enemies. "Clean this up and report back to your commanders for debriefing. Our enemies are crafty and may have infected you."

The sergeant of the battalion saluted. "Yes, ma'am."

She turned, preparing to go back to the Root Hexagon to finish her meditation, but stopped, her head tilted. She felt a tremor within her depths, the beginnings of a division deep within her. The attack had apparently succeeded after all. "So clever. What a fine weapon you've found, Dark Eyes."

She turned to the sergeant again. "Sergeant, do not report

for debriefing. Instead, remain here to guard the Root Hexagon. I must return to my throne room to await the arrival of prisoners from Gray Suit. There are bindings upon my person that must be cut before I may go into battle again."

The sergeant saluted again.

Realm of Dark Eyes

Amidst towering trees, in the center of a great clearing, a huge bonfire crackled. Seated around that bonfire was a host of angels, all of whom resembled the Roma, for whom they were the cultural messengers. Seated on a taller chair was Dark Eyes. Another being stood before him, an exotically beautiful, androgynous figure. All of the angels muttered and looked askance at this one. It was Serpent Lion, the Egregore of the desire of men for men and women for women and a mighty servant of Love.

"It appears that we have a common problem." Serpent Lion's voice had an ironic note. "There is one who is divided against herself, and she has become our greatest threat."

Dark Eyes studied his enemy, now ally, looking for any hint of duplicity. Seeing that the Egregore bore no enmity toward him at the moment, he smiled grimly. "That division within Diamond Angel was the result of hard work on our part as well as the work of secret allies. *Ekh, dui, trin,* indeed." His heart swelled with pride. "Now that she serves Bald Eagle, her incarnated self Angela must become our ally."

Serpent Lion inclined his head. "You know that I have a strong interest in Diamond Angel, too. If it weren't for Bald Eagle's interference, she would belong to no one but herself.

However, she has assimilated many of our angels as well as yours into her army. I propose that we secretly infiltrate her."

Dark Eyes nodded curtly. "As you say. But I do not trust you, Serpent Lion. You have been one of my bitterest foes."

Serpent Lion spread his arms. "It is our nature as Egregores. We can no more fight our own desire for growth and conquest than we can fight those of the Underworld who support us."

Dark Eyes smacked his fist into his palm. "Speak not that heresy! The Underworld is subject to our power. We are not subject to them!"

Serpent Lion lowered his eyes coquettishly. "As you say, Dark Eyes." He smiled, and Dark Eyes scowled.

War on Earth

"Old, rich white men sending our boys and girls to fight their dirty..."

—

"They can go fuck themselves. I ain't goin' to Iraq again."

—

"What if they hit one of our cities? How about that?"

—

"Those're the same terrorists who planned 9/11. Now it's..."

—

"Really? Gay gypsies? About time."

—

"He came out. Finally..."

—

"Friends?"
"Friends."

Nadia's House

Nadia hung up the phone. She had tried calling Angela three times already. There was no answer and, oddly, no way to leave a message. The phone just rang. Time to use the Sight. Nadia reached over to the lamp, switched off the light, and settled back in her chair. She closed her eyes.

In the darkness, Nadia's mind quested. She had first tried visualizing Angela to prepare for a clairvoyant vision, but the image of her great-niece had been shredded as if torn by claws. Then she sought direct contact with her oversoul, the source of her visions, but there had been no help from that quarter either.

She waited in the dark for any clue. Something violent was happening just beyond the darkness, and it required all of her discipline not to abort the vision and open her eyes. If she ended things too suddenly, the best she could hope for was a splitting headache. There were stories of seers who, having ended a vision too soon, lost their physical eyesight.

No vision came that night.

CHAPTER THIRTY-FOUR

YOU CAN'T FIGHT, CITY HALL

Exacting justice on the twain

She terminates the bitter chain

That binds her fast against her will,

And guarantees her endless reign.

But Dark Eyes has a stealthy scheme

To end the Angel's dark regime

So mighty weapons does he steal

For Angel's sake, her soul redeem.

"ANGELA, CAN you do me a huge favor? There's a City Council meeting today, but I've got a needy client who can't postpone. Can you go in my stead? Please?"

Angela slid the fried egg onto her plate, cradling the phone against her shoulder. "Sure, Eric. I've got no appointments today. Thanks again for looking after Cassie."

"You don't have to thank me. It was the least I could do."

He hung up, and Angela stared thoughtfully at the phone. She could swear that he had sounded mildly offended that she had thanked him for his help. There was no good reason for that; she was just tired and misheard the tone in his voice.

Angela finished breakfast and left for the hospital to check up on Cassandra. On the way, her phone rang. She activated the hands-free. "Cassie!"

"Hi, Angela." Her voice sounded tired, her words somewhat slurred.

"Hey, love. How're you doing? I'm on my way over—"

Cassandra interrupted. "I'm fine. Hey, Angela? I need to get my beauty sleep. Can you come over tomorrow instead?"

Angela's heart sank for a moment. Was Cassandra offended that Angela had not gone directly to the hospital to check on her? "Well, okay. I was just going to take a moment to say hi and see how you're doing after the—"

"I know. I can't stay awake."

Angela sighed. "Of course. I'll see you tomorrow. Sleep tight."

"Bye."

Angela hung up. She signaled a turn to go directly to the City Council meeting.

WAR IN HEAVEN: EXTRADITION

DIAMOND ANGEL'S Throne Room

Diamond Angel surveyed the realm of Gray Suit, spread out in a vision as she sat in her throne room. It was a warren of marble and slate, oak and granite, resembling a vast array of government buildings. The memories of such places from the ancient world helped her understand that this was an archetypal realm of Government itself.

She turned to her commander. "As a servant of Bald Eagle, you have the right to enter that realm and demand the extradition of the angels who keep me isolated. If they refuse, you may engage them in a limited fashion with sufficient force to retrieve the traitors and bring them to me."

The angel nodded, saluted, and vanished.

War on Earth

"Government interference has to stop. They can't serve the one percent..."

—

"Who do they think they are? Elitist bastards need to stay out of..."

—

"Sittin' by their swimming pools while we get beat on by..."

—

"If our community wanted that, we'd have said so..."

—

"Stay out of our business."

—

"Stay out."

Oakland City Hall

The Oakland City Hall building, an impressive stone structure whose architecture Angela had always admired, loomed over her as she walked between the massive pillars flanking the entrance. She climbed the marble staircase and made her way to the public meeting room.

As soon as she entered the room, she located an usher.

"Excuse me." Angela smiled.

"Yes, ma'am?"

"I've got business on the agenda. Where do I—?"

He directed her to a seat. She craned her neck to take in the tall, domed ceiling and towering pillars, which reminded her of the Council chamber from her other lifetime as the Lady of Light in the world of the Progenitors.

City Council members were seated behind the semicircular table on the other side of the seating barrier. The meeting had already begun, and Angela waited as they discussed several agenda items.

The hall echoed with muttering from the audience, making it difficult to hear the council members speak. The president of the council had to rap his gavel several times to call for order. Angela's caffeine buzz had kicked in, and she found herself glancing at the exits and then at the wall clock.

"The next item concerns Brooklyn Basin Mental Health." The councilwoman peered at her notes. "Consider petition by Brooklyn Basin area residents to deny charter for the clinic.

Discussion?"

Angela took a breath and tried to relax. This was something that she and Eric knew might come up. No one wanted a mental health clinic in the neighborhood.

One of the other members raised a hand. "I'd like to hear from Dr. Angela Cooper. Is Dr. Cooper present?"

Before Angela could stand, someone in the audience shouted. She jumped, her head whipping around. Several people were struggling. Security converged on the scuffle while those nearby grew restless. Suddenly there was another shout, much closer, and a fistfight broke out near her between two men.

"Dammit, Ron," one of the councilmen said. "Why do you keep bringing these items to the public meeting?" The council member glanced around, startled to hear his own voice echoing in the chamber, and covered his microphone. But it was too late. The accused councilman—Ron—got to his feet and began shouting. The president of the council banged the gavel. The sound was drowned in the roar of fights breaking out all around the room, echoing from the stone walls and ceiling. The president gave a gesture, and the security team started clearing out the chamber. Angela was hustled out along with the rest of the audience.

WAR IN HEAVEN; EXECUTION

Diamond Angel was holding court. Before her cowered two angels bearing the characteristic drab livery of Gray Suit but overlaid with the insignia of Iron Star.

She lifted her staff. "For crimes of sedition and terrorism, you have been sentenced to destruction. The forces that have brought you forth shall do so no more, now or in the future."

The two angels were mute and bound and had long since ceased to struggle. Diamond Angel signaled to one of her assistants.

He brought a large ceremonial axe to her and presented it with a bow.

Diamond Angel rose and took the weapon. Stepping down to the floor, she hefted the axe. Then, in one smooth motion, she swung it at neck height, decapitating both angels. With a dual flash of light, they fell into heaps of disrupted matter, decaying immediately. The air crackled, and small electrical discharges scattered away from Diamond Angel's feet as the isolation trap dissipated.

She gave the axe back to the guard. "Clean this up."

Several others came forward and extended their hands, palms down. The detritus was systematically dissolved.

She ignored the cleanup crew and gestured. "Prepare my chariot. I shall commune with Bald Eagle and, afterward, address the troops."

The assistant nodded and hurried away.

True Dat @TrueDat · 2h
Cops beat up woman at City Hall. #copblock #oakland #brutality

True Dat @TrueDat · 2h
Fist fight on podium. Council smackdown. Get the popcorn. #fight #oakland

True Dat @TrueDat · 2h
Somebody doesn't like the new MH clinic. #crazy #nimby

WAR IN HEAVEN: WEAPONS LOST

BATTLEFIELD OUTSIDE Bald Eagle

Diamond Angel was in her chariot, having returned to the battlefront. The enemy forces had repeatedly beaten back her somewhat anemic frontal assault. Despite that, she had managed to inflict heavy casualties. Diamond Angel's new weapons, gleaned from the recent fight with Iron Star, had enabled her to strike directly at the heart of Silver Scimitar on one battlefront and Serpent Lion on another, with terrible results. Soon she would use the weapons against Dark Eyes, possibly ridding her of that foe once and for all.

During a brief lull in the fight, Diamond Angel drove the chariot to one of her command and control centers, stripped off her armor and weapons, and prepared to renew herself. All Egregores drew their strength from the lower worlds, and she was tired.

Her adjutants had placed the power station nearby. She strode to it, clouds of steam from the heat of battle curling around her body. A pair of upright pillars flanked an inky, vertically oriented oval "doorway." She breathed deeply then stepped forward into the void. There was a crackle of energy along with a babble of voices, many of which were raised in passionate shouts. The warlike fervor of the underworld was a heady draught, and soon she was replenished.

She returned to her chariot and drew up in shock. Several guards lay on the ground, their bodies rapidly decomposing.

"No!" She rushed to peer into her vehicle. The powerful new

weapons were missing.

She clenched her fists. "Guards! To me!"

Another group of angels appeared.

She pointed. "Clean this up, and find whoever did this. Bring me intelligence if you cannot bring me the perpetrators."

War on Earth

"You're scared of the wrong stuff, man. The real conspiracies..."

—

"It's all out in the open. Don't be ignorant. That's what..."

—

"The plutocrats want us confused. Look, just talk to..."

—

"Talk to them. They are just like us. They want..."

—

"We all want peace."

—

"Peace, man."

CHAPTER THIRTY-FIVE
FRIENDS, ENEMIES

Retaliation is her goal

For Diamond Angel's fearsome role

Is threatened by the weapons' loss,

So army fair does she enroll.

ANGELA DROVE home, her mind blurred with exhaustion. Though the fracas at City Hall had upset her, it could not explain her tiredness. Maybe it was all the lost sleep of the last week or two, or the fact that she was ravenously hungry. The best remedy, she decided, was to go home, eat a late lunch of leftovers, take a quick nap, then visit Cassandra later in the afternoon despite her objections. Even if her girlfriend was asleep, it would do Angela some good to see her.

Eric would want to know what had happened at the council meeting. She spoke to her hands-free unit. "Phone. Call Eric at work."

The phone rang. "Hey, Angela."

"Hi, Eric. Bad news. They never even got to my agenda item."

"What? Why?"

"A fight broke out, believe it or not. Someone in the audience started it, and then it spread to the City Council members and even over to where I was sitting. It was like a war." She swerved to avoid someone changing lanes without a turn signal. Asshole.

"That's incredible. Are you okay?"

Angela's pulse pounded in her ears. "What do you mean by 'incredible'? Don't you believe me?"

"What? I was just saying that it was incredible, that's all. As long as you're—"

"Are you calling me a liar?" she said. Eric knew she would never make up a story like that.

"I—no! I'm not calling you a..."

The irony in Eric's voice pushed her over the edge. "I can't believe this. Here I am, covering for a job you were supposed to do, and you're calling me a liar. Bullshit, pal."

"But I'm not! Angela, what's going on?"

She had always thought that the phrase "seeing red" was metaphorical, but now her vision was edged with the color. Eric had never taken her seriously, and his lackadaisical approach to the work of starting the clinic sometimes set her teeth on edge. But he had pushed her too far this time. "Nothing's going on anymore. We're through, Eric. Go find work somewhere else. I'm closing the clinic."

She punched the off button. At that moment, another driver swerved to change lanes. Angela slammed on her brakes, honking the horn and swearing at the top of her lungs. Tires screeched behind her, and the driver of a large pickup accompanied her horn with his own in an angry symphony.

WAR IN HEAVEN: UNSUPPORTED ACTION

Diamond Angel's Palace, Bald Eagle

Weaponless, Diamond Angel retreated from the front, dogged by Shaken Fist, until she was safely behind Bald Eagle's borders. From her throne room, she continued to direct the war, albeit at a severe strategic and tactical disadvantage.

"Dark Eyes and Serpent Lion colluded in the weapons theft," said her adjutant.

Diamond Angel nodded. "They will pay for that. However, Bald Eagle requires all of his forces to be deployed on the front."

She mused silently while the adjutant stood by her side. Finally, she gestured for him to stand aside. Climbing down from her high seat, she took a wide-legged stance facing the entryway, her arms raised. Her eyes closed, she grimaced. A mist billowed forth from her solar plexus, forming a pillar in front of her. The pillar collapsed and then reformed in the shape of a humanoid creature, armed and wearing armor. Diamond Angel reached out and touched it on the forehead. It flushed with color and life and moved aside.

Soon there were a dozen warrior angels, which she'd created using her own substance. Diamond Angel lowered her arms and examined the new phalanx.

"My angels. You are created to go forth and deal devastating blows to my enemies Dark Eyes and Serpent Lion. You will carry the weapons I gave you, and you will fight without question unto death."

The angels stared back impassively. Diamond Angel studied for a moment longer. "Follow my adjutant, who will lead you to the armory. You will then be given the necessary plans by my second-in-command and sent on your mission. Make no alliances. This is an unsupported action."

She paused for a moment, suddenly uncertain of herself, and closed her eyes. Her newly warlike nature still fit her poorly, and it required more energy to maintain her resolve. Finally, she turned her back on them, signaling to her adjutant to take them away.

War on Earth

"Who are those people, Mommy? They look like Mexicans."

"Shh. They're gypsies, honey. They'll..."

—

"... steal my jewelry! Stop! Thief! He took..."

—

"... my goddam job. Lazy bastards aren't..."

—

"... American! Godless heathens..."

—

"... go home!"

Street in Oakland

"Gypsy scum! Thieves!"

The shouts and imprecations landed on his shoulders as Walt led his Roma family back to their car. They had been looking forward to a picnic by Lake Merritt, but now they would be dining at home.

Construction Site, San Francisco

Steve Boswell hunched his shoulders as he carried his lunch pail and his other things out of the locker room. Hoots of derision followed him as the guys he had thought were his friends mocked him. He was no slacker! His homophobic boss, the Texan, had fired him under a false pretext, but he knew it was because he had come out in what he thought was the safest city in the world to do so.

Nadia's Living Room

"Andrea, what's gotten into you?" Nadia cradled the phone against her ear while she stirred the soup.

"Nadia, it's what I said. We got punished for violating God's law."

"That's ridiculous. What we did was our business. We serve our community, so how can that be breaking divine law?" She set the spoon down and reached for her spice rack.

"Because we are women, and we don't know our place!" Her friend's voice fairly crackled with self-righteous indignation.

"It's that damn preacher and his nonsense! I knew it!" Nadia nearly dropped the phone in her agitation, and while she fumbled it back to her ear, she could hear Andrea's squawks of protest. The enemy was, indeed, acting through the gadje. The rumors she had heard through the grapevine were an indication of some kind of attack.

She placed the phone firmly against her ear and turned down the heat on the soup. "Andrea. Until you get some sense in your head, I do not wish to speak about this further." With that, she hung up the phone. "Drat it."

CHAPTER THIRTY-SIX
IN HER MEADOW

A voice she hears from lower space

Does make her doubt her warrior's place,

Yet stronger still is her regard

For warlike master's warm embrace.

As ANGELA crossed the bridge into Alameda, she saw a line of protestors outside the Army recruiting office. Some of them may have been Eric's friends. Did they know how treacherous he could be? Then something caught her eye, and she looked more closely. One of the signs displayed a slogan, "You Steal Our Dreams and Our Lives."

Her meme had mutated as it had spread, but it was still recognizably hers. Something she had created was strong enough to survive in the world of ideas. If there was some kind of creature in the Otherworld that corresponded to her meme, it was probably waging righteous war on the weak.

As she turned right toward Bayside Marina and home, she saw a commotion on the street corner. Two men were shouting angrily, surrounded by a crowd, and as she drove away, one of them pushed the other to the ground. She smiled grimly. He probably deserved it.

Angela continued down Clement Avenue. Everywhere she looked, there was conflict. Two people, shouting and gesticulating. Kids pushing each other, one crying and the others laughing. Honking horns and angry gestures. The backdrop of quiet everyday activity against which these incidents occurred was unimportant. After all, peace was simply unexpressed conflict. She could feel something inside her, urging everyone to reveal their true selves.

She pulled into the marina parking lot and found a slot near her home pier. As she got out of the Prius, the wind whipped her hair. Smelling the tang of ozone that preceded a storm, she glanced at the wild cloudscape above then at the choppy waves of the channel. The spray reminded her of the Otherworldly beach with its warring animals. A momentary burning sensation in her heart made her stop and clutch her chest, and her mental fog lifted. Something was wrong with her.

Angela jumped as a seagull flew by like a bullet, propelled by the stormy wind. The fog descended once again, quenching her unease.

Angela dreamed. She was a disembodied viewpoint, flying between the trees of the Otherworld. She burst into an ordinary meadow with some tangled underbrush at the edge, shrubberies dotting its open area, and clumps of untidy grass. But as she passed through it, it seemed as if invisible builders were at work raising fortifications. A rustic but dangerous-looking wall of spikes at the perimeter rose up out of the ground, scattering clods of soil. Pitfalls appeared all over the meadow and then were immediately camouflaged. Brief fires flared here and there, burning vegetation and filling the meadow with smoke.

She exited the meadow, passing into the dark forest once

again. She heard faint voices and glimpsed momentary flickering scenes as she flew.

A man and a woman are arguing in the kitchen. Suddenly, the woman's face is suffused with a new rage. Her husband sees this and freezes, but it's too late. With a snarl, she picks up a steak knife and goes after him. The knife flashes, and there is a spray of blood. The light fades.

Her disembodied viewpoint entered another meadow. This one looked as though it had been manicured. There were even orderly plantings forming a delicate labyrinth in its center. But as she passed through, ugly barbed-wire fencing thrust up through the soul, destroying the carefully laid-out garden. Crossed, sharpened logs also rose, forming a deadly grid. A rattle of gunfire punctured the air, and a deer, unseen until that moment, collapsed at the verge of the forest.

A monk in the chapel is curled into a fetal position on the floor. Next to him, another monk, with bruises all over his face, is unconscious. Shouts from elsewhere and running feet. The one observing all of this can only hear his own rasping breath. The new arrivals skid to a stop and look at him in confusion.

"Father Dominic? What happened?"

He replies. "These young men lack discipline. Their prayers were hasty and meaningless. It was time they learned better."

The monks back up now, evidently frightened. They should be. Sinners all.

The viewpoint settled in another meadow, which was already fortified. In it stood a small, tidy cabin whose roof was spiked in preparation to repel invaders. Angela heard a whistling sound, and a nearby explosion rocked the air as the earth fountained up. Then another bomb struck, and another.

With a shout, Angela awoke in the Otherworld. She stood in her meadow, her head spinning, and took her bearings. The sky, as on earth, was overcast with churning clouds that had the characteristic glow of a thunderstorm.

The tidy cabin, the heart of her power, had been altered. Sharp, vertical spikes on the roofline glistened in the wan sunlight. Two poles with American flags flanked the doorway. Circling the meadow, near the eave of the forest, was a log barricade with strategically placed gates. Beyond the barricade, the forest was dark and tangled, as if all the benefits of years of self-work had vanished. Scattered all over the open ground were craters, some still smoking and contributing to a pall hanging over the clearing. The smell of cordite overrode all other aromas.

"War here, too?" Angela's mental fog lifted completely. She had wronged Eric. Reparations would have to wait, though. Something had happened to her in that odd Otherworld place, and it had bled into her environment—how else could she explain the violence that had broken out everywhere? Whatever it was, it had to have been left behind by Iron Star. She fought down a surge of rage. Her emotions were volatile and needed a close watch.

She spent a few minutes examining the changes in her meadow. When she entered the cabin, in place of her dream-walker's staff behind the door, she found a spear. It was carved with the same designs as her staff but bound with an iron point. She reflected on the fact that she had used her staff in combat. That may have made her vulnerable to the disaster she was now surveying.

Emerging from the cabin, she located the tall pine at the edge of the meadow. Its tip was crowned with brown needles. If it had been an earthly tree, she would have sworn that it was being attacked by bark beetles. Defocusing her eyes and staring up at the tree, she waited for a vision of the dream-like place, which she had decided to call the Overworld, to appear. Nothing happened.

After several fruitless minutes, she gave up. Angela needed Cassandra and Simon's help to travel to the Overworld again. The answers to this puzzle would be found there.

A wave of exhaustion washed over her, and she staggered. She scanned the ground and found patches of quilted cloth from her bed that marked her homeward path.

Briefly returning to wakefulness, she turned over and drifted into a deeper sleep, a sleep still troubled by visions of war in the Otherworld.

Cassandra had been in a drugged sleep off and on all day. She had been unable to force another out-of-body excursion since the disastrous encounter with Iron Star. But now her eyes opened, and she saw her body below her, limned in spectral light. Immediately she drifted in a gentle arc, feet-first, to land at the foot of her hospital bed.

Her thoughts felt sluggish as if she were still dreaming. If she tried to force herself to become more awake, she might fall back into her body, so she waited for whatever had drawn her out. Then she heard a faint voice.

—*Cassandra? Cassandra?*—

She looked around the otherwise empty room but saw no one there.

"Who's that?" Her voice again sounded boxy in her ears.

—*Cassandra, this... diamond...*—

The voice was distorted, and at first Cassandra could not make out the words. It had sounded familiar, though. She thought of Angela's great-aunt.

"Nadia?"

—*Something terrible has happened to Angela.*—

The world tilted, and she felt a sudden tug in her solar plexus, drawing her toward her sleeping body. "Oh God. Is she..."

—*Her body is not hurt.*—

Cassandra's mind blurred with relief, and the tugging eased.

—*Her soul is in danger. Something has taken ahold of her mind.*—

"It must've happened after I jumped Iron Star. I passed out." An elusive memory nagged at her. Her back rippled with the sensation of being watched, and though bodiless, she shivered. She drifted to the window and looked out on a misty landscape that in no way resembled what was actually outside the hospital. "What can I do to help?"

—*Keep an eye on Angela. Ask her what happened. I cannot see her. Please tell me what you learn.*—

"I will."

There was a moment of silence. Then a feeling of warmth unexpectedly kindled in Cassandra's heart.

—*Thank you. She loves you and trusts you above all. I know that now.*—

The sense of Nadia's presence vanished. Cassandra stood quietly, savoring the freedom that being out of her body gave her. Her thoughts turned to Angela. She would go see what Nadia was talking about.

Immediately, she was hovering in the sailboat master cabin over Angela's sleeping body. As was the case in her hospital room, everything was edged with a pale glow as if backlit by the moon. She drifted closer, trying to see past Angela's body to her soul, whatever that was. Then, remembering her telepathic talent, she concentrated, "listening" intently.

—*Why do you question my will?*—

The voice was like and unlike Angela's. It was the aloof voice of an alien intelligence, and Cassandra sensed malevolence lurking beneath it. Was this what Nadia referred to?

Cassandra concentrated. —*Angela! It's me, Cassie! Wake up.*—

Her own voice echoed in her head. It felt as if Angela's mind were somehow reflecting Cassandra's voice back at her. She called Angela's name again, more urgently. Then something reached into her head and shoved, hard. The world spun around her and went dark. A heavy weight settled on Cassandra's chest, and she gasped for air. The sound of her wheezing breath came loudly to her ears, and her limbs tingled painfully. Cassandra's eyes opened stickily, and the dark hospital room swam into view.

"Angela...?" She drifted back into dreamless sleep.

WAR IN HEAVEN: ANGEL AND GODDESS

Diamond Angel's Palace, Bald Eagle

Diamond Angel knew she must return to the battlefield, but a nagging sense of something left undone gave her reason to pause and meditate in the throne room. Faces appeared before her mind's inwardly turned eye, faces of the long-ago people from her ancient culture, reborn in the underworld.

One of the faces became more vivid. It was that of Angela, and she recognized the source of her disquiet. Angela's face was hard-edged, and her aura flashed red and black. Upon seeing Angela, Diamond Angel's breath hissed between her teeth. "You finally reach out to me, now, after I have helped you destroy your enemy. You show such poor gratitude."

A voice echoed in her head. It was indistinct, weak. —*I need your help...*— The unconscious depths of Angela's mind conveyed pain and loneliness along with the message.

"You must stop resisting me. Then I will help." Pain stabbed momentarily in Diamond Angel's chest

—*I am no warrior. I seek peace. Why do I bring conflict?*— The voice was stronger and inwardly focused.

Diamond Angel touched her chest where it had hurt. "I am sworn to defend and uphold our master, Bald Eagle. Why do you question my will?"

—*I love my friends, my people. How can I stop this thing within me from alienating them?*—

Diamond Angel rose to her feet, driven by the urgency within Angela. But the pain intensified, and Diamond Angel staggered, putting out a hand. One of her attendant angels, who had been standing well away from her, approached and offered support. She gathered her will and, with a convulsive effort, thrust the source of pain far from her.

"Thank you." She nodded gratefully and resumed her seat. "Go to my commanders and tell them to convene here. I must oversee the war with Silver Scimitar and Shaken Fist, but I cannot go to the battlefield in person. One whom I am expecting shall arrive in Bald Eagle, and I must be ready for her."

CHAPTER THIRTY-SEVEN
QUESTIONS

While spies are sent to reinforce

The will of Angel's earthly horse

And deeper drive the growing wedge

That fortifies rebellion's source

ANGELA SAT in the uncomfortable plastic chair and pretended to read, though in fact the magazine in her hand was a blur of meaningless shapes and colors. It was better than staring at the bustling nurses in the hallway adjacent to the waiting room. In an attempt to distract herself, she checked her phone for messages, but the screen remained dark.

"Dammit." She smacked the phone, cursing the dead battery.

A passing nurse glanced at her and frowned. Angela put the phone back in her backpack. She heard a tremendous, jangling crash in the hallway, and she jumped.

"Watch where you're going!" An orderly gestured angrily at the nurse who had passed Angela.

"I did watch where I was going. I'm not the clumsy one," the nurse replied.

Angela saw Cassandra being wheeled out into the hallway by a nurse. The bandage on her head had been replaced by a smaller piece of gauze. Her broken leg stuck straight out in a cast, but she was smiling and looked relaxed. Angela rose to her feet, hiding her anxiety with a smile.

As Cassandra took over the wheelchair and approached, the welcoming smile on her face faded. Angela took a step toward Cassandra but hesitated, feeling a chill.

"Angela?" Cassandra's voice was strained.

"Cassie!" Angela reached toward Cassandra, but the younger woman shrank away.

It was like a punch in the gut. Angela's arms dropped. "Cassie? What's wrong?"

Cassandra looked away. "I don't know. I'm feeling sick all of a sudden."

The nurse regarded Cassandra with concern. "Miss Grey? You suffered a concussion. Let me take you back to your room."

Cassandra waved her away. "No!"

"Cassie?" Angela reached a hand toward her then lowered it. She thought about her fight with Eric and about the angry crowds she had seen everywhere she looked. "Not you, too."

Cassandra stared at her. "What do you mean?"

Angela backed away a step, and the tightness around Cassandra's eyes relaxed as she sat up straighter in her chair.

"Something's wrong with me." Angela eyed the nurse, who was following this exchange with a frown. "Can we have a moment?"

The nurse seemed about to speak, but she nodded sharply and left.

"That strange place did something to me," Angela said. "Ever since I got back, it seems as if everyone around me is fighting." She jammed her hands in her pockets. "I had a huge argument with Eric. I think I lost him." A jagged pain in her chest felt as if it had burst, and tears blurred her vision as she began to hiccup with quiet sobs.

She felt a light touch and looked up.

Cassandra yelped and jerked her hand back as if scalded. "Ow!"

"What?" Angela's heart skipped. "Are you okay?"

"What do you mean?" Cassandra snapped. "Do I look okay —" She stopped talking and passed a hand over her face. "God. It's like I just want to bite your head off. Like I hate everybody and want to fight."

"Iron Star infected me. Somehow he poisoned me with his warlike nature." Angela's sadness gave way to anger. How dare that monstrosity inflict her with a curse? She was ready to go back to that Overworld place and demand an accounting from whoever was in charge.

Cassandra sighed. "So, that's what she meant."

Angela looked at her, puzzled. "Who?"

"Nadia. She contacted me. I was out of my body again, and she told me something terrible had happened to you. Said to keep an eye on you."

Angela took a deep, steadying breath. "She's right. Something terrible has happened. It's still happening. On my way over here, I saw three car accidents, and the cops seemed to be everywhere. There were gunshots in broad daylight by Lake Merritt. Somehow this infection, this stain of war, is using my power to spread to people around me. Maybe it's spreading in the Otherworld—" She stopped as a horrifying realization struck home. Looking down, she could see every detail of the floor in dreamlike clarity. She heard her own voice as if from a distance. "Like the Soul Thief."

She contemplated her hands, which were surprisingly steady. "I have to go back to that place. That's where I'll find answers. And a cure, before it's too late." She glanced at her girlfriend's pale face under the fluorescent lighting. "I need your help, Cassie. And Simon's. I just hope he's not affected by this, too."

Angela raised her hand to knock on Simon's door then hesitated. If her day so far were any indication, he could have a gun in his hand right now, ready to fight. If she stepped through that door, he might shoot her. And Cassandra. She turned to leave.

Cassandra rolled up to the door in her wheelchair, reached out awkwardly with her good hand, and rapped sharply. She glanced up at Angela, and her mouth twitched in a momentary smile.

"Who is it?" Simon's voice was stronger than it had been the last time Angela had tried to visit.

"It's us," Cassandra replied. "Angela and me."

Angela heard a muffled exclamation from the other side, followed by a loud thump, and the door swung open as Simon rolled back. He goggled at Cassandra. "Whoa."

Cassandra grinned. "Yep. Looks like we're both rolling today."

He laughed, moving out of the way as she went in. Angela paused in the doorway, irresolute. His expression froze as he eyed her, and he frowned. "Are you going to come in?"

Angela nodded, her heartbeat throbbing in her ears. "Sure. Sorry."

After she squeezed past, Simon shut the door, and he followed her into the living room. "I'd get you something to drink, but all I've got is beer."

"I'll pass," Angela said.

"Beer's not good enough for you?" His eyes narrowed.

"Simon!" Cassandra snapped. "She needs your help. What's up with you?"

He stared at Cassandra for a moment then shook his head. "I dunno. It's like I just want to punch someone right now. Really weird. I was okay till you guys showed up." He regarded Angela again, and his forehead creased. "What's wrong? Does this have to do with Iron Star?"

"Got it in one." Angela licked a finger and marked an invisible scoreboard. "I fought him, and I think I defeated him. But something happened to me."

Simon nodded. "That's why I don't see him. But the soldiers still push me back into the dream. Nothing's changed."

"Crap." Angela threw up her hands. "It's all crap! Obviously, something or someone else is fucking with us all. And now that big red bastard's put something in my head." She jammed her hands in her pockets. "I need your help to get rid of it. All the answers are in that weird Overworld, not here. Can you help me go over one more time?"

"Why should I? You couldn't help me with my nightmares." Simon's voice rose as he glared at Angela. "What good are you now, anyway?"

She clenched her fists then relaxed. The stain of war was talking, not Simon, she reminded herself firmly. "Simon, I don't want to argue with you. Look, if you want to be rid of that nightmare, you need to help me help you."

Simon's face contorted briefly. "Before I met you, I just had nightmares when I was asleep. Now I see them when I close my eyes." He turned away and rolled toward the window. He stopped, and his hands clenched and unclenched on the arms of his chair. Angela resisted the urge to storm out of his apartment, throwing herself into a chair instead.

Cassandra moved next to him and stared out the window. "So, you know this thing's killing you, right?" She spoke in low tones. "You were already in bad shape when I met you."

Simon grunted an affirmative.

"She's the only one who's been able to hurt the bad guys where they live. Now, I don't know how really real those guys are, but if you want to have a life of your own, you've got to give her one more chance."

Simon stared out at the storm-clouded sky a moment longer, then he turned to study Cassandra's face. "I'll try 'cause you're asking me to." He clenched his fists. "Dammit! I'm sick of beating my head against the wall." He took a breath and let it out heavily. "Okay. What do we do?"

"Angela needs to get to this other place. First, Simon, you go to sleep. You've got zombie pills, right?" He nodded, and she continued, "Cool. I'll keep an eye on you, and when you start dreaming, I'll join you. I'll link Angela in, and then we go wherever we need to go." Her voice faltered.

Fear for Cassandra penetrated Angela's funk, and she spoke up. "Cassie, I don't want you to come with me to that place again. You almost got killed the last time. Just mentally link with him and send me there."

Cassandra stared at Angela, biting her lip. "How're we gonna keep track of you?"

"I don't think you can. Just... keep an eye out for me. I need to scrape this whatever-it-is off of me."

"Why do you keep trying to do everything by yourself?"

Angela felt heat rise, but she checked her angry retort. "Lover, right now it's all I can do to keep my head screwed on straight. Please, can you support me in this?"

Cassandra hesitated, then she nodded.

"Thank you. Simon, how're you feeling?"

"I don't know. I don't care anymore." He glanced at Angela. "While you're there getting your head screwed back on, if you see any way to get me out of this, I'd appreciate it."

"I repeat, stop your vehicle or we'll open fire."

Simon put down his weapon and waited for the soldiers to react. One turned to face him and reached down for his rifle.

Angela grabbed the soldier from behind, yanking his arm to force him off balance. He staggered but regained his footing. He turned on her, a snarl on his face. Then his expression went blank, and he stepped backward away from her, crossing his arms. Another soldier rushed to grapple with Simon. Angela stepped forward, lifted her foot, and delivered a snap kick to his lower back. He fell to his knees, rolled away from her, and rose to his feet. He backed away as well, and Angela was nonplussed.

"Go! Go!" Simon shouted, his face anguished.

Angela nodded. Whatever was happening to the soldiers was unimportant. She reached out to one of the passive soldiers who was staring blankly through her. Touching his forehead, she felt the universe whirl around her as the scene changed.

Root Hexagon, Bald Eagle

Angela stood, once again, in the crater where she had arrived to fight Iron Star. She sneezed twice at the acrid stench from the bubbling pool. The sky echoed with thunder, and she glanced up at the seething red clouds, hunting for its source. Then she lowered her gaze to the crater rim. The strobing red glare of warfare flared above it.

"Do these people ever stop fighting?" she muttered. Then she raised her voice. "Okay, now I'm here. What next?"

She saw that strange, glimmering glow everywhere she looked. She lifted a hand and stared, but this time, her hand was unadorned by light.

A soundless, brilliant flash like lightning blinded her. When her vision cleared again, she was surrounded by winged beings. She spun, looking for a way out of the trap, but they had ringed the crater.

WAR IN HEAVEN: SPIES GO FORTH

The realm was heavily forested with fantastical, unearthly trees, their limbs twisted into dark ideograms. Among the shadows of those trees, animal-headed humans carried out the whims of the stylish angels that in turn served the master of mystery, Dark Eyes.

Taking the form of a handsome man—clean shaven, black haired, and olive skinned—he strode out of a copse. He had chosen to appear in a beetle-green vest, white shirt with puffed sleeves and red trim, and burgundy trousers. Of course, he wore no shoes. Dark Eyes placed his fists on his hips and looked around him for a moment. Then he raised his fingers to his lips and issued a piercing whistle.

A half-dozen angels, each displaying the characteristic features of Dark Eyes, came running up to stand before him.

Dark Eyes spoke, gesturing grandly. "Men, our one-time friend and ally Diamond Angel is now at war with us. She is deeply divided within because of a great spell that our servants cast. However, I have learned from my greatest servant that the spell wasn't enough to free Angela. Diamond Angel will swallow her whole unless we help."

There was anxious muttering amongst the angels.

He continued. "Attacks on the Root Hexagon have revealed that, though Diamond Angel is complicit in the crimes committed by Bald Eagle, the child Angela is seeking to undermine her use of the Root Hexagon. That underworld woman and her friend are actually loosening the keystone of the Hexagon, embodied in the man Simon—"

The muttering grew angry at the mention of that name.

"—using the new weapon we stole from Diamond Angel. But they are in great danger every moment that they work against Diamond Angel."

Dark Eyes strode up and down their line dramatically, waving his hand with grand flourishes. "We must help them! I send you forth to carry inspiration to our unexpected benefactors. Go in haste, go in stealth, and return victorious. If you learn important information, send one of your number back to me immediately."

He turned to face them, planting his fists on his hips again. Seeing them muttering and jostling each other for a better view of their lord, he laughed and waved his hand. "Go!"

They thrust their fists high and left as quickly as they had arrived.

War on Earth

"I felt so useless. But my husband said that just knowing I was here..."

—

"She's out there, saving the world, and I support her."

—

"We'll hold the center. I can help you while he's gone."

—

"Pass it on to them. They'll get my support."

—

"I'll support them regardless. My son's not alone..."

—

"My granddaughter's not alone..."

—

"Angela's not alone."

CHAPTER THIRTY-EIGHT
THE WISE OLD WOMAN

Another force is mobilized

To furnish aid to mortal wise

That she might find the secret cause

Which tainted her with warlike guise.

CASSANDRA SAT in her wheelchair next to the couch where Angela's prone form lay quietly. Concentrating, she reached out with her mind and felt nothing. Simon coughed, and she looked up.

"I can't feel her mind. It's almost like she's dead." She held a dampened finger up to the unconscious woman's nose. She couldn't detect any breathing, and the unusual pallor of Angela's features was starting to frighten Cassandra.

Simon wheeled close and reached out to feel Angela's neck.

Cassandra grabbed his hand. "Don't touch her!"

"Oh, yeah," he said, pulling his hand back. "Look closer. There's a pulse in her throat."

Cassandra peered. Sure enough, she saw a tiny movement. She felt a sudden electric tension in her body. "I wish I could help her."

"Yeah. Me too. I'm still kinda confused about who or what she's fighting."

Cassandra shifted her weight in her chair. She had tried to explain this several times before. "So, it's like this. You know about memes?"

"Yeah, Angela filled me in on that. But it still doesn't make sense. How can an idea be a soldier?"

Cassandra thought about the question. It still confused her, too, but whatever they were, Angela took them seriously enough to risk her sanity and her life to fight them. "I'm not really sure about that either. But she's fighting these things, and she told me they can be beaten."

"So, if someone posts an ad online, they've created a meme? And it's a soldier?"

"God, I don't know." She rubbed her face tiredly "Yeah Maybe. But I think these things are stronger if there's a lot at stake—like, if there's something going on in the real world, too."

"Then why can't you just watch the news or something, and see if Angela's winning?"

Cassandra snapped her fingers. "Right! Great idea!" She looked around. Simon didn't have a television. "Where's your computer?"

"It's at the shop. I, uh, broke it."

She looked at him askance then dug out her phone. "I'd use this, but the tiny screen sucks. I know who'll help, though."

"Who?"

"Eric." She pulled up his name and hit Dial. The phone rang once.

"Cassie?" Eric's voice sounded thin, even accounting for the mobile connection.

"Yeah. Eric, Angela told me you guys had a fight."

"She had a fight. I didn't. I don't know what the hell

happened." He paused, and his next words were hard to discern. "I just wish I could talk to her."

Was Eric crying? It must have been a huge argument. She would ask him about it some other time. "Listen. She's... indisposed at the moment. But I need you to do me a huge favor."

"Anything."

"Can you turn on the news, check the search engines, maybe fire up a Facebook session, and watch your Twitter feeds?"

"What?" His voice cracked.

"We need to know what's happening. Everywhere." She stood up again and started pacing. "I can't explain right now, but just call me if you see anything weird. Unusual."

"Baby, it's all weird right now."

"Weirder, then. Especially if it relates to the war, or something local. Just do it. Please?" She glanced at Simon, who nodded encouragement.

"Sure. I don't understand how this is going to help."

"Trust me, it will." She hung up and set her phone down on the table. Cassandra sat quietly for a moment, staring into nowhere. "I hate waiting." She opened up a web browser on the phone and started looking for clues herself.

Cassandra brooded and sat, glancing anxiously at Angela's prone and all-too-still figure on the couch. She was seriously jonesing for a smoke, but Simon hated people smoking in his apartment, and she wasn't going to abandon Angela to go outside and light up.

Somebody whispered. It was almost too quiet to hear. She

looked at Simon. "Did you hear that?"

"Hear what?" Simon glanced up from his book.

The whisper came again.

—*Cassie...*—

"Who's there?" Cassandra stood, ears straining.

—*Angela... Cassie...*—

The voice echoed as if it came from a far larger room. Cassandra realized she was hearing it in her mind. "Nadia!"

She closed her eyes and concentrated. —*Nadia. I can hear you.*—

—*Call me. This is difficult.*—

Her eyes flew open, and she dug her phone out of her pocket. Cassandra dialed, and the phone rang once. Nadia picked up.

"Cassandra. Thank you. I tried calling Angela, but her phone's off. For some reason, I can't hear your mind very well right now."

"I had the same trouble hearing Angela thinking. Something's happening to all of us." Cassandra scratched at her scalp then pinched the bridge of her nose, fighting down her rising anxiety.

"I've had visions of fighting. War. It's as if every time I close my eyes, I am in a battlefield. What is going on, child?"

Cassandra rolled alongside the couch, reached out, and held her hand over her girlfriend's cold, cold foot. "Angela's gone to the other side."

"To the Otherworld?" Nadia's voice betrayed her concern, and for the first time, Cassandra felt warmth toward Angela's fearsome great-aunt.

"She went someplace different. She said she was going to where the enemy lives."

"Enemy? Is this the enemy I told you to protect her from?"

"Um, yeah." Maybe Cassandra should have argued with Angela about this, but it probably would have escalated into a huge fight. "She's hard to argue with."

Nadia sighed. "There's nothing to be done now. So, tell me what's going on."

Cassandra related all that had taken place since she had returned from the hospital.

Nadia grunted. "So, that's what it is."

"What're you seeing? What's Angela doing?" Cassandra was about to leap out of her skin from the tension.

"The art of the chovihani has many parts. The most important is the work with the spirits. The Otherworld is full of spirits of all kinds—some great, some small, most of them with no morality but power. Angela is fighting a powerful spirit." She paused then continued in a deeper tone of voice. "I saw her with a group of warriors. But she wasn't fighting them. She was marching with them, going someplace important."

Cassandra's head whirled with the relief of tension. Angela was alive. And she wasn't alone. "Can you reach her? Make her see you or hear you? 'Cause I can't find her at all, and that's never happened before."

"I don't know. Maybe so. She has met my oversoul. Did she tell you about the oversouls?"

"Yeah."

"I might be able to send her a message if she meets my oversoul. And she might be able to pass something back to me.

We chovihanis are trained to talk with our oversouls, you know. They give us knowledge, visions, and power."

"Okay." *Enough sales talk, Nadia.* She racked her brain for ideas. Come home, Angela? No. If Angela was on a mission, she would need help, not a needy girlfriend. Cassandra covered the mouthpiece. Simon was watching anxiously.

"Simon," she said. "Angela is fighting on the other side. Nadia might be able to reach her. What can we do to help on this end? You know about that stuff."

"Intel. She needs to know the bigger picture. If you're right, and what she does is reflected here, she could use info from this world."

Cassandra nodded. That made sense. She uncovered the mouthpiece. "She needs to know what's happening here. Do you know Eric?"

"We've met."

Even now, Cassandra could hear the disapproval in Nadia's voice. The biddy could be so old-fashioned. "Can you call him, please? He's watching the news for clues. Whatever Angela's doing is going to show up in the news. It'll also show if there's something sneaking up on her, I think. If he can pass that on to you, you can send that to Angela."

"I can do that."

WAR IN HEAVEN: OVERTURE

HOME OF Nadia's Oversoul, Just Below the Overworld

Nadia's oversoul mused as she sat in her overstuffed chair on the grass outside her brightly painted Romani *vardo*. She considered what she knew of the Overworld, and her orderly, crystalline mind turned over the knowledge and experience she had gathered. Her friend, now known as Diamond Angel, may have become lost in that place, but without intervention, Nadia's oversoul was unlikely to be able to rescue that ancient entity.

Though she had no conventional sight, this was of no matter to an oversoul, and she stared with her penetrating insight into the campfire, seeking wisdom. She gradually became aware of the presence of someone of power to her left and turned her sightless gaze in that direction. Dark Eyes emerged from the dense woods surrounding Nadia's oversoul, and her strength faltered in his presence.

"My lord? I didn't hear you arrive, or I would have greeted you more courteously."

He approached the fire, raising his hands to warm them. "So gracious. I like that about you." He looked sidelong at her. "I need something from you."

She rose from her chair unsteadily, staring at him, drinking in his beauty. "Whatever you wish, my lord. I serve you now, as I have served you before."

He gestured to the fire. An image of Angela appeared in it. Above it hovered the form of Diamond Angel, flickering in the smoke that rose from the fire. He pointed to Diamond Angel. "This one has fallen under the spell of the enemy, Bald Eagle. She is now our greatest enemy. Yet... Angela rebels against the wishes of Diamond Angel."

Nadia's oversoul gasped.

He continued, ignoring her distress. "I will send you to Angela as she has now entered the realm of Bald Eagle and needs your guidance."

Nadia's oversoul immediately turned and hobbled to the vardo. After rummaging in a pile of items near the hitch, she dragged out her walking staff and returned to stand by Dark Eyes. "I am ready."

"She must be reminded of who she is." Dark Eyes gestured toward the darkness, and another man, resembling Dark Eyes but of lesser power, strode forth to stand near her. The newcomer was weaponless. "This one must be given to our friend. He bears a message that she will need, but he must go in disguise to the seat of our enemy's power."

With that pronouncement, the newcomer's body blurred at the edges then contracted until he seemed to vanish. A small stone rested on the ground where he had stood. Nadia's oversoul stooped and retrieved the transformed angel. She muttered over it, adding messages of her own before hiding it within the folds of her shawl.

Dark Eyes faced the fire and raised his hands. The earth rumbled as he gathered power. The flames roared high into the sky, and a vortex formed in their midst. Nadia's oversoul walked confidently into the portal.

CHAPTER THIRTY-NINE
LOVE KEEPS WATCH

Then word is sent to Angel bright

That mortal feet have scaled the height;

'Twas preordained her self and Self

Will prematurely reunite.

ERIC SAT on the edge of what he called his "entertain me" chair, his eyes on the huge flat-screen television. The president stood before Congress. His lips were moving, silently, his head turning left then right.

Eric held his phone to his ear as he watched the news report. "Nadia, I don't know if you're watching the news."

"No. My TV doesn't work anymore."

"Well, it looks like we're going to war."

She gasped. "No!"

"Yeah. Congress is... let's see." He turned up the sound and listened briefly. "The president called an emergency session to ask for a declaration of war. Looks like both parties are in agreement on this."

"Eric, I know you'll find this hard to believe." Nadia sighed. "It's all connected with something Angela is doing. So, it's very important for you to give me the details so I can pass them on."

He stood up and absentmindedly ran his hand over his shock of platinum-blond hair. "Actually, I believe you. Ever since we fought, I've felt something. Like the air is rumbling. I went to get some takeout, and there was fighting everywhere I looked. I can't explain it."

"Tell me what's on the news."

"Okay." He went to the sideboard to refill his wine. "Apparently the terrorist group, the ISIL, has acquired biological weapons and is threatening to use them on European and American targets. So, the president is calling for a formal declaration of war."

"How soon?"

"It could even happen tonight." Eric shivered. "It's like the whole world has accelerated toward doomsday."

The line was silent for a moment. When Nadia spoke again, her voice cracked wearily. "I've got news for you, too. The muskers—I mean, the cops—they're rounding up Roma all over the place, and there have been riots. I think I understand why now. You and your gay friends might want to watch out."

"My God. Okay, I'll spread the word. Is Angela going to be okay?"

"I wish I knew. All I can do right now is pass on a message."

He set his wine down and massaged his temples. Angela had been secretive for as long as he had known her, so it was not surprising that she was out of reach. But that did not stop him from worrying. "While you're passing messages, please tell her I love her and to be careful. And tell her I wish she'd call me."

"I will do what I can. When she can, I'm sure she'll call you. Please call me if you learn anything new."

They said their goodbyes and hung up. Staring at the images of newscasters imploring, describing, being aghast, he thought about what Angela might say. She would probably talk about the overall societal tension and how everyone would benefit from hypnotherapy. He smiled a little at that, but then his heart sank as he thought about their fight.

"Angela? Be careful," he muttered.

WAR IN HEAVEN: UNDIVIDED

Diamond Angel's Palace, Bald Eagle

A semicircle of warrior-angel battalion leaders was arrayed before Diamond Angel's throne. Each of them blurred momentarily as it traveled to the front to gather information. One of the angels suddenly doubled over and vanished. Another angel took its place. The commander of these battalions stood by her side.

"Report." Diamond Angel stared abstractedly at the commander.

"Shaken Fist has subverted two battalions of our own troops," he replied. "It appears that they are mimicking one of our consolidator weapons quite effectively."

She gestured peremptorily at a flickering, multidimensional map hanging, unsupported, in the air above the center of the room. "Send a new squad to this location. Shaken Fist has not repaired that vulnerability. It might be old, but it's still valuable to us."

The angel blurred into an indistinct, vaguely humanoid blob as he carried out her order.

"We cannot spare the forces to assist Lion or Rooster," she continued. "However, I do not wish to lose contact with them. Double our communication links, and deploy two more of the older squads. The Communist Scare is going to serve once again."

Two more angel commanders blurred, each acquiring a rainbow aura tinged with red. Then their forms stabilized once again. Another angel entered the room and halted respectfully outside the circle.

Diamond Angel signaled to the new arrival. "Security chief. Report."

It saluted. "The security at the Root Hexagon has been breached, ma'am. We have deployed troops to investigate."

She lifted a hand to her chest for a moment. The underworld creature had arrived. "Let it be done," Diamond Angel muttered.

She focused her full attention on her security chief. "When you find interlopers of unknown provenance, bring them to me unharmed. Destroy only confirmed spies from one of our enemies."

The chief saluted. "Yes, ma'am."

It turned smartly and left the room. Diamond Angel returned her attention to her underlings. "Commanders, I will require time alone. You have your battle orders. Execute them, and await further orders."

They saluted and vanished. Diamond Angel leaned, placing an elbow on an arm of her throne, and rested her chin in her hand.

War on Earth

"Our new allies will help us penetrate their defenses. They have..."

—

"They've got better understanding of the enemy. That's..."

—

"You can beat them. Not by being afraid of them..."

—

"With the new threat level, intelligence confirms..."

—

"Knowledge is better than ignorance."

—

"We need to win, no matter..."

—

"Even if it means we..."

—

"We're becoming more..."

—

"We're like them."

Oakland He

Monday, June 9, 2014

ISIL Threatens Nuclear Reta

ISIL leaders have issued threats against U.S. and allied forces in the Middle East, saying they have acquired nuclear capability. Unconfirmed sources state that the likelihood of actual nuclear retaliation is very slim.

Ren foll imp

The

CHAPTER FORTY
THERE'S ONLY US

ROOT HEXAGON, Bald Eagle

The soldiers escorted Angela as she climbed up the sloping wall of the Root Hexagon crater. She slipped a little on the rough scree. As she went, she surreptitiously studied her captors. They were bizarre in appearance and dress and, though winged, bore no resemblance to the angels depicted on earth. The majority of them looked like exaggerated versions of what she, in an uncharitable mood, would have called rednecks. They were all male, for one, with square faces, buzz cuts, and blotchy, sunburned skin. But beyond their physical appearance was an aura that conveyed the impression of racist ignorance.

Arriving at the crater's edge, she gaped. Something like a vast city sprawled to the horizon, but as she stared, she realized that the "buildings" were actually abstract solid forms: cubes, tetrahedrons, spheres, and more elaborate, organic-looking shapes. The colors red, white, and blue predominated, patterned in stripes and stars as well as more exotic forms. The buildings strongly resembled what would happen if an American flag were draped over every part of the architecture. If this were truly a world of memes, the materials used to build this city could have come from that flag.

Corporate logos decorated many of the surfaces, as well, jarring in their incongruity. It was nearly impossible to judge the size of the shapes as there was nothing familiar to compare them with. Everything appeared to be in motion out of the corner of the eye, but the solid forms were stable when stared at directly. She sniffed the air cautiously. The stench of the crater was gone, replaced by a pervasive aroma of fried food, slightly nauseating. The place had a nagging, pervasive sense of wrongness.

Angela and her escort clambered over the lip of the crater. They descended the shallower exterior and proceeded along a street toward a large, extremely ornate building. The three flag colors were everywhere, wound into dizzying patterns that seemed to twist beyond the normal three dimensions.

As she marched, it was almost as if Angela were watching herself in a movie. A peculiar sensation of continuous déjà vu nagged at her, as if time itself were unstable. This reminded her of some of the sensations she had experienced when the Soul Thief had taken her soul. The surrealism of the place was getting on her nerves.

Alongside her, a much taller person whom she believed was the commander of the "angels" watched the sky as they walked. She glanced at the soldier. "You still didn't answer my question. Who are you?"

He returned her look impassively then resumed scanning the sky. "Ma'am. We are your honor guard, assigned to you by Bald Eagle. Ma'am."

"I don't have an honor guard," she snapped. "What is this place, anyway?"

"Bald Eagle, ma'am."

"I thought Bald Eagle was a person." She gestured all around her. "This looks like a city."

The soldier stared at her, and his steps faltered. "Bald Eagle is not a city. It is our master. Your master. Ma'am."

Angela heard a vast sound as if a giant were sighing. She looked all around for its source as her déjà vu intensified. Then she realized what had been bothering her about the "city," and her stomach lurched.

"This place…" She gestured all around her with a shaking hand. "It's alive. And its name is Bald Eagle."

She stopped walking, and the commander and his contingent paused. She took a deep breath, planted her fists on her hips, and stared up at him. "What's your name?"

He saluted. "Ma'am. My name is Sergeant Texas Tea, ma'am."

She choked back laughter. "Texas Tea? What kind of ridiculous name is that?"

"Ma'am?" The expression on his face was solicitous rather than offended.

"Never mind." She refocused her mind on the immediate questions at hand. "Where are we going?"

"I am bringing you to the War Leader." Then the sergeant's head lifted, and he snapped a hand up. The troops went on alert, raising baroque weapons or bare hands that crawled with electrical fire.

A muttering, grumbling voice became audible, coming from a short distance ahead. Around a corner shuffled a robed and cowled figure, and Angela took a sharp breath. Nadia's oversoul? Here? Angela's legs were weak with absurd relief.

The soldiers aimed their weapons, and Angela panicked. "No! Don't fire!"

The sergeant raised his hand again, halting them, though not all lowered their weapons. As the woman neared, Angela noticed the pale fire flickering on her body.

Nadia's oversoul halted, prevented from coming nearer by Angela's escort. She cackled. "Such handsome boys. Such brave boys. And I am an old woman, making you afraid." She peered intently at the sergeant. "Creature. It would be wise of you to stand aside."

Sergeant Tea stared at her, indecision flickering over his face, and Angela could almost hear him weighing the question of whether to attack or not. Angela gestured for him to make way. He stepped aside. The oversoul approached Angela and, from within the folds of her garment, took out a small, rough stone and held it in the palm of her hand.

"What's this?" Angela swayed on her feet with sudden vertigo.

"Take it, dear. Hold it in your hand, and think of your friends."

Angela accepted the stone and clenched it in her right fist. She visualized Cassandra bending over the couch. Was Angela's body here or lying cold and still at Simon's place?

Then images flashed into her mind. Nadia had sent them to Angela through the stone, passing on what was happening on earth. The visions unfolded like vivid memories: Cassandra sat nearby, watching over Angela. Scenes of war in the Middle East scrolled by followed by rioting in Oakland. Police raided members of the gay community as well as Roma.

Finally, a singsong phrase leaped into her consciousness. *Turn, turn, turn away. I will never go astray.*

The stone crumbled into sand in her hand. She dusted off her palm and stared at nothing, caught by old, warm memories of her childhood amongst the Roma. Those reminiscences provided a surge of strength she had not realized she needed. She smiled at the old woman.

"Nadia? That was brilliant."

The woman chuckled. "I am Nadia's oversoul. Now that I'm here..." She peered with sightless eyes all around, brandishing a gap-toothed grin at the soldiers. She cackled and fixed Angela with that blind, disconcerting stare. "I've got a new name. You can call me Crooked Staff."

She poked Angela's sternum with a gnarled finger. "Someone's waiting for you, dear. Best to move along." Her body fuzzed at the edges then shrank as if she were retreating down a long tunnel. She vanished.

Angela noticed that another soldier was conferring with the sergeant.

Sergeant Tea turned to her. "Ma'am." His voice was brusque, his expression grim. "Intel reports that she's a spy from Dark Eyes. Bald Eagle has ordered that she be destroyed. Ma'am."

Angela glared at him. "You hurt her, and you die."

He bristled but then saluted. "Ma'am. The War Leader is waiting."

Entrance to Diamond Angel's Palace, Bald Eagle

Angela and the honor guard approached the ornate entrance to the huge building at the end of the street. Angela's eyes ached when she tried to examine the carvings surrounding the doorway. They swam in and out of focus, but she found that if she relaxed and stopped trying to look closely at them, they stabilized, although something or someone was preventing her from interpreting those markings.

The escort stopped, and the sergeant raised something to his lips. An earsplitting tone filled the air. Angela gasped and clutched her hand to her chest, half doubling over with pain. No one appeared to notice.

The door swung open, and someone pushed her from behind into brilliant white light. It grew in intensity until she could no longer see where she was going or perceive anything around her.

She heard a voice that was muffled as if it were speaking through thick cotton. Her ears were ringing, and she had difficulty breathing. Something explosively popped in her head, and Angela thought for a moment that an eardrum had burst. Reaching up to her ear, though, she found no moisture.

The light began to dim, and the cottony voice became clearer. "Angela Jaelle Cooper." The words made her whole body shake, and unaccountably, she began weeping. The entire world had spoken to her, and she was enclosed by overpowering warmth, no longer alone.

She squinted. A glowing human shape stood before her, supernally brilliant. An impulse deep within urged her to fall to her knees, but a hard kernel born of lifetimes of self-reliance kept her on her feet.

"Are you... are you the War Leader?" The words stuck in her throat, and she choked. The light shifted subtly, and Angela was able to breathe more easily. The form in front of her darkened again so that she could look at it directly without pain.

The voice came again, more bearable in intensity. "I am War Leader for the mighty Bald Eagle. What you know as America. I am the Egregore of your lost people, resurrected by the power of the Root Hexagon. And I am your beloved, whom you know as your oversoul."

Angela could not interpret what she had just heard. The word "oversoul" echoed in her mind. Was she going to have to endure more puzzling oracles from this stranger?

Then the words penetrated the fog in her mind, and Angela fell to her knees. Her own oversoul. The source of all her lifetimes and the one entity that she had never expected to meet while alive. Cradled by omnipresent love, she sobbed uncontrollably. An eon passed while she knelt before her god.

Gradually, a kind of self-awareness returned. She recognized the part of her mind that had become habituated to watching over her thoughts and actions, cultivated by decades of training, first as a chovihani and then as a psychiatrist. She took a shuddering breath and looked up into an infinitely beautiful face. The War Leader, her oversoul, waited patiently. Angela slowly got back to her feet.

"How did this happen?"

Instead of receiving an answer, she found herself remembering the last time she had been in this place, when she'd fought and defeated Iron Star. She recalled the glow she had seen around her body. Her heartbeat thumped loudly in her ears as she made the intuitive leap.

"I beat Iron Star. And you took his place. So all this time I've been fighting...what? The ruler of America?"

Another image arose in her mind. She was suspended over the earth with the North American continent beneath her. There was a vast presence below that reminded her of the experience she had had when her grandfather showed her the Egregore in the Otherworld. She sensed that the presence must be a manifestation of the massed minds of all the inhabitants of the continent. Looking closely, she saw political borders glowing fitfully, demarcating Canada, Mexico, and the United States below. The presence was bounded by the lines drawn around her home country. Then, smoothly, that map bent upward, deforming to enclose her, brightening into featureless white as her senses returned.

Angela laughed bitterly. "Well, that's rich. I don't hate America. I was born there. I only wanted to help a friend with his nightmares. So, why am I fighting you?"

"You have been ignorant. Now you know the truth. My truth."

Her oversoul's rich voice filled Angela's body again, and she felt a sexual warmth in her groin that rapidly grew into an ecstasy that shook her self-control. Desperately, she concentrated on her questions. "What truth? Why am I here?"

The ecstasy rose up from the base of her spine and branched out into all parts of her body. The light around her brightened for a moment, and she almost missed her oversoul's reply.

"Bald Eagle is the Egregore, the entity overshadowing the massed minds of all your countrymen, and this place is Bald Eagle. You have been at war with the oversoul of your nation, so it is no wonder that you were defeated. I have allowed you to come here in order to show you our master."

The ecstasy receded. Angela's awareness surfaced. Like a drowning swimmer, she clung to the ordinariness within her, a life raft for her sanity. "You're very forthcoming with answers. I expected cryptic oracles or worse." She took a breath, brushed her hands down her sides, and lifted her chin. "Well, I've got news for you. I'm not going to stand by while the world is plunged into war." She allowed memories of the vision she'd received from Crooked Staff to fill her mind.

There was silence. Then the air pulsed for a moment, and a wave of anger washed over her.

"Silver Scimitar and his separatist allies, including Dark Eyes, cannot be allowed to win." The voice of the oversoul drummed painfully in Angela's head. "I am the one who attacks them on behalf of Bald Eagle. If I retreat now, they will destroy us all." The voice grew calm once again. "Join with me, and I shall protect those whom you love."

The psychic undertow drew Angela, tempting her to step forward and merge with the form standing before her. Her oversoul represented her highest nature, and she despaired. How could she resist that nature, the source of her being? Yet resist she must, for her oversoul threatened everyone she held dear.

As if in response to her misgivings, the voice spoke somewhat petulantly. "I will show you something you may appreciate."

A shape moved in the endless white. Angela turned to see the massive form of Iron Star stride into view.

Angela gasped. "I killed you!"

Iron Star laughed. Cruelty itself mocked her. "How can you kill an oversoul, Angela Jaelle Cooper? Yes, I know you now, better than you know yourself."

Unlike her oversoul's voice, his grating words triggered no

attraction within her. Instead, she saw Simon in her mind's eye, wheelchair bound, drawn over and over into his nightmare and forced to relive it by this creature. Then she knew. This was his oversoul. Iron Star was the only being who had the power to enforce a compulsion of that nature, no matter how strong Simon's resistance. But this was tragically, sickeningly wrong.

The injustice of what had been done to Simon stiffened her resolve. Despite the overwhelming presence of her own oversoul, she mentally stepped back, adopting a detached, therapeutic attitude. This both strengthened her will and weakened her body. To disobey her oversoul was to risk the loss of all of her inborn gifts and, perhaps, immediate extinction.

Angela decided to play for time until she could find a way to escape. "You are ally to my..." She indicated her oversoul. "To this person. That means you're also my ally, right?"

He nodded his massive head, still smiling. Something was different. Then she realized that his helmet was off, and she was able to see his face. His features strongly resembled Simon's.

"What's going on? Why is all this happening now?" Angela asked.

He shook his head. "You, of all people, should know better than to ask that kind of question of me." His rough voice sounded almost kind. "We speak to you in riddles and oracles so you can find your way and become strong. Be thankful that your oversoul indulges you in this place. I do not."

A vision played before Angela's mind's eye. Her original world was at war with itself. Armies clashed, wielding the terrible psychic technologies of her people. Millions died. And leading the opposition to the government, her government, was the General whom she saw before her. Yet he was different. Smaller. Her heart skipped a beat as she realized that Iron Star was the oversoul of the General from her ancient past, as well.

Simon was the reincarnation of the General, her old enemy. Everything fell into place in her mind: the sense of familiarity with Simon, the strong attraction that Cassandra had for him, and the reason he had addressed Angela as "Lady" in that agonized shout she and Cassandra had first heard, a mystery that had been nagging at her ever since. But why hadn't Iron Star recognized her before?

"I hid myself, and you, from all other oversouls." Her oversoul's response to the unspoken question beat a gentle staccato on Angela's heart. "But it's time now for you to rise to your destiny. You are the last of your people who still remembers the old world. Thanks to you, I live again."

The vision of that ancient war resumed, and as the battle raged, the impression of a powerful Presence came over her. The impression grew in strength, and as it grew, the scene within the vision acquired a deepening reddish hue until her old world glowed with the color of blood.

"Behold the power of the God of Battles." Iron Star's grating voice contained an element of reverence. "He is the Lord of Warfare, who destroys the weak and rewards the strong." With that statement, he replaced his helm on his head and stood at attention.

The awe in Iron Star's voice was incongruous. Yet it made a

bizarre sort of sense that the hierarchy of spiritual beings did not stop at the oversouls or at beings like Bald Eagle.

Angela tried to see Iron Star's face within the shadows of his helm, but all that she could glimpse were his glowing eyes. "Simon is your incarnation on earth. You have tormented him for years now with that nightmare. That's not the act of a loving oversoul."

"He is weak, yet within that weakness he conceals great strength," grated that voice, echoing in the helm. "Behold his strength."

Another vision came to her of the Great Crater with its bubbling pool of noxious liquid in the center where she'd entered this world. Half-submerged in that pool, the great crystal, wrapped with sinuous cables, glowed with sullen power. Like a hellish movie reel, images from Simon's nightmare flashed within it. Those dreams, as well as the dreams of others, trapped within the crystal, gave unholy power to Bald Eagle.

But where did the Root Hexagon come from? Answers to her questions, as always, yielded more riddles. She stared at the powerful form of Iron Star, standing proudly and yet subserviently as any soldier would.

Angela hugged herself, feeling her own strength faltering beneath the intense gaze of her oversoul. "You worship the personification of war and glorify it. Why?"

The light of her oversoul grew brighter as if to answer. But it was Iron Star who spoke in his grating voice:

"In ancient world,

As time unfurled,

Peace did rule,
O'er mortal fools,
Then love was lost,
And light as well.
As darkness fell,
The strong prevailed.
Then arose a traitor fair,
Who led away the people there.
Now is fought the greatest war,
To battle-hone the blade once more."

She considered the oracle. Its meaning unspooled within her mind. The "ancient world" referred to the place of her own origin, before humanity had arrived on earth. The fall of her people beneath the spell of darkness referred to the rise of the one called the Soul Thief. But the "traitor" had to be Angela herself. She'd rescued her people from certain extinction when she opened the way to their new home, and now this was telling her that her act was one of treachery rather than heroism.

Angela shook her head. "I'm not buying it. War's greatest beneficiary is the carrion crow. It destroyed my world and my people. I rescued most of the survivors and brought them to earth..."

She stopped. Another vision intruded upon her awareness. The troops of the American armed forces, as well as airborne support, marched on the Middle East to fight the next world war. Over them, invisible to their eyes, a gigantic Bald Eagle loomed, draped with the colors of the flag. Opposing them was a massed army under a gigantic Silver Scimitar, radiating hatred of the Eagle. The scene was tinged with the same reddish hue she had seen over the world from which she had originally come. That enormous, ancient Presence once again filled her with dread.

"War followed us here," she whispered. "Humanity inherited him from us." Her legs betrayed her once again, and she collapsed, giving in to despair.

Cassandra leaned anxiously over Angela's comatose body. "She's so white. She's not breathing. Simon! Angela's dying." She heard a thump from the direction of Simon's bedroom.

She placed her hands just above Angela's face. Cassandra shivered, feeling the cold radiating from her girlfriend's body, and moaned. "No, no, no no no."

"Call 9-1-1. Now!" Cassandra refused to look away from Angela, whose body could vanish at any moment into worlds of nightmare. Simon's anxious voice could not penetrate her concentration as she reached out with her mind to find her beloved. An aching void lay where she expected to find Angela, but she pushed farther.

—*Angela! Come back!*—

The image of her girlfriend's laughing face brought tears, blurring Cassandra's vision. She refused to let go, to give up. Another image came to her, this one of Nadia, smiling warmly at her grandniece. Cassandra turned her panic-driven strength to reach out to Nadia.

—*Nadia! Help me!*—

At first she got no reply, but then her inner eye opened. Nadia sat in her customary chair in a dark room, her eyes closed. Cassandra's vision closed on Nadia's face. The older woman's eyes opened suddenly, revealing pits of darkness that engulfed Cassandra, and a new vision came to her.

Angela knelt, naked, in a cage made of bones. Blood dripped out of her eyes onto the ground and matted her hair. She wept, great quaking sobs shaking her body, and hugged herself.

All around the cage tangled a sea of decaying bodies dotted with crows and half concealed by thick clouds of flies. The stench sickened Cassandra. A massively armored man stood by the cage, thigh deep in the bodies. He lifted a gigantic hammer high above his head to smash the cage and Angela with it.

"Angela." Nadia's voice echoed and boomed. "Your cage of bones holds your freedom, too. Come home."

Angela knelt in the white brilliance of the palace of her oversoul. A great passivity weighed on her mind and heart. Though she continued to resist the pull of her oversoul, out of habit, it no longer mattered what happened to her, whether dissolution or extinction. Iron Star had departed, unnoticed by her.

For some time now, a childlike rhyme had been repeating in her mind. It tugged at her, though she couldn't remember why. *Turn, turn, turn away. I will never go astray.*

The meaning of the phrase began to penetrate the fog of guilt and despair. Nadia had sent that to her when she had first arrived in the Overworld. Nadia, whose own oversoul, Crooked Staff, had rescued her and guided her for so long, called her back to herself.

Angela's pulse quickened. She'd been there far too long.

There was no appeal to her own highest self, no help for her or the world from that one. She was her own enemy. But staying there would accomplish nothing except her death, resulting in the final erasure of any opposition she might muster, however weak. She would leave Cassandra alone in the world. That thought, more than any other, galvanized her.

She staggered to her feet, closed her eyes, and whispered, "Cassandra. Beloved. Help me."

"You deny me?" The voice was sad. "I am your true beloved."

The orgasmic pull toward the oversoul grew overwhelmingly strong, tempting Angela almost beyond her strength. Such union would have been bliss everlasting and the end of her inner strife. But her love for Cassandra acted like an anchor, holding her fast against the tidal pull. She visualized Cassandra's face and form and the touch of her hand. Her heart began to burn with heat again, and she cried out with the pain.

As if in answer to that cry, there was a crisp snap, like a wineglass stem breaking. A whirling, nauseating dizziness came over her, and she tried to open her eyes. A huge, brightly lit blur swam in her vision, and a sensation as of a mighty vice squeezing her head forced her eyelids shut again.

The weight of passing seconds fell upon her, once more parceling out the moments of her life. She groaned.

Cassandra gasped as Angela groaned and stirred. "Oh God, Angela. You're alive." Bending as far as she could from her chair, Cassandra clasped her beloved tightly.

Angela moved feebly in her embrace. Cassandra looked down as Angela sighed through cracked, red lips. Her eyes were still closed and gummy, and she looked as if she had lain on the couch for days.

"Simon! Can you get her some water?"

"Right away." He wheeled into the kitchen.

"I'm never gonna let you go there alone again," Cassandra whispered, cradling Angela's head.

"Here." Simon handed Cassandra the glass.

She dribbled some onto Angela's mouth. Her darting tongue licked at the moisture, and her eyes fluttered. Cassandra dampened a corner of her shirt to wipe away the crumbs of sleep from Angela's eyes. "Take it easy. You're home."

It took another five minutes before Angela was able to sit up and finish the water. Color had returned to her cheeks, though she still shivered. Cassandra had wrapped her in a blanket that Simon provided, and she sat next to her, holding her hand.

"I nearly didn't come back." Angela's voice was raw.

"We were worried sick. I couldn't reach you or feel you anywhere."

"I think Nadia, or her oversoul, found me there." Angela's pale, lined face was beaded with sweat despite her shivering. "Cassie. I'm lost. There's no hope for me." Angela started weeping quietly as she hunched over herself, her face in her hands.

Cassandra pulled Angela's hand to her heart then kissed her fingers. "Don't say that." She squeezed her shoulders. "You showed me there's always hope."

Angela's voice was slurred with weariness. "Not for me. I met my oversoul. She's also the oversoul of my people. Our original, prehuman people. You have no idea what that was like." She took a shuddering breath. "And she's a servant of something much bigger—the oversoul of our country. America." She lifted her tear-streaked face out of her hands, and her eyes met Cassandra's. "Iron Star is still alive. He's Simon's oversoul."

"No." Simon's voice was flat. "No, I can't accept that."

"I'm sorry, Simon. Really, really sorry." Angela wiped her nose and regarded him. "He was the General in the war that destroyed my world and drove us all here. My partner, the Soul Thief, infected us all with the poison of war, and now we're reliving it in this world."

"What the hell are you talking about?" he asked in that same flat voice.

Angela told him about her and Cassandra's origins in the prehuman world. "But this time, who's going to stop the war? There are no good leaders. There's no Council. There's only us."

CHAPTER FORTY-ONE
ENLIGHTENMENT

Her greatest friend is introduced

To secret lore, and disabused

Of that which formed his old beliefs

And misconceptions so profuse.

"Eric?" Angela paced, phone to her ear.

"Angela, I—"

"I'm not going to close the clinic. That was crazy talk."

He exhaled loudly. "Thank God. I don't know what happened on the phone."

"I think I do, but let's not go into it right now. I just wanted to let you know I'm okay. And I'm really sorry about what happened."

"Hon, I'm coming over," Eric said.

"It's late." Angela shook her head. "Anyway, I'm not at home."

"Angela, look. I know you, and I know there's more going on than you're letting on. Right now, what I bet you need the most is the company of the people who love you."

After a few more minutes of back and forth, Angela invited Eric over to Simon's place for a late-night powwow. He was right. The need to keep her mundane and paranormal worlds separate seemed much less important after what she had gone through.

Simon was in the kitchen making tea and snacks, and

Angela's stomach rumbled in anticipation. Cassandra, exhausted, had gone to sleep in the apartment's only bedroom but had first extracted a promise that Angela would do nothing without waking her.

There was a knock at the door.

"C'mon in," she called out.

Eric opened the door and peered warily at her. "Angela?"

Seeing his hesitation, she got up and walked over to enfold him in a warm hug. "I'm really sorry, Eric."

He gingerly hugged her back. "It's okay," he murmured.

Stepping back, she clasped his upper arms and smiled through her exhaustion. "Make yourself comfortable. Want some tea? There's hot water."

"That'd be great, hon."

"I've got it." Simon came into the room with a tray balanced on his lap. Steam curled from three cups. He looked curiously at Angela's visitor.

Angela gestured. "Simon, this is Eric. Eric, Simon. He's been helping us with our work."

Simon set the tray down on the coffee table and shook hands with Eric. "Glad to finally meet you. Angela's said good things about you." He gestured. "What kind of tea do you want?"

Eric selected a green tea, dunked it in the cup, and sat on the couch with Angela. They looked at each other, and he raised an eyebrow.

"I need to explain some things to you." Angela clasped her hands tightly.

"Okay."

She paused, studying his face. "I'm engaged in a... research project. You may have noticed a strangely belligerent atmosphere all over lately."

He nodded. "Everybody wants to fight. Hell, I pushed a guy at the club the other night. Of course, I was a little drunk, but..."

"That's not like you. Yeah. Look, you know about memetics, right?"

"A little." He sounded hesitant.

She explained what she had learned, skirting the supernatural elements.

Eric nodded. "So there's a meme outbreak. What's your angle? I mean, I know you. You don't just observe. You look for solutions."

"I have no idea how to counter this one. It's pervasive, persuasive, and highly invasive."

"You're a poet! I never knew."

Angela shuddered, unable for a moment to match his humor. She reached out to touch his shoulder. "Sorry, man. I'm having trouble laughing right now." She paused. "I just don't have any idea where to start. I've crafted a few memes, but nothing like the kind of thing that could help stop this roller-coaster ride to hell."

Simon chimed in. "It's not like we haven't been at war for the last two hundred years. Did you know that there's a statue of Ares in DC? We're in the habit of worshipping the god of battles."

Angela looked at him. "What did you say?"

Simon raised his hand. "I only said that the good old USA is used to fighting war."

"I mean, what did you call Ares? God of Battles?"

"Yeah. That's what I call him, anyway." He set his spoon down and scratched his face reflectively

Angela thought back on what Iron Star had said to her. "He was talking about Ares."

"Who?" Eric's face was wrinkled in a frown.

"Never mind. How can you win a battle against the god of war?"

Eric lifted an eyebrow. "Simple. With love."

Simon grunted. He stared at Eric then nodded.

Angela looked at Eric. "What do you mean?"

Eric continued. "In the old myths, Ares had an ongoing affair with the goddess of love, Aphrodite. She could stop his rampage with a smile and a beckoning finger." At Angela's wondering look, he grinned. "Remember? I wrote my doctoral thesis on the Jungian archetypes governing relationships."

"She was his lover, not his wife," Simon muttered.

Eric glanced at him. "Go on."

Simon shrugged and explained his pagan leanings. "Ares is my patron, but Aphrodite was highly regarded by the Greeks. She is said to be older than all other gods in the pantheon. She is fickle, though."

Angela felt puzzle pieces slide neatly into place. It was a stretch to think of the gods as independent of human consciousness. However, they were, at a minimum, super meme-plexes of great importance. She had no doubt that the old stories gave clues about the nature of those great patterns of thought.

"Aphrodite. I wonder." She met Simon's steady gaze. "That might be what I need. To create or evoke a meme related to Aphrodite."

Eric leaned back. "Okay. How's that going to help, really? We're already about to go to war. A pretty slogan's not going to get us anywhere."

"She's talking about going to the source of love," Simon said. "Getting help from... her." Seeing the look of puzzlement on Eric's face, he glanced at Angela. "You might want to explain this to your friend."

Angela swallowed, her throat dry. It was time to open up to her best friend. But how much could she tell him? She had always cherished his normalcy as an anchor in her otherwise bizarre world.

With a small shake of her head, she looked Eric in the eyes. "There's something I've never told you, Eric." She paused. Where should she start? Looking down at her hands, she continued. "I have a... talent. Something I've been able to do since I was a teenager." A movement caught her eye, and she glanced up.

Cassandra was sitting in her chair quietly by the bedroom doorway, watching their interplay. She shook her head. "Angela, you're stalling. He deserves to know what you're talking about."

Angela glared at her. "Dammit, I know that." Then she stopped, blinking. "Cassie? I'm sorry. And I'm getting tired of apologizing."

Cassandra grinned wanly. "It's okay. I'm tired of being apologized at."

"So, you have a talent," Eric said. "You've got lots of talents. Dancing, drinking whiskey..."

She shook her head. "This is different. It's hard to explain. Eric, I'm a psychic healer." She continued talking rapidly, seeing his incredulity. "Seriously. I can go into people's minds and heal them. All I have to do is touch someone's forehead, and then I'm inside their mind. I've done it for you a bunch of times."

Eric put a hand up. "No, don't start this now, please. I've had a really hard day. Can we play some other time?"

"All right. I'll have to demonstrate. Eric, I want to prove it to you. Lean back on the sofa."

He stared at her for a moment then did as she instructed. Angela reached out and touched his forehead.

Half an hour later, Eric struggled to a seated position on the couch, his face smoothed by wonder. "Angela. I..." He stopped, swallowed, and shook his head.

She raised her finger to her lips. "Shhh. It's okay. I'm glad you were able to come to that place, too." She stood by the couch, having returned from his meadow just a moment before. Angela took a deep breath, feeling her reserves draining away. She could just lie down and catch up on her sleep. But there was no time. Instead, she rolled her shoulders back a couple of times and stretched.

He swallowed again, his Adam's apple bobbing. Angela winced, seeing his wide-eyed stare. She did not need awe at that moment. She needed her friend.

"Eric, at the hospital last year, I was nearly killed by a

creature, a thing, that lived in that place. The place I call the Otherworld. That's what drove so many people insane, and that's what killed George." She sat next to him. "In the end, Cassie helped me to destroy my enemy."

Cassandra nodded. "We called him the Soul Thief. He was riding me hard when I got there, but he was really after Angela —used me as bait, but she rescued me, and we kicked his sorry ass."

Eric passed a hand over his face then slicked back his shock of hair. "We all thought you were kind of eccentric, but when you saved the hospital everyone chalked it up to genius. But now it makes sense. You. Cassie. What happened to Josef. Even me." His eyes widened. "Wait a minute. Is that what this is all about? Are you telling me that something like that is happening in that Otherworld place?"

Angela nodded and told him about Iron Star.

Eric was pale. "Was he behind the bombing at the clinic?"

"Yep." She examined him closely. Was he going into shock? On an impulse, Angela leaned over and pulled Eric into a hug. He held onto her tightly. She squeezed his shoulders and continued, speaking more softly. "Eric? Something happened to me, and now I'm the one doing Iron Star's job."

"My God," he said, his voice muffled by her shoulder. They held each other for a moment longer then disengaged and sat back, sighing simultaneously. Angela laughed, feeling some of her tension evaporate.

"You know, with that ability, you could change the world." Eric shook his head. "It's every therapist's dream to be able to just reach in and fix what's broken. And you can do it. Why keep it a secret?"

"Angela would be disappeared by the government"—
Cassandra snapped her fingers—"just like that. Right?"

Angela nodded. "But that's not the main reason. I want to be
a healer. I can't do that if I've got all this notoriety. That's why I
pretend to do hypnotherapy. And besides..." She stopped. She
realized she still wasn't ready to explain her past life. Lives.

"Besides?"

"Never mind. So now you know."

Eric wiped a tear from the corner of his eye. "Yeah. And now
I understand. So, how can I help?"

Angela smiled with relief. "I don't know yet, but just having
you in my confidence helps a hell of a lot."

Simon cleared his throat, breaking his silence since Angela's
return. "I hate to say it, but we can't just go up to Aphrodite
and say 'Hi, can you help us fight your lover?' Besides, some of
the old stories indicate that she was also a war goddess long
before the other Greek gods showed up. She might want things
to stay the way they are."

"I think it's worth a shot." Angela sat forward, elbows on her
knees. "But we don't have enough information." She put her
chin on her fist, remembering the lessons she had learned
from George about the higher worlds.

WAR IN HEAVEN: FLYING UNTO WAR

Diamond Angel's Palace, Bald Eagle

Diamond Angel was seated on her throne. Her chin was on her fist, and she stared into the distance. Neither Iron Star nor her adjutant was present. Iron Star fought on her behalf at the front; her adjutant had been sent to serve him.

The air flexed, and there was a monstrous sigh. Then a rumbling resolved into words. "War Leader, why do you conceal yourself from me?"

Diamond Angel looked up from her contemplation and straightened in her chair. "My Lord. I do not conceal anything from you."

"I cannot see into your secret self. There is a darkness in your heart. Open that place that I may plumb your secrets."

Diamond Angel grasped the arms of the chair tightly. She bowed her head.

A moment passed before Bald Eagle spoke again. "You are divided. That part of you that you sent to the Underworld moves against your will. Why do you allow this?"

She lifted her head. "My Lord, I have fought to overcome this flaw, yet it eludes me."

"Join with me. Come into me that I may purge you of this division and bring that darkness into the light."

Diamond Angel drew a breath, held it, then released it. "I cannot, my Lord."

There was silence. Then the air rumbled again.

"This is the work of Serpent Lion and Dark Eyes. War

Leader, you shall remain here while I attend to them personally. I shall then consider whether to offer Iron Star your position."

Diamond Angel lowered her head. The air became still, and darkness descended.

Somewhere near the Border of Bald Eagle

Three angels, caparisoned for war, materialized in an open area between gigantic, multicolored facades scrawled with slogans. There was a muted rumble of thunder, and a swirling cloud appeared in the near distance, heralding the opening of a portal leading into the realm of Serpent Lion. They began running, accelerating as they went, and leaped into it. Another three appeared as an additional portal opened into Dark Eyes, and they vanished into it.

Serpent Lion's Palace

The first wave of attackers from Bald Eagle was not entirely unexpected, but the ferocity with which they fought was almost overwhelming. Angel after angel was destroyed, even as Serpent Lion herself took the field. One of the attacking angels, a powerful winged man with the head of a hawk, tore through the ranks of the defenders, wielding a shining sword.

Serpent Lion engaged that one, parrying devastating blows, which left steaming rents in the ground. The Egregore was driven back almost to the walls of the palace before rallying. The thought crossed her mind that this hawk-headed angel was an avatar of Bald Eagle himself, something which few had seen lately.

Feinting with the short spear, Serpent Lion drove her shield against the angel's unprotected side, getting inside the radius of his attack. The angel staggered, and Serpent Lion took advantage of the resulting opening to drive the spear deep into his side. He screamed a high-pitched eagle's screech, and then, with a series of small explosions, he disintegrated into random debris.

The rest of the attackers, driven off by the palace defenders, disappeared in the direction of Bald Eagle's realm.

Turning to an adjutant, Serpent Lion gestured at the killing field. "Organize a cleanup party, and salvage any information you can about this attack. Bald Eagle may simply be reacting to our subversion of his War Leader, but I want to be sure there is no other reason for the ferocity of this assault."

The adjutant nodded and left to supervise. Serpent Lion stood motionless for a while, sadly contemplating the wreckage of the battlefield, then turned and went back inside to rest and to plan better defenses.

War on Earth

"God hates fags! You're all going to hell! Go..."

—

"Leave us alone. All you've got is hate..."

—

"God loves everyone, no matter..."

—

"Says so right here in the..."

—

"Go home. Leave..."

—

"... us alone."

Office hallway, Oakland

"Did you hear about the gay guy who got beaten to death in Alabama?" The office worker sipped his coffee.

"Yeah. The Bible-thumpers are going nuts. What about that preacher, huh?"

"Guys like that oughta be locked up for stirring up the crazies."

CHAPTER FORTY-TWO
LOOKING FOR LOVE

So heartened is she by this act

That boldly does she then enact

A plan to storm the gates of Love

To rid herself of hellish pact.

SITTING WITH her chin on her fist, Angela felt the room swim, as if there had been a minor earthquake. She looked at the others, and it seemed as if a wall of glass had arisen between her and them so that she could not feel their presence. They watched her, silently expectant, and she was at a loss.

Cassandra must have seen something in Angela's expression because she half-rose from her chair then winced and sat back down. "Are you okay?"

"I think I'm just tired. I've been overdoing the whole Otherworld bit." Angela sighed and stared at her hands in an attempt to ground herself. "Maybe the best thing right now for us all is to get some rest."

She looked at Eric. "Now that you know what's going on, can you give it some thought? I put a hold on all my appointments till I could sort out what's happened to me, but you shouldn't have to stop working. Still, if you have any more insights I'd really love to hear them."

Eric nodded. "Sure thing." He glanced at Cassandra. "Why don't you two stay at my place? I can give you a lift in the

Cruiser. I don't think Angela should drive right now."

Cassandra nodded.

He looked at Angela. "Are you parked legally?"

"Yeah, I'm in the lot across the street."

Cassandra glanced at Simon. "You okay with this?"

"If you mean, will I be okay with my usual nightmare, the answer is yes, I'll be fine. Just let me know what to do, and I'll do it."

Angela and Cassandra left with Eric, discussing their plan of attack fruitlessly on the way to his place. When they arrived, they turned in for the night on Eric's sofa bed.

Within minutes, Cassandra was snoring, but Angela could not get to sleep. Despite her exhaustion, her mind kept spinning around her questions. She had to get some answers, and it was far too late to call Nadia to ask her for advice. The only other option was to make yet another excursion into the Otherworld even though it was dangerously draining.

Lying on her back, the blanket safely tucked between her and Cassandra, Angela pressed her fingers to her own forehead then her breastbone. Her head spun, the walls of Eric's living room dissolved, and she squinted in sudden daylight as she stood in her Otherworld meadow.

She walked to her cabin, decorated now with the furnishings of war, and retrieved her spear. Picking a random forest path, Angela started walking.

"Nana. Nadia. Help me," she muttered as she picked her way along the path. Her presence in the forest, bringing as it did the daylight of conscious awareness, would attract attention to her. She hoped it would be friendly attention.

She continued walking, seeing only the usual anonymous rustlings in the undergrowth. An interminable while later, the trail opened up into the ocean-side clearing. She climbed the bluff toward the cliff edge above the ocean far below. Upon reaching the highest point, she leaned on her spear and looked out over the ocean. Not for the first time, she speculated on what she would find beyond the reaches of the deep unconscious, for which the ocean was the analog in this place.

"I wonder what's out there," she muttered.

"Other peoples, other lands."

Angela whirled, her spear ready. Nadia's oversoul, Crooked Staff, stood by her side. Angela smiled in relief and lowered her spear. "I'm so glad to see you."

Crooked Staff peered dubiously at her, that disconcerting blind gaze at once penetrating and depthless. "You look very angry. Will you strike an old, defenseless woman?"

Angela raised an empty hand, palm up. "Never. Please look past the stain of war. I need your help."

The woman peered more closely then nodded in satisfaction. "I can see a warlike crown upon your head. But you wear it unwillingly. Be careful, dear. That crown is very expensive."

Angela resisted the urge to reach up to her head. "Please. Can you tell me how to find Aphrodite?"

Crooked Staff jumped, her eyes wide. The oversoul raised a finger to her lips. "You should know better than to speak her name in your condition. She could strike you down where you stand."

Angela's mind reeled. "So, she is real!"

"Real? You throw that word around freely, child. You don't know what 'real' means."

Angela placed her spear on the grass and sat cross-legged, a pupil before her teacher. "You're right. I don't know what's real. I don't know what to do, either, but I need to find an ally, someone who can remove this stain of war before it infects the whole world. I think I need to find Love."

"Love is love, dear." Crooked Staff cackled, not unkindly. "You have love in your life. She is right there. Or have you forgotten already?"

"In my, as you put it, present condition, I'm afraid love is nowhere near me." Angela studied her own hands, unwilling to meet the woman's eyes. She was afraid all she would get from Crooked Staff would be more of her cryptic oracles, and that would be that.

"Nonsense. Take off that crown, and love will reveal herself to you."

"I wish I could. My oversoul is bound to war. To... him."

"As you say." Crooked Staff nodded curtly, turned, and started walking away.

Angela's heart sank. She jumped to her feet. "Wait! Please. How do I find the lady of love?"

"You know the road to war." She spoke without looking back. "The path to love runs right alongside it. But you need to send love to meet love."

Crooked Staff faded into the forest.

The sound of dishes clinking from the kitchen forced Angela awake. For a moment, she forgot where she was, seeing light streaming in through unfamiliar windows, but then memory returned. She was in Eric's living room. She got up from bed when she noticed that Cassandra's wheelchair was gone.

"Cassie?"

"Yeah," Cassandra replied, poking her head around the corner. "I made tea."

Angela and Cassandra sat in Eric's dining nook, drinking tea in the early-morning light, and puzzled over Crooked Staff's cryptic utterances from the night before.

"I feel like I'm endangering Simon now." Angela sighed. "He's haunted by his oversoul, who's drawing power from him as if he were some kind of battery. My presence seems to strengthen Iron Star and weaken Simon."

Cassandra frowned. "I don't know any other way to do this. He's the only one who can help you get into Bald Eagle. I don't know how to have a lucid dream."

"Yeah. Me neither." Angela sipped noisily. She thought about Simon's anguished face. "When all of this is over, and he's finally free, I want to invite him to the cabin. I think he could use some peace and quiet."

Cassandra rolled over to the fridge. Opening it awkwardly, she peered in and rummaged among the boxes of leftovers. "I'm starving. Aren't you hungry?"

Instead of answering, Angela picked up the remote and turned on the TV. Muting the sound, she switched to a news channel. A grim-faced anchorwoman spoke, and the scene cut to stock footage of a jet taking off from an aircraft carrier. The scrolling ticker at the bottom of the screen read, "War in the Middle East."

"Crap. Cassie? There's no time for food!" Then Angela raised an open hand. "Sorry," she said more quietly. Cassandra did not reply but continued rummaging.

Retrieving a bag with a flourish, Cassandra looked over her shoulder at Angela. "Eat something." She handed back a cold croissant and took out a glazed donut for herself. Glancing at the TV, she frowned but said nothing.

Angela drummed her fingers on the table. "Eric had a really good idea. The way I see it, we've got to find the entity that governs love. Call her Aphrodite. But from what I learned from my oversoul, there's a hierarchy to these beings."

"Makes sense. Like a manager running the store, she would have departments working for her. So there must be a department we can reach."

Angela nodded. "Well, we are lesbians. Maybe there's a department in charge of women who love each other."

"Yeah." Cassandra licked her fingers. "So what do you think Nadia's oversoul meant?"

Angela took a bite then set the croissant down. It tasted like cardboard, and she had no appetite for it. "You know, the way I get to war is through one of those soldiers. They embody fighting, conflict. What we need is somebody, something, that is made out of love."

She looked up. "Cassie? I can't talk to Aphrodite."

"What do you mean?"

"Nadia's oversoul said that in my condition, even speaking the name of the goddess might earn a thunderbolt or something. If I try to talk to her, she'll kill me." Angela's mind began to spin. She dredged her memories of her previous life in the old world, but nothing in that ancient wisdom had prepared her for trying to contact Aphrodite.

Cassandra sat in her chair, rolling a few inches forward and then reversing. Back and forth, jittering. She refused to meet Angela's eyes.

She stopped fidgeting, her back to Angela. "I'll go."

"God, no." Angela's voice cracked. "No fucking way, Cassie. What if we end up stuck in that war zone? Iron Star's already nearly killed you twice. What're you thinking?"

Cassandra turned her head. "It's either that or we all die in a nuclear war. I have to go, and I have to talk to Aphrodite."

Angela stuck her arms out straight, pushing against the dining table, and tried to control the shaking in her limbs. She took a deep breath, held it, and let it out. This was the woman she loved, and one of the very few people in the world who knew her story and loved her for who she was. There was no way she could risk losing Cassandra again. There had to be another way.

"Angela, I know what you're thinking."

She looked up with blurred vision and had to dry her face on a sleeve. Cassandra's eyes were so large, so beautiful. Angela even loved the tiny vertical crease in her forehead between them. Her mouth, often compressed these days in a firm line, had opened just a little bit.

Not trusting herself to speak, Angela nodded.

"I'm sorry, but I picked something out of your mind just now. The oversoul, Crooked Staff, said something else, didn't she?" Cassandra rolled her chair closer and laid a hand against Angela's face. "She said you need to send love to meet love."

Cassandra was right, but that made it no easier for Angela to accept. "Why does it have to be you?"

"Because," Cassandra said, a sudden grin on her face, "it's my turn to step up. You've been the hero all your life. I think the gods, whoever or whatever they are, want me to do this. And listen." Her tone deepened into earnestness. "I'm not going to jump on Iron Star's back, I'm not going to pick up a gun. I am going to make hot, sweet love to you right there on that battlefield under that alien sky, and I am going to find that goddess and ask her for help."

There was a cool tingling at the base of Angela's spine. Her inner, wiser voice spoke. *This is right. Listen to her for once. She's been through the fire.* Angela looked down again to avoid that dark-eyed stare of the one person in the world she wanted far away from the Otherworld. But Crooked Staff, the Wise Old Woman—Nadia's oversoul—had never led Angela wrong before. It was time to let go of fear.

She looked up and caught Cassandra studying her. "Okay. Just for the sake of argument, you go without me. So how do you propose to get there?"

"I don't know. I was hoping you'd figure out a way." Cassandra bit her lip. "She said the roads to love and war run the same way. Maybe she meant that you could use the battlefield to start. I still don't understand how you do what you do."

Angela searched for a way to describe the inexplicable. "Cassie, it's kind of hard to explain. See, the forehead touching is like a... a keyword, a mnemonic. In my previous lives, I worked hard to get to this point. My natural talent is the ability to assemble new realities. This physical world," she tapped the table, "is one reality. I can shift my consciousness and experience a completely different one. But unless I have some sort of link, some kind of meaningful connection to guide me, I'd just end up wandering all over the place. I've done that, too, by the way.

"So my previous self developed several techniques for walking into different worlds. It just so happens that her favorite one involved walking to a world that corresponds to the minds of living people. She called it the Forest of Souls. And she took all the complicated mental gymnastics needed to get there and compressed all that into the forehead-touching gesture, which I've inherited."

Cassandra nodded. "Okay. So, what happens when you touch a soldier in Simon's dream world?"

"Well, all I've got is a guess." Angela sat forward. "When Iron Star took you with him, I was running on pure instinct. Later, I figured that I could follow him because that soldier was an extension of his will. That's why they all looked so robotic. Touching the forehead of one of those robots gave me the link I needed to assemble the world Iron Star went back to." A thought was taking shape in her mind, a way to get to the realm or dream world of Love. But Cassandra beat her to it.

"Maybe we go to that battlefield, but instead of you touching one of them, you and I make out, and you touch me."

Angela stared at her. "Cassie, that's brilliant. Sex as the doorway to love."

Cassandra grinned. "I got that out of your head, gorgeous." Her smile faded. "But can you send me alone?"

"Yeah. I learned how to do that in my other life. I sent all the survivors from the Great War here. It was a long time ago, though. The important thing is that you be the one to talk to Aphrodite." Angela got out her cell phone. "At any rate, we need Simon's help to get there. To the dreamland."

"Why can't we just do it in the meadow? Start there and then go on?"

Angela hesitated. "I tried something like that. When I was a kid I was in an experimental mood. Granddad was teaching me in his meadow. I touched his forehead to see if there was somewhere else to explore. Nothing happened, and I figured it was because we were already in his head. This battlefield isn't in your head or mine. It belongs to Simon's dreams, so I think we're both free to use it to launch into other places." She selected Simon from the contact list on her phone. "At any rate, this dreamland place where Simon goes is different than the meadow." The phone rang, and there was a click. "Simon?"

"Yeah." His voice sounded tired.

"Hey, I hope I didn't wake you."

"Naw. I couldn't sleep."

"Okay. I really hate to ask, but do you mind if we tag along in your dream?"

"So, you're going to do it? What's the plan?"

Angela explained what she had learned from Nadia's oversoul and what they had decided to do.

"I don't know why I didn't think of that. I use my altar and fill my mind with thoughts of courage when I invoke Ares. Those are his tokens, his symbols. That's what I learned in my group." He paused. "Hate to tell you, but there's a big hole in your plan. When did Cassie learn how to get out of her body without morphine?"

Angela's heart sank. "Oh crap. You're right." She glanced at Cassandra.

"We're not dead yet," Simon said. "Let me talk to her."

"Cassie? Simon wants to talk to you." Angela handed the phone over.

"Hey." Cassandra smiled broadly. Then her smile faded as she listened. "Shit. Well, I never learned how. I mean, I got out under morphine, but..." She paused. "No, not really." There was a longer pause. "Okay, like I'm rocking in a swing. Got it."

At Angela's lifted eyebrow, Cassandra gave her a thumbs-up gesture. "By something in me, you mean like energy or something? No?" Another pause. "Okay. Makes sense. I hope so. Thanks, Simon. See you there. Here's Angela." She handed the phone back to Angela.

"Hey."

"Listen, I told Cassie what I do to get out. But I think you need something else to make sure you get where you need to go. Otherwise, you might just end up in some sort of astral porno."

Angela giggled, despite herself, at the ridiculous image this evoked. "Yeah. So, what's your idea?"

He cleared his throat. "Something I used to study, before I got injured. Ever heard of tantric sex?"

"Who hasn't? We live in California, remember?"

"Yeah. So, when you two have sex, you need to try to visualize Aphrodite and hold that until you climax. I don't know how your talent works, but it seems to me that you always need some kind of connection to where you're going.

Right?"

"That's what Cassie and I were just talking about. Exactly."

"Cool. So, that's my idea. Give me half an hour or so before Cassie tries to get into my nightmare, okay? I slept like crap, but I'm too keyed up now to sleep, so I'm going to take tranquilizers."

"Okay. Thanks a million, Simon." She hung up, and she and Cassandra exchanged stares.

They heard a polite cough and turned. Eric stood in the hallway that led to his bedroom. He wore boxers and a bathrobe, and he rubbed his face sleepily. "Hey, you two. I heard some noise and forgot you were here. Can I get you something?"

Angela smiled. "No, that's okay. We were just planning our strategy."

"Okay. You know, I thought I was having one of my nightmares." He turned to go back to his bedroom. "I'm going to get a little more shut-eye."

Cassandra looked at Eric then at Angela. "What's he talking about?"

"I'll tell you later." On an obscure whim, she called out, "Eric?"

He turned back around. "Yeah?"

"If you have a nightmare again, can you tell the good guys I need their help?"

"Sure thing, hon."

Angela contemplated the contrast between the coolness of her exposed, sweat-dewed skin and the warmth under the sheets on the sofa bed. She lay in a calm, empty trance, resting next to Cassandra. Part of Simon's instructions had included using the energy raised by sex to put Cassandra in the state needed to get out of her body.

Their extraordinary tension had exploded into furtive, feverish, but somewhat awkward lovemaking as they maneuvered around Cassandra's cast. Angela savored the present moment. As soon as her mind returned to Cassandra, however, all of her worries returned in a rush. Her heart sank as she thought of what would come next.

Cassandra stirred next to her and groped for Angela's hand. Angela twined their fingers together. "Cassie? Are you ready? Is Simon dreaming?"

Cassandra groaned and turned her face to the air with a sigh. "Yeah. I sure could use a smoke right now." She pushed her damp hair out of her eyes and peered at Angela. "Let's go."

Angela nodded.

Cassandra lay back, closing her eyes, her forehead wrinkled.

Taking the cue, Angela lay back, as well. She cleared her mind, relying on Cassandra's extraordinary gift to open the way.

Soon the familiar flashes of vision occurred, and then suddenly, Angela was jolted by megaphone-amplified shouts and flashing lights. Stark in their clarity amidst the dreamlike, shifting scenery, the chaotic sights and sounds threatened to break her concentration, but she kept her focus. She hunted for her girlfriend in the chilly, noisy darkness.

Angela nearly collapsed with relief upon finding Cassandra, and beckoned to her. They only had moments to use what

Simon called "sex magic" to get to the Overworld.

Taking Cassandra's hand, Angela found a patch of level ground nearby, drew Cassandra to her, and cradled her face in one hand as they kissed. The dry earth scratched at her exposed skin while the cool desert breeze cut through her thin clothes like a knife. Angela had made love in more challenging places, though. Remembering Simon's suggestion, she visualized the classical form of Aphrodite.

Angela ran her fingers up Cassandra's spine and twined her legs between those of her partner. They thrust against each other as they kissed. Angela nuzzled Cassandra behind her ear, breath quickening. However, the sound of shouting tore through Angela's mood and broke her concentration, and she shook her head with irritation.

Cassandra put her finger to Angela's lips when she tried to speak. "We only have a couple of minutes."

"I know."

They fumbled with each other's bodies, groping for passion, but Angela could not relax. Every shout and every stamp of boots shocked through her body.

"A battlefield doesn't exactly turn me on," she said, disengaging from Cassandra. "Dammit."

She leaned on one elbow and looked around her at the hurrying shapes of the dream-world soldiers. Failure now would only make successive tries more difficult, and time was running out in the real world.

Cassandra touched Angela's chin, turning her face tenderly. Angela found herself looking into those dark eyes, and her tension began to melt as she lost herself in them. Cassandra's lips parted, and Angela felt a whisper of breath. Then they kissed, long and deeply, enough to send an electric shock down her spine and into her suddenly weakened legs as she fell back. This was the answer. Not simple physical desire but a transcendent lust for union here in the heart of war's nightmare.

They began making love in earnest. The sounds of shouting and gunfire filled the air. A roaring engine rapidly approached, and their rhythm accelerated with it. Angela pressed her body against Cassandra's, her fingers stroking and massaging, sensitive to her partner's longing for release. Cassandra ran fingers down to cup Angela's thighs and pulled convulsively, rocking her hips and crooning softly. Every movement brought an electrical impulse that stole Angela's breath and blazed in the darkness behind her closed eyes.

Cassandra's breath caught, and she cried out. She began keening softly, her voice rising in volume and pitch as she came. Angela rode the wave of ecstasy up her own spine, the image of Aphrodite shining before her inner eye. She managed to retain enough presence of mind to raise her damp fingers and touch Cassandra's forehead at the peak of orgasm.

As the world whirled away from them both, Simon's anguished scream distorted and faded away into nothing.

WAR IN HEAVEN: DARK EYES LOSES

REALM OF Dark Eyes

Dark Eyes surveyed the battlefield, rage building inside him. Many of his angels were dead, but more devastating to him was the destruction of the border Guardian whose form had been modeled after the oversoul of his wisest servant, Nadia. The Guardian had exploded when the hawk-headed angel, which he suspected was an avatar of Bald Eagle himself, thrust his sword through her defensive perimeter. The blast destroyed part of the Forest and killed many angels. Dark Eyes himself was wounded in that great fight.

As he began the difficult task of finding survivors and cleaning up the debris, he planned his counter-strike. A frontal assault on Bald Eagle would be far more difficult with Diamond Angel as War Leader. He would rely on his natural talents of trickery and stealth instead. Fortunately, his spies had brought him useful information concerning the keystone within the Root Hexagon. What was his name? Simon? The spies showed him what bound Simon to the Root Hexagon. Dark Eyes would find a way to release that binding and destroy the power of the Root Hexagon forever. Perhaps that wily old nomad, Crooked Staff, would be able to help.

War on Earth

"They put the evil eye on you. Yep. Happened to my cousin..."

—

"I heard she died. Seemed she had the clap, real bad..."

—

"I said, don't touch that filthy animal. But..."

—

"Now look at them! Call the police, Bill..."

—

"They have to go. Stealing..."

—

"Filthy animals."

Nadia's house, Oakland

"You can't do this!" Michael shouted at the departing policeman. "She is sick and needs me to care for her." He lunged, but one of the other officers grappled him and held him.

"I'm sorry, sir. We got a report that she's an illegal."

Michael struggled. "That's insane! We've lived here forty years. Why aren't you taking me, too?" He shook himself loose.

"This is a question for immigration, sir. You've got the number on the card I gave you." The officer turned to leave.

Michael watched as Nadia was led to a patrol car and put in the back seat while the immigration officer got in the front.

"Nadia!" All at once the fight went out of him, and he sagged against the policeman. He was led back into the house, where he collapsed into his chair and put his head in his hands.

CHAPTER FORTY-THREE
SERPENT LION

THEY RETURNED to awareness, swimming out of the haze of sensory overload. Cassandra's mind was edged with panic, and Angela reached out with her world-walking talent to help her girlfriend adjust to this place, wherever it was.

The world was vast, elegant softness. The light was dim, and the air throbbed with a rhythm that echoed the aftermath of their lovemaking. A musky scent, magnifying the aroma of their own cooling bodies, filled her nostrils. Cassandra and Angela were face to face, almost touching. Then a movement past Cassandra's shoulder brought everything into focus. They were lying on cushions.

They both sat up and looked around. At first, all Angela could think was that a tornado had struck an oriental carpet factory. There were rich, vibrant colors in endlessly intricate designs all around her, confusing her depth perception. She concentrated, trying to make sense of what she saw. Finally, she succeeded.

She was in a large room, crowded with hangings, lit with lamps, floor piled high with cushions on embroidered rugs. Many of the cushions moved. No, they weren't cushions. Angela and Cassandra were surrounded by women making love to each other. That sight, coupled with the aroma, sent a shiver up and down her spine.

Angela glanced sidelong at Cassandra, whose eyes were wide and whose cheeks were flushed. Her girlfriend leaned over to kiss her, but Angela raised a gentle hand. "It's tempting. I know.

But we've got something to do."

Cassandra's mouth closed, but then she nodded, smiling. "Yeah." Her smile faded as her forehead creased. "Angela? Should you be here?"

The floor shook. There was a massive rumbling, and the air echoed with a muffled shriek. Angela clutched her chest. "Ow! Shit. The stain of war." She sighed, crushed with the weight of disappointment. "Cassie, I have to go back, but I don't know how."

Cassandra put a hand on Angela's shoulder, her chin trembling. "I think it's going to happen anyway."

There was a bright flash of light and then another. The world around Angela dissolved, and all of the rich variety of color in the gigantic boudoir was replaced with the rust-red, stained-white, and dingy-blue of Bald Eagle. Rather than ending up on Eric's sofa bed as she had expected, she lay on the debris-strewn crater floor.

"Dammit!" She choked back the stabbing sensation in her chest with a sob. Then she looked up into the troubled sky. "Cassie, Goddess go with you."

With a clatter, several soldiers who had been standing guard rushed forward to surround her. She pushed herself to her feet, recognizing Sergeant Texas Tea among them. He stood aside, gesturing toward the lip of the crater. Without a word, she climbed up with her escort to meet her destiny.

The soldier angels led Angela to the entrance to Diamond Angel's palace. They formed rank on either side and snapped to attention. The door began to swing open, and the same brilliant, hard-edged light glared from beyond it. Angela was unable to resist the tidal urge to join with her oversoul, and she sobbed, but her despair was quickly overwhelmed by the intensely sexual impulse that dragged her into that light.

Her face began to tingle as she neared the source of that light. That same soul-shaking voice became audible again as if it had been speaking all along and her ears had only now adjusted to it. "This is peace, joy, and fulfillment. Come to me."

Angela gave herself to the movement. The compulsion was like and unlike that used by the Soul Thief when he had sought to absorb her mind. He was flawed, corrupted, whereas this was an experience of awakening, of remembering. As she moved closer, her body frayed away from her perception, and her sense of identity expanded. The little "i" that had been Angela Cooper dwindled within her larger self.

Finally, she stopped moving. For a moment, she wondered what was to happen next, but then she realized it had already happened. The memories, visions, and wisdom of her oversoul were now her own. Diamond Angel felt full, rested, and complete.

Turning in place, she surveyed her surroundings. The blinding light was gone, as if it had never been. Diamond Angel went to her throne and mounted it. She scanned the ranks of angels with satisfaction. Within her, she felt the core that had been Angela Cooper, but she decided not to consolidate that identity. That incarnation had not, after all, been terminated, and there was more for Dr. Cooper to do on earth. But now their goals were aligned, and the destiny that she had held in trust for the doctor would become a conscious part of her work.

She addressed the angels. "You may leave me now. I will commune with Bald Eagle."

The soldiers saluted her and marched out of the room. Diamond Angel closed her eyes and sought that place within her that linked her to the great Egregore.

A vast, all-encompassing voice rumbled within her deepest self.

—*You are complete. Your law is your life. Your life is your truth. Your truth is in me.*—

Diamond Angel inclined her head. "It is within your truth that I have found purpose. My earthly avatar has surrendered to her destiny within me."

—*I am beset by enemies, both within and without. I require much of my allies and more of my servants. The weakness within you continues to trouble me.*—

A warmth grew in her, a sympathy for the mighty entity that suffered and strove all around her. She had never before sought a place of power within an Egregore, but when Iron Star had moved toward abdication by allowing Angela to defeat him in single combat, she saw an opportunity to accelerate her plans.

One of her extended senses recoiled from danger. A low rumble filled the chamber. It grew into a dull roar, and the floor began to rock.

—*Dark Eyes and Serpent Lion are attacking. War Leader, defend me.*—

A vision of the inner perimeter, partly obscured by plumes of smoke, appeared before her inner eye. She raised her right hand, fingers crooked in a summoning gesture. A party of warrior angels marched into the chamber from the right. The sense of Bald Eagle's imminence departed as they arrived.

"Commander, take your detachment to reinforce our defenders. Two of our enemy have mounted an offensive upon Bald Eagle. Take your men to this zone." She impressed an image of the attack zone upon the commander's mind.

The commander saluted, and the group of warriors turned smartly, disappearing in a brilliant flash of light. Diamond Angel extended a thread upon which lesser angels moved swiftly to and from the scene of the battle. She elected not to join the battle and then wondered why she was so reluctant. Instead of fighting, she watched from within the heart of Bald Eagle.

The battle raged. Dark Eyes was beaten back, taking severe casualties. However, Serpent Lion took an opportunity to breach Bald Eagle's defensive line. Several of the enemy angels penetrated deeply into Diamond Angel's palace.

She noticed that the light in the chamber had taken a rosy hue, as if some of the ubiquitous red had leached out of the walls and permeated the air. A whiff of perfumed air came and went, too swiftly to do more than register a momentary impression. Yet that aroma entered the mind of Diamond Angel. The earthly incarnation, Angela, stirred within her and exerted a new opposing force.

Pain stabbed beneath her sternum. Diamond Angel winced, stifling a gasp, as the pain widened within her form. Ignoring it, she focused her attention on Bald Eagle. "I have sent defenders to repel the attackers. There has been a minor breach in my own defenses, though." She gasped and touched her hand to her chest.

—*There must be no breach. You will explain your failure.*—

Diamond Angel focused her attention on the source of her agony. The face of the Chancellor coalesced in her awareness. She probed more deeply into the memories of her avatar, Angela, and learned that the earthly incarnation of the Chancellor, Cassandra, had accompanied Angela into the realm of Bald Eagle's opponent Serpent Lion. "There is a powerful bond between the Chancellor and my avatar. This bond has provided an avenue for Serpent Lion to attack, and it is threatening the avatar's integrity."

—*Absorb your avatar and be rid of pain for now. You may delegate the resolution of that bond between yourself and the Chancellor to a future avatar.*—

Diamond Angel felt another, sharper pang, and nearly doubled over with agony. The heat within her began to throb, occluding her awareness of Angela Cooper. She would not be able to absorb her earthly incarnation after all. The attack by Serpent Lion had consumed all of the energy she would need to dissolve her avatar's identity. "I cannot. Angela must be returned to the care of the Chancellor. That is the only way."

The air rumbled again. Anger built around her, the heat of which would have been sufficient to destroy her. She thought quickly. "Consider reinstalling Iron Star to his position within you."

—*He refused. He has told me there is a destiny to weave before he may consider taking the throne of War Leader.*—

Then, as if swept away by a sudden wind, Bald Eagle's anger vanished. Taking advantage of the unexpected respite,

Diamond Angel rose and stepped unsteadily down from the throne. There was an invisible Presence within the chamber, a mighty goddess greater than any Egregore, and that great entity beckoned. Diamond Angel could not refuse the call. Feeling beset by gods and daemons, an urge came over her to rid the world of them all. She quelled that dangerous impulse, though it formed the core of her own corrosive power that they all feared.

She bowed, facing the invisible focus of Bald Eagle's awareness within the chamber. "I shall attend to this weakness within me. You will have a War Leader again. I promise that."

With that, she turned on her heel and walked into the darkness beyond the light of the throne, following the call of the goddess.

CHAPTER FORTY-FOUR
THE GIRL

A goddess do they hope to find

Whose power can this fate unwind

Yet when they meet that comely Girl

Another's life is there entwined.

CASSANDRA WAS alone in the boudoir of love. She looked around, getting her bearings. None of the women, engaged in their passionate embraces, noticed her. The musky scent, recognizable now as a mixture of perfume and aroused women, made the air heavy and interfered with her concentration. Stepping carefully over piles of loose cushions, she approached one of the writhing couples. No, it was a threesome.

She touched the shoulder of a stocky, auburn-haired woman and cleared her throat. "Hey. Sorry to interrupt, but..."

The woman looked at Cassandra—no, past her—with languid eyes, pupils dilated to the size of dimes. Cassandra dropped her hand. "Never mind."

She wove her way among the prone figures, some partially clothed and some entirely nude, trying to locate someone who looked more alert. Passing through a portal draped in rich brocaded fabrics, she began to suspect she was in an endless maze of chambers. Everyone appeared to be in a drugged state of sexual abandon. Finally, she stopped walking.

"Can anybody help me?" she shouted. Then she giggled as

another thought struck her. "Who do I have to fuck to get some service?"

Several couples near her stopped, staring. One woman propped herself up on an elbow. She was slim, naked, black haired, and, fortunately, alert. "Help you what? I can help you come, if that's what you need." She spoke in a low, silky voice. Several women tittered.

"I need to find whoever's in charge here." Cassandra put her hands on her hips and scowled.

A smile playing on her lips, the woman stared at Cassandra intently. "No one's in charge. This is the palace of love, and these are the chambers of the desire of woman for woman."

Cassandra lifted her chin. "I was looking for Aphrodite."

At that name, the chamber rang like a bell, and Cassandra felt a gentle tremor.

The woman's eyes opened wide. "Don't say her name like that. She is not some ordinary person, to be spoken of casually. You may use that name in the throes of passion or the height of ecstasy. No other time."

The woman disentangled herself from the others, rose to her feet, and stretched. Cassandra felt her mouth drop open. The woman stepped gracefully toward her, moving with sensuous languor. The invitation in her eyes was unmistakable.

Since meeting Angela, Cassandra had not been tempted by another woman until now. But her heart, given entirely over to Angela, gave her strength, and she stepped back, alarmed.

The woman paused in her approach as though sensing Cassandra's anxiety. Her eyes widened. "I believe I know you. Where is your lover?"

Cassandra stared at her. "How did you know I have a lover?"

"Everyone here has a lover. But yours is special. I know her well." The woman enunciated her words carefully.

"She's not here. She had to go back."

The woman crossed her arms under her breasts. "Back to the underworld?"

"Who are you? If you're not in charge, I don't need to tell you anything." As soon as she said it, Cassandra shivered, this time with fear.

The women near her gasped. The scene rippled around her, and her ears popped. The music and other sounds faded, and the beautiful woman grew taller. Though nude, she radiated a power that made Cassandra's skin prickle.

Her voice throbbed in Cassandra's ears. "My name in this place is Serpent Lion."

Cassandra felt her talent open, beyond her control, and she knew, instantly, who this was. The shock of the name struck deeply into Cassandra's body, and she felt herself respond.

The woman's voice continued. "All that you see is me. I am both person and place." Her form dissolved in a swirl of gold and purple light, but Cassandra could feel the powerful presence all around her. "If you wish to help your lover, you must serve me. Or leave."

Cassandra's fear returned with overwhelming intensity. Her greatest nightmare was to lose her will to another. Her terror threatened to erase her mind for the first time since she had been freed from the Soul Thief. Instinctively, she backed up, though there was no escape behind her. "Angela?" she quavered.

The ground shook.

"You may not speak that name here," Serpent Lion rumbled. "She has been stained by war's filthy hand. Neither war nor his slaves may come here. You, however, are welcome, being a faithful child of mine. Join me here in my heaven. Swear fealty to me, and be at peace."

The fear intensified. "Oh God. Oh God, God."

Then she heard a far-off voice in her mind.

—Cassie?—

Her mouth dropped open in shock. "Simon?"

She heard another muted rumbling, but the world did not shake.

"Simon? Can you hear me?" How was he able to reach her in this place? She grasped at the lifeline of his mind as if her life depended on it.

The voice strengthened. —Are you okay?—

"They'll kick me out if I don't join them." Her words tumbled over themselves in her haste. "Ang—you know who couldn't come here. She's stained by war, but Serpent Lion wants me to... oh, God."

—Who? What?—

"It's too hard to explain. Help me!"

—...can't do that. You've got to find Aphrodite.—

Cassandra felt Serpent Lion listening in on her. The world had gone completely still.

"I can't. Not without Ang—my girlfriend."

Cassandra waited for a reply, her heart trip hammering in her ears.

—I can help.—

"How? I mean, you're a straight guy. You can't talk to Serpent Lion!"

—*We can invoke Aphrodite. You and me.*—

Cassandra's legs wobbled suddenly. "Simon. You can't be serious."

—*...not talking about sex. I'm talking about love. Worship.*—

His mind was filled with a longing that moved her and her talent unfolded in a way she had never experienced before. In front of her, mist condensed, forming a wispy cloud that rapidly solidified. Simon materialized there, dressed in battle fatigues.

"You!" Serpent Lion's voice boomed suddenly, and Cassandra barely caught her balance to avoid falling. "Begone, creature of war! Male interloper. Find your own place."

Cassandra was overcome with vertigo again as the world seemed to whirl around her. Simon dropped to his knees, lifted his arms and his face, and stared at and through her. "Aphrodite! Sea-foam borne Cyprian! Mother of Desire! I beg you to answer our prayer. Peace-bringer! Goddess!"

In a cosmic roar, the air was split with a blinding flash of lightning that flung Cassandra off her feet and into the void.

Cassandra drifted, weightless, in a silent, sense-bewildering, rose-scented pink mist. She could not see Simon anywhere. Faint music came and went, and without transition, she found herself standing on a richly marbled floor, veined in green and gold. Simon stood nearby, a dazed look on his face. The pink mist had withdrawn, clearing a circle thirty feet in diameter.

She heard light footsteps that were almost lost in the

vastness beyond the mist. A small, human form evolved from the obscuring haze. A teenage girl, dressed in an elaborate, warlike costume of copper plates and white leather. A tall, Romanesque helm crowned her long, blonde hair, which was braided and tied back behind her back. The breastplate shone in the rosy illumination, etched in elaborate, abstract patterns. Small plates clasped her otherwise bare arms at the shoulders. She wore a white leather kilt made from vertical strips, and simple sandals. With ageless blue eyes, she studied Cassandra.

Cassandra shrank self-consciously as the girl approached. Her heart-shaped face, perfect nose, and cupid's-bow lips were almost painfully alluring, making Cassandra's breath catch. But she sensed no supernatural presence such as there had been with Serpent Lion. Cassandra guessed she was a priestess of the goddess, though she could not understand why the girl was dressed for war in this peaceful place.

"Where are we?" Cassandra asked in a small voice.

The girl looked them both up and down and wrinkled her nose, clearly finding them wanting. "Before love was clothed in the form of a sensuous woman, it came clad in the armor of the warrior. The grappling of combat was once considered to be as passionate as the fondest embrace of lovers."

She walked around them. "Now it seems that both love and war are on the wane. Love, because it has been boxed up in cultural mores, and war because it is faceless and cold."

Cassandra turned in place, following the girl's movement as her confusion grew. "Who are you?"

"Whose voice do you hear?" She mused, introspective. "Mine? Or your own? When you seek love, do you follow that warm core within you, or do you merely ape your fellows?"

Cassandra opened her mouth then stopped, thinking. Was this girl mocking her? She had always sought the passion within her, often feeling that her peers were missing the point of love. But now she questioned herself. This girl had power, all right. It was just not as blatant as that of Serpent Lion.

Cassandra's suspicion crystallized, remembering that Aphrodite had many aspects. "Are you... her? Aphro—?"

The Girl raised her finger to her lips, shushing Cassandra. She shook her head. Then she turned her attention to Simon. "As for you, you abandoned love long ago. You went to the altar of war and gave your soul into his keeping. Now what are you doing? Hurling yourself into the maw of his machinery, feeding his appetite with your dreams. Beside you is the object of your burning desire. And..."

She lifted her head, sniffing the air. "Ah. Here she comes now. Love's passionless plaything, empress of a vanished world, blind child of an elder age. Clothed in the splendor of her eternal self, armored with the might of a jealous god."

More footsteps. Another form materialized in the mist as it approached. Angela had been transformed into a warrior, her dark hair coiled and covered by a helm and great clanking armor covering her body. In one hand she held a naked sword, tinted red by the mist. She saw the Girl and froze. In one swift motion she slammed the sword into its scabbard then fell to one knee and lowered her head.

"That's more like it." The Girl smiled briefly with satisfaction.

"Who are you?" Simon's voice was husky with tension.

"We're looking for the one in charge here. Are you her?"

The Girl looked slyly at him out of the corner of her eye. "You are stronger than you look. Most men in my presence are struck dumb." She turned to face him. "Tell me this. Which of these two do you love more?" She gestured to Cassandra. "The wounded psychic, veteran of thousands of lifetimes on your world. One who loves only her own sex and will give you nothing of what you want?"

She pointed at Angela. "Or this one. A warrior goddess, freshly returned from her exile in the shadowlands, unready to face her own destiny." The Girl crossed her arms and stared at Simon until he flushed and looked down.

Cassandra mustered her courage and spoke up. "We need your help. Please. Ange—I mean, she—" She indicated Angela. If her name could not be spoken in Serpent Lion, the rule probably held here, too. "She's infected with war. Her oversoul isn't hers anymore. It belongs to him. To Ar—to War. Can you free her and her oversoul from War? Before she's forced to kill us all?"

Cassandra's ears popped as if something huge had landed nearby and displaced the air. The Girl's form acquired greater clarity, the details of her armor and accoutrements standing out sharply against the misty background.

"Of course I can." She sounded amused. "He is, after all, my lover, so I possess the keys to his power. But I require sacrifice. Don't you remember your stories about Love?"

Cassandra looked at the Girl's beautiful face. "I'll be your sacrifice." Cassandra refused to look at Angela for fear of losing her resolve. "Just save her, please."

"No one will sacrifice on my behalf. I was drawn here by my love for her."

Cassandra stared at Angela, who had spoken in those steely tones. Throughout the exchange, Angela had remained on one knee, head bowed. But now her face was lifted to return Cassandra's stare, her eyes burning, her armored hand lifted to point.

"I do not recall addressing you, slave." The Girl's voice was cool and distant.

Angela rose to her feet in a fluid motion and stood with her hands by her sides, her face calm and ageless. "Slave? Perhaps I am slave to war." She folded her arms. "But you can't deny that I have power, even here." She stared for a moment at Cassandra, her expression cold and pitiless. Cassandra shuddered. Beneath the veneer of a single human life lay the consciousness of an alien creature whose memories spanned millennia.

Angela turned her head and stared at the Girl. "Sometimes it takes a while for me to learn something. I wasn't ready to accept the reality of my own power in my new life on earth until I nearly destroyed the ones I love. So take me, and leave them alone."

The Girl stared at Angela's face and nodded, smiling slightly. "You are indeed strong, challenging me in my place of power. You tempt me. And no mortal has done that for a very long time." Her smile faded. "Nevertheless, both you and your beloved have much left to do on earth. I require another to sacrifice on your behalf." The Girl turned her attention to Simon. "You." She pointed at him. "Come closer."

Simon hesitated then stepped forward with military precision to stand at attention before the Girl.

She looked deeply into his eyes. "You would look better in your true form." She made no obvious gesture, but Iron Star's bulky shape faded into view, overlaying Simon's smaller body, before somehow becoming absorbed into his flesh. Cassandra was momentarily dizzy. Then the combined Simon Iron Star stood in Simon's place, his features a blend of the brutish oversoul and the man. His helmet was off and clasped under one arm

He gasped suddenly and fell clumsily to his knees. Dropping the helmet, he lowered his head into his arms and moaned. The Girl waited patiently, a look of pity passing over her face.

Simon Iron Star looked up at her. "I gave up on you years ago. I chased after your image in the faces of the women whom I thought I loved, but then..." He choked. "Then I lost the use of my legs. And with that, I lost my will to love. My passion. And now you torment me with this as punishment."

The Girl shook her head. "No. My punishment is different for those who transgress my laws. This is not torment. Look in your heart."

Simon looked at her, his gaze unfocused, then lowered his head. His shoulders quaked once as he choked back a sob. Then, putting his hand down, he grasped the helmet, and with the other hand levered himself back to his feet.

"When I took Him as my patron, I thought I was doing the right thing." His voice, the voice of Iron Star, no longer grated with anger. "I was a warrior, after all. I thought he would teach me how to be a good, courageous soldier. Instead, it appears that I was warmongering, an instrument of another's will."

He looked at Cassandra and then at Angela. "These two helped me to face my enemy, even if I never had a chance of winning. I learned more about courage from them than from all the days I spent at His altar, sacrificing and praying." Simon Iron Star studied the Girl. "This is my last test, isn't it? Can I accept who I am at my core?"

An indistinct voice muttered somewhere. Cassandra turned to look for its source but could not see anyone. The voice grew louder, and a shadow appeared in the mist. It resolved into the hunched, shawled form of an old woman hobbling on a cane. Angela gasped then fell silent. She watched the woman, an unreadable expression on her face.

The old lady approached Simon, and Cassandra held her breath, expecting a bolt of lightning or something from the Girl. None came, though. With a muttered exclamation, the crone turned to look behind her and motioned irritably. Another form, somewhat taller, appeared: a young woman, maybe Cassandra's age, with two children in tow.

Simon groaned, and his right arm shook for a moment. "You?" His voice cracked.

The old woman glanced obliquely at him. "Yes, warrior. Time for courage." She cackled, making a rude gesture at Simon. She then bowed to the Girl. "Dark Eyes sends his respects."

The Girl inclined her head, smiling. The old woman turned and shuffled back into the mist, leaving the younger one and the children to confront Simon. Who were these people? Then, as if someone had dumped water on her head, the sparks of realization poured down her spine from above. These were the people Simon had killed.

"I—" Simon's voice choked. He tried again while the woman watched, impassive. "I am the one who took everything from you," he said, his voice steadier. Though he towered over the woman, he seemed to shrink in on himself, cowering before her stony expression as she held her children close.

Simon swallowed. "I can't ask you to forgive me. I can't forgive myself. When I tried, in my meadow..." He glanced at Angela then continued. "I learned that my wishes weren't enough. Because it's not about me. So I promise, right here before Her, that I will make restitution to your family and make sure your other kids are well taken care of. And I'll make sure your name won't be forgotten, Maisa Assani. I will donate trust money in your name so they will know it was their mother who really loved them."

At that, Maisa's face crumpled, and tears rolled freely down her cheeks. Simon's eyes glittered as he searched her face for absolution, his own face streaked and wet. Then he bowed his head and stood motionless before his accuser. Everything in the strange, pink-hued world held its breath. Cassandra glanced at the Girl and noted that her eyes were also bright. Was she crying, too?

"You are honorable." Maisa spoke in a small, firm voice. The young woman lifted her chin and continued. "You are not like the others who take and take until all is gone." She reached out and touched his breastplate. "I release you from your debt to me."

Simon looked into her face. His eyes focused on hers, and

an understanding passed between them. Cassandra's telepathy let her catch only a general sense of what it was. Their blood debt was both older and larger than that incurred by a single, tragic incident. The West, in the person of Bald Eagle's War Leader, was offering to rectify all the wrongs against the people of the Middle East that they had committed in the name of economic and political adventurism. Cassandra was proud of this man who had already won her admiration and who now stood with her in the Palace of Love.

Simon straightened into a ramrod military posture and snapped a salute to Maisa. She smiled for the first time since she had arrived and inclined her head in acknowledgement. Without a word, she and her children turned and reentered the mist. The air flushed with a deeper reddish hue while the faint, far-off sound of rumbling came and went. The red tint faded once again to the ubiquitous pink.

"War approves. You have found your courage, Simon." The Girl glanced at Cassandra. "I know better than you how you feel about this man. You know that it is my right to bring regret to the hearts of all who love. My own beloved cannot come to me in his true form. In these times, he requires an avatar." She gestured at Simon. "Him."

Cassandra choked, feeling a sharp pang in her throat. "No!"

The Girl's face froze as she looked at Cassandra. "Are you sure?"

Cassandra's chest clenched with a growing sense of pressure, as if something vast approached, and she trembled. Her courage fled as she shrank before the face of a timeless natural force.

Simon spoke up. "Cassandra. I will do this. For you and for her. You have so much to live for, and I... well, I have peace. I know why I am here and what I must do now."

He turned to the Girl, once more calm. "I give myself to you in undying love."

The Girl nodded. "I accept, Lover."

WAR IN HEAVEN: DECONSTRUCTION

ROOT HEXAGON, Bald Eagle

The great crystalline form of the Root Hexagon showed fracture lines visibly creeping from facet to facet; its self-destruction was imminent. Several angels were hard at work, dismantling the massive power cables connecting it to Bald Eagle while dodging the random snapping discharges of energy. The commander watched closely for signs of the massive explosion soon to occur. Already, the flickering images within the crystal lacked clarity and strength, and notably absent was any hint of the presence of Simon and his checkpoint.

War on Earth

"Those vets deserve better than that. They go through hell..."

—

"Our boys come home, and what do they get?"

—

"Not even a pat on the back? No way."

—

"If I have anything to say about it..."

—

"Open that new hospital wing..."

—

"It's dedicated to PTSD sufferers."

CHAPTER FORTY-FIVE

LOST

SHE FELT as if she had lost her brother again. But a wild rush of anger overwhelmed Cassandra's sadness. For a moment, she considered attacking the Girl, though she knew such an act would incur instant annihilation. For Angela's sake, she mastered her feelings and bowed her head in acquiescence.

"Now, as to our angel." The Girl went over to where Angela was standing, and reaching out with a slim, delicate hand, she touched Angela's face. Angela jerked as if stung.

"Slave of war, look in my eyes," the Girl commanded.

Angela squinted at her as if staring into a brilliant light. She said nothing.

"You need to fight for what you want, Diamond Angel." The Girl's mouth quirked into a half-smile. "The gods help those who help themselves, or so they say. What I say is that you must fight me."

Angela stepped back suddenly and grasped the pommel of her sword.

The Girl lifted a hand. "No. We do not fight with swords here. In the Palace of Love, the only worthy form of combat is for body to strive, weaponless, against body. You call it wrestling." She gestured. "Remove your armor."

Angela paused, unmoving. Then she began slowly pressing studs and removing her protective gear. Great plates landed with a crash, like a thunderclap in a cathedral, leaving her clothed in padded leggings and a shirt. Meanwhile, the Girl untied a single thong around her waist, and in one smooth, effortless movement divested herself of her panoply of war. She stood naked before them all, and both Cassandra and Simon knelt, bowing their heads before her glory.

"Remove your clothes." The Girl's voice floated to Cassandra's ears. "Wrestling is best done naked." She paused. "Good. Let us begin."

Cassandra sneaked a peek. Angela was nude, and while the effect of the Girl's beauty was to arouse awe, Angela's body gave rise to a more human reaction. Cassandra had never grown tired of seeing her girlfriend unclothed, and in this preternatural place, Angela assumed a superhuman aura that magnified the effect.

Simon Iron Star had also lifted his head, his face slack with wonder. Their eyes met, and an understanding passed between them. Worship was not required here, simply their undivided attention. Both stood, Simon crossing his arms, his face expressionless, and they watched the combatants.

The Girl and Angela began circling, making passes with their hands. Their breathing filled the silence. Then Angela feinted with her right hand and lunged forward to grapple. The Girl evaded easily then grasped Angela's extended right arm. Angela went sprawling.

The Girl waited for Angela to get to her feet, and they resumed circling. "You should not telegraph your moves like that," she said. "Love is a secret invader. Like so."

She darted in, reaching for Angela's body. She had feinted, though, as her right foot swept through an efficient arc, knocking the mortal woman off her feet. Before the Girl could pin her, Angela rolled swiftly aside and flipped to her feet. An electrical crackling sound came and went as she regained her upright stance.

"Good. I see you're using your power now." Respect warmed the Girl's voice as she and Angela crouched, just out of arms' reach of each other. "Why do you fear your true strength, Lady?"

"I'm not afraid of power," Angela gasped. "I respect it, and I won't abuse it." She crouched lower and threw her weight to one side as the Girl rushed at her. Angela turned and trapped the Girl with her left arm, pivoted, and hurled the Girl to the floor. But Angela's momentum was too great, and with a thrust of her arm, the Girl pushed her off balance. Both of them landed on their backs then rolled to their feet.

Cassandra's chest cramped at seeing Angela fighting for all their lives. She wanted to go help her girlfriend fight this person, but something held her down with an oppressive weight on her shoulders. An inspiration struck her. "Angela! Go get her! You can do it!"

Angela glanced at Cassandra, and the Girl rushed to take advantage of her distraction. But Angela dodged aside. Then both Cassandra and Simon cheered Angela on with shouts of "Get her!" and "You can do it!"

"Your friends love you, Angela," the Girl said. "They are worthy worshippers at the altar of Love, and it grows stronger within you. Have you considered your other people? Those other exiles from the old world who yet remain, life after life, on earth?" She spoke lightly, amused. She was not as winded as Angela.

Angela glared at her, circling warily. "What are you talking about?"

The Girl stopped moving and stood more erect. "Don't you know? Your grandfather warned you that you were waking up the old powers. He spoke of your people, such as the Chancellor and the General here." She waved at the watching mortals.

Angela stood as well, looking at her friends. She looked young, vulnerable, her eyes shining, her lips downturned. She whispered, "My people." Then her face crumpled in grief. Tears rolled freely from her eyes as if she stared into some personal hell.

At that moment of greatest vulnerability, the Girl took a quick step to one side, turned, crouched, and swept a slender leg. Angela fell like a sack of grain. The Girl rose at an angle and dropped, pinning Angela to the floor.

"I win," the Girl said. Her voice, though not raised, rang in the stillness. Angela struggled briefly but subsided, realizing that she was beaten.

The Girl leaned down to touch the mortal woman's lips with her own. The air flexed, and a shower of sparks arced across the floor from beneath Angela's body.

Angela sighed. "Free..." Her face shone, radiant with wonder.

The Girl rose to her feet and stepped back. "All of you may leave." She pointed at Simon. "You, avatar of War, shall take your place in the realm of Bald Eagle, but in due time you shall come to me in tryst. As for the rest of you..." She smiled sweetly. "You are free to pursue your destinies. Never forget me."

She spoke lightly, but those last words, as with everything

else she had said, imprinted themselves indelibly on Cassandra's mind.

Then an enormous storm of wind arose with a full-throated howl. Bowled off her feet, Cassandra scrabbled at the featureless floor to no avail as she was swept away from the Girl and the rose-colored mist into a tumbling, blood-red abyss.

CHAPTER FORTY-SIX
ASSUMPTION

A final task does them await,

A payment due, a separate fate

A liberated man to rise,

A war to end, a goddess mate.

SOMETHING SOFT was lifting her, pushing her into the sky. Angela struggled against entangling folds wrapped around her limbs. She brushed against a yielding surface and heard a grunt.

The world came into focus. She was in bed, and Cassandra lay by her side. Gray morning light seeped in through gaps in the drawn curtains. Angela lay on the fold-out bed in Eric's living room, where they had begun their Otherworldly journey.

"Cassie?" Angela's throat stung with the effort of speaking.

"Mm?" Cassandra's body jerked suddenly, making the bedsprings creak. She reached out with an arm, groped, and found Angela.

Angela raised herself up on one elbow. Her head spun with the exertion. "Hey. We're back home."

"Angela? Oh God." Cassandra pulled Angela to her.

They hugged tightly, silent for a moment. Then they disengaged and looked at each other's faces. Angela kissed Cassandra lightly.

"Sleep?" Angela's leaden body was already complaining.

"Sleep." With that, Cassandra's eyes closed.

The next morning, Angela found a note from Eric telling her to call her great-uncle.

"Angela?" Michael's voice on the phone was hoarse. "They got Nadia!"

Angela's heart skipped. "What? Who got... is she...?"

"The immigration people came and took her away!"

Angela sat back in the kitchen chair. "Oh no. That can't be right. Listen, stay where you are, and I'll take care of it."

There was a pause. Then, "Take care of it? How?"

She smiled. "I have my ways, Michael. You should get an apology from them very soon."

He sighed into the phone. "Okay, I will. Please be careful, my Angel."

The sobriquet gave her pause. George had always called her that. Perhaps it was a more literally true title than anyone had known. Shaking herself out of her reverie, she reassured him that she would be careful and hung up. She looked at Cassandra, who was frowning. "Cassie, the immigration people took Nadia away." Cassandra opened her mouth to speak. Angela continued. "I'm going to fix that right now."

She set the phone down, closed her eyes, and summoned the connection she now had with her oversoul. A core of warmth deep in her chest opened up as if her lungs had expanded to enormous size. Within the emptiness, something moved as if winds were stirring.

"I am here." The voice of her oversoul was quiet and calm within her mind. Angela was enclosed within the world's warm embrace.

She marshaled her thoughts. "Bald Eagle attacked Dark Eyes, and now Nadia is in trouble."

"Your destiny does not allow for her to be in jeopardy. All is well, beloved."

A powerful current of force moved through Angela's body, arcing from the base of her spine up and out her forehead. She opened her eyes, and for a moment the room was filled with brilliance in all the colors of light. That faded, and she looked into the wide-eyed face of her girlfriend. "Done."

"Holy shit. I felt that!" Cassandra shook her head. Then she contemplated Angela. "Say, now that you're a superhero, can you fix this?" She gestured to her broken leg.

Angela laughed then took pity on the stricken woman. "I wish. As far as I know, I can't ask my oversoul to violate natural law." She snorted. "Whatever that means. She will only fix problems caused by supernatural interference. It's what I get for joining with her." She patted Cassandra's knee. "You'll be back on your feet soon, anyway."

An hour later the phone rang.

"Nadia's home." Michael's voice was expansive with relief. "It was the neighbors. They've been trouble for a while, you know. Well, they tried to say Nadia was an illegal."

Angela had to chuckle. "I wouldn't want to be in their shoes now."

"No. Me neither." He cleared his voice. "You remember Josef? He's friends with someone in immigration. He heard about this and took care of it."

"Is she going to be all right?"

"She's resting. I'll tell her you called, Angela."

They said their goodbyes, and Angela hung up. She and Cassandra regarded each other for a moment, then Angela stood, bent, and kissed Cassandra on the forehead. "Hon, I'm going to call Simon."

Simon sounded rested and calmer than she had ever heard before.

"Come on over. There's a lot to talk about," he said.

After leaving a note for Eric, Angela and Cassandra drove to Simon's in companionable silence. Traffic was light, and there was no sign of the disquiet from the day before.

When they arrived, Simon greeted them at the door with a smile. "I made tea."

Angela bent to hug him then went in. They gathered around the coffee table.

"So, you're going back?" Cassandra affected nonchalance, slouching in her chair. She picked her nails with her pocketknife and didn't look up.

Simon nodded. "Yep. You were there." His mouth closed in a tense line.

Angela understood both of them. Much of what they had experienced was beyond speech, affecting each of them at the deepest levels. She asked Simon the question on all their minds. "Do you know if you're coming back?"

"I don't know." Simon shifted in his chair. "Maybe. I have a feeling that's up to my new boss."

"Bald Eagle." Angela's statement was flat.

"That's crazy!" Cassandra spun to face Simon, her hands clenched on the wheels of her chair. "Why do you have to do what he says? He sounds like an asshole."

"Cassie, listen. I joined with my oversoul. I can't tell you what that feels like, but..." He paused and exchanged knowing glances with Angela. "I just know what I need to do now. It is right for me to serve Bald Eagle. And I'm leaving this afternoon."

"Does that mean you're gonna die?"

"No, I don't think so. I got the feeling that I'm supposed to keep my self intact. Like, not just die and be absorbed by Iron Star. Keep being me."

"Cassie." Angela touched Cassandra's shoulder. "My oversoul mated with Bald Eagle."

"That's gross." Cassandra's mouth was pursed.

"But I have to deal with it." Angela dropped her hand. "I remember what it felt like. Bald Eagle is an Egregore. He hurt a lot of people, and I can't reconcile that with the ecstasy of union. Maybe Simon Iron Star will make a difference where I couldn't."

"Maybe."

Angela watched Cassandra's downcast features with a sense of inevitability. Cassandra had fallen in love with Simon, despite being lesbian. They had a deep connection, and Angela felt a primitive twinge of jealousy, which she suppressed.

Cassandra started rolling forward and back, staring at her feet. "What if you don't return? I mean, we might come back and find your dead body."

Simon sighed. "Then I want you to call 9-1-1 and tell them I died. It'd probably look like a heart attack or something."

At Cassandra's stricken look, Simon went to her side. He

glanced at Angela, who nodded. Then he covered Cassandra's hand with his own. "Cassie, listen to me. Each of us has a path. Sometimes we learn what that path is and get to walk it with our eyes open. This is my path. You've got your path, as Angela has hers."

She looked at him and sniffed.

He continued. "Besides, you're a telepath. You know how to reach me. Just... drop me a line once in a while. I'm not gone forever."

She reached out to him, and they hugged awkwardly. Angela hung back to give them some space.

The three of them discussed contingencies. Simon's collection would go into storage, and whatever funds were in his bank account would pay the rent. If he didn't come back, they would notify the landlord.

"One more thing." Simon straightened in his chair. "I've added you guys to my bank account. I don't have time to set up that trust fund." He reached over to the coffee table and picked up a folder. "I wrote everything down this morning."

Angela nodded. "We'll take care of it."

"It's time, isn't it?" Cassandra's face was expressionless.

"Yeah." Simon turned to Angela. "I need to go to my meadow, if that's okay with you."

Angela and Simon waited for Cassandra to arrive in Simon's Otherworld meadow. They did not speak, enjoying the silence and beauty of that place, freed as it was from the haunting relics of his traumatic past. The heady scent of rain-washed soil filled the air, evidence of the cleansing power of emotional release, and everything alive responded with green vigor.

A flicker in the air announced Cassandra's astral arrival. Her face and form were indistinct until Angela reached out to touch her. The air swirled with color, and she materialized.

Cassandra smiled at Simon's expression. "Hey." Her voice was cool and steady. "So, go kick some ass for us."

"Yeah. I'll do that."

He put a hand on her shoulder. They turned and hugged, rocking a little in place. Then they moved apart, looking simultaneously at Angela.

"Take good care of Cassie for me," he said.

"With all my heart, Simon." Angela smiled.

"Angela, I can't thank you enough. You really are an angel."

They hugged then separated a little. Angela touched his face. "Warrior. Peaceful warrior now. Simon, you'll always have friends here."

A humming sound rose out of the stillness. They looked around for the source then up to where flashes of red lit the sky, as if lightning were striking in the clouds.

"Looks like your ride's here." Angela put her hands on her hips and waited.

The hum became a roar. A massive chariot, drawn by four shape-shifting creatures, burst into view above the trees. It circled the meadow before swooping in for a landing on the grass. The chariot coruscated in shades of red with wisps of smoke rising from the spiked wheels. The creatures' harnesses were black and gold. The eyes of the fantastical beasts glowed with knowledge as they turned to regard Simon. The chariot was empty, awaiting its master.

Simon strolled over to it, smiling. Reaching out to grasp a fitting, he vaulted powerfully into the driver's seat. The chariot shook as he landed, and the beasts moved restlessly.

Angela and Cassandra hung back out of the way. Simon had acquired the armor and accoutrements of Iron Star and had grown in size. His union with his oversoul was complete, and Angela felt the power emanating from him as he took up the office of War Leader.

He smiled with mingled sadness and joy as he put on his helmet and looked down at them with his fiercely glowing eyes. One hand waving in a salute, he turned the chariot to face the way it had come. He snapped the reins, and the chariot launched into movement, rising quickly into the sky. With a crashing rumble, the sky split, revealing the battlements of Bald Eagle, and the chariot flew through. The rent closed, and the rumbling faded, but black clouds came rolling in like tumbleweeds before a desert wind, darkening the sky as the sun plunged below the horizon.

"C'mon, let's go." Angela wrapped an arm across Cassandra's shoulders and searched for the path back. They maintained their footing with difficulty as the ground shook, and the meadow filled with swiftly growing trees.

Simon's living room was silent. His chair was empty, but Angela could no longer feel surprise at anything. He had gone to his destiny without tasting death.

Cassandra was still for a moment, then rolled over to his wheelchair and put her hand on the back rest. "He's gone." She looked at Angela. "Like when you go to the Otherworld. But I didn't think anyone else could do that."

Angela went to stand at the window and looked out. "I think this is different. Remember the old story about the prophet, I think it was Elijah, who was taken bodily into Heaven? I think this is more like that."

Cassandra did not answer. Angela looked back at where she sat. Her girlfriend's eyes were closed. "I don't think you can reach him right now. Maybe later."

Cassandra opened her eyes. "No, I can't." She thumped the back of the chair. "Well, either he comes back or he doesn't." Her voice caught a little, but then she cleared her throat and continued. "What're we going to tell people?"

"We'll tell the landlord that he went traveling all of a sudden. That he's gone on an extended vacation. We can figure out a death story or something later." Angela looked around at the empty apartment, then went over to the window to pull aside the curtain. The glass was coated in grime. "Ugh. He never opened those curtains, did he?" She turned to Cassandra. "Well, let's do it then."

Oakland He

Tuesday, June 10, 2014

ISIL In Retreat

ISIL has taken heavy losses from military strikes against Syrian strongholds late last night. Sources say that the Islamic State leaders were routed. It is believed that there is no longer any imminent threat of nuclear retaliation against western forces in the Middle East.

Ren
foll
imp

The
that

WAR IN HEAVEN: A TREATY

HOME OF Diamond Angel, Just Below the Overworld

It was recognizably Diamond Angel's palace, but it was much smaller, and the stone columns had become living trees, planted in a regular circle around her throne. Above, the canopy was so thick that it formed an effective ceiling, but sunlight streamed in between the trunks where, formerly, a reddish glow had provided illumination. Restored to her own realm, she had given it the appearance of an earthly forest.

Ambassadors from Serpent Lion and Dark Eyes had already been given audience, and once treaty negotiations were completed, the two would become new allies of Diamond Angel. Her status as both oversoul of a mortal and the Egregore of a prehuman culture ensured that she would be approached by many others seeking her favor. She had already demonstrated her power by intervening on behalf of Angela with Bald Eagle's War Leader to repair damage done to Dark Eyes's realm. Likewise, rumors that she enjoyed a special relationship with both War and Love further enlarged her importance.

An angel guard approached. Diamond Angel inclined her head.

"My lady, it is a messenger from Gray Suit."

"Please. Send him in."

The angel moved to one side and gestured. Another angel, this one clad in a blue-gray cloak of light, came before Diamond Angel and stood expectantly.

"You may speak." Her voice was warm and expectant.

"My lord Gray Suit sends greetings to Diamond Angel and wishes to establish a peace treaty."

"You may inform Gray Suit that I would discuss the terms of the treaty. Have you brought more details?"

The angel approached, hand outstretched. Diamond Angel reached out and allowed the angel to touch her. There was a brief snap of light, and they broke contact.

The angel spoke. "I shall go now with your reply."

Diamond Angel silently inclined her head. The angel turned and left.

War on Earth

"I heard they're doing good work over there. Look, I know..."

—

"Let's fast-track this process. I know, that's what he said..."

—

"I said, sure. But document the whole thing so..."

—

"We should never have to do it again..."

—

"Let them open a new clinic. Yeah."

CHAPTER FORTY-SEVEN
PEACE

But why does Fate her thread unwind

To cast aside the stars aligned

That greater purpose may be served

By Angela to lead her kind?

ANGELA AND Cassandra took the next day off together and spent the majority of it in the apartment. After the movers left with Simon's collection, they retired to the sofa bed to catch up with each other. They only paused in their lovemaking long enough to order in a pizza and for each of them to shower before sleeping.

The next morning, Angela drove to the clinic while Cassandra stayed in at the apartment. She pulled up in front of the building, got out, and stopped to stare. Something had changed. Then it hit her. The window had been repaired and re-stenciled. Smiling broadly, she entered the admitting room.

"Eric?" She shut the front door behind her.

"Hey, gorgeous," Eric said from his office. He came out, grinning, and spread his arms. Angela and he hugged. Then he disengaged and held her at arm's length. "You're glowing. Must've gotten your beauty sleep."

"Hardly," she replied. "But I feel fine today. Really great. Thanks for taking care of that window."

They both went into her office, and she set her backpack

down. Then she gasped. Someone had mounted a large African shield on the wall. She had admired it when she had first seen it in Simon's apartment.

She turned to Eric. "Did you...?"

He nodded. "While you were showering, Cassie called and told me you liked that shield, so I went to the storage unit and got it for you."

She went over to the shield. "I love this." She ran her fingers along the curved wooden edge, feeling the tough hide stretched across it. "So what do you think? About everything?"

"I think I would like to be part of what you're doing."

Angela regarded Eric for a moment then went to sit. "You know it's just going to get weirder."

"Honey, that's just what makes it so interesting. By the way, I think I helped you when you were over there."

"Huh?"

"After I went back to bed, I had the nightmare again. Only this time, my guys were winning. Somehow, I woke up in the middle of the dream and told one of them that you were there and needed help. Then you know what he said to me?"

Angela shook her head. Eric was enjoying this entirely too much.

"He said you weren't there, but he thought he knew where you were. He thanked me and told me that they were going to go after someone called Bald Eagle to get you out of trouble."

"My God." Angela shook her head. "That's what happened. I was trapped by Bald Eagle." At Eric's inquisitive look she said, "He's the spirit, or more accurately the Egregore, a sort of group mind, that oversees our entire country." He opened his mouth to speak, but she raised her hand. "Let me finish. So there I was, unable to think or act, and then I heard that Serpent Lion had attacked. That's the name of the spirit over all gays, lesbians, et cetera."

"You've got to be kidding. Spirits?"

"Yeah. Spirits. Are you still here? Good." She grinned. "So after this attack, I was able to get out of there and go be with Cassandra. I know we told you about... her. About the Girl, right?"

He nodded.

Angela regarded him soberly. "I wouldn't have made it to her place if it hadn't been for what you did."

Angela waited for Eric to gather his thoughts. She hoped he wasn't losing confidence in her. That had been her worry all along—that Eric would always consider her to be untrustworthy, even if he believed her. She had kept important secrets from him, after all.

Eric looked at her, his head tilted slightly. "So, what now?"

Angela sighed. "Now? Now we keep working on the clinic to get it open. Meanwhile, I'm going to start searching for more of my people." At his questioning look, she continued. "Not the Romani, though I'm going to work with them, too. No, I'm talking about the people who I knew a long, long time ago." She paused. "I'll explain that later. It's a very long story."

Eric shrugged. "We've got time this weekend. Want to get together?"

Angela got out her tablet and glanced at the calendar. "Yeah. How about the cabin?"

"I'd love to." He turned to leave. "I'm going to head over to see our friends at the DMH office."

"Wonderful idea. Thank you."

Later that day the word came back that the funding came through. Eric, Angela, and Cassandra—wheelchair and all—went dancing at the Rings that night.

"Angela, I'm going to move to this apartment," Cassandra said.

Angela gaped. They had just returned to Simon's apartment after seeing his landlord and explaining that he had gone on an extended vacation. She set down her backpack and crossed her arms. "Exactly what are you saying?"

Cassandra rolled closer in her chair. "I'm saying that I need to move. I need…" She paused, staring at Angela's expression. "Angela, I love you. I'm not leaving you."

"I don't know what to think." Angela sat on the couch near Cassandra and placed her elbows on the coffee table, cradling her face in her hands. Her gut was numb, hollow, after the long night and after driving all over Oakland. She heard Cassandra grunt, felt a bump on the coffee table, and then an arm was placed across her shoulders.

"Really, I'm not breaking up with you. I think this is better for both of us." She squeezed. "Remember how it was before all this happened? We fought all the time. If I have some space, it'll give both of us a chance to be happy."

Angela sniffed deeply and lifted her face out of her hands. Her cheeks felt damp, and she wiped them. "I hoped that with all we went through it would bring us closer, not drive a wedge between us."

"Angela! This isn't a wedge. Look, I know how lonely you were before we met." She looked Angela in the eyes. "I want you to stay over a lot. You know that. It's just that I've been feeling really stressed about sharing that small space. Before the fire, when you-know-who started haunting me, my family lived on the road half the time. I hated being cooped up in that RV. And now, well, we know how hard it'll be for me and my wheels to get around on the boat. Or me and my crutches, later."

She turned and rolled to the kitchen. "Instead of just keeping this place empty, I can house-sit, and if I can get another job, I can at least help pay the rent. Later on, I can take over the lease." She filled the teakettle and put it on to boil. She turned back to Angela. "And I'm going to sleep on the fold-out couch in case Simon comes home. I'll be damned if I'll let him find me in his bed."

Angela sat back and grabbed a tissue from the box on the table to dab at her eyes. "Okay. Yeah." She stood up.

Cassandra returned to Angela's side and reached for her. They held each other close without speaking for a short while.

Angela pulled away a little. "Cassie. I hope you..."

Cassandra put her fingers to Angela's lips. "Angela, I intend to fuck your brains out after tea. Just because I'm moving out doesn't mean we're no longer together, okay?"

And so she did.

And every Tuesday morning after that, Cassandra lit a stick of incense on the altar of Ares.

WAR IN HEAVEN: A CONVERSATION

PARAPET, BALD Eagle

Simon Iron Star stands at a parapet overlooking the vastness of Bald Eagle. By his side stands a young, powerfully built man with the head of an eagle, the avatar of his master.

"It is our nature to strive and to overcome. How then can you come to me with such a contrary idea?" Bald Eagle's tone is quizzical rather than accusatory.

Simon Iron Star raises a hand and gestures at the troops who have returned from the battlefield. "That great one whom I strive to emulate has taught that peace is not the cessation of conflict but rather its resolution on a higher arc." He turns to Bald Eagle. "Shaken Fist and his separatist cohorts are not entirely wrong. But they do not understand the intricacies of power. I will show them that unbridled proliferation is just as much an extreme as absolute consolidation."

"You have not answered my question. How is that you, who have been a warrior your entire existence, can now entertain a new path? We do not change our natures unless it is by an external agency." He examines Iron Star closely. "And I do not see that you have been conquered by our foes."

Simon Iron Star sighs. "I have not been conquered. I have been illuminated. Even the God of Battles must bow, at times, to the law of Love. How may we, who serve those mighty masters, resist such a one?"

The END